INVISIBLE
WOMAN

Brenda

SARA FRASER
INVINCIBLE WOMAN

WARNER BOOKS

A *Warner* Book

First published by Macdonald & Co in 1991
Published by Warner in 1992
This edition published by Warner in 1994
Reprinted 1997

ISBN 0 7515 0029 1

Printed in England by Clays Ltd, St Ives plc

Warner Books
A Division of
Little, Brown and Company (UK)
Brettenham House
Lancaster Place
London WC2E 7EN

Introduction

The terrible scourge of cholera attacked Great Britain in the year of 1832.

This is the story of one small town and its people during that time of grief, suffering and death, and of one young woman in particular - Tildy Crawford.

Chapter One

THE MURDEROUS CHOLERA Morbus was on the march! From India in 1826 it had invaded Persia and Afghanistan, following the great rivers, and the trading routes and struck into Russia, its deadly bacilli reaching Moscow by August 1830. The cruel Russian winter appeared to defeat it, but it only lay dormant, recruiting its strength, and in the spring of 1831 it reappeared in Moscow, then swept victoriously across the whole of eastern and central Europe. In a vain attempt to halt its seemingly inexorable advance Russian soldiers cordoned off stricken towns and villages, shooting down any who attempted to flee from the scourge. Warlike Prussia mobilised its entire army and threw an impenetrable barricade of bayonets along its eastern frontiers. But King Cholera's legions brushed aside that barricade with a contemptuous ease, and by September 1831 people were dying in the streets of Berlin. In Cairo and Alexandria 30,000 died in only days, and from June to September 1831 100,000 Hungarians paid the ultimate price.

Poland, Austria, Sweden, France, Italy, Spain, North Africa, the Middle East were all attacked and mourned their countless dead, and in all of the Old World it seemed that only Great Britain, protected by its defensive moat, was secure from King Cholera's invasion. Then on 23 October 1831 a 60-year-old Sunderland keelman named William Sproat was taken ill at his home on the Fish Quay, overlooking Sunderland harbour. At twelve noon on 26 October 1831 he died. The Sunderland medical authorities reported

7

that the Cholera Morbus had claimed its first official victim in England. By December 1831 Newcastle and Gateshead had been attacked, and in January and February 1832, Edinburgh and Glasgow. Almost simultaneously in the foetid slums of London, at Limehouse, Lambeth and Southwark people were struck down, and by erratic leaps and bounds the seemingly invincible legions of King Cholera began to extend their reign of terror across the length and breadth of the British Isles.

It was the first Monday in August 1832 and from long before dawn the roads leading into the centre of Redditch Town, in the Parish of Tardebigge, Worcestershire, had been thronged with loaded carts and waggons, cattle and horses, sheep and pigs and people on foot and on horseback. Today was the beginning of the annual Horse and Cattle Fair, and for the next three days and nights there would be noise and bustle and varying types of tumult in the streets of the town. Innkeepers and shopkeepers rose from their beds on this day with an eager anticipation of the profits to be made. Needle Masters and other employers of labour sighed resignedly at the prospect of absentee workers, and the local magistrates and constabulary braced themselves to face drunken mayhem and riot.

Joseph Cashmore stood at the door of his cottage and glowered at the clear, sunlit blue skies, and the carts and animals and people passing along the Evesham Street before him. As Parish Constable of Tardebigge, it was mainly on his own broad shoulders that the maintenance of the King's Peace would fall, and from bitter experience, he knew that the load would be a heavy one to bear. In a violent age, the inhabitants of his home town were notorious for their propensities for violence, and even without the added excitement of the Fair, Joseph Cashmore and his deputies were hard-pressed to preserve law and order in the hilly streets of Redditch Town.

He turned and shouted back into his cottage, 'Wife, bring me things here. I'm gooing out.'

His diminutive, mouselike wife, who lived in fearful awe of her formidable husband, hurried to bring him his ornately brocaded tri-corn hat, his long crowned staff of office, and his blue frockcoat with its huge brass buttons.

When he had donned the latter garment, and arranged his archaic hat on his close-cropped, bullet head, she handed him his staff, and enquired in a timid whisper, 'When can I expect you back for your dinner, Mister Cashmore?'

'When I arrives, wife, when I arrives,' he told her grandly, and then marched away.

The central area of the town was built on a small plateau, which was the termination of the northernmost spur of the long high hill known as the Ridgeway, running like a raised spine from the northwest towards the south of Worcestershire. To the east, west and north of the town centre the land fell away sharply to a broad valley in which the River Arrow curled around the northern and eastern boundaries of the town.

Joseph Cashmore walked north along Evesham Street to its debouchment at the central crossroads of Redditch. There was a large open-spaced triangular Green here, and the Chapel of St Stephen, the Anglican place of worship, stood near to the crossroads on the Green's southwestern corner. The Green itself was bounded by terraces of buildings of varying types and purposes and along its western edge ran the road towards Birmingham which plunged steeply down Fish Hill at the northern apex of the triangle.

The constable stood opposite the squat, single-storied, cupolaed chapel and regarded with jaundiced eyes the clusters of lowing cattle and bleating sheep stretching all across the Green. The iron railings mounted on the low wall which surrounded the Chapel Burial Ground were being utilised as hitching posts for horses; and travellers and gypsies were tying awnings of sailcloth to the spiked tops to create their temporary camping shelters. The road known as the Market Place ran eastwards from the crossroads, and even at this hour of eight o'clock in the morning rows of stalls and booths had been erected, and showmen were building up their carousels and swingboats and seesaws, and a big four-armed dipper.

The air was filled with noise and bustle and the acrid stenches of animal urine and excreta. Snatches of a score of different accents reached Cashmore's ears. He scowled as he visualised what this scene before him would resemble in a few hours time when the local people swarmed to take their pleasures. Even now dozens of excited children were clamouring around the showmen, and despite himself Cashmore's lips twitched in bleak amusement knowing that soon many of these small truants would be shrieking with a different type of excitement as the canes of their schoolmasters and monitors drove them to their lessons.

The constable resumed his slow patrol of the town, his shrewd eyes noting the myriad packmen, cheapjacks, beggars and all the other trampers and doubtful looking characters that the Fair had drawn to it like a magnet draws iron.

'I reckon that's what more nor a few o' you lot 'ull be tasting afore this is all done wi',' he thought grimly. 'All you'll likely get from here is a bar of iron across your yeds, and your goods robbed from you. Times are too hard here, for you to be finding charity. Theer's too many hereabouts needs all the charity that they can get for themselves, ne'er mind giving it to the likes 'o you.'

Times were indeed hard in the district, which bore the distinction of being the world centre of the needle manu- facturing industry. During the last couple of years machines such as the foot stamp and eye press had been introduced which did away with many of the old hand-worked processes in the town's staple trade of needle making. Many workmen had been forced out of their employments and they and their families were now miserably existing on the Poor Relief doled out grudgingly to them by the Parish Authorities.

Cashmore's gaze fell upon a particularly fat-bodied cheap- jack, who was voraciously tearing at a large hunk of bread and cheese.

'I reckon the Pointer Lads 'ull have a bit o' fun wi' you, my bucko, later on this night, when they'se got the drink in 'um. But it wunt be no use you acoming crying to me about it if they does you an injury because I'll have me hands too full by that time to be able to do anything for you, and that's as sure as maybe, or my name arn't Joseph Cashmore.'

Chapter Two

THE PEDLAR CAME trudging up the long hill, sweating beneath the weight of his heavy pack. The fierce noontime sun baked the ground and his heavy boots kicked up puffs of reddish dust from the rutted surface of the road. Some hundred yards ahead of him were the clustered buildings of the town's outskirts, and he sighed with heartfelt relief as he neared them. He passed the tall many-windowed walls of a needle mill, and came abreast of a small wayside public house, outside which a group of men wearing rolled white aprons around their hips and square brown paper caps on their heads were sitting on a bench. The sight of the tankards in their hands caused the pedlar to hesitate. Although he was eager to reach the Fair, his long hard trudge had made him very thirsty, and his dry throat and mouth clamoured for moisture. He slowed his pace and came to a halt by the seated men.

'Good day to you,' he greeted them, and his well modulated, educated accents were oddly at variance with his shabby appearance. 'Could you tell me please how far I am from the Fair?'

'Not so far, pedlar,' one of the men told him. 'But I wouldn't bother rushing to get theer. It wun't ha' warmed up yet awhiles.'

The pedlar smiled, showing clean even teeth. 'No, it's early still, is it not. I think I'll take a glass before continuing on with my journey.'

He went inside the low doorway, and the men outside nudged and winked meaningfully at each other. When the pedlar reappeared with a leather drinking-jack of ale in his hand, he was invited to take a seat on the long bench.

'My thanks to you,' he accepted politely, and once he was settled and had taken a long draught of ale, asked, 'What part of the town is this?'

'You'm in Bredon,' he was informed. 'That's Tommy Bayliss's needle mill over theer. That place a bit further down from it is Whittle and Lambert's factory. This here's the Wagon and Horses, and that pub a bit nearer on to Redditch is the King's Arms. What's you got in your pack?'

The pedlar took his wide-brimmed hat off, revealing a rounded florid clean-shaven face, and brown hair with long side whiskers. He looked to be about forty years of age, and his body was taut and muscular beneath his shabby black jacket and grey flannel shirt.

'I've got ribbons and hand-mirrors. Some Sheffield knives and thimbles, threads and needles and buttons of various patterns,' he told them pleasantly. 'Do you wish to see my wares?'

They grinned and winked surreptitiously at each other. 'In a little while maybe, pedlar. You take your drink fust. It's a dusty walk you'se had be the looks on it. Wheer is it you'se come from?'

'From Birmingham last. I needed to get more buttons, and that's the best city to buy them in.' The pedlar seemed pleased to have someone to talk with. 'But before that I've been in Scotland, and the North Country.'

'What's the news from theer?' one man asked.

'The cholera is very bad, there are thousands dead of it in Scotland and more in Yorkshire and Lancashire. It's reaching the Midlands and the Black Country as well,' the pedlar informed them gravely. 'There's been riots because of it in Paisley and other parts, or so I've been told.'

'Riots? Why so?' he was asked.

'Because of ignorance and of fear.' The pedlar smiled wryly, 'The people in Paisley believed that the surgeons were deliberately poisoning the victims of the cholera to obtain their corpses for dissection.'

'I 'udden't put it past the bastard sawbones to do just that,' one of the men declared angrily.

The pedlar shook his head, 'I think not.' He drained his leather jack and went to rise. 'Well, I must be on my way.'

From Bayliss's needle mill came the ringing of a bell.

'Theer, that's our snap-time finished.' The other men rose also, leaving their empty tankards on the bench.

'Come on down to the mill wi' us now, pedlar, and show us what you'se got for selling. I needs to buy some ribbons for my missus.' Others joined his urgings.

'Yes, come on down wi' us, pedlar.'

'You'll be sure to do plenty o' business wi' the wenches theer. They'll all be wanting ribbons for the Fair, wun't they?'

The pedlar shouldered his pack and accompanied the gang back into the mill. In the small inner courtyard they indicated a clear space on the cobbles where he could lay out his wares, and as he did so the other workers in the mill began to crowd the windows overlooking him.

He quickly spread a large piece of white cloth and laid out upon it his reels of cotton and hanks of thread. Ivory, bone, brass and enamelled buttons, swirls of brightly coloured ribbons, shining hand-mirrors, small knives and decorated thimbles. Also some small wrapped packets of needles.

As these latter were laid down, a concerted growl sounded from the men standing closely about him, and he looked up at their scowling faces with surprise.

One of the men bent and snatched up a packet of needles.

'What the fuck is this then?' He snarled angrily, and holding the packet aloft so that the workers leaning from the windows above could see it, he bellowed, 'Does you see what this bastard has brung wi' him? He's brung fuckin' foreign sharps!'

Howls of execration and fury greeted his words, and the pedlar straightened in alarm.

His puzzlement was plain as he asked anxiously, 'What's the matter with them? I bought them in London. There's naught wrong with them as far as I know.'

More packets of the needles were snatched up and examined by the men around him, and one of them cursed and spat out, 'These be fuckin' Frog sharps, pedlar. Bloody foreign muck!'

'You bastard!' a man hissed. 'You'm taking the bread out on our mouths selling this chape rubbish.'

The pedlar's own indignation roused at this insult. 'I'd advise you to have a care in what you say,' he warned and went to take the packet of needles from the man's fingers.

As his own fingers closed about the garish wrapping paper, a fist thudded against the side of his face and he gasped in pain and shock. Then the storm broke upon him, and from all directions punches and kicks rained. Powerless to defend himself he was sent crashing to the cobbles, senses dazed with pain.

'Clear away! Clear away!' The shout went up, and his attackers scattered back as from the upper windows buckets of filth and thick grease were hurled down upon the helpless pedlar's sprawling body. Howls of laughter and catcalls resounded in the confined space.

Blinded by oily filth he could only roll into a ball and try as best he could to shield his most vulnerable parts as more kicks crashed into his body, and then he felt his ankles gripped by brutal hands and he was dragged face downwards across the cobbles and with a parting salvo of kicks heaved bodily onto the road outside the gates of the mill. His wares were kicked through the streaming filth and stamped into ruin by heavy boots and his pack was slashed and ripped to shreds. As he crawled away on hands and knees volleys of missiles accompanied by curses, threats, cruel jeers and laughter went with him. Racked by pain he crawled on, unable to see through his streaming eyes, then slumped down and lay still, fighting to hold back the darkness that threatened to engulf him.

'Whoa now, whoa.' Daniel Lambert reined in his horse and stared closely at the filthy, bloodied man lying face downwards in the roadway outside a terrace of mean tumbledown cottages. A trio of haggard, ragged women were standing staring at the motionless body, and Daniel Lambert asked them, 'What's happened to him? Did you see?'

One of the women hawked and spat onto the sprawled man and beneath her greasy mass of frizzed hair her pallid face bore an expression of virulent hatred.

'He's a fuckin' cheapjack, master,' she hissed. 'He had French needles in his pack. The lads from Tommy Bayliss's got ahold of the bugger. Serve him bloody well right as well. That 'ull teach the sod not to come here making mock of us.'

'There was no need for them to serve the man so badly, was there?' Lambert remonstrated and the woman was quick to round on him.

''Tis alright for you to talk, Master Lambert. You'm making plenty o' money wi' your fucking stamps and presses, arn't you! But my man anna worked for more nor a twelvemonth, and my kids goes to their beds crying wi' the hunger more times than enough. You bloody Stamping Masters has done too much harm to us already, without these bastard cheapjacks acoming here to rub our noses in it by trying to sell fucking French sharps here as well.'

Daniel Lambert could make no defence against this assault. He and his partner, Brandon Whittle, had indeed been among the first of the local Masters to introduce stamps and presses into the district. Although he had been forced to do so through the necessity to survive, he still felt a great sense of guilt for the hardships this introduction of machinery had caused for many of the 'soft workers', those who made needles by hand.

He dismounted and, keeping hold of his reins with one hand, knelt to examine the injured man. The thick filth and grease and the weeping of blood from cuts and abrasions made it difficult to ascertain the extent of the man's injuries and Daniel Lambert asked, 'Can you hear me?'

The torn swollen lips mumbled an indistinct reply and one hand weakly indicated the eyes, still streaming with tears from the effects of the oily filth.

'Don't try to speak any more,' Daniel Lambert instructed. 'Just lay quiet until I can get help. I'll look after you now.'

He stood, and asked the women. 'Will you help me to move him?'

All three of them merely glared venemously at him, and turned their backs.

Again he spoke to the injured man, 'I'll needs leave you here for a few minutes. But don't worry, I'll be back.'

Chapter Three

THE SMELL OF the fresh-baked bread was a fragrance on the heated air and Tildy Crawford smiled with satisfaction as she used the flat-bladed wooden shovel to lift the big round golden-crusted loaves from the baking oven and set them on the massive white-scrubbed table in her kitchen.

'You'm a dab-hand at the baking, Tildy, of that theer's no doubt at all,' said old Esther Smith and the younger woman's face glowed with pleasure at the compliment.

The old crone's bright black birdlike eyes were warm and loving as they regarded her companion. Just a month short of her thirty-second birthday, Tildy Crawford was still a beautiful woman. Her dark brown hair was glossy with cleanliness, and her eyes, a deeper lucent velvet-brown, set off to perfection the olive-tinted skin of her oval face. Beneath the plain grey gown her body was slender and shapely, and her high firm breasts jutted out against the bodice of her long white apron.

'My nephew is a lucky man,' Old Esther's toothless jaws worked up and down beneath her hooked nose as if she were chewing on that statement. 'Just think on it, Tildy, in three weeks' time you'll not be a Crawford any longer, but a Lambert like I used to be, afore I was stupid enough to wed that bleeder Smith.'

Tildy's even white teeth glistened between her soft full lips. 'I'm looking forward to it, Esther.' Then she paused for a moment before continuing thoughtfully, 'But truth to tell, Esther, I couldn't feel more married to Daniel than I do now. All the church services in the world won't alter that. After all, we've lived as man and wife for nigh on two years, haven't we?'

She touched her fingers to the loaves to test their heat, then fetched a piece of clean cloth from the dresser drawer and wrapped one of the loaves in it.

'I'll just take this along to Emma,' she told the old woman, whose withered brown features frowned at this information.

'You tell Emma Duggins that her needs to get in here and do some bloody filing. Her arn't done a tap for days now. Bread must be earned.'

'Now you're being over harsh, Esther,' Tildy reproved her quietly. 'You know well that both her youngest are ill. The poor woman can't be expected to leave them neglected to come and file needles with us, can she?'

Old Esther subsided with muttered ill grace; Tildy lifted the wrapped loaf and went outside.

The dwelling place that she shared with Daniel Lambert, her schoolboy son, Davy, and Daniel's aunt, Old Esther, was in Salters Yard. An ancient huddle of buildings with a long cobbled frontage behind a low crumbling brick wall in Alcester Street, some two hundred yards east of St. Stephen's Chapel. The castellated Town Lock-up reared midway between the Salters Yard and the Chapel, and further along to the east was the stinking, green-scummed Big Pool, with its floating population of drowned rats, cats and dogs, and its pullulating swirls of foetid rotting sewage. On a hot day such as this, the vile smell emitted by the Big Pool hung like a miasma in the air, and Tildy's nostrils twitched as the stench assailed them.

The Salters Yard had once been considered a very desirable residence, but now its seven tenements were ramshackle and ruinous and had been subdivided constantly. Its teeming population was for the most part drawn from the poorest elements of the town.

Tildy and her family had come to live here some two years previously, during a period of hard times. But now, her lover and husband to be, Daniel Lambert, held a partnership in a small yet flourishing needle factory, and their fortunes were improving steadily.

As she walked along the yard she saw that Alcester Street was busy with Fair Day traffic, and she smiled with pleasure at the prospect of going to the Fair that evening with her son and her lover.

Emma Duggins and her husband Charlie rented one single room with a minute attached lean-to scullery at the end of the yard. When Tildy reached their door she found it half-open. She knocked and called, 'It's Tildy, Emma, can I come in?'

'Come on, my duck.' It was the woman who answered, and when Tildy entered she saw that, apart from the two sick children lying in the bed that almost filled the available space, Emma Duggins was alone.

The air was foul and a momentary queasiness caused Tildy to clench her teeth hard, but she would not allow her reaction to show in her expression and smiled at the pale, haggard Emma Duggins, noting with concern her badly bruised and swollen eyes.

'Has he been battering you again, Emma?'

The other woman nodded resignedly.

Tildy's heart welled with pity. She herself had endured a loveless, violent marriage and knew how her friend was suffering. But in her world a wife was merely the chattel of her husband, and he could use her in any way he pleased. Tildy said nothing, knowing how useless words would be, instead she proffered the hot loaf.

'I've brought you this, Emma. I've told Davy to call and buy some cheese on his way back from school, and when he comes I'll send him round with it.'

She saw the other woman's eyes begin to brim with tears and, to spare her embarrassment, went to the bedside and bent over the two small figures lying quietly on the soiled sheeting.

'How are you feeling today, honey-lambs?' Her hands gently stroked the hot foreheads and tears threatened to brim in her own eyes as she saw their grey, wasted faces and their huge, pain-wracked eyes.

'It's just running out on 'um, Tildy,' their mother told her, 'and now they'm starting to pass blood.'

'Have you had the doctor to them?' Even as she spoke Tildy could have bitten on her own tongue, knowing the stupidity of such a question. Penniless paupers could not afford doctors. She didn't wait for any reply, but went on, 'Listen Emma, I'll pay for the doctor to come and look at them.'

The other woman raised her hands and protested, 'No, Tildy! I can't keep taking from you.'

'Nonsense!' Tildy would not accept any refusal. 'They must have a doctor to them if they've started to pass blood.'

'But Charlie 'ull goo mad iffen he finds out I'se took your money, Tildy. He's so bitter agen the Stamping Masters that he can't even abear me ataking a bit o' grub from you, because you'm wi' Daniel Lambert.'

'I can't say that I blame him for being so bitter, Emma,' Tildy remarked ruefully. 'If I was Charlie, I'd more than likely be feeling so myself.'

Charlie Duggins had been a soft worker at Henry Milward's needle mill until Milward had introduced foot stamps and eye presses, and Charlie Duggins had become redundant.

'Where's Charlie now?' Tildy wanted to know.

Emma Duggins shrugged her thin bowed shoulders. 'God knows wheer the bugger's got to, Tildy. He went off this morn to see if he could get a bit o' work at the Fair.' She sighed heavily, 'Mind you, even if he's found work, I doubt that I'll see any of the bloody money he'll earn. He'll drink it all away afore he comes back here.' Tears now fell freely down her cheeks, but she made no attempt to wipe them away. Her hands remained in her lap in a posture of hopeless resignation. 'He's changed so much, Tildy, since we'se bin forced onto the Parish. He's like a bloody stranger to me now. He arn't a bit like the man I got wedded to, I take me oath he arn't. He's become a bloody stranger.'

'Listen, don't worry about Charlie finding out about the doctor,' Tildy reassured her. 'I can send for him to come to my house first, and then I can make sure that Charlie's not here when I bring the doctor to see to the kids.'

She didn't wait for any further protests but hurried from the room, thankful, despite her liking for the other woman, to escape from its nauseous stench.

To her surprise she saw Daniel's horse tethered at the gate in the low wall, and hurried into her own tenement to find him in the kitchen with Old Esther.

'What brings you home so early, Daniel? Is anything the matter?' she asked with a note of concern in her voice.

Since she had met this man, Tildy had known a happiness that she had never experienced before in her harsh life, and always deep down, she feared that something would happen to take that happiness away from her.

He smiled and kissed her cheek. 'Nothing for you to fret yourself about, sweetheart.' He hesitated a moment, then asked her, 'I hope you won't mind, but I'm having an injured man brought here. The cart's following me up.' Quickly he went on to explain about the pedlar, 'I couldn't just leave the poor fellow bleeding in the dirt. So I'm having him brought here, and I'll bring the doctor to take a look at him.'

Tildy was forced to smile herself at this coincidence. 'That makes two of us who are wanting to bring a doctor to see to somebody, honey. You go and fetch one, and I'll make ready here.' Then she asked Esther, 'Help me clear this table, Esther. So we can lay the poor man on it when he arrives.'

Even as she spoke she heard the excited babbling of her neighbours' voices as they came from their rooms to see the injured man lifted out of the cart and carried into Tildy's house.

The men who laid him out on the kitchen table were unsympathetic to his plight. 'Bloody fool should have had more sense than to let a crowd get him into a mill like that,' the oldest of them sneered as they all left.

Tildy stood looking down at the filthy, bloodied head and the clothes ruined by the thick oily grease, and could not help but agree with the carter's statement. It was something of a sport locally to inveigle an unsuspecting pedlar or pack-man into a mill yard, and then handle him and his wares roughly.

'You would think that the cheapjacks would pass the word among themselves not to be caught so,' she remarked to Old Esther. 'Because as long as I can remember they've been getting similar treatment in Redditch.' Then she went to fetch water to cleanse the man with.

As the wet cloth touched his skin the man stirred and mumbled incoherently and Tildy soothed him, 'Be still now, I won't hurt you. I'm just trying to clean you up a bit.' She turned to Esther, 'We'll needs take his clothes off first, I think. The doctor won't be able to see what other harm's been done to him else.' She leaned over and spoke into the man's ear, 'Look, you'll have to help us to undress you. The doctor's coming to examine what harm you've suffered.'

'Can you cleanse my eyes first?' Although his lips were so badly cut and swollen that he could only speak with difficulty, Tildy was able to understand.

'Alright, good man, I'll do that.' With great care she started to sponge the caked filth from his eyelids.

'There now, I've done.' The young and dandified Doctor Hugh Taylor considered by many to be the handsomest man in the entire needle district smiled down at his patient, 'You've no bones broken, but you'll be stiff and sore for a few days.'

He nodded towards Tildy, 'And you've had the finest sick nurse in the parish tending to you, so all in all I consider you to be a lucky man.'

The pedlar, wrapped only in a blanket and looking much cleaner after the ministrations of Tildy and Old Esther, painfully pushed himself into a sitting position on the table. 'My thanks to you, doctor.' He tried to smile at Tildy, Old

Esther and Daniel Lambert. 'And my thanks for your great kindness to me, sir, and ladies. Now, if I could have my clothes, I'll not trouble you further.' He looked back to the doctor, 'I'm afraid that it may be a little while before I can pay your fee, sir. But I do assure you that your bill will be settled at the earliest I can manage.'

Hugh Taylor grinned easily, 'My bill has already been met.' Turning to Tildy he said, 'And now, Mistress Crawford, I'll go with you to see those other patients you have for me.'

The pedlar appeared deeply embarrassed and when the doctor and Tildy had gone from the room he asked Daniel Lambert, 'Tell me sir, is it you who have paid the doctor?'

Daniel shrugged deprecatingly, 'It was but a trifle. Think no more of it I beg of you.' He stared at the small pile of ruined clothing lying on the floor, and smiled wryly. 'As to giving you back your clothes, I think they are beyond repair. However, we look to be about the same size, and I have clothes to spare. I'm sure we can find something to suit you.'

The pedlar was obviously very moved by this added kindness, and for some moments appeared unable to speak. Then he said haltingly, 'I am very grateful to you, sir. I can only trust that some day I may have opportunity to return your kindness to a stranger.'

'I think it is time we introduced ourselves, I am Daniel Lambert, this is my aunt, Mistress Esther Smith, and the other lady who was tending you is my wife-to-be, Mistress Matilda Crawford.'

The pedlar bowed his head courteously. 'I am honoured, sir, and ma'am. My name is Brown, Charles Claude Brown.' A smile hovered on his damaged lips. 'But on the road most people know me as Mister Smith, the Gentleman Pedlar. I prefer it so.'

'Very well, I shall call you Mister Smith then. So, let's find you something more suitable to wear.' Daniel grinned, and asked Old Esther, 'Aunt, could you prepare some refreshment for Mister Smith while he is getting dressed?'

When Tildy returned home she found the three of them sitting at the table, drinking ale, eating cold beef and bread, and chatting as easily as if they had all known each other for years. She knew Daniel well enough to sense that he had conceived an instant liking for this stranger and, confident in Daniel's judgement of human worth, she was content to accept the pedlar at her table.

An hour passed and then the pedlar told them, 'And now, regretfully, I must take my leave of you.'

'Forgive me if I intrude unduly upon your privacy, Mister Smith, but might I enquire where you go to?' Daniel asked. Tildy had been correct, Daniel had conceived an instant liking for this stranger, and was reluctant to lose his new friend.

Mister Smith smiled warmly, 'Why Mister Lambert, I go to repair my fortunes. I must seek for lodgings and for work so that I can earn money to repay you and to replace my stock of goods.'

'What sort of work do you seek?' Daniel asked.

'Anything at all,' the pedlar shrugged. 'I'm not a man who thinks certain types of occupation to be beneath him.'

Tildy, although normally reserved with new acquaintances, had also found herself unaccountably drawn to this stranger, and, like Daniel, had conceived a sympathy for him. Now she suggested tentatively,' Esther and me need help with the filing, Daniel. Since Emma's kids have been badly, she's not been able to work with us and we can't keep up with what you're bringing here.' She spoke directly to the pedlar. 'The work is filing the heads of the stamped and eyed needles, Mister Smith. It's tedious and there's a need for speed and a sure eye. The trouble is, that it's not very well paid. You see, it's mostly counted as women's work.'

The pedlar's hazel eyes, still badly bloodshot and watery from the effects of the filth and grease, shone with gratitude.

'Well, ma'am, I've never made any distinction between male and female work. It's all one to me. I'd be most happy to give it a try.'

'So be it then.' Daniel beamed happily, then added, 'On one condition though. And that is, that from this moment on we shall call each other by our Christian names, I can't abide unnecessary formality.'

'Here is my hand on that,' the pedlar grinned, and shook hands with each of the others in turn.

'Now lodgings are not a problem either,' Tildy put in. 'Widow Sprake, two doors along the yard here, has a spare room she is eager to find a lodger for, and the rent is very cheap.'

The pedlar abruptly threw back his head and laughed aloud. Then grimaced as that action sent sharp pain lancing through his badly bruised ribs. Sobering, he said quietly, 'It could be termed miraculous, could it not. Not two hours ago I was laying in a gutter, my world in ruins, and here I am now, with fresh work, and fresh lodgings, and fresh friends. I do declare that it seems as if it were all pre-ordained that this should happen.'

His words struck an answering chord in Tildy's mind, and she thought silently, 'You're right. That's just what it does seem to be, pre-ordained.'

Chapter Four

'COME NOW, THREE shots a penny! Three shots a penny! Three shots a penny! Knock down the boxes and win a fine prize! Three shots a penny! That's the style, young sir, here you go!'

The showman handed three short throwing sticks to the boy, and frowning with concentration Davy took careful aim and hurled them one after the other at the cigar boxes balanced on upright poles at the opposite end of the booth. Two of the sticks struck the boxes, but they only shook and did not fall.

'Try agen, young sir, you'm a fine shot, so you am!' the showman urged, but Tildy took her son's arm and pulled him away.

Walking between her son and her lover, Tildy felt proud of her menfolk. Davy, twelve years old, had grown straight and tall, and his cropped black curls topped a face that drew longing glances from girls and young women, and interested stares from some of their older sisters. Daniel was also strong-bodied and tall, with his face deep tanned by the savage suns of distant lands. Dressed in well-cut brown frockcoat and pantaloons, with a tall tan tophat on his thinning brown hair, his light blue eyes clear and confident, he was an attractive and very masculine man.

It was late afternoon, and the cattle and horse sales were done for the day and now people were turning their minds to pleasure. At this hour the crowds were mainly composed of the more staid and respectable elements of the population: soberly dressed artisans, shopkeepers, skilled tradesmen and masters, farmers in wide-skirted coats and leather gaiters, countrymen in smocks and billycock hats, housewives wearing their 'Sunday go to Church' dresses, their children with scrubbed shiny-clean faces clutching their Spend-Fair half-pennies and farthings in fingers made sticky by spun-sugar, toffee-apples and ginger-snap.

The older siblings trailed reluctantly behind their families, resentful of the censorious eyes of parents and elders. The young girls dressed in high-brimmed, be-feathered bonnets, their flounced skirts drawn up out of the dust to display neat white-stockinged ankles and dainty shoes and bootees; their hair dressed in elaborate cascades of ringlets and curls. The youths and young men with tight pantaloons strapped beneath their footwear, slender-waisted, shoulder-padded cutaway coats, high-stocked collars, froths of lacy cravats and dashingly tall tophats, preening like peacocks beneath the demure glances of bright eyes, and slyly purchasing the posies of ribbons called fairings, which they would later present to their sweethearts if parents grew careless and opportunity arose.

'Who'll cast a hazard? Who'll cast a hazard? You sir, you'se got a knowing eye, take the dice.' A ferret-featured gentleman handed his dice to a red-faced, leather-gaitered farmer, portly in good broadcloth; blue and white smocked countrymen pressed close around the table to watch the cast and bet their pennies on the result.

'An eight! Hard luck, sir! Hard luck!' Ferret-face commiserated, 'Try agen, sir, you mun try agen, and your luck 'ull surely change!'

'Come and buy, come and buy me, before I go me way. Just a paltry penny for the news of all the town.' A broadsheet seller, festooned with his wares came carolling through the thronging crowds.

'Ride the cock horse to Banbury Cross, and see the fine lady upon her white hoss!' The glassy-eyed wooden horses of the carousel went tirelessly round and round and round, and up and down went the seesaws, higher and higher soared the swingboats, and the great four-armed dipper carried its squealing cargoes towards the skies and plunged them earthwards in dizzying circles.

'Gingerbread! Fine gilt gingerbread! Who'll buy my gingerbread?' Old Mother Jennens' plump pink face beamed good-naturedly on her eager customers. 'Fine gilt gingerbread! The finest money can buy? Who'll ate my gingerbread?'

'See the fattest 'ooman in the world, and her sister who'se the thinnest 'ooman in the world. Half a penny to see one on 'um only. Three farthings to see 'um both!' A garishly clothed dwarf bellowed in a voice that sounded too massive for his tiny body.

'It ought to be a farthing only to see the thin 'un because there aren't a lot to see, is there?' one of his audience objected loudly.

'Ahr, but the fat 'un is so big that by rights I should be charging a penny to see her. There's so much on her that afore she lost a bit o' weight, it used to take a whole day to walk right round her. So you'm getting a fine bargain, my lord,' the dwarf retorted sonorously.

'Roll up, roll up for the Welsh Giant. He was found at the bottom of a coal mine, wheer his dad had abandoned him because he cost too much to feed. Roll up, roll up, roll up for the Welsh Giant!'

'No, not a shillin'! Not a six-pence! Not a twopenny piece 'ull I take for this jug. This masterpiece o' the potter's art! No! My lords, ladies and gentlemen, this masterpiece is here to be sold for a single penny-piece! Two bloody ha-pennies! Four measly farthings! I'm a fool to meself! I knows I am, but I canna help it! I'm agoing to let you rob me blind! A single penny for this magnificent jug, fresh from the bloody kiln!'

Cheapjack Farmer threw the painted vessel high in the air, and caught it with one hand, only inches from the ground. 'Come now, who wants it, afore I bloody well smashes it? Thank you, my lady! You'm a very clever woman, so you am. You knows a bargain when you see it.

'And here's a platter fit to grace the table o' King

William hisself, but I'll not take a shilling for it. No, I bloody well refuses to take what it's worth! I wants to sell it so bloody chape, that I'm practically giving it away, fool that I am, and I knows it!'

'Find the pea, good sirs. Find the pea,' Brummagem Charlie invited. 'Which thimble is it under? Is it there? Or is it there? By Christ, but you'm a fly cove, you am, my buck. You'm a real Jack Artful, ain't you? It's under this 'un, you say? Put your money down, my master, and then we'll see.'

'Ahhhh nooo! It aren't there arter all, is it? Ne'er mind, my buck, I'll tell you true that you nearly copped me there, and that's a fact. Come now, whose next to try? Where's the pea? Where's the pea?'

A gong rang and through a speaking trumpet a man challenged. 'Be there any strong men among you? Is there any man in this town who thinks he can lift a weight to match the 'Mighty Hercules' here? Just look at the thews on this man, my lords and ladies. Just look at the thickness of his arms, and the size of his chest. In just one minute, my lords and ladies, the Mighty Hercules will perform his amazing feats of strength. He'll bend iron bars, and lift massive weights, and challenge any two men in the world to match him. Pay at the desk, my lords and ladies. Pay at the desk and come inside. You'll be able to tell your grandchildren that you'se seen the strongest and mightiest man in the history o' the world. Pay at the desk and come inside!'

'Buy my beads and buttons! Buy my beads and buttons!'

'Ginger snap, loverley ginger snap! Ginger snap, loverley ginger snap!'

'Hot meat pies! Hot meat pies! Hot meat pies!'

From the platform of a garishly painted booth came the martial rattle of drumbeat and blast of trumpet played by two boys clad in ancient shabby scarlet regimentals, and a man dressed in the red coat and battered black shako of a soldier saluted the crowd with a rusty curved sabre and bellowed, 'Inside these walls is one o' the wonders o' this modern age. A panorama that has been displayed, before all the crowned heads o' Europe. A creation that created riots in London, because people were fighting to get in and see it. It is the one and only true panopticon representation o' the great battle o' Waterloo!

'I knows it to be true because I was theer on that blood-soaked field o' glory meself, in the division of brave General Picton who fell most gloriously at the head of his men, fighting for his King and Country like the true hero he was, God bless his immortal memory!

'Come inside my lords and ladies, come inside and see great Wellington, the noble Iron Duke hisself! See that evil villain, Old Boney! See how he gnashes his teeth and slinks away before our bayonets. See our gallant matchless infantry and our valorous cavalry and our glorious artillery pound the French to atoms! See the Prussians coming onto that bloody field, led by the gallant old Marshall Blucher hisself! See the French Imperial Guard running from our own brave Guards! Come inside and live again through the most glorious day for British Arms that has ever been known!'

Tildy smiled at Daniel and took his arm, 'Do you want to go and have a look at it, Dan? It might bring back memories to you.'

He shrugged, and grinned, 'Some of those memories are bad ones, honey. I lost some good old comrades there. Truth to tell, I was sore frightened most of that day, and I wouldn't like you to see me so if my likeness is pictured inside.'

'Let's go in, Daniel. I want to see where you were fighting when you were a soldier,' Davy begged eagerly, and the man smiled fondly at him.

'Alright, son, we'll take the Grand Tour.'

'You're spoiling this boy, giving way to his every whim,' Tildy rebuked him, but her loving smile belied her words.

They strolled through the tent, lit by oil lamps and viewed the long crudely painted mural displayed there. Tildy was disappointed by the poor draughtsmanship of the pictures, but Davy was thrilled by the lurid scenes of battle.

So Tildy held her peace and made no criticism of what she saw.

They came from the tent and were instantly confronted by a group of beggars. Ragged, filthy, stinking creatures, some of whom lacked arms, or legs, or eyes.

'Spare a penny, my lord, for an old soldier who lost his arm at Waterloo!'

'I was a Colour Sergeant wi' the old 28th, sir. Can you spare a trifle?'

'Help an old soldier who's fought and suffered for King and Country, lady!'

'Left me eyes in Spain, I did. Left me eyes in Spain! And for all I knows, they'm alaying theer still in the breach o' Badahoos walls.'

'Mam, I'm going to give them something!' Davy told her. 'It's a shame to see brave soldiers reduced to this.'

Tildy took a few half-pence from the pocket of her gown and handed them to the boy, and he added his own meagre store of pence to them and distributed the coins among the clamorous beggars.

As they walked away from the tent Tildy asked Daniel, 'Do you believe that they really were at Waterloo, those men back there?'

Daniel smiled grimly. 'It's very doubtful, but perhaps some of them were. I know it's all that a lot of crippled old soldiers can do, is to beg.'

A sudden flash of angry resentment burst from him, 'A damned rotten country is it not, that treats men who fought and suffered for it so shamefully. Those men back there are probably fakers and cheats, but I know myself of fine men who can't obtain a pension for their wounds from the fat-bellied bastards who rule us, men who are forced to beg for a crust from those who stayed safe and snug at home and grew rich, while the rest of us went out to fight the French.'

He sighed gustily, 'I do declare, Tildy, there are times when I think that we were all fighting for the wrong side. At least Napoleon Bonaparte cared for his old soldiers, and made sure that they received a just recompense for their sufferings and their wounds.'

'I'm Aston from Dudley, and this is Aston's famous Learned Pig. The only animal in the whole o' Christendom who can see into the future!' The showman's fat red greasy face and broad flat snout gave him more than a passing resemblance to his animal. 'What is more, this wonderfully gifted and sagacious creature can not only see into the future, but even more miraculous than that, it can tell us what is to be.'

His audience looked suitably impressed by this statement, until a wag at the rear of the crowd shouted, 'Ask it if me old 'ooman's agoing to let me have a bit tonight, then?'

'You doon't need to ask the pig that, Jimmy, just ask your missus's Fancy Man!' another wag quipped, and the crowd roared with raucous laughter.

Aston ignored the interruptions. His massively fat pig was standing in a close-fitting boxlike structure of canvas and wood, and the showman bent over the beast and asked loudly, 'Can you hear these fools, O Learned One?'

The huge beast suddenly jerked and grunted loudly, and Aston smiled broadly and turned back to his audience, 'Theer now, you all heard it answer didn't you? It grunts once to say "Yes", and twice to say "Nay".' Again he bent to the pig, 'That's true what I say, arn't it, O Learned One?'

Another jerk and grunt, and Aston straightened and spread his arms wide. 'Theer now, the proof o' the puddin's in the ateing of it. You'se all seen and heard what this marvellous creature can do. Now for a single penny, you can ask it any question you so desires. One single penny!' He paused, then nodded portentously, 'To my way o' thinking, that's dirt chape to know what the future might hold.'

'I'se got a question, master.' A smock-clad young ploughboy lifted his hand and stepped forwards from his group of grinning friends, and Aston held his own grimy paw out palm upwards.

'Then pay your penny, good sir, and you shall put the question and have your answer in a trice.'

The yokel handed over the thick coin, then asked. 'Can you tell me, master, if I'm agoing to be give Old Jasper's brown mare?'

The showman bent to his pig, and appeared to whisper in its ear. There was a slight pause, and then the pig jerked and grunted twice.

The young ploughboy's jaw gaped with astonishment, and behind him, his friends stared at each other, then at the pig with wonderment.

Aston grinned, and loudly questioned. 'O Learned One, is the reason that this young man wun't get that mare, is it because that mare is already dead?'

A single loud grunt came in reply, and the group of ploughboys broke into excited exclamations.

The showman's greasy red face was very severe. 'You see, Ladies and Gentlemen, not even a deliberate trick question like that 'un was, can gammon this marvellous beast. Like I told you afore, it can see the future, and knows what's gone before. The proof o' the puddin's in the ateing, arn't it, and you'se all now witnessed the proof.' He swung with upraised arms and beseeched dramatically: 'I pray you! I pray you all, ladies and gentlemen, let us have no more attempted trickeries here. Let us have only genuine questions. Now who comes next to have the future revealed?'

Others pressed forwards with their own questions and for a while the pig was continually jerking and grunting.

Daniel drew Tildy and Davy close to him, and whispered. 'Do you see how it's done, honey? Do you see, son?'

Tildy shook her head in mystification, but Davy grinned and made a stabbing motion with his hand, and Daniel chuckled and nodded.

Tildy suddenly understood, and laughed at her own previous dullness, in not realising that the showman had a needle concealed in his hand, with which he pricked the pig through the canvas wall of the box, to elicit a grunt of pain.

Three Pointer Lads joined the group, wearing the leather aprons, square paper caps and red flannel shirts that their particular trade favoured. Tildy noticed them, and knew that within a short time there would be some sort of mischief created by these notoriously wild young men.

The newcomers pressed through the group until they stood next to the canvas box, then one of them offered a penny to Aston. The showman frowned doubtfully, knowing the reputation of Needle Pointers for violence and general misbehaviour.

'I'se got a question for that bloody piece o' bacon.' The brawl-scarred face of the Pointer was suffused with an unholy pleasure.

'What is it?' Aston frowned, and tried to watch the other two Pointers who had pushed through to the opposite side of the box away from their friend.

'I want's to know iffen my old feyther is agoing to turn in his grave agen this week?' the first Pointer grinned.

Before Aston could reply, the pig suddenly jerked and emitted a high-pitched squeal, then started to kick and jump in an effort to escape the box.

'You bastards!' the showman bellowed, as the pig's squealing crescended, and the crowd roared with laughter and applauded wildly.

'Ahhr, your bloody pig arn't bin used to a big sharp up its arse, has it?' the first Pointer shouted gleefully. 'It's only ever felt that bloody little bodkin you'se got in your hand.'

The struts of the canvas box suddenly gave way and the huge pig came roaring, squealing, battering its way to freedom, and the crowd scattered from its path, whooping and laughing. With a howl of mingled rage and despair the showman set off in pursuit of his wage-earner, followed by the cheers and catcalls of his audience.

The horseman guiding his mount through the jeering crowd appeared oblivious to the uproar. He was a small man, wearing a black clerical coat and high neck-stock, with a broad-brimmed beaver hat shadowing his gaunt pale face.

He bent low in his saddle to ask a passerby, 'Tell me, my man, where is the house of the Reverend John Clayton?'

''Tis down the Fish Hill theer, master.' The passerby pointed to the northern end of the Green. ''Tis the big lime-washed 'un down on the right hand side o' the roadway.'

'Many thanks,' the small man nodded curtly and went on.

John Clayton, a youngish man with a remarkably ugly face, and an equally remarkable muscularity of physique was in his shirt-sleeves, working on a sermon in his book-lined study when his manservant knocked and entered. 'It's the Reverend William Leigh of Bilston come to see you, Parson Clayton.'

John Clayton frowned in surprise, and with inkstained fingers re-tied his cravat which he had loosened in the throes of his literary endeavours, and pulled on his black, wide-skirted coat.

He rose and went forwards with an outstretched hand as his visitor came into the room. 'Why William, this is a most pleasant surprise. To what do I owe the pleasure of seeing you here?'

The smaller man frowned and sighed heavily, his gaunt pale features displaying his troubled mood. 'I've this day conveyed my wife to her sister's house in Bromsgrove, John.'

The ugly face of the younger clergyman showed concern. 'Is she ill?'

'No, thanks be to God.' The other man answered. 'I do believe I've moved her in the very nick of time.' Seeing the puzzlement on his old friend's face, he went on quickly. 'The cholera has come to my parish, John. Three died on Saturday last. A woman of thirty-six, a youth of sixteen and a small child.'

'Dear God save us all!' Clayton exclaimed with concern. Bilston was only some eighteen miles distant from Redditch. Another worrisome thought occurred to him. 'Was not Saturday the day of Bilston Wake?'

'Indeed it was,' his companion confirmed. 'With people come there from all over the Midlands. If the contagion is carried by human beings, then I fear by now it could be spreading far and wide across another half a dozen counties as they all go back to their homes.'

Clayton gestured to a chair. 'Please, William, be seated. I'll send for some refreshment and then we'll talk more of this. Say nothing in front of my manservant. The fellow's an incorrigible gossip, and he'll enjoy nothing better than to carry wild tales around the town.'

After they had eaten and drank the two clergymen returned to the subject of the cholera epidemic.

As early as January 1831 The Lords of His Majesty, King William the Fourth's most Honourable Privy Council had directed their secretary, C.C. Greville, Esq., to write to a Doctor Thomas Walker, an English physician resident in St. Petersburg, to propose that he travel to Moscow and investigate the disease which by then was rampaging through the Russian Empire. Accompanied by four other physicians who had been sent out by the Prussian Government, he had done so, and by April of 1831 was able to report to the British Government that it was indeed the Asiatic cholera.

The Privy Council acted upon his report with a commendable speed, and by June 1831 a National Board of Health had been established in London, which was ordered to . . . 'Prepare and digest rules and regulations for the most speedy and effectual mode of guarding against the introduction and spreading of infection, and for purifying any ship or house in case any contagious disorder should unhappily manifest itself in any part of the United Kingdom, notwithstanding the precautions taken to guard against the introduction thereof, and to communicate the same to all magistrates, medical persons and others of His Majesty's subjects who may be desirous, and may apply to be made acquainted herewith.'

The said Board to hold their meetings at the Royal College of Physicians, and to be composed of the following persons: Sir Henry Halford, President of the Royal College of Physicians and President of the Board of Health.

Doctors Holland, Maton, Turner, Warren and Mac-Michael, Fellows of the Royal College of Physicians, and others including the Comptroller of His Majesty's Navy, the Director General of Army Hospitals, the Deputy Chairman of the Customs, the Commissioner of the Victualling Office and the Superintendent General of Quarantine.

Although this Board was only an advisory body with no executive powers, nevertheless two very powerful Ministers of State were particularly concerned with its work, The Home Secretary, Lord Melbourne, and the Vice President of the Board of Trade, Charles Poullet Thomson.

Acting on this London Board of Health's advice the Lords of the Privy Council ordered that in any parish attacked by the cholera a local Board of Health should be set up, to consist of the magistrates, the clergyman, two or more physicians or medical practitioners, and three or more of the principal inhabitants. One of the medical members to be appointed to correspond with the Board of Health in London.

An Order in Council was also issued which empowered the local boards to enforce quarantine on the sick and various other coercions.

By November 1831 widespread dissatisfaction with the London Board of Health's coercive regulations caused it to be virtually disbanded and a new Central Board of Health constituted, composed of a Colonel Rowan of the police department, Sir William Pym the Superintendent General of Quarantine, and two physicians newly returned from a mission to St. Petersburg, Doctors Russell and Barry. The Honourable Edward Stewart was appointed Secretary, and the new board was instructed by the Privy Council to ' . . . devoted their whole time to the details, and take upon themselves the entire executive department . . . '

The new Central Board then issued their own Order in Council concerning the steps to be taken to combat the epidemic, but the coercive methods were abandoned in favour of suggestions.

Unfortunately neither suggestion or coercion had any effect on the spread of the cholera, and no matter what measures were taken to combat it, people continued to be stricken and to die in ever increasing numbers throughout the length and breadth of the British Isles.

'And so now I return to my parish and, pray God, will do all that I can to aid my flock,' William Leigh sighed wearily. 'But from what I have experienced of this dreadful affliction, I fear that that will be little enough. There is no known cure or even palliative. I saw the corpses of the three victims, John, and they resembled monkeys more than humans, they were so shrivelled and wasted by this scourge.'

'Stay here and rest yourself tonight,' John Clayton urged, but the other man shook his head.

'I'd not be able to rest, my friend, even if I did stay.' His sunken eyes mirrored his despair. 'It may be that we shall not meet again in this life, John.'

'That is up to the will of our Master, William,' John Clayton shook the other man's hand. 'He will do with us as He sees fit. We can only trust in Him.'

For the first time since his arrival a wry smile curved William Leigh's thin lips. 'I would suggest, John, that as well as trusting in Our Lord, you also take immediate steps to set up a local Board of Health, and make all possible preparations to cope with this epidemic here in Redditch. Although until now you have enjoyed immunity, I can tell you from bitter experience that this Asiatic cholera can strike anywhere and at any time. There seems to be no discernible pattern in its spread. I fear that like Satan, it lurks all around us, and seeks only opportunity to wreak its evil upon us. Palace or hovel, mountain or valley, city or hamlet, it comes when it chooses and nothing can stop it.'

'Nothing can stop it! Nothing can stop it! Nothing can stop it!' His friend's words reverberated in John Clayton's mind as he sat alone once more in his candlelit study, and filled him with a sense of terrible foreboding. Finally he knelt and prayed:

'Dear God, protect this parish and its people from this terrible scourge, I beseech You. Protect Your servants, and those who trust in You. Protect also those others, miserable sinners, who are still sunken in wickedness and unbelief, Oh Lord, that even yet there will be time to bring them to know Your mercy. Protect us all, Lord, I beseech You. Protect us all . . . '

Chapter Five

THE MORNING AFTER the Fair the pedlar, Charles Brown, came early to Tildy's house to begin his instruction in the art of needle filing. Although his features were still bruised and swollen, and plasters covered the cuts on his head, he assured her that he felt well able to commence work.

In the workshop at the rear of their rooms, Tildy demonstrated how to grip the needle in the narrow jaws of the tongs and use the fine-toothed slender files to shape, clean and smooth the head and eye. She looked doubtfully at his large, strong hands and said, 'Are you sure that you'll be happy to do this work, Charles? As I said yesterday, it's counted as women's work mostly, because there's so few men have the necessary lightness of touch and speed of hand.'

He chuckled, and very slowly manipulated the tongs and files until he had finished a dozen needles. Then invited Tildy, 'Pray do me the favour of examining those, Tildy, and give me your honest opinion as to the quality of my work.'

Carefully she scrutinised the finished needles, and nodded. 'They're truly excellent, but . . . '

'But I'm far too slow at the business,' he interrupted and laughed happily. 'Now watch.'

With a lightening rapidity he again manipulated tongs and files, and Tildy frowned doubtfully as she saw the finished needles beginning to form a small heap. Again he paused and invited her, 'Please, inspect these now.'

With increasing wonderment Tildy picked up the needles one by one and scrutinised them for flaws but was able to find none. She stared at him, and he laughed at the expression of astonishment on her face.

'Truly, I've never seen a man so dexterous with his fingers,' she told him. For a moment his smile faltered, and he murmured, 'That's been said to me before, Tildy.' Then shook his head as if to drive away unasked and unwelcome memories.

Tildy went to the door of the workshop and shouted for Old Esther to come to her. When the old woman appeared, Tildy told her excitedly, 'Come and see this, Esther. You've never seen the like of it, I'll venture.'

She entreated Charles Brown to demonstrate his skill once more, and as he did so Old Esther's beady black eyes slitted shrewdly, and her withered head bobbed in knowing nods.

When the man finished, she also examined the filed needles and again her head bobbed in that knowing nod, 'I knowed it, Master Pedlar, I knowed it from the fust time you was spaking to us yesterday. You anna bin a cheapjack all your life, you'se bin summat a sight more skilful than that. I knowed it all along, so I did.'

He frowned slightly, and then shrugged and tried to make a joke of that unexpected skill. 'When I was a small boy, I was instructed in sewing and fancy needlework instead of the more masculine pursuits, ladies. That's the only reason for my dexterity with the needles, I do assure you.'

The three of them settled to their day's work, and soon the only sounds to be heard in the room were the faint metallic shirring of the files and the tinkling of needles falling from the jaws of the tongs.

The two girls made a charming picture as they walked demurely side by side along Alcester Street in the late afternoon; the pattens strapped beneath their dainty cloth bootees keeping their feet raised from the roadway left muddied by the intermittent rain squalls of the day.

Both were dressed alike in slender-waisted, bell-skirted, voluminous gigot-sleeved, pink day pelisses, with wide brimmed, flowered bonnets covering their hair. They carried closed parasols in their small kid-gloved hands which swung in unison with their step, and the tight bodices of their dresses emphasised the high pert firmness of their shapely breasts. Men's heads turned to watch them as they passed, and compliments were shouted and invitations issued, but the girls only exchanged amused glances from beneath demurely lowered eyelashes and ignored their admirers.

At the Salters Yard they halted, and for a few moments stood facing each other, as if uncertain of their next move.

'Do you think we should, Maria?' The speaker was the pretty, blue-eyed blonde one of the pair. 'Only my pa will go mad if he comes to know that I've been here.'

'I shall go mad if we don't do as we agreed, Charlotte.' Maria Pitts had raven-hued hair and huge grey eyes. Her friend, Charlotte Benton was wholesomely pretty, but she, Maria Pitts, was sensually beautiful.

Charlotte Benton seemed nervous. 'But they say that she is truly a witch?'

Her friend's white teeth glistened between her full red lips as she giggled delightedly, 'But of course she is! At least I hope that is so. Otherwise there is no point to us coming here, is there?'

'But my pa says that she's an evil old crone. And that she lives here with an ex-convict and his trollop. He says that no decent person would ever so much as acknowledge any of them.'

Charlotte Benton's nervousness was making her whine petulantly, and the more spirited Maria Pitts abruptly lost patience with her friend's timidity.

'Go you on home then, Charlotte, and wait for me there if you've a mind to. I'm quite determined on seeing the woman, and naught that you say will serve to make me change my mind.'

She turned and her pattens tapped rapidly across the

cobbles of the Salters Yard. Charlotte Benton's lips twisted angrily, and then she also turned away and went flouncing back along Alcester Street.

Standing outside the rough weather-stained door Maria Pitts hesitated for a moment, as momentarily her courage waned, then she drew a deep breath and lifting her small hand rapped determinedly on the dirty wooden panels.

When there was no immediate reply, the girl's determination only increased, and she hammered on the door so loudly that a frowsty head appeared from a window above her head, and a man's voice bawled angrily.

'Jasus, Joseph and Mary! Can't a body get a bit o' fuckin' slape wi'out you amaking all that fuckin' rattle? Iffen I get up from me bed I'll leather the fuckin' arse offa ye, so I will! Jasus strike me clane dead iffen I don't!'

This unexpected threat almost overcame Maria Pitts' resolve and she might have fled before another verbal onslaught, but then the door opened and Tildy Crawford's low melodic voice asked, 'Yes, my dear, what is it you want here?'

'If you please, ma'am, I want to see Mistress Smith.'

Tildy frowned slightly and for a moment or two made no reply. Then she sighed resignedly, and invited, 'Please to step inside.'

Maria Pitts stared interestedly around the room. Surprised at its sweet-smelling, immaculately clean neatness, so much at variance with the decaying tenement it was housed in.

A wry smile tugged at the corners of Tildy's mouth as she read the girl's expression, 'Tell me, Miss?'

'Pitts. My name is Maria Pitts.'

'Tell me, Miss Pitts, what is it you wish to see Mistress Smith about?'

For a moment the girl's fresh face flushed with an uncertain embarrassment, and she fumbled for words.

Not wishing to torment her, Tildy smiled reassuringly and told her, 'Don't be flustered, my dear. I was only teasing you a little. Do you want Old Esther to read the future for you? Is that why you're here?'

Her visitor sighed with relief, and giggled. 'Yes, ma'am. That is so. My friend Charlotte came with me, but at the last moment she lost her courage and ran away. I nearly took to my heels myself when that man above shouted at me for waking him, I do declare.'

The girl's artless simplicity and complete naturalness instantly won over Tildy, and she giggled like a young girl herself and explained, 'That's my neighbour, Master O'Leary the carrier. He was out on the drink last night, and it always makes him liverish next day. But he wouldn't do any harm to you. He's really a very nice man.' She gestured to a wooden armed chair by the side of the hearth. 'Would you care to sit down, Miss Pitts? Old Esther has popped out on an errand. But she should be back very shortly. I'm Matilda Crawford, but everyone calls me Tildy.'

'I know.' Maria Pitts was now completely at her ease. She regarded Tildy with admiring eyes, thinking how lovely the older woman looked even though so plainly dressed in a simple grey gown and her unadorned hair coiled in glossy plaits around her head. 'I've seen you many times walking in the town, Mistress Crawford. I've always wanted to talk with you. My father is Arnold Pitts, the Attorney at Law; we live up on the Mount Pleasant in the large house next to the Parsons Lane.'

'I know it.' Tildy nodded and in her mind's eye visualised the girl's father. A stoop-bodied, sour-faced man whose fat frumpish wife always looked as if she had swallowed something unpleasant. She marvelled inwardly at how that ugly couple could have produced such a striking young beauty as this.

The girl continued to talk, telling Tildy how boring and constricted she found her life to be and how she wished that she were a man so that she could travel and have adventures, and be independent in life, and Tildy listened and smiled gently to herself as she recognised the myriad similarities of thought and desire that she had shared with her visitor when she herself was a young girl.

Tildy herself had been left an orphan when still only a

very small child, and with her younger brother had been taken in by her father's sister and her maniacally religious husband in a tumbledown cottage in the Brockhill Woods just outside Redditch Town. While still a very young child her brother had been sent with a cartload of other pauper children from the Tardebigge Parish to work as virtually slave labour in the grim cotton mills of the North Country, and she had never seen or heard of him since that day. She was forced to accept that like so many other of those tragic child-slaves he had long since died from overwork and harsh treatment.

Tildy herself had been kept on in her aunt's house as an unpaid and badly-treated drudge, until on her eighteenth birthday she had rebelled and run away to the Redditch Hiring Fair. There she had met her future husband, Tom Crawford. Who, taking advantage of her youth and inexperience had made her incapable with drink before raping and impregnating her.

A forced marriage and long years of suffering had followed, and Tildy had experienced many vicissitudes of fortune, but all through those years she had gloried in the possession of her only child, her son Davy. Conceived in violence, but inheriting none of the viciousness of his father, Tom Crawford, the boy was a constant source of joy and pride. And now, Tom Crawford was dead. Transported to the penal colonies in Australia, he had been killed out there. Her husband-to-be, Daniel Lambert, was himself a returned Transportee, who had been sentenced for poaching when still a wild young man. It was he who had brought her the news of Tom Crawford's death. An event that Tildy was honest enough to admit to herself had been a blessed release for her, since she had only ever known torment and brutality at his hands and had not even liked, let alone ever loved him.

With a slight start, Tildy came out of her reverie and back to the present.

'Do you think it unladylike of me to want to travel and to seek for adventure, Mrs Crawford? Ma and pa both scold me constantly for it. They wish me to marry with Dick Boulton, the woollen draper's son. They say that now I'm nineteen years old, I am of an age when I should be married and having children of my own. What think you, Mrs Crawford?'

Tildy smiled warmly at the young woman. She always wished that she had a younger sister, and could well imagine that if she had, then that sister might well have resembled Maria Pitts.

'Do you love this Dick Boulton?' she questioned and Maria Pitts chuckled and devils of mischief danced in her huge grey eyes.

'Would you think me shameless if I said that there are times when I could wish to make love to him. He is very handsome and has a fine athletic form.'

Tildy could not help but chuckle also, and her heart warmed towards this young woman whom she found herself liking more and more.

'You had best not let your parents hear you say such a thing. I'm sure they would be most grievously shocked if they knew that thoughts such as those ever came into your mind. But I must confess that I can't really think you shameless. After all, I'll wager there is not a woman in this town who has not had such thoughts regarding some man or other at some time in her life.'

Maria Pitts laughed delightedly, 'I knew that if ever I talked with you, Mrs Crawford, I should come to like you. Can we be friends?'

'I don't know if your parents would look upon our being friends with any favour?' Tildy answered doubtfully.

'Phoo! A fig to that!' Maria Pitts made a dismissive snapping with her fingers. 'I don't care whether they view it with favour or not. I want you for a friend. I feel so easy with you. May I call you Tildy? And you must call me Maria.'

Tildy smiled. 'Very well Maria, we will count each other as friends. But do not advertise that fact too widely throughout the town. There are many more people other than your parents who do not look upon me with a deal of kindness. I have quarrelled with a deal of the ones who think themselves to be people of much importance.'

'I know,' Maria crowed happily, 'and that is one of the main reasons that I admire you so much.' At a tangent she asked, 'Old Esther Smith, can she really foretell the future?'

Tildy hesitated, then said simply, 'She believes herself that she can. I have to admit that she has foretold events for me which have come true.' Again she paused and then went on reflectively, 'But truth to tell, Maria, I can't help but think that perhaps we do wrong in trying to see into the future.'

'But it fascinates me so,' Maria exclaimed. 'I find it wonderfully exciting.'

'It fascinates me also,' Tildy confessed, 'but it makes me very uneasy as well. I wish you would give it more consideration before asking her to do this thing for you.'

'No!' The flowered bonnet shook decisively, 'I am quite determined on it, Tildy. There's naught you can say which will make me reconsider.'

Even as she spoke the outer door opened and Old Esther's tiny black-clad form came into the room.

'This is Maria Pitts, Esther,' Tildy informed her. 'She wishes you to read her future.'

'Does her now.' The old woman seemed a trifle crabbed in her mood. 'And does her dad know that her's here?'

'Indeed he does not, Mistress Esther,' the young woman smiled gaily. 'He thinks you to be a Black Witch, in league with the Devil. If he knew I was here then he'd take a whip to me, that I do assure you.'

For a moment the old crone scowled and then her bright black eyes began to twinkle and she laughed wheezily, 'Why Tildy, this pretty maid is saucy enough to be a younger sister to you. But then, I like women to show a touch o' spirit and not to pay heed to what menfolk tells 'um they mun do.'

She spoke directly to Maria Pitts, 'You hold fast for a minute or two, my maid, and when I'se had a bit of a rest, then I'll see what's to be done about looking into the future for you. But I make no promise o' success mind you, for I'm lacking the practice these days. My sweet wench here wun't let me do the scrying iffen her can help it. Her's a bit like your dad, my maid, her reckons it's the Devil's work as well.'

Tildy accepted this barb with a good humour. There was a deep bond of affection between herself and this old woman; they were like mother and daughter to each other.

The old woman cleared the white-scrubbed table and placed upon it a shallow saucer which she filled with a black oily liquid from a small bottle. Then she fetched two candles and setting them at each side of the saucer she lit them. She motioned for Maria Pitts to sit at the table, and seated herself opposite to the girl so that the saucer and its flanking candles were directly between them.

''Ull you draw them curtains, Tildy?' she requested.

Tildy did so and then sat down by the hearth from where she could see both of the others' faces.

In the darkened room the light of the candles sheened the black liquid and the flames were reflected upon its oily surface.

Old Esther placed her outstretched arms alongside the candles and nodded for Maria Pitts to take her hands.

The darkened room and the eerie pale glow of the candle flames appeared to curb the young girl's high spirits, and her huge grey eyes were shadowed with nervous apprehension as the old woman's clawlike hands gripped her own soft fingers. Old Esther began to rock gently backwards and forwards, her eyes closed and her lipless, toothless mouth muttering unintelligible words as if she were chanting an incantation to mysterious gods.

Despite having witnessed Old Esther doing this 'scrying' many times before, Tildy was still powerfully affected by it, and she felt a vague sense of foreboding burgeoning within her and her breathing shallowed and quickened.

The old woman's rocking motion abruptly ceased, and a

low keening moan sounded from deep within her throat. Then her eyes opened and fixed upon the oily sheen of the saucer.

'Yes, yes I see it,' she whispered hoarsely. 'There's a young man. He's in love wi' you, my maid. But you care naught for him. You only wants him for your own vanity.'

Maria Pitts started visibly, and she drew in a sharp intake of breath. 'Will I marry him?' she questioned eagerly.

Old Esther kept her eyes fixed upon the shining liquid, and another keening moan sounded from her.

'Tildy, watching closely, knew the old woman so well that she could sense that something was happening to cause Old Esther distress.

'Cannot you tell me Mistress Esther, will I marry him?' Maria Pitts' normal light-heartedness seemed to be reasserting itself and she smiled gaily, 'Cannot you tell me whom I shall marry, if it's not to be Dick Boulton?'

The keening moan came again from Old Esther's mouth, and then her hands began to shake violently and her right hand suddenly struck a lighted candle and sent it toppling.

Maria Pitts cried out in shock and pulled free of the old woman's clutch; Old Esther slumped back and shaking her head from side to side gasped out hoarsely, 'The spell is broke and the spirits ha' left me. I can see no more this day. I can tell you no more.'

Sensing the young girl's sudden alarm, Tildy quickly rose and drew back the curtains to let the daylight flood into the room, then went to Maria Pitts and forcing a smile, told her, 'There's naught for you to concern yourself about, Maria. This often happens. Esther will be alright in a little while. She needs to rest now, that's all.'

Reassured, Maria Pitts giggled breathlessly, 'I was quite frightened for a moment, Tildy. But isn't it exciting. When can I come again?'

Tildy glanced at Old Esther and saw that the old woman was struggling to calm herself. Then told the girl, 'I'll let you know, Maria. In a few days perhaps. You see, it's as I told you previously, Old Esther doesn't read the future very often these days, and she must accustom herself to it again by easy stages. It's a great strain on her you see.'

'Oh yes, I do see that,' Maria Pitts agreed readily.

'I think it's best if you leave us now, and I'll get Old Esther to her bed,' Tildy suggested gently.

With obvious reluctance the young woman rose to her feet. 'You will send to tell me soon, won't you Tildy?' she beseeched, and Tildy nodded and smiled.

'Of course I will, my dear. Just as soon as Old Esther feels able enough, then I'll send for you to come.'

She accompanied the girl to the door, and they parted the best of friends. Then, with a sense of dread, Tildy asked the old woman, 'What was it you saw, Esther? What was it that you didn't wish to tell her?'

The old woman's eyes were filled with sadness as she answered quietly. 'I saw Death reaching out for that poor sweet maid, Tildy. I saw Death.'

Chapter Six

IT WAS THURSDAY, the ninth day of August and the Fair had come to its close on the previous night. By now the showmen had packed their carousels, swingboats and show-stalls onto their waggons and were gone on their separate roads. The cheapjacks had shouldered their packs; the dealers and gypsies driven away their animals and the Market Place and the Chapel Green had reverted to normal. The people of the town were left with their empty pockets, their queasy hangovers, the broken bones, cuts and bruises of their brawls, and in the case of certain of the women, an anxious time of waiting to discover whether their moments of loving weakness had left them with a more permanent reminder of the Fair.

The Reverend John Clayton walked across a Green littered with the leavings of the festivities, his mind still grappling with the dread news that his friend, William Leigh, had brought to him on Fair Monday. At the northern point of the Green the clergyman came to a halt, and stood staring down the long steep length of the Fish Hill, reluctant to return to his home, knowing that all he would be able to do once back there would be to restlessly pace his study floor and worry fruitlessly about the possibility of the cholera epidemic reaching his own parish.

From his position he was able to see right down the straight hill to where the steepest part of its slope eased at the imposing façade of the British Needle Mills, owned by the redoubtable Samuel Thomas. As he looked he saw the shabby old black-painted stagecoach of Richard Humphries draw to a halt and disgorge its passengers. They would have to walk up the hill because the four horses only had strength enough to draw the coach and baggage and Richard Humphries himself up into the town centre.

Clayton watched the passengers approach, idly curious as to who had made the tedious and uncomfortable journey from Birmingham that day. There were two ladies and several men, and it was the man who strode briskly ahead of his fellows that took John Clayton's attention. He was tall and lean-bodied, fashionably dressed in a claret coloured frock-coat and dark-grey strapped pantaloons. A large black 'water-fall' cravat hid his shirtfront from view, and on his head he favoured the ultra fashionable 'Cumberland Hat', eight inches high with the crown tapering upwards and a very narrow brim upturned at the sides. He carried a rolled brown-silk umbrella which periodically he swung in a sideways arc as if in time to some martial tune.

As the oncoming man came nearer vague flashes of recognition crossed Clayton's mind, but each time he tried to grasp at those fleeting flashes the memory eluded him. The man was now only some twenty yards away, and Clayton was able to see the pale face framed by curled hair and side-whiskers, the moustache and the fashionable tuft of hair beneath the lower lips known as the 'Favourite'.

The clergyman's lips curved amusedly, 'My word, whoever you might be, you're most certainly an Exquisite. I can only hope for your own sake that you don't fall foul of any of our Pointer Lads. They enjoy nothing more than breaking a peacock's feathers.'

'My God, Clayton! Are you still here in this benighted hole?' The Exquisite had halted some three yards away from him, and was smiling at him.

John Clayton stared questioningly into the other's remarkably fine dark eyes, and suddenly whistled through his teeth in surprise.

''Pon my soul! It's yourself! Lucas Royston! Do you know when I saw you coming up the hill I felt a sense of recognition. Well, I'm damned! I never thought to see you in these parts again!'

The man laughed easily. 'And neither did anyone else in these parts expect ever to see me again, that I'll warrant.' He had a faintly discernible Scottish accent. 'It just goes to prove the truth of the old saying, does it not, the bad penny always turns up. However, the locals need have no fear, for I'm not intending to remain here for long. I'm come to reconcile myself with my Uncle Alexander. Not so much a case of the ''Prodigal Son'', but rather the ''Prodigal Nephew''.' Again he laughed. 'The old fellow has been writing to me for these last three years, Clayton. Who would ever have thought him capable of being so forgiving and tender-hearted towards me?'

He looked back over his elegantly padded shoulder down the hill. 'I see Master Humphries has nearly climbed the mountain.' He turned and smiled at the clergyman, 'I must press on to the Unicorn Inn, Clayton, I've no wish to lose the race. I trust we'll empty a bottle or two in company before I leave here again.'

He saluted with his umbrella and went off across the Green blithely whistling, leaving John Clayton staring after him.

The clergyman returned the greetings of the coach driver and the other passengers as he continued on his own way down the hill towards his house, his mind flooding with recollections of the man he had just met again after a period of almost eleven years.

Lucas Royston was the nephew of Doctor Alexander Pratt, one of the town's surgeons, and was himself a doctor of medicine. He had appeared in Redditch in 1821 and Doctor Pratt had used his influence to procure for his nephew the position of 'Surgeon to the Poor' in the Tardebigge Parish. The young man had proven himself to be a modern-thinking and skilful doctor, and had been instrumental in introducing the practice of vaccination against smallpox in the parish.

But Lucas Royston had two fatal weaknesses, one for

drink and the other for women. He had embarked upon a tempestuous affair with a local widow, and at the same time had paid court to the nubile daughter of one of the town's most influential citizens, arousing the fury of her father. His predilection for strong drink had also got him into other difficulties and he had quarrelled violently with his uncle.

His insisting on using new methods of treatment also aroused the prejudices of the local poor against him and eventually, through no fault of his own, a young girl he was treating had died. Her father had brooded and blamed Lucas Royston for her death, and had finally attacked Royston and injured him severely, leaving him for dead. When he had recovered from his injuries, Lucas Royston had gone from the town, and no one had heard or seen of him since.

A grim smile lurked on John Clayton's face as the memories flooded back. Despite Lucas Royston's peccadillos he had always had a liking for the rogue. He also respected the young Scotsman for his refusal to identify the attacker who had left him for dead. Clayton felt that he understood the reason for that refusal. He believed that Lucas Royston considered that the man had already suffered sufficiently by losing his daughter, and that he, Royston, had realised that it was the instinctive and unthinking reaction of an ignorant brutish man to try and strike back at the person he held responsible for the death of a loved one.

Now John Clayton chuckled wryly. 'I just hope that Lucas Royston manages to leave the parish without being attacked this time but, knowing him as I do, it's hard to say what mischief he will find to get himself into.'

Chapter Seven

ALTHOUGH THE RED Lion Inn stood next to one of the worst slums in the town, Silver Street and Silver Square, it did at times cater to the needs of the town's elite. Adjoining the rear of the inn was a very large room which contained a stage and raised balconies along three of its walls. It was this 'Red Lion Assembly Room' which was utilised for any balls or public meetings held in the Parish.

Tonight, Saturday the eleventh night of August, the room was the venue for the annual Ball of the Tardebigge Parish's own military unit, the Hewell Troop of the Worcestershire Yeomanry Cavalry. This year's Yeomanry Ball was creating even more than its usual frissons of excitement throughout the respectable population of the parish because it was strongly rumoured that the Right Honourable Other Archer, The Earl of Plymouth himself, was to attend in his capacity as the officer commanding the Hewell Troop.

By eleven o'clock the dancing was in full swing and the Assembly Room was crowded. The dancers swirling to the waltz presented a glittering kaleidoscope of shifting colours. The scarlet and gold of the Yeomanry Cavalrymen. The blue and black evening coats, brilliantly hued waistcoats and white satin cravats of the male civilians. The gorgeously flowered silks, satins and velvets of the ladies' ballgowns, shimmering beneath the golden light of the hanging clusters of tall wax candles.

On the stage the musicians of the Leamington Band,

specially imported for this single night at great expense, sweated in their black evening dress and white powdered queue-wigs, and standing beneath the stage watching the dancers, the Master of Ceremonies, Augustus Bartleet, wearing full court dress of lavender coloured coat and breeches, with white stockings and dainty leather dancing pumps, winced visibly as a clumsy young farmer, red-faced with exertion came clod-hopping past.

Augustus Bartleet had been considered a poetic-looking youth and now in his middle thirties still did his utmost to retain that youthful appearance. He was a slender-bodied man, with slender hands and a slender neck and long slender legs. His face and head also were slender and his great mass of once blond, but now greying hair still fell in long sweeping locks around his ears and neck. Although his father, William Bartleet, belonged to a family which boasted several Needle Masters and was himself a manufacturer of that article, Augustus Bartleet had always considered himself to be too sensitive and artistic to enter the rough and tumble of the needle trade. Instead he managed to survive as a Dancing Master in the parish, and paid court to adoring elderly ladies of property in return for their lavish hospitality.

He also had much appreciation for the younger ladies, and had taught many of those now present their dancing steps. Now he smirked in gratification as one of his pupils, Maria Pitts, looking very lovely in her white satin ballgown, came whirling gracefully past him in the arms of a young Yeoman, dashing in scarlet coat and black red-striped overalls.

Augustus Bartleet caught the young woman's grey eyes, and he smiled and half-bowed towards her and his susceptible heart thudded as she smiled radiantly back at him.

The next instant his own smile disappeared as her partner glared fiercely at him over the girl's deliciously rounded bare shoulders, and his mascaraed eyes gazed with sudden interest at the chandeliers above his head.

'Goddamn it, Maria! Why must you encourage that painted fop?' Dick Boulton demanded angrily.

Maria Pitts' small white teeth glistened and she widened her beautiful eyes in mock alarm. 'La, how fierce you are!' she teased. 'I do declare that if looks could kill, poor Augustus would even now be gasping out his final moments.'

Ranged on chairs around the room and in the balconies overlooking the floor, the mothers and aunts and grandmothers of the dancers vigorously wielded their large ornate fans and watched with beady eyes, smiling and frowning by turns as their offspring either appeared to be making headway towards a desirable match, or a disastrous one.

Standing behind the chairs of their turbaned, befeathered and bejewelled womenfolk the stalwarts of the town's trade and industry gave their attention to the doings of their fellows. Evaluating why one spoke to another in such a secretive manner. Why this one scowled. Why this one grinned with satisfaction. Important, hard-bitten Needle Masters, wealthy smooth-mannered shopkeepers, ambitious artisans, opulent farmers, each one acutely aware of his own importance in the scheme of things. Gatherings such as this gave them the opportunity to display their social standing, and perhaps to gain a march upon one or other of their rivals by words whispered into the right ear at the right moment.

Herbert Willis, the ageing, fat-bellied landlord of the Red Lion, drove his waiters and serving maids harder and harder as the night progressed, and trays of drinks and food circulated constantly around the over-crowded room, adding their own rich odours to the hot fugged air thick with the smells of perfumes and powders and scented maccassar oils and pomatums, and sweet and foul breath, and washed and unwashed flesh. Outside the large windows the ragged, underfed children of the slums pressed their noses against the glass and stared with greedy eyes at the glittering wonderland from which they would be forever excluded.

Lucas Royston, elegant in black, came through the double doors at the end of the assembly room which were guarded by Yeoman Cavalrymen, and when the Yeomanry corporal asked him his name gave the man his embossed ticket and indicated that he did not wish to be announced. The Scotsman moved a little further into the room, and then stood quietly beneath the balcony and regarded the scene before him. At first it was the older people who took his attention, and his eyes moved across their faces, periodically gleaming with recognition as names came into his mind. Milward, Gould, Chillingworth, Cutler, Holyoake, Bartleet, Hemming, Boulton, Horton, Clark, Mence, Huins, Humphries, Allcock, Smallwood, Terry, Pursal, Scambler. All eleven years older with spreading bellies and faces etched with new lines, the pretty young girls he had known now stately matrons, and the children become adults.

A momentary sadness of nostalgia touched Lucas Royston and a sense of regret for all the might-have-beens, then he grinned inwardly and chided himself, 'Don't be such a dull dog, Royston. The night is still young, and so is your heart.' His eyes locked onto a very lovely, dark-haired young woman dressed in a white satin ballgown, dancing with a young Yeoman, and all at once his spirits soared, and he felt very glad that he had come to the Ball.

While their self-regarded social superiors danced and preened, the remainder of the town's population passed away the hours of Saturday night in their own individual ways. The taverns and beer-shops rang with laughter and dispute and song. In the foetid hovels of the slums, and the houses of the more respectable alike, men, women and children took their respite from the hard labours of the week beneath the flickering, guttering lights of rush-dips and tallow candles. In some homes only the children were present, their elders having gone to the public houses to drink and carouse. In other homes a woman would be sitting with her children about her skirts, waiting in dread for the return of her drunken man, fearing the violence that drink engendered. And in yet other homes the family gathering was complete and harmony was reigning.

Down at the Bredon Chapel where the road leading eastwards from the town parted into its separate courses towards either Beoley or Studley villages, the Methodists were holding their Saturday Meeting.

> 'O Sacred head, sore wounded,
> Defiled and put to scorn;
> O Kingly head surrounded
> With mocking crown of thornnnn;'

The fervent chorus of singing voices echoed along the neighbouring terraces of mean cottages, and in the roadway outside the red brick chapel a group of half-drunken youths hooted and jeered,

'Methody Pisspots! Methody Pisspots! Methody Pisspots!'

In the Salters Yard in the darkness of their bedroom Tildy Crawford and Daniel Lambert lay entwined in the tender aftermath of their lovemaking, and talked fondly in low voices of their coming marriage, and their plans for the future. Along the passageway young Davy lay sleeping, his arms outflung from the covers of his narrow bed, his lips smiling as he dreamed of scarlet coats and streaming banners, of bugles, drums and glory. Downstairs in the candlelit kitchen Old Esther Smith sat staring into the black oily liquid in the saucer on the table before her. As she scryed she rocked her bent body backwards and forwards and keened low in her throat and muttered sibilantly, 'He's acoming. He's acoming towards this town. Death is acoming. I see him . . . I see him . . . '

Chapter Eight

I T HAD BEEN a hot morning and a hotter afternoon, but
now as the sun started its long decline to the western
horizons a soft breeze began to cool the air.

Tildy sighed thankfully and laid aside her file and tongs,
and next to her Charles Brown gave the finishing strokes to
the needle he held and did likewise. From the kitchen Old
Esther's cracked voice shouted, 'I'se got the tay brewed.'
Smiling at each other the couple left the workbench and
went through into the other room to join her.

As she sipped the hot, fragrantly scented drink Tildy
mentally computed the amount of needles that Charles
Brown had filed that day; she felt a growing sense of
wonderment. The man was the fastest worker she had ever
known, and she still marvelled at his speed and dexterity
even though he had only been working with her for about a
week.

He finished his dish of tea, and leant back in the wooden
chair, closing his eyes as if to rest them. Tildy studied him
covertly, wondering what his personal history really was.
Although he was always agreeably chatty, and could
converse knowledgeably on many subjects, yet he never ever
divulged anything of his antecedents, and when driven by
natural curiosity Tildy or Daniel or Old Esther had tried to
lead the talk into that subject, Charles Brown had somehow
evaded giving any information.

Now his eyes opened and he smiled, 'Do you know, I'd
like very much to take a stroll now that work's done. Will
you ladies join me?'

''Tis all I can do to hobble about the kitchen these days, what wi' me rheumatics,' Old Esther demurred. 'But you goo wi' him, Tildy. You'm looking a bit peaky. A breath o' fresh air 'ull do you good.'

'Please come,' Charles Brown urged. 'I'd like very much to be shown the town. All I've seen of it so far is a little bit of Bredon, and Salters Yard.'

'Very well,' Tildy agreed, tempted by the prospect of being outdoors on such a beautiful afternoon. 'If Davy or Daniel come while I'm out, will you tell them where we've gone Esther. I'll not be long away.'

Outside in the yard she told the man, 'If you wish we'll make a perambulation around the centre parts. Then when you know how it lays, you'll be able to explore further at your leisure.'

He agreed happily, and they set off side by side down Alcester Street towards the Big Pool.

Even without seeing it the presence of the stagnant stretch of water could be detected at a considerable distance by the foul stench its green-scummed surface emitted as decaying matter constantly bubbled up from its depths.

As they skirted its edges, along the western side of which were huddled erratic rows of low-storied decaying cottages, Charles Brown snorted with disgust, and pointed to the rotting, bloated corpses of the rats, cats and dogs which floated in company with the rubbish and vegetable waste and human excrement that had been hurled into it.

'Why in heaven's name is that cesspool allowed to exist? Do not the people hereabouts know that such foul pollution is deadly to their wellbeing?'

Even as he spoke a small girl came from one of the cottages carrying a wooden bucket and knelt by the pool's edge. With her hands she scooped away the floating excrescences and then filled her bucket with the discoloured stinking water, and carried it back to the row of cottages.

Again Charles Brown snorted with disgust, 'I doubt that even a self-respecting dog would drink such muck as that. What's the name of those houses?'

'That's Paoli's Row,' Tildy informed him, 'and you mustn't judge the poor souls who dwell there so harshly, Charles. The Big Pool is their only water supply. They've not much choice but to use it.'

'But there must be a parish pump somewhere hereabouts?' Brown challenged.

Tildy shook her head. 'The water on the Flat here is all drawn from very deep wells, and those wells are on private property. Some of the owners are willing enough to let others draw water, but when you live in Paoli's Row there's precious few people hereabouts will let you come onto their land. The people who live in the Row have a very bad name in this town. We're lucky in Salters Yard to have a good pump for our own use.'

'But surely something could be done for the people here?' Brown persisted.

'Oh yes, there have been attempts made to help them by the charitable.' Tildy's tone was tinged with irony. 'One man paid to have a well sunk close by the Row, but the people complained that the water was no good because it tasted so different to what they were used to, and then the pump-engine itself was stolen. So now they draw their water from the Pool again, and one of the Row women told me years since that she liked that better. She said it was less trouble to take the water direct from the Pool, rather than have to queue up and wait to pump it out.'

Her friend could only shake his head silently. She smiled and pointed ahead up the long slope of the road known as Ipsley Street. 'Come, we'll walk up that way and up the Back Hill to the Mount Pleasant. I want to show you the Round House. It's the most peculiar building you ever did see, that I'll swear to.'

'Do you know the history of the Round House, Doctor Royston?' Maria Pitts enquired, as she looked up at the bizarre structure.

'Please, I wish you would call me by my given name, Miss Pitts. Surely we need not be so formal.'

On the other side of Maria, Charlotte Benton giggled and squeezed her friend's arm.

'But I hardly know you, sir.' Maria smiled coquettishly. 'I could not be so forward. It is unbecoming in a lady.'

'You have known me for at least three days, Miss Pitts.' Lucas Royston was enjoying himself hugely flirting with this delicious girl. 'It is now Tuesday and we met last Saturday night, did we not. Therefore I think it to be high time that we dispensed with such stiff and unnecessary formalities. So, I shall from this moment address you as Maria.'

'La sir, I do declare you are very bold. I'm beginning to fear that you are not quite a gentleman,' she rebuked him archly, and again Charlotte Benton dissolved into giggles.

'There are many varieties of gentlemen, Maria,' Lucas Royston countered, 'and I think that on the whole I prefer to be numbered amongst those who have boldness enough to pay court to beautiful women, rather than to stay at a distance, too timid to make any approach.'

Maria's full red lips quirked slightly with sudden annoyance, 'Indeed sir, your boldness in approaching me at the Yeomanry Ball caused me some considerable embarrassment. My parents were much displeased.'

Royston laughed heartily, 'And your friend, Master Dick Boulton likewise, if I'm any judge of men.'

Behind her façade of annoyance, Maria Pitts was delighted with this handsome admirer's reaction to her statement, and although she frowned angrily, in her grey eyes the familiar devils of mischief were dancing.

'You'd best have a care that you don't provoke Dick Boulton too sorely. He's very hot-tempered, and he told me that he was eager to challenge you to a duel,' she rejoined tartly, and Charlotte Benton stared at her with admiring awe. 'It took all my endeavours to prevent him from issuing that challenge there and then.'

Lucas Royston smiled with great tenderness, and in a low husky voice told her, 'If I could have but one loving kiss from your lips, Maria, then I would happily risk death in any duel.'

Maria glowed radiantly. This was indeed the very essence of romance, and this present game was by far the most exciting and delightful she had ever played.

'If I ever did give you a kiss, sir, then you may rest assured that Dick Boulton would indeed kill you. You would not be the first man to fall to him.'

Charlotte Benton cried out faintly with shock. 'Oh Maria, how could you say such a terrible thing?'

Maria's own sense of humour now betrayed her. 'I really don't know,' she confessed, and dissolved into helpless laughter.

As Tildy and Charles Brown approached the Round House which stood on the western side of the Mount Pleasant some hundred yards or so from the junction of the Front and Back Hills, Brown's tongue clucked against the roof of his mouth and he asked facetiously, 'What was it meant to be, Tildy? A landlocked Martello Tower?'

The Round House was a massive red brick tower some four stories high, topped with a steep-sloping conical cone of red-tiled roof, the apex of which ended in a tall chimney stack bearing a cluster of long chimneypots. At the base of the tower, like spokes on a wheel, were two sets of back to back cottages, with their own tall chimney stacks, and steeply gabled roofs. Spaced all round the walls of the tower itself were elongated, horizontal, bricked up slots, and small leaded windows.

Tildy smiled and shook her head, 'Daniel tells me that it was built forty years ago. A Quaker named Sherward had it constructed to the plans of old Charles Avery. Avery still lives in Redditch. Apparently it was going to be a windmill, but with the sails inside the tower. The wind was supposed to pass through those big slits that you can see in the walls there, and so drive the sails around like a carousel.'

Brown grinned, 'A curious story, Tildy, and a most curious building. What is it used for now?'

'Why for dwellings,' Tildy told him. 'It's all been divided up into separate apartments, and the people who live there say that they've the most snug and comfortable homes in the parish.'

'It seems that it attracts considerable attention from every visitor to the town,' Brown remarked, and indicated the two bonneted girls and the elegant man standing staring up at the great tower.

'Oh see there, it's Tildy Crawford.' Maria Pitts noticed the couple and even though they were still some distance away, instantly recognised Tildy. She called and waved.

'Tildy? Tildy, it's me, Maria Pitts.' Then she beckoned, 'Do come here a moment, I beg of you.'

Tildy waved back, and said to Charles Brown. 'I'd best go and say hello to her. Otherwise she might think me churlish.'

'I'll wait for you here, Tildy,' Charles Brown told her. 'Forgive me if I seem to be rude. But for the time being I've no wish to be presented to anyone.'

Although this puzzled Tildy, she only smiled, 'Alright then, I'll not be more than a few moments.'

Lucas Royston stared keenly at the approaching woman, who, despite being so simply dressed in her dark grey gown, with a shawl about her shoulders and no bonnet covering her neatly-coiled glossy hair, yet had an air of quality emanating from her. Abruptly his breath hissed between his teeth.

'Well God strike me, if it isn't the Poorhouse woman, Crawford!' he exclaimed softly. 'And she's still pretty enough to turn any man's head.' He became aware that the two girls were staring at him curiously, he smiled and told them. 'This pauper woman is an old acquaintance of mine. She and her baby were the first people that I vaccinated against the smallpox in this district. She was in the Poorhouse then, but I obtained for her a position as servant to a lady I was friendly with at the time.'

'Well she's not a pauper woman any longer, Master Royston.' Maria Pitts' colour had risen and she snapped her words as if to defend Tildy from any aspersions. 'She is a personal friend of mine, and soon to be married to a Needle Master. I'll not stand by and see her denigrated, so you'll do me the favour of addressing her with all due courtesy.'

'Hold fast, I beg of you.' He held up his hands jokingly as if warding off a blow. 'I shall be politeness itself to the lady. I do assure you.'

True to his word, as Tildy came up to them, he took off his hat and bowed gracefully, 'You'll maybe not remember me, ma'am. But my name is Lucas Royston. I was the doctor who vaccinated yourself and your baby against the smallpox. It must be nigh on eleven years since.'

After the first shock of recognition, Tildy smiled, and completely at her ease, answered, 'But of course I remember you, sir. I was in the Poorhouse at Webheath at that time, was I not?' She turned and told the two girls. 'I owe this gentleman a great deal, because not only did he protect my Davy and me with his vaccination, he also taught me much about nursing the sick, and since then I've often had cause to make use of those teachings and remember Doctor Royston with much gratitude.'

Tildy forebore to tell the girls that the lady she had gone as servant to had been a Mrs Anna Coldericke, a widow who was Lucas Royston's then mistress, whom he had later heartlessly abandoned. But inwardly she resolved that if her newly-found young friend, Maria, ever confided to her that she was becoming emotionally involved with this undoubtedly charming and attractive man, she would at least warn her to take care in the affair.

Now, although her curiosity was aroused by finding Lucas Royston in the company of these two young women, Tildy's natural reserve prevented her from attempting to pry further into the matter.

'What brings you up here, Tildy?' Maria Pitts wanted to know.

'I'm just taking a stroll with Mr Smith there, to show him something of the town. He's just lately come to work at the needles with us.'

'Why doesn't he come and be introduced to us?' the girl asked next.

Tildy shrugged slightly, 'He is a little shy of new company.'

'Something that Doctor Royston here could never be accused of,' Maria Pitts said with a hint of malice. Although she was greatly attracted to the elegant and worldly Scotsman, she still found that his very confidence created within her an uneasy sense of being lacking in the sophistication she was sure he was accustomed to in the ladies he mixed with.

Lucas Royston stared curiously at Charles Brown, who was standing half-turned to them, waiting for Tildy to rejoin him. The Scotsman frowned thoughtfully. 'Strange, but I think I've met that fellow before,' he remarked.

Tildy smiled, 'You may well have done, Doctor Royston. Before he came to work with us, he was a travelling pedlar, and I believe he spent a deal of time in Scotland. Perhaps you have seen him there?'

'I think not, ma'am. It's several years since I was in my native country.' He gave a brief shake of his head. 'No, I think that I've seen that man somewhere abroad.' He smiled charmingly at Tildy. 'Since I was last here I've been serving in the Army as a Regimental Surgeon for some years, ma'am, in the West Indies and also in the Canadian garrisons.'

'Are you still in the Army?' Tildy asked; he shook his head.

'No, I resigned some two years past. Now I'm giving much consideration to putting up my plate here in Redditch again.'

He grinned at Maria Pitts, who much to her mortification could not help but blush. Royston saw the blush, and his fine dark eyes gleamed with pleasure, and he went on, 'I find that there is much to please me in this Parish. I was always happy here, as you know, Mrs Crawford.'

For a moment Tildy was strongly tempted to be spiteful, and to ask him whether he thought that Anna Coldericke had been as happy as he. But she suppressed that urge, and instead merely took her leave of the trio and returned to Charles Brown.

As they walked back down the Mount Pleasant towards the town centre, she asked him, 'Did you take note of the man who was with the two girls, Charles?'

'No, not really, except to notice that he appeared something of a dandy,' he answered casually, but his eyes had become instantly wary. After a moment he asked, 'Why do you ask me that?'

Tildy had not noticed the wariness and she replied dismissively, 'Oh, it's nothing really. It was just that he thought he knew you from somewhere.'

'Did he now.' The wariness in his eyes became tinged by concern, but with well-assumed disinterest he merely shrugged and dismissed the subject by saying, 'Well, as a pedlar there must have been many people who have seen me during these last years, Tildy. I've travelled widely, after all.'

'Did you travel abroad at all, before you became a pedlar?' Tildy wanted to know.

'Yes, I have travelled abroad. When I was a younger man.'

'To the West Indies, perhaps?' By now Tildy's curiosity, aroused by Lucas Royston's claim to have met this man before, was clamouring to be satisfied. 'Or to Canada?'

Charles Brown's hazel eyes were troubled, and there was a long pause before he told her, 'Yes. I was in both the West Indies and Canada.'

Tildy waited for him to enlarge upon this but he stayed silent, and she did not like to press him further. So she changed the subject and they chatted easily enough until they parted back at Salters Yard.

Daniel Lambert's horse was tethered on the front cobbles, and when Tildy went into their rooms she found him waiting for her. He kissed her fondly, but she could see by his grim expression that something was troubling him.

'What is it, Daniel? You seem unhappy?' she asked anxiously.

'I've got to go up to Sheffield, honey. I must start out this very night,' he told her glumly. 'They're having a deal of trouble casting the new dies that we wanted, and they've written with much urgency to ask for either Brandon or myself to go up there and discuss the patterns with them. Brandon's unwell, so unhappily it's I who must go.'

'Is that all?' Tildy smiled with relief. 'Judging by your face, I thought it to be something serious.'

'It is serious.' His strong hard-etched features were still glum. 'I could be up there for weeks getting this problem solved. That means we can't get married straight after the banns are called, as we planned to.'

She stroked his cheek tenderly. 'What does a small delay matter, sweetheart? As far as I'm concerned we could not be more married than we are already.'

'That's as maybe, but I'll not be content until we're churched, and then no one will be able to point the finger and say that we are living in sin.'

Tildy chuckled, 'I don't care how many fingers are pointed, Daniel. So long as we are together.'

'I care, honey,' he told her huskily, 'because you are so precious to me that I want to bind you to me with every means that exist, and when you're my lawful wedded wife, then the whole world will be able to see that we are truly sworn to each other for the rest of our lives, and for eternity beyond.'

He drew her to him and held her close, his lips buried in her glossy hair, and Tildy smelled the clean masculine scent of his body and felt the taut strong muscles of his shoulders and back beneath her fingers, and her heart welled with love for this man who had brought her so much happiness.

Tears stung her eyes as a little later she watched him ride away up Alcester Street and she was forced to swallow very hard to dispel the lump in her throat as she went back inside her home to join Davy and Old Esther.

Chapter Nine

'MISTER PITTS, WILL you have words with this shameless hussy? Will you deal with her?'

Maria Pitts' mother stood with her arms akimbo on her massive hips, her broad fat face mottled with temper.

Her stoop-bodied husband's sour, sallow features bore an expression of disgust as he regarded this woman whom he disliked so heartily.

'Will you cease from caterwauling like a slum alley cat, madam, and have the goodness to state your case against the girl,' he mouthed contemptuously.

'Don't you insult me, sir!' his good lady hissed savagely. 'Don't you screw up your mealy mouth and talk down to me! This is no law court, and I'm not standing in a dock before you.'

'By God, I could wish you were so, madam. I'd do my damndest to have you transported to Van Diemens Land, that I swear.'

Sitting on a straightbacked chair between her parents, in the over-furnished drawing room of her home, Maria's face was a pattern of shifting emotions. Anger, resentment, fear, distress, all battling for domination.

'Will you deal with this strumpet?' Mrs Pitts screeched.

'You have not yet given me any indication of what she has done to cause your anger,' Arnold Pitts stated icily.

'Oh I'll give you indication alright. Be assured I will.' The woman's turbaned head nodded so fiercely that her flabby cheeks and jowls quivered like jellies. 'She's only been parading around the town with that scoundrel Lucas Royston, as bold and shameless as a sixpenny whore!' Mrs Pitts flung her arms heavenwards. 'Just think of the disgrace she brings on our name, Mister Pitts, behaving with such wickedness, and her betrothed to such a fine young man as Dick Boulton, as well.' She turned on her daughter and with spittle spraying from her lips screamed into the young woman's face, 'I would to God that he had laid you in the grave before you could shame us so in the eyes of this town!'

Maria bowed her head to avoid her mother's foul breath and, taking this gesture as submissiveness, the older woman screeched, 'Oh yes, my fine lady, you may well bow your head in shame! You have good cause to do so. But when Dick Boulton comes to hear of your whoring with that wicked man, Royston, I'll warrant he'll withdraw from your betrothal. And who can blame him for doing so? No respectable young man wishes to take a whore for wife!'

Maria's justifiable indignation brought her head up and she faced her mother boldly, and stated angrily, 'I'm no whore! All I've done was to walk a space in company with Charlotte Benton and Doctor Royston. Just to walk and talk that's all. Our conduct was most seemly.'

'You lie!' Her mother's head shook from side to side in vehement jerks. 'It was not only with Charlotte Benton and Royston you kept company was it? You also shouted after that Crawford woman and had speech with her, did you not? In full view of anyone who cared to look! Have you no shame, you hussy? Have you no shame?'

'Is this true, Maria?' Arnold Pitts intervened.

Maria had some degree of physical fear of her mother, but her father's cold rage could strike utter dread into her. Now as her grey eyes swung to his, she quailed inwardly and swallowed hard before mumbling, 'Yes, pa, I did have speech with Tildy Crawford.' She drew breath and summoned her courage, 'I like Mrs Crawford, she is a good living and respectable woman.'

'There now!' Satisfaction throbbed in Mrs Pitts' voice. 'Did I not tell you as much, Mister Pitts, and now this little whore brazenly admits to her guilt. Good living and respectable woman, indeed? That Crawford whore has always been too saucy towards her betters for her own good. And now she lives openly with Daniel Lambert. An ex-convict! Good living and respectable, you say?' Her livid lips emitted a snort of derision, 'Sixpenny whore, I say!'

Her rage suddenly boiled over and she struck out wildly at Maria's head and face with her pudgy hands. The young woman cried out and tried to shield herself from the flurrying blows, but then with a strength that belied his weakly looking physique, Arnold Pitts grabbed his wife's thick shoulders and pushed her away.

'Control yourself, madam!' His voice trembled with temper, and he jerked his head at Maria, 'Get you to your room, girl. I'll come there and deal with you presently.'

Maria, sobs of distress tearing from her throat, ran quickly up the stairs and into her room, where she threw herself face downwards on her bed and buried her face in her hands.

By the time her father came upstairs she had managed to regain control over her distress and sat on the edge of her bed with a pale set face, her hands clasped together in her lap.

For a moment or two Arnold Pitts stood in the doorway of the room, gazing unhappily at his wayward daughter. Despite his cold, unprepossessing manner, he genuinely loved this young woman, but victim of his own harsh upbringing and repressions, had always been unable either to express or demonstrate that love to her.

'You have caused your mother much distress this day, daughter,' he now said in a harsh voice. 'Why must you so behave yourself, as to bring shame upon our name?'

'I've not brought shame upon our name, pa.' Despite his lack of outward demonstration, Maria knew that her father loved her more than anything else in his bleak life. And although she could never nerve herself to try and break down the protective walls he erected to shield his emotions, yet she loved him dearly in return.

'I went walking with Charlotte and Doctor Royston happened to meet with us. He stayed in our company for a while, and we walked and talked. That's all that happened. Nothing untoward passed between us and Doctor Royston behaved as a gentleman should.'

Arnold Pitts' narrow head nodded acceptance of what she told him, but then he asked, 'And this Crawford woman? What of her?'

Maria drew a long shuddering breath, and nerved herself. Then told him matter-of-factly, 'I met Tildy Crawford some days past in Redditch and had speech with her.' The girl thought it best not to tell her father the full details of that first meeting, and comforted herself with the thought that a lie of omission was a very minor sin. 'I find Tildy Crawford to be a woman of considerable intelligence and pleasing to talk with. She always conducts herself as a lady should, pa. At least in the brief moments I've spent in her company she has done so. I cannot understand why people should be prejudiced against her. As far as I know, she has never done any harm to anyone in this town. Why does ma hate her so? There is no reason for it, is there?'

A bleak smile flickered across the man's sallow face. 'Your mother has never needed reasons for her myriad hates, daughter. As to this Crawford woman, the only charge that can be laid against her with any justice is that she has never seemed to be able to accept her lowly station in life. I know of several instances where she has displayed insolence towards her betters, and been defiant of their strictures.

'Everyone is born to their allotted station in life, daughter, and should keep to that station, and be accepting of it as the Will of God. The lower orders must show the proper respect towards those of us whom the Lord has placed above them. Otherwise this country will go to rack and ruin in very short order. If Jack is allowed to think himself to be as good as his master, then bloody revolution could quickly follow. Look at the example of France. Surely you would not wish such a terrible event to happen here?'

'No, pa, of course I do not wish for anything like that to

happen. But truly, I can see no harm in there being friendship between those of different social position. After all, was not Jesus himself merely the son of a carpenter?'

Again the bleak smile momentarily softened Arnold Pitts' features. 'It's a pity you were not born a male, daughter. I do believe you have the makings of a lawyer. However, while I accept the point that you have made, it is my duty as your parent to forbid you to have any further intercourse with the Crawford woman. Worthy woman she may be, but it does not befit your station in life to have her for a friend.'

'That is not just, pa,' Maria protested.

'In this life, daughter, justice is a very rare thing to find. You will obey me in this matter. Do I have your word that this will be so?'

For a while she made no answer as inwardly she fought to clarify her thoughts, and the man waited patiently. At last she regarded him with steady eyes and told him quietly but firmly, 'If I wished to deceive you, pa, I would give you that promise without hesitation. But in all truth I cannot promise any such thing. I have the right to make my own friends in this life, have I not? I think all this talk of social betters and inferiors to be a nonsense. And a wicked nonsense at that. I like Tildy Crawford a deal more than any of the silly empty-headed creatures that are reckoned to be of my own social position in life. And I truly think that she is a woman who has more real value than they.'

Arnold Pitts frowned. 'So then, you would defy me in this matter?'

Maria's dark ringlets swung about her softly rounded cheeks as she shook her head in helpless frustration. 'No, pa, I would not willingly defy you in this matter. I would only ask you to be more understanding and less rigid in your outlook. What possible harm can there be in my being friendly with Tildy Crawford?'

'The harm lies in the fact that she is your social inferior, daughter,' the man snapped curtly. 'The barriers between the classes are there for a very good reason. Without them this country would be ungovernable. I do not intend to argue the matter further with you. Either you give me your most solemn word that you will have no further intercourse with this Crawford woman, or I will keep you pent up in this house until you come to your senses.'

The girl's red lips set in a stubborn line, and she shook her head. 'I cannot give you my word on that, pa. Because I think it to be a monstrously unjust thing that you ask of me.'

'Very well, daughter. As from this moment, you are confined to the house and you shall not step one yard outside these walls until you have repented of the error of your ways.' He swung on his heels and left her alone.

Maria remained seated motionless on the edge of the bed, then smiled ruefully and looked around the room. 'Ah well,' she murmured aloud, 'at least my prison is a comfortable one.'

Chapter Ten

AT MIDDAY ON Saturday the 18th of August, the Reverend William Leigh again called at the house of his old friend John Clayton. John Clayton was shocked and horrified to see how gaunt and ill-looking the other man had become in the few days since they had last met. He was even more shocked and horrified by the news his friend conveyed.

'I'm on my way to Birmingham, John, to buy a supply of coffins. We cannot get a sufficiency made in the parish to bury our dead in.'

While John Clayton listened in horror, Leigh went on to tell him. 'There have been over one hundred and fifty fresh cases of the cholera reported in Bilston in this last week alone, and of those taken ill some thirty-six had died before I left home last night to travel to Bromsgrove and see my wife.'

'Lord save us!' Clayton muttered.

'Amen to that, for only He can do so,' Leigh sighed heavily. 'Our medical men are performing heroically, but nothing that they do in the way of treatment appears to have any efficacy. This scourge is spreading all across the Black Country like a wild fire, John. I fear it is only a matter of time before it appears here in your own parish.'

He drank a glass of brandy and ate a biscuit, then took his leave and went on towards Birmingham.

The very minute his visitor departed, John Clayton shouted to his manservant to saddle his horse, and within a very short time he was spurring the beast towards the hamlet of Tardebigge, some three miles distant, where his employer and clerical superior, the Right Honourable and Reverend Walter Hutchinson, Lord Aston, Vicar of Tardebigge, Parish and Justice of the Peace of the County of Worcestershire, lived in the opulent vicarage overlooked by the beautiful slender-spired parish church.

Lord Aston was in the process of demolishing a fine roast goose when the tiny maidservant brought his curate into the dining room; he scowled at this interruption of his favourite pastime.

'Damnee Clayton, cannot I eat a simple meal in peace, without you must come crashing into my home like a raging bull?'

Nearing sixty years of age, the noble clergyman's fat body strained the seams of his black coat, waistcoat and knee breeches, and his sallow face, greasy with the juices of the bird, resembled a great tallowy full moon beneath the bushy white tie wig that perched on his bald pate.

Clayton bowed. 'Forgive this untimely intrusion, My Lord, but I have news of the utmost urgency to impart to you. However, if it pleases you, I'll wait in the hallway until you have finished your meal.'

Aston belched loudly and his petulant lips curled in self-pity. He was a martyr to self-inflicted chronic indigestion. In a sudden fit of pettishness he thrust the half-devoured goose away from him and snarled, 'The damage is already done, damn you! You've quite ruined my digestion bursting in upon me like this.' He lifted his glass of claret wine and sucked the ruby liquid noisily. Then belched resoundingly once more and wheezed sulkily, 'Come then, speak out man. What is it you wish to tell me?'

Clayton quickly related all that William Leigh had told him of the progress of the cholera and the terrible mortality taking place in the Black Country, and finished by questioning. 'Do you not think it to be a prudent measure for us to embody immediately a local Board of Health in this parish, My Lord, and make preparations for the onset of this epidemic?'

78

Lord Aston could be accused with justification of possessing many faults and shortcomings, but he was not lacking in shrewd intelligence. His small eyes, half hooded by puffballs of fat, made a brief but keen study of his curate. A smile lurked in their depths as he asked, 'Tell me, John. Do you not trust in Our Lord to protect this parish from the cholera. After all, have I not led my congregation in prayers for that Divine protection these three weeks past, and have I not instructed you to do that very same thing down at the chapel in Redditch?'

'Indeed you have done so, My Lord, and I have complied with your instructions.' The young clergyman's pleasantly ugly features wore an expression of doubtful unease. He was well accustomed to his master's eccentricities of thought, and wondered now what was to come next.

'Then, John, let us trust in the Divine providence, and wait to see what is His will in this matter, shall we?'

'But, my Lord . . . ' Clayton began.

'But nothing, John!' his master snapped curtly. 'Listen to me well. I know of the progress of the cholera. Indeed I have talked only yesterday with the Earl concerning it.'

The Right Honourable Other Archer Windsor, Earl of Plymouth, whose seat at Hewell Grange was only a mere half mile distant from the vicarage, was the chief magistrate and landowner of the parish, and was its virtual ruler.

'I know that you regard me as a cantankerous old fool, John Clayton,' Aston's mocking smile now reached his lips as he saw the discomfiture this latter statement caused to his curate, 'but I have not yet become completely senile in my dotage. I have studied the reports from the North Country and from London and Exeter concerning the attacks of this plague, and I have reached certain conclusions. One of those conclusions being, that any premature actions taken by ourselves will do more harm than good. If we now embody a local Board of Health before there is any outbreak of the cholera in this parish, then we shall only create a panic among the local population. All trade and commerce will come to a halt, and outbreaks of lawless behaviour will undoubtedly take place. We shall be faced with riot and mayhem.'

One of Lord Aston's obsessions, and favourite topics, was the ever present likelihood of the lower classes rising in bloody revolution. Particularly at this time when the question of the Reform Bill was creating great agitation throughout the country.

'We, the ruling class of this district, must maintain a calm and confident demeanour, John. We must not let it appear that the cholera causes us any alarm. As I have told you before on many occasions, once a dog sees its master in a state of fright, then that animal can no longer be controlled by that master.'

'I do not dispute what you say, My Lord, but still I do believe that if we make preparations now, we can only benefit ourselves if the worst should happen and the cholera strike here.'

Lord Aston waved his pudgy hand dismissively, 'I have already taken the necessary steps, John. At my request the Earl has sent to London to obtain the warrant empowering us to embody a Local Board of Health should that need arise. The Earl and I have discussed what measures we might take to combat the disease and contain it.'

Clayton could not help but inwardly acknowledge with a grudging respect that he had underestimated his employer's capabilities.

Lord Aston grinned with a sly smugness at his curate, as if he could read the younger man's thoughts. 'Well John are you somewhat easier in your mind now that you have discovered that I am not a complete fool?'

Clayton's face flushed and he fumbled for words, but the Vicar laughed and told him mockingly, 'Go you now, John, and keep watch for the first sign of this dire epidemic. Then, if you should find it, come post haste to me and I'll do whatever is necessary. But remember what I have said, and in the meantime do not give way to unnecessary panic like an old maid.'

As John Clayton rode slowly back towards Redditch, he

frowned in remembrance of what had just passed. He was a man of considerable physical and moral courage and deeply resented the imputation implicit in Lord Aston's words, that he was acting like a panicky old maid.

Unfortunately, John Clayton was also a very poor man, and in a Derbyshire village there were a widowed mother and unmarried sisters dependent on him for support. Apart from a few private pupils whom he taught, the stipend from his curacy was his sole source of income, and although there had been many occasions when he had been sorely tempted to take his employer's fat throat and squeeze it hard between his powerful hands, he had been forced by the sheer necessity of his loved ones to swallow all insults from Lord Aston.

'Ah well, what cannot be cured, must be endured.' He sighed resignedly. 'But I still think that we should be making all preparations now, and not wait and do nothing until the cholera arrives here. Judging from what William has told me, it strikes with such dreadful rapidity that it could decimate the parish before we could even begin to act against it.'

Instead of turning down the long, lonely Salters Lane which would eventually lead him to the north western edges of the town, he decided to continue on along the main road through the hamlets of Foxlydiate, Webheath and Headless Cross, and come down Mount Pleasant to the south of Redditch.

He had almost reached the White Hart crossroads at Headless Cross when he overtook a man wearing sailor's rig. A short blue, brass-buttoned jacket and white duck trousers, a round tarry straw hat on his head and a long tarred pigtail hanging down his broad back. Over his shoulder he carried a bulging canvas sack, and in his other hand a short cudgel.

When John Clayton passed him, the clergyman could not resist asking with a smile, 'Are you seeking a ship in these parts, Jack?'

The man's sun-browned features creased in a grin.

'That's right, your honour. But the ship I'm seeking must be carrying a cargo of good ale and grog. Might ye know where one like that is to be found?'

'Just steer straight over the crossroads, Jack. The ship you seek bears the name of the White Hart.'

'Well that's great news to hear, I'm sure, your honour. I'll lay a course for it.'

'I hope you find a good berth there. Good day to you now,' Clayton wished him, and rode on past.

Chapter Eleven

'NOW THEN MATEY, can I get food and a bed for the night here?' the sailor wanted to know.

'Nail' Styler, the landlord of the White Hart inn, had been a Needle Pointer and local prizefighter in his younger days but had had the good sense to leave the former trade before the 'Pointer's Rot' could kill him, and to give up prizefighting before his sight had been damaged and his brains addled.

Now he grinned bluffly at the sailor in his tap room, and told him, 'I reckon I can fix you up, Jack. Does you want a drink afore you ates?'

The man nodded, 'Have you got good rum?'

'The best,' Nail Styler assured him. He filled a small horn tumbler from a keg behind his tall narrow counter and pushed it across to the other man. 'Tell you what, Jack. You just take a taste o' that. Iffen you don't like it, then there's no need to pay me for it. Is that fair enough?'

'By Jase, it is!' The sailor tossed the dark drink down his stubbled throat and gusted a sigh of satisfaction. 'It's good stuff! Here now,' he casually tossed a gold coin onto the bar, 'just kape filling me tot, and tell me when that's all gone. And have a drink yerself while ye're at it.'

The landlord glanced at the empty room, and accepted the offer. 'Many thanks, I'll take a dram wi' you afore my customers starts coming in. I wun't have time later on, because Saturday's allus a busy night.'

As they drank their drinks in a companionable silence, Nail Styler covertly studied this new customer, trying to estimate how much potential profit he represented.

'You'm not from these parts, am you?' he sought to know, and the sailor shook his head.

'No. I'm a Dublin man be birth. But I've been gone from there for many a long year.'

'What brings you up here?'

'I've been visiting wi' me brother over in the Black Country. Now I'm heading back to Portsmouth. I've heard tell that my old ship is commissioning agen, the Agamemnon. So I'm going to re-enter on her books.'

'You'm in the King's Navy then, am you, not the merchant service?'

'That's just right,' the Irishman grinned. 'I'm rated gunner's mate. I've been a man-o-wars man for nigh on twenty years.'

'I hear tell that there's cholera over in the Black Country?' Nail Styler questioned.

'Sure, isn't there cholera all over the bloody country,' the sailor remarked unconcernedly.

'You doon't seem much feared on it, Jack?' Nail Styler was surprised that the man was so casual about it. He himself, like nearly all of his fellow townspeople, was very nervous about the prospect of the epidemic coming to his own area.

The sailor shrugged his brawny shoulders and drained his horn-tot before saying, 'I've always believed that when you're birthed, then the date o' your death is written on your forehead.

'I was with Admiral Codrington at Navarino back in twenty-seven and Johnny Turk sent over a shell that struck down every man but me on our gun. Nobody could believe how I hadn't a scratch on me.' Again he shrugged, 'But it's like I say, nothing 'ull harm ye until it's your time to go. And then, nothing 'ull save ye.'

Nail Styler drained his own tot. 'I reckon you could be right there, Jack.' He lifted the other's horn tumbler and refilled it. 'Here, have this one on me, and I'll goo and see about some vittles. 'Ull a beefsteak do for you?'

'It'll do me grand, matey. It'll do me grand. And the sooner the better, because me stomach is starting to think that me throat is cut.'

By nine o'clock that night the White Hart tap room was packed with noisy half-drunken men and women, and the air was thick with tobacco smoke and the exhalations of sweating bodies and reeking mouths. The White Hart was the favoured haunt of many of the local prize-fighters and their hangers-on, and this in turn attracted the younger sporting elements of the district, and the whores and gay girls out for a good time.

The Irish sailor, John Earns, was enjoying himself hugely. His good humour, and liberality with his money, had ensured his ready acceptance into the company, and now he laughed and joked and sang with his new acquaintances as if he had been a regular customer of the White Hart for years, instead of only hours.

'Now, I'll give ye a song ye've never heard before,' he announced, and to the cheers and plaudits of the crowd he clambered unsteadily to stand on a table top, and stood swaying violently. He flung his arms wide and in a strong tuneful voice began:

> 'It was in the month of April, upon the fourteenth day,
> This expedition did embark to cross the raging say;
> Our fleet then being well prepared,
> Our anchors we did weigh,
> To sail against the Burmese
> For to show them British playyy.'

'Hurrah!' the crowd cheered and punched the air with their clenched fists, and John Earns beamed and bowed and flung his arms to and fro in time with the tune.

> ''Twas early the next week, upon the break of day,
> Each man being well prepared, and eager for the fray.
> Our squadron formed a brilliant line,

> To show a grand half-moon,
> And with British colours flying,
> We sailed against Rangoon.'

'Go it, Jack! Go it!' A young pointer bellowed. 'We'em the Bulldogs, we am!'

> 'The Lilly frigate led the way when clouds of smoke
>   did rise,
> The Leander sloop in company, which did the foe
>   surprise.
> The Sophia brig and gunboats their cannon loud did
>   roar,
> Like thunder rent the elements all on the Burma
>   shore . . . '

'Hurrah! Hurrah!' the crowd bellowed, and again a forest of clenched fists punched the air.

On his table top, the sailor abruptly staggered, and almost fell off his makeshift stage, but a dozen hands grasped and steadied him, and he shook his head as if to clear it, then took a horn tumbler from a proffering hand and tossed the contents down his throat. He grinned hugely, and once more began to swing his arms and sing.

> 'All hands prepare for landing, resounded through the
>   fleet,
> Let every man have sixty rounds, the enemy for to
>   meet.
> Like lions bold we rushed on shore,
> At twelve o'clock that day.
> Those cowardly dogs could not us stand,
> We forced them to give way.'

Another storm of cheering burst out, and mugs and pots and hands hammered on the tables while feet stamped thunderously.

A pretty young whore, whose hair hung in a wild mass

down her back and whose rounded breasts almost spilled from her low-cut bodice, clambered up onto the table and threw her arms around the sailor's neck.

'Come on, Jack, dance the fuckin' hornpipe wi' me,' she invited, and wriggled her hips lewdly against him, while the crowd roared with laughter and offered obscene advice.

The sailor kissed her lips passionately, and then, abruptly, he thrust her away, and clapped both hands to his ears.

An expression of pure fear crossed his face and he moaned, 'Me head's ringing like church bells.' Then his eyes rolled upwards, and he toppled from the table and crashed down upon the people sitting directly below him. Pots smashed and drink spilled, men bellowed curses, women shrieked, and those who were seated further away howled with laughter and slapped their hands on their knees with gleeful delight.

The uproar brought Nail Styler hurrying from behind the counter and he bulled his way through to the side of the fallen man who was lying on his back, breathing in short, harsh pants, his eyes wide with fearful bewilderment.

As the landlord bent down to pull the sailor upright, Earns broke wind loudly and suddenly his bowels emptied, exploding a vile stench, and fluids stained and spread from beneath his hips.

'The dirty bleeder's shit hisself!' a man howled, and there was a general scramble away from the sailor's vicinity.

Nail Styler's shrewd brain raced with lightning speed, and instinctively he realised the truth of what was happening to this fallen man.

'Cholera! It's the cholera taking hold of the bugger!' The thought screamed in his mind, and inwardly he shuddered with fear and horror. But in another instant he clamped down on those emotions. He knew that if anyone else in that room guessed at what was the matter with the sailor, then he might just as well put up his shutters and abandon his business. This would ruin him, unless he kept his nerve.

Even while he tried to think out what was his best course

of action, his body and voice seemed to take on a volition of their own, and he could hear himself bawling angrily, 'Out you go, you dirty bastard! I'll not stand for anybody shitting in my pub! Out you go, and doon't try coming back agen ever!'

Grabbing the sailor's ankles he dragged him across the floor and out through the door onto the front yard of the inn. He glanced around him and seeing no one, pulled the sailor around the side of the inn where thick clumps of bush and uncut weeds and grass would hide him from view. He knelt by the man and told him, 'Just lie here for a bit, until I comes back to you. And doon't make a fuckin' sound, or I'll break your fuckin' yed. Does you hear me?'

The sick man groaned with pain, and nodded.

'Right then, just stay theer and wait for me.' Nail Styler assumed a joviality he was far from feeling, and went bustling back into the tap room, rubbing his hands together and shouting, 'That's the last we'll be seeing o' that dirty bastard in my place.' He bawled for his serving man, 'Jamie, get a bucket o' water and sluice that shit away.'

Within a few minutes the incident appeared to have been forgotten, and the tap room was once again a hubbub of uncaring drunkeness.

Outside in the darkness John Earns underwent his purgatory. His hands, arms, feet and legs stung with a painful prickling sensation; it felt as if a broad band of steel were being unbearably constricted around his waist, and clammy sweat gushed from every pore in his body. An agonising throbbing pain lanced through his head and every time he tried to move he either vomited, or purged and was left too drained and spent to lift himself up from the pools of his own excretions.

In the tap room Nail Styler had recovered from his initial panic and was now battling with his own conscience. Although a hard, tough and at times a brutal man, he was not vicious in his temperament, and as he served drinks and laughed and joked with his customers, he mentally disputed with himself over what he had done.

'It might not be the cholera. It could be that sailor had just took summat what disagreed with him?'

'But he's just come from the Black Country, arn't he. He told you that hisself.

'That don't mean that he's got the cholera, does it. Theer's thousands living theer who arn't got it.

'Maybe so, but you'se got a wife and childer to think about. Can you risk them catching it? And what about your business here? Iffen it got about that you'd bin serving a cove who'd got the cholera, then nobody 'ud step foot across your doors. You and your family could well end up in the bloody Poor'us, and sooner nor than later as well. You'se got to look arter your own, my bucko. The sailor's no concern o' yourn. You must look to your own fust.'

A further thought struck Nail Styler, which for a moment or two filled him with an awful dread. 'Supposing it is the cholera that cove's suffering wi'. Then it could well be all across the pub already. We could each and every one on us already have caught it.'

His heart thudded fearfully, and he stared blindly across the crowded room, his fancy picturing the dark figure of Death hovering over the heads of those present. The terrible picture brought a cold sweat starting on his forehead.

'What the fuck's up wi' you, Nail? You looks like you'se sin a ghost?' a crony demanded, and Styler took a grip of himself and forced a grin.

'It warn't a ghost, Sammy, it was the shock you gi' me when you offered to pay for this round.'

'I anna fuckin' offered to pay for naught,' the other shouted in protest, and Nail Styler's momentary loss of control passed without further notice.

For a while he toyed with various plans of action concerning what to do with the sick sailor. Then reluctantly accepted that whatever he might decide on, he would need help. His attention fixed upon a stocky, hard-featured man who was sitting quietly by himself on a bench at the side of the serving counter, keeping deliberately aloof from any company.

'Yes, John Lea. You'll do.' Styler knew that he could trust this taciturn, unsocial man to ask no questions and to keep a still tongue in his head – for a price.

He moved along the counter and crooked his finger, and John Lea came to him. With their heads close together, they talked for a few minutes, and then John Lea nodded and unobtrusively slipped away out of the tap room.

When closing time came, and 'Stop Tap' had been called a score of times and the last drunken reveller ejected from the inn, Nail Styler took a lantern and went up to the attic where the sailor had left his canvas sack. It was gone. Next Styler went outside and into the bushes at the side of the inn. Only flattened grasses and weeds showed where the man had lain. Styler abruptly sucked his teeth in wonderment and bent to feel the ground beneath the flattened area. It felt cold and damp to the touch, almost as if a bucket of water had been thrown down some hours previously and left to soak into the soil.

'Jesus Christ! Who'd 'a believed a human being could have so much wetness in 'um.'

He stifled a twinge of conscience. 'Theer was naught else I could ha' done. I'se got childer to think on, arter all.' He went back into his inn and bolted and barred the doors.

Chapter Twelve

THE SHARP RAPPING on his front door brought Joseph Cashmore out of his doze; he yawned and rubbed the sleep from his eyes. The rapping sounded again, and the Constable cursed softly, and growled, 'Alright, alright, I'm acoming.'

The candle on the table by the side of his hearthside chair was now only a guttering stub, and Cashmore squinted his eyes to see the time displayed on the ornate face of the grandfather clock in its corner.

He frowned, and went to the outer door to open it. 'What time does you call this?' he demanded sourly. ''Tis half past midnight. You'm supposed to report to me at midnight, on the hour, arn't you.'

'Give over moaning 'ull you.' The old man pushed past the Constable and entered the room. His toothless jaws waggled as he grumbled querulously, 'We anna all got jobs as soft as your'n, Joe Cashmore. I doon't get paid for sitting snoring by the bleedin' fire. It took me nigh on three hours to sweep up arter the mart this arternoon. I ne'er got home 'til gone nine o' the clock. I needs a bit o' slape doon't I, afore starting work agen. Iffen you was to do your job proper them bleedin' stall holders 'udden't be making such a bleedin' mess for me to clane up, 'ud they?'

'Alright, alright,' the Constable said wearily. 'I'se heard all this afore, too many times.'

The old man, Anthony Spragge, was his father-in-law and made his living as the town's night watchman, and sweeper of the market place.

Joseph Cashmore regarded the smelly, scrawny-shanked, great-coated and shawl-muffled figure, whose lank strands of long greasy white hair were topped with an ancient, shapeless, broad-brimmed hat, with an acute distaste.

'Does you know summat, feyther o' my missus?' he snorted disgustedly. 'You'm the scruffiest old bugger that ever come over my doorstep, and the bloody smelliest.'

'Bollocks!' the disreputable old man ejaculated, 'and you'm the meanest souled, most miserable bleeder of a son-in-law that's ever bin birthed. I'll take me oath on that. I curses the day that my daughter ever wed wi' you.'

Despite himself, the Constable's dour features creased in a fleeting grin. For all his cantankerous ways and physical dirtiness, there was still something likeable about this old reprobate before him.

'You may as well set yourself down for a minute while I primes the lantern for you. Arter all, it's your daughter who'll have to clane the chair arter you'se bin on it, not me.' Cashmore's grin showed again as the old man cursed horribly in reply to this sally.

'What's the town like, is it all quiet?' Cashmore asked as he primed the big lantern and lit it.

'You'd know what it was like iffen you didn't spend all your time setting on your arse in front o' the fire,' the old man rejoined.

'That's what I'm paid to do, old 'un. To stay here and wait to be sent for. It arn't any part o' my duties to patrol the town. I does that as an extra, and well you knows it.'

The other could make no reply to this truism, and could only mutter disgruntledly as he rummaged in the pockets of his coat to take out a filthy stub of old clay pipe, which he lit from the fire and then proceeded to suck noisily and belch out great clouds of foul-smelling smoke.

'Well?' Cashmore prodded. 'Is it quiet?'

'Ahr. As quiet as the grave.' Anthony Spragge seemed inclined to call a truce. 'The Fishers and the Allcocks had a bit of a barney in the Red Cow yard earlier on. But that was soon settled.'

'Did you notice anybody hanging about on your way here?'

'No.' The old man hawked and spat into the glowing embers of the fire. 'No, it looks like everybody's gone to their beds early for a change.'

'Well, I don't expect they've got too much to spend at present. What with the Fair only just being over. Most on 'um are probably still paying off their slates in the pubs.'

'That's sure to be right,' the old man agreed amicably.

'Come on then, get yourself shifted.' Cashmore handed the old man the lighted lantern and also a brass-cased pocket watch. 'I'se wound it and set the hour. So you arn't got any excuse for not calling it out accurate tonight. Have you got your stick?'

Anthony Spragge nodded and produced a lead-weighted cudgel from within his coat.

'Off you goo then.' Cashmore opened the outer door and ushered the old man through it. 'Send for me if there's anything amiss.'

'Phoo, who needs you? I can handle any trouble that might be,' the old man declared defiantly, and went shuffling off into the darkness.

Surrounded by a pool of lantern light Anthony Spragge slowly perambulated the streets and alleyways of the town through the hours of the early morning.

'It's two o' the clock and all's well. It's two o' the clock and all's well. It's two o' the clock and all's well.'

His cracked wavering voice echoed through the still air, and sleepers stirred and shifted and turned over in their beds.

But not everyone lay sleeping in their beds. A horse and cart came lurching slowly down the steep Back Hill, and when it reached the bottom of the slope the man leading the horse guided it into the shadow of a warehouse wall, and tethered it there. He moved to the rear of the cart and stared down at the inert figure lying curled into a ball on its floor. Only the sound of half-strangled, whining breath showed that the sailor still lived. John Lea put his mouth close to the sick man's ear, and whispered hoarsely, 'You lay quiet now. I'll bring help.'

He moved off, travelling with silent rapidity, his ears straining to detect any sounds. Then in the distance came a faint cry.

'It's half-past two o' the clock and all's well.'

Lea grinned with satisfaction, and halted, listening intently. When the cry came again through the darkness, he pin-pointed the direction from where it had originated and went running towards it.

The pool of lantern light was moving slowly across the eastern edges of the Chapel Green in the direction of the Lock-up. John Lea watched briefly to be sure of its direction, and then ran back through the silent streets to where he had left the horse and cart. Again he led it on down the long gently sloping Ipsley Street, until he reached the foetid Big Pool. There he halted the horse, and as gently as he could he pulled the inert man from its floor and laid him on the roadside. Then he took the canvas bag from the cart and put it at the sick man's side.

Before he left him, he bent and whispered, 'I dunno if you can hear me, Jack. But theer's a Watchman coming along this way shortly, and he'll be sure to find you. You'll be alright then, so just lay quiet and wait 'til he comes.' Then he turned the horse and cart and led it back towards the Back Hill.

When Anthony Spragge reached the Big Pool he would normally have turned southwards and patrolled up Ipsley Street and the Back Hill. John Lea knew the old Watchman's patrol route, and it was for this reason he had left the sick sailor on the roadside by the pool. Nail Styler's instructions had been to leave the man where he would be found by the Watchman, who could then be expected to summon help from the Constable, who in his turn would undoubtedly fetch a doctor. Thus giving the sailor a chance of life.

Unfortunately for John Earns however, tonight Anthony Spragge knew that his bosom drinking crony, old

Ben Wardle, the night watchman of the Fountain Mill, had gone to his work with a bottle of brandy tucked into his snap-bag, and Anthony Spragge was determined to share that bottle with him. So instead of turning southwards, he shuffled on down towards Bredon and the Fountain Mill.

For almost an hour John Earns lay where Lea had left him, and then he stirred and groaned as excruciating cramps gripped his fingers and toes and then with lightning rapidity spread across his entire body. He cried out in pain, contracting his body into a clenched ball, and as the pain lessened his tautened muscles slackened and he lay gasping with exhaustion. A raging thirst added to his torments, and mindlessly driven by atavistic instinct he began to inch his way towards the Big Pool, his hooked fingers clawing at the ground to drag his body onwards. He reached the top of the bank, and then the cramps struck again. His body jerked uncontrollably, and he rolled down the bank and splashed into the stinking stagnant depths. The foul water closed over his head, and flurries of bubbles burst on its surface. He rose once, twice, water splashing and heaving, then sank, and that same water gave him a swift and merciful release from his sufferings.

The first palings of the dawn were spreading along the eastern horizons when Anthony Spragge came shuffling back up Ipsley Street his mind swimming in a drunken haze. At the Big Pool he halted and fumblingly drew the skirts of his greatcoat aside and let down the front flap of his breeches. The steaming stream of urine arched high and fell spattering into the scummed water, some of its droplets hitting the semi-submerged corpse of John Earns.

Swaying and muttering to himself, the old man re-arranged his clothing and went stumbling on, then came to an abrupt halt. For a while his bleared eyes gazed owlishly down at the canvas sack lying on the roadway. Then with an exaggerated air of cunning caution, the old man peered all about him, and lifting his lantern high called out, 'Is anybody there? Who's dropped this ditty-bag?'

Only the soft soughing of the early morning breeze

answered, and Anthony Spragge's toothless mouth gaped wide and a wheeze of laughter issued from its reeking depths. He slumped down on his knees and his arthritic fingers fumbled with the bag's tie-rope. He peered inside and pulled out some of the clothing it contained, then wheezed with laughter again and congratulated himself.

'It's your lucky day, my bucko.' Then he spoke to the bag, 'You'm coming home wi' me, you am. You'm my property now.'

Groaning with the pain of stiff joints, he clumsily clambered to his feet, and hoisting the bag across his shoulder went staggering off homewards.

Chapter Thirteen

SHIVERING SLIGHTLY IN the early morning chill, the small, ragged-dressed girl came out of the mean hovel in Paoli's Row carrying a wooden bucket in one hand, and dragging her whining younger brother along with her other hand.

When they arrived at the edges of the green-scummed Big Pool, the girl was forced to release her brother as she needed all her puny strength to fill and lift her bucket out of the stinking water. The boy's bare feet squelched in the mud as he scurried to escape her, and she shouted after him, 'You come back here, Benny! Or I'll fuckin' well kill you!'

The boy ignored the threat, and whooping excitedly went scampering around the waterline.

'Benny!' the girl wailed, and then abandoned the heavy bucket and went running after him, her own bare feet leaving a clearly etched pattern in the soggy ground. Quickly she began to gain on the tiny boy, and then suddenly she skidded to a halt and stood staring with wide eyes at the water.

'Benny!'

The frightened shriek caused her brother to halt also, and to stare back in puzzlement at his elder sister. Then, when he saw her turn and begin to run back the way she had come, he followed after, shouting plaintively, 'Wait for me, Sue! Wait for me! I'll tell me mam if you doon't!'

'Mam! Mam! Theer's a man in the Pool!' Shrieking at the top of her voice the girl burst into the foetid hovel. 'Theer's a man in the Pool, mam!'

Aggie Cook slapped out wildly at her daughter and hissed, "Ull you stop blartin', you little bastard! You'll wake your feyther!'

The girl dodged the blow, and again shrieked at the top of her voice, 'Theer's a man in the Pool. I just see'd him. He's in the Pool, mam!'

On the rickety creaking bed in the corner of the single room, Thomas Cook rolled over and his dirty unshaven features glowered furiously over the edge of the greasy torn coverlet.

'I'll break your fuckin' yeds for you lot!' he roared.

'Theer now, look what you'se bin and gone and done, you little bastard!' Aggie Cook screeched. 'You'se woke your feyther!'

The girl emitted a frightened sob, but still shrieked out, 'Theer's a man in the Pool. I see'd him. I see'd him! He's in the Pool!'

"Ull you give over?' Aggie Cook went forward with upraised arm and the child cowered before her, but before the woman could strike her husband bellowed, 'Hold hard, Aggie!'

Obediently she did so, but still kept her arm raised in threat as her husband lifted the bedclothes and swung his dirty, pallid, hairy legs out from under them. Dressed only in his shirt, he sat on the edge of the bed, and scratched vigorously through his lank lice-ridden hair.

'Get here to me, you,' he growled at his daughter, and with frightened eyes she advanced timidly towards him.

'Get here, I arn't agoing to hit you, you stupid cow,' he assured her gruffly. When she was standing directly before him, he asked, 'Now what's you trying to tell us?'

'Theer's a man in the Pool dad! I just see'd him!'

'What does you mean, theer's a man in the Pool? What the fuck is he doing in theer?' Thomas Cook's drink-dulled, brutish features masked an equally drink-dulled and brutish brain.

'I reckon he's dead, dad,' his daughter informed him, and now her previous fright of discovery was being overlaid by this unaccustomed novelty of being listened to by her parents instead of just being treated as a dumb drudge.

The information seemed to galvanise Thomas Cook; he quickly lifted his breeches from the floor and pulled them over his hairy legs and buttocks.

'You'd best come and show me wheer he is,' he told his daughter.

John Earns was floating on his back, his face just below the surface of the water.

Thomas Cook stared at the drowned man for long, long moments. Then he told his daughter, 'Run and tell your mam, that's she's to goo and fetch the Constable. And tell her to be quick about it.'

As the child ran off, Thomas Cook gingerly waded waist-deep into the slimy water, gasping at its coldness. He was able from there to stretch over and grasp the drowned man's floating pigtail and pull the corpse with him back to the bank. He made no attempt to drag the heavy body from the water but, after a quick glance round to make sure he was unobserved, he removed the stout leather boots from the dead feet and put them on his own bare feet, then started to search the pockets of John Earns' clothing.

The Horse and Jockey public house stood on the east side of Ipsley Street facing Paoli's Row across the Big Pool. And since the boundary between the parishes of Ipsley and Tardebigge was reckoned to run along the centre line of that street, then the Horse and Jockey was in the former parish. So Dick Quiney, the landlord of the Horse and Jockey, was within his legal rights to refuse Joseph Cashmore's request to be allowed to leave the corpse of John Earns in his premises until such time as the Constable's enquiries were completed.

All licensed premises were legally obligated to give shelter to unclaimed corpses if the authorities so required, but since Joseph Cashmore was the Constable of Tardebigge Parish only, he had no legal powers over Dick Quiney. However, the landlord of the Horse and Jockey knew well that there would be many people who on one pretext or another would want to see the corpse, and he foresaw that there was a healthy profit to be made.

The cellar being the coolest room in the house, Dick Quiney had a trestle table rigged up between the barrels of ale and porter and John Earns was laid upon it. As the word of his death spread through the town there came a constant stream of viewers, and Dick Quiney charged each a penny. Many of these viewers also stayed on to take a glass or two of ale, and to discuss the mysterious corpse.

Many commented on the strange dusky hue of the dead man's skin, and the curious shrunken appearance of the corpse. But it was generally agreed that these things were caused by the foul waters of the Big Pool.

'You only needs to look at the buggers who lives in Paoli's Row, to see the truth o' that,' one wag commented. 'You'd think yourself to be in bloody Africa to see them buggers. Theer arn't a patch o' clane white skin on 'um, is there?'

'I reckon you'd have to boil 'um to get the dirt off 'um,' another man quipped.

'That's the truth. You'd need to boil the skin right off 'um, to get rid on it, it's grimed that thick. And then I reckon that you'd find dirt on their bones,' the wag came back at him.

When Joseph Cashmore returned to the Horse and Jockey, John Clayton was with him. 'Doon't let anybody come down while we'em theer,' the Constable told Dick Quiney, before he and the parson went into the cellar.

The landlord grinned as he replied jokingly, 'Well try not to stay down theer too long then, Joseph. It could cost me money. This is a very popular peepshow.'

The two men descended the narrow stone steps and Cashmore lifted high the lantern so that its light fell across the face of the corpse.

'Now please to look real close at this 'un, Parson,' Cashmore requested with a grim expression on his dour face. 'Just the colour he is. That arn't natural, is it? I'se seen a few drowned 'uns afore, and I arn't never yet seen one wi' that colour o' skin.'

In the pale light the dead man's skin looked to be a livid purple, and John Clayton shivered slightly. 'Not a pleasant sight, Master Cashmore,' he murmured. 'But then I've often heard that death by drowning sometimes produces peculiar discolourations.'

The Constable appeared unimpressed by this. 'Well, that's as maybe, Parson Clayton. But I arn't never seen one like it afore. And as I say, I'se pulled a few out o' the water.'

Reluctantly, John Clayton was forced to confront his own fearful dread.

'What do you think to be the cause of this man's discolouration then, Master Cashmore?'

'I don't rightly know what to think, Parson,' the man stated bluntly. 'But he's a stranger in these parts, arn't he. And I'se made enquiries at the houses hereabouts, and theer's nobody who recollects seeing him afore. So it's my opinion that he only come into the town last night. And I'm wondering what he might ha' brought wi' him, so to speak?'

'You're wondering if he might have brought the cholera, aren't you, Master Cashmore?' Clayton's own fears made him speak with an acerbity alien to his normal pleasant manner. 'Well might I suggest that you keep such opinions to yourself, until this man is examined by those properly qualified to diagnose diseases.'

Cashmore flushed with resentment at the other's tone, and Clayton instantly regretted his words. 'Forgive me, Master Cashmore,' he apologised, and smiled ruefully. 'I will confess frankly to you, that my own fear of the cholera reaching this town provoked me to react with such ill-manners. You are quite right to point out such a possibility.'

Cashmore nodded his acceptance of the apology. 'There's no offence took on my part, Parson. But what am we to do?'

The clergyman considered briefly. Then stated, 'For the

present, I think it best that we do nothing, Master Cashmore. My Lord Aston has most positively instructed me, that on no account are wild rumours to be allowed to be spread concerning the cholera. So, we must be sure of our facts before we do anything. My Lord Aston will be coming into the town later this morning. He is to take the service at the Chapel. Since many of the leading citizens will also be present at the Chapel, I think our best course is to consult with them, and so decide in concert what is to be done.

'In the meantime, I shall bring Doctor Taylor to view this poor fellow, and solicit his opinion regarding this discolouration of the skin. It may well be as I said. Nothing more than the effects of drowning.'

'Very well, Parson,' the Constable agreed. 'I'll attend on you directly after the service. Meanwhiles I'll make a few more enquiries about this cove.'

And with that mutual accord the two men went back up the cellar steps and into the light of day.

While John Clayton went in search of Doctor Hugh Taylor, Joseph Cashmore made his way to the hovel of Thomas Cook. He found Cook and his wife sitting on a crudely made bench before the rusted, fireless grate, sharing a flask of cheap gin.

'Why if it arn't Master Cashmore come avisiting.' Cook was already half drunk. ''Ull you take a sup, Master Cashmore?' he offered the flask.

Cashmore shook his head. The Constable was not an educated man, but he possessed a considerable fund of native shrewdness, and a doggedly enquiring and retentive mind. He was certain that someone or other knew who this mysterious drowned man was, and he was equally certain that the man had not come into the town wearing only the shirt and trousers he was now lying dead in.

'Wheer's your girl?' he asked.

'Her's gone out on an errand,' Aggie Cook told him, and there was a sly defensiveness in her manner which confirmed to Cashmore that either she or her husband had done something that they did not want him to find out.

He grinned inwardly, as the thought struck him, that it would be a very rare man or woman who had not done something or other that they would wish to hide from the law.

'I arn't going to beat about the bushes wi' you, Cook,' he said aloud. 'You knows me well enough to know that I'se got me own ideas concerning what's right, and what's wrong.' He stared meaningfully at the stout leather boots on Thomas Cook's dirty sockless feet. 'I'm not one o' them who thinks that a dead man has got any use for boots. After all, he arn't going to do any more walking, is he?'

A furtive expression flashed across Cook's unshaven, begrimed face and the man tried to bluster, 'I arn't done nothing, Master Cashmore, so doon't you goo accusing me of anything.'

'Hold your tongue!' Cashmore shouted suddenly. 'Does you think me a bloody numbskull, Cook. Because if that's the case then you'd best start saying your goodbyes to this stinking hole, because I'll have you in the other Hole up the town theer in bloody short order.'

The other man blanched, and mumbled, 'I'm sorry, Master Cashmore. I warn't trying to be flash wi' you. Honest, I warn't.'

Cashmore mollified his own tone, 'That's alright then, my buck. Just so long as we understands each other. Now listen to me very careful. I arn't interested in anything else, other than trying to find out a bit more about that cove you found in the Big Pool.

'Judging by his pigtail and tattoos he looks to ha' bin a sailor. But if that's the case, then wheer's his ditty-bag got to. And what's happened to the clothes he was wearing. He certain sure never come here to Redditch in his bare feet, wi' only a shirt and trousers to cover his nakedness, and wi'out a penny piece in his pockets.'

The Constable paused deliberately and his hard eyes went very slowly from man to woman, and back to the man.

'Now then, Cook,' he said softly. 'You tell me what you

got from that dead 'un. And I'll promise you that whatever you tells me, 'ull not goo further than me.'

Thomas Cook stared at the earthern floor, his tongue flickering out along his suddenly dry lips.

'All Tom got was them boots he's wearing and a crown piece he found in that dead 'un's trousers, and this jacket.' It was Aggie Cook who answered, and she rose from the bench and from underneath a pile of dusty rags in a dark corner of the room she unearthed a short blue jacket, with big brass buttons.

Cashmore took the saturated article of clothing from her and briefly examined it, then handed it back to her.

'Are you sure that you seen nothing like a ditty-bag anywheres?' he questioned.

Cook shook his head, and his bloodshot eyes stared nervously at the Constable.

'I swear on me babby's life, Master Cashmore, that what you'se bin told about is all I'se took. Just like Aggie's said, I never sin any bag.'

'Is there any chance that your kids might ha' found the bag, and be keeping it from you?' The Constable smiled grimly, 'Arter all, they might take arter their dad in the way o' being light-fingered, mightn't they?'

Again it was Aggie Cook who replied. 'No, Master Cashmore. The kids come running to tell us straight off when they found that chap. I'd know iffen they'd found a bag, and you can take it from me, that they arn't hid nothing away.'

Her words carried the ring of truth, and Cashmore was satisfied.

'Alright then. Now, listen to me, both on you. As far as I'm concerned, I know naught about boots, jacket or the crown piece.'

The couple looked visibly relieved.

'But what I wants you both to do,' Cashmore went on, 'is to keep your eyes and ears open. And if you comes to know anything else about that drowned bloke, then you'm to come straight off and tell me of it.'

'We'll do that, Master Cashmore,' Thomas Cook assured him vehemently, and his wife added her own assurances.

'Fair enough.' Cashmore nodded a curt farewell, and went from the stinking hovel.

He walked to the Big Pool, and for a while stood staring into its foetid depths, then pulled out his pocket-watch and checked the time. He saw that he had some two and a half hours before he need report back to John Clayton at the Chapel Vestry, so decided to use that time in making enquiries at the various pubs and inns around the town. He reasoned that since the dead man seemed almost certain to have been a sailor, then he would have had the sailors traditional love of carousing and must have been drinking locally before his death.

'Let us pray . . .' From the high pulpit of Saint Stephen's Chapel the Right Honourable and Reverend Lord Aston waited until the serried ranks of heads beneath him bowed and hands were raised and clasped in humble supplication, before bowing his own head and intoning in the mellifluous sing-song chant favoured by Anglican High-Church clergy: 'Most gracious Father and God, who hast promised forgiveness of sins to all them that with hearty repentance and true faith turn unto Thee, look down, we beseech Thee, from Heaven, Thy dwelling place, upon us, Thy unworthy servants who, under an awful apprehension of Thy judgements, and a deep conviction of our own sinfulness, prostrate ourselves before Thee . . .'

Aston frowned, as from the high seat set into the pulpit beneath him, Joseph Davis, the Parish Clerk, called out loudly, 'Amen to that!'

' . . . We acknowledge it to be of Thy goodness alone, that whilst Thou hast visited other nations, and other parishes of this country with pestilence, Thou hast so long spared us.

'Have pity, O Lord, have pity on Thy people both here and abroad; withdraw Thy heavy hand from those who are suffering under Thy judgements, and turn away from us that grievous calamity, against which our only security is Thy compassion . . . '

A sibilant chorus of agreement with this sentiment hissed along the pews nearest to the pulpit, but Aston forebore to frown at this. After all, these were the pews occupied by the town's elite.

' . . . We confess with shame and contrition, that in the pride and hardness of our hearts, we have shown ourselves unthankful for Thy mercies, and have followed our own imaginations, instead of Thy holy laws . . . '

At the rear of the packed chapel old John Adams, the sexton, moved down the aisle with a swiftness that belied his advanced years and brought his long slender rod sharply down upon the head of a small boy who was following his own imagination and fidgeting restlessly, instead of devoutly listening to the words of wisdom issuing from above.

The boy emitted a yelp of fright and pain, then held his breath and went red in the face with the effort of doing so, as his father scowled fiercely at him to be silent.

' . . . Yet, O merciful Father, suffer not Thy destroying angel to lift up his hand against us, but keep us as Thou hast heretofore done in health and safety, and grant that being warned by the sufferings of others to repent of our sins, we may be preserved from evil by Thy mighty protection. Preserve us from the dreadful pestilence, from the scourge of the cholera, O Lord, and let us enjoy the continuance of Thy mercy and grace, through the merits of our only Mediator and Advocate, Jesus Christ . . . Amen.'

'Amen.' The gusted response from the congregation was a compound of sanctity and relief.

George Sutton, the organist, played solemn chords as the congregation filed out of the Chapel. But those among them who were looking forward to shaking the hand of Lord Aston, and perhaps having a friendly word or two with that august personage, were to be disappointed on this day.

The noble clergyman came down from the pulpit and with an imperious gesture indicated to John Clayton that he should immediately go into the Vestry, together with those others who had been invited to attend this special meeting.

The Chapel Wardens and Overseers, medical men, Needle Masters and other leading townsfolk almost filled the small Vestry, and Lord Aston wasted no time in preamble.

'Gentlemen, this morning a male tramper was found drowned in the Big Pool, and the question has been raised as to the possibility that the unfortunate fellow might have been afflicted with the cholera at the time of his death.'

His listeners exchanged looks of concern and alarm.

'Apart from my curate, how many of you other gentleman have viewed the corpse?'

Only the exceptionally handsome Doctor Hugh Taylor answered, 'I have, My Lord. I accompanied Parson Clayton here to view the deceased.'

'What is your opinion, Doctor Taylor? Do you think that the deceased was afflicted with the cholera?'

The handsome dandy was loath to commit himself. 'I have no personal experience of the cholera, My Lord. Certainly the deceased was curiously discoloured and his skin corrugated. But whether or not those manifestations were a result of cholera, I really cannot state with any certainty.'

'Might I ask who it is who is spreading this rumour that the man had the cholera?' William Hemming, one of the town's leading Needle Masters, and a considerable landowner in his own right, seemed angry.

'I have made the suggestion to My Lord Aston that it is possible that the man was so afflicted. But I have not spread any rumour,' John Clayton spoke up.

'Then, Parson Clayton, it may well prove the case, that you will be responsible for inflicting upon this town one of its worst calamities,' Hemming stated aggressively.

'How so, sir?' the curate demanded.

'How so, sir? Because, sir, if false report that the cholera was in this parish was spread abroad, then the trade of this district would be ruined.'

A chorus of agreement came from the other Needle Masters present.

'How so?' Clayton demanded again.

'Because, sir, we would be unable to despatch our goods. Not only would the carriers refuse to handle our packets, but our customers would also refuse to receive them.'

'Nonsense!' John Clayton snapped.

'It arn't nonsense, Parson.' Henry Milward, fat and red-faced, and another of the town's leading Needle Masters, was quick to support his colleague. 'My cousin lives in Lancashire, and he writ to me only a sennight past and told me that since the cholera's been in that county, trade has all but come to a standstill.'

'But I cannot believe that intelligent men would refuse to carry or receive a packet of needles,' Clayton persisted.

'Any man who did carry or receive a packet from an infested district would be a damned fool, 'udden't he!' Milward riposted. 'Nobody knows for certain how this disease spreads. It seems to me to be very likely that it's carried by packets and suchlike.'

Several voices were raised in agreement with this statement, and Clayton realised that to argue further would only serve to waste valuable time.

'Well, gentlemen, the question is, what are we to do about this dead man? If he was suffering from the cholera, then should we not take immediate measures to prepare ourselves for the onset of the epidemic in this Parish?'

William Hemming was still smarting from Clayton's earlier scathing comment, and now he seized the opportunity to strike back.

'Oh really now, Parson Clayton,' he scoffed. 'A tramper gets drunk and drowns himself in the Big Pool and you expect us to ruin the trade of this entire district because of it? We are not vaporous old maids, Parson, but men of sense. We do not fly into needless panic, do we, gentlemen?'

His appeal to the audience met with a concerted support,

and encouraged by this, he went on. 'Can you prove that you are correct in what you say, Parson? Can you assert in all truth that this man had the cholera?' He jeered openly. 'I would not think that a degree in Divinity qualified a man to diagnose diseases. We have heard Doctor Taylor here state that he could not tell if the man was afflicted with the cholera. As to the poor fellow's discoloured and corrugated skin, I hold the opinion that even the briefest of immersions in the Big Pool would be sufficient to discolour and corrugate the toughest of hides.'

Voices were again raised to support Hemming, and John Clayton's heart sank as he realised that most of these men present were deliberately refusing to accept the possibility that the cholera had come to Redditch. Greed, fear, stupidity, desire to ingratiate themselves with the important and influential Needle Masters, all these traits were playing their part in erecting an impenetrable barrier against which he, John Clayton, would struggle in vain.

He made one last despairing assault against that barrier. 'The cholera is in the Black Country, only a few miles from this parish. If my Lord Aston will permit me, then I will go there and engage a doctor who has experience of this disease so that he may come here and examine the dead man.'

Lucas Royston had been standing quietly with his uncle, Alexander Pratt, listening and watching intently. His quick and acute mind had fully appreciated that the majority of the men present would regard with hostility any doctor who supported the Parson. Trade and Profit were the idols worshipped here, and these men were prepared to risk even their own well-being in order to ensure the uninterrupted continuance of that worship.

Royston was very desirous of establishing a practice in the town, but knew that his previous sojourn and escapades were well remembered by many of those now present. He needed to re-establish himself in their good opinions if he was ever to have any chance of succeeding as a doctor in this district. Now he saw a way in which he could begin his rehabiliation into their midst.

'May I speak, My Lord?' he asked Lord Aston politely, and received a curt nod of permission.

'As some of you gentlemen already know, I am a qualified physician.' Royston met their hard stares with a bland expression.

'It is not necessary for Parson Clayton,' he bowed slightly towards the cleric, 'to go to the Black Country in search of a doctor with experience of the cholera. I have been in Liverpool for some months earlier this year, and while there I assisted the physicians in that city with many of their patients who were afflicted with that dread disease.'

He smiled with an air of self-deprecation. 'While not wishing to appear conceited, gentlemen, I may state with justification, that I became regarded as something of an expert in the cholera's manifestations.'

'If you wish, I am prepared to make an examination of this dead man and give you my own diagnosis.'

His offer did not meet with immediate acclaim.

'Do you really think it necessary that any further examination should be carried out upon a man whom we know died of drowning, Lord Aston?' William Hemming challenged.

The Needle Master and the noble cleric were old antagonists, and although Lord Aston was equally reluctant to countenance any possibility that the cholera had come to his Parish, he could not bring himself to agree with the Needle Master.

'It is not the cause of his death that we seek to know, Mister Hemming,' he retorted acidly, 'but what other disease may or may not have been present.' He nodded his head at Lucas Royston. 'Very well, Doctor Royston. Go now and make that examination. We will await your diagnosis.'

'Certainly, My Lord. I'll not be any longer than is absolutely necessary.' He bowed to the clergyman, and then to the other men in the room. 'Gentlemen.'

As he passed the glowering William Hemming, he smiled pleasantly, and thought to himself, 'I hope I can bring a grin back to your miserable face, you surly old bastard.'

At the Horse and Jockey people were still coming to look at the drowned man and Lucas Royston was forced to invoke the name of Lord Aston in order to be alone in the cellar when he looked at the corpse.

Lucas Royston had not been lying when he had told of his experience of the cholera. He had assisted the Liverpool physicians, and what he had seen and learned of the disease enabled him now to judge that there was a strong possibility that the dead man had indeed been infected with it.

His judgement put him into a quandary. He knew that if he was to go back and tell the meeting that the cholera had come, then like all bearers of evil news, he would be regarded with great disfavour by those who had no wish to hear such tidings. He was sufficiently experienced in the perversity of human nature to know that there would be some who would even blame him for the onset of the epidemic. It was a certainty that his chances of establishing a successful practice among the Needle Masters and tradespeople of the town would be greatly harmed, because they would undoubtedly hold him partly responsible for any loss of trade.

On the other hand, if he reported that the man had not been afflicted with the cholera, and then the disease spread throughout the parish, he would be morally guilty for not having issued the warning.

As he walked slowly back towards the Chapel he wrestled mentally with his dilemma, and regretted that he had pushed himself forward with his offer of examination.

'Well, Doctor Royston, what is your diagnosis?'

Anxious, frowning faces surrounded him, and suddenly the image of Maria Pitts' lovely face came into his mind's eye. 'If I'm to progress with you, Maria, then I need to establish myself in a good practice here,' he thought, 'and I can't afford to antagonise these fellows. Not with my previous record in this town.'

With level eyes he faced Lord Aston, and said confidently, 'In my opinion, My Lord, the man was not infected with the cholera.'

Relieved sighs sounded. Smiles replaced frowns, and the almost palpable tension in the room dissolved in sudden loud talk and laughter.

William Hemming clapped the Scotsman's shoulder as if in congratulation. 'I could tell that you were a clever fellow at your trade, Royston. A smart young doctor like yourself could do very well in this town, you know. Have you thought of setting up in practice here again?'

'Yes sir, I'm thinking of doing just that.' Royston smiled, and that smile broadened as the Needle Master told him, 'Well, if you do so, then I for one will certainly recommend you.'

John Clayton frowned unhappily and asked Doctor Hugh Taylor, 'What do you think, Hugh? Is he right?'

The handsome face was very serious, 'I can only hope that he is, John. Because if he is not, then this town could be facing tragedy.'

Chapter Fourteen

'THEY SEEM TO be perfectly well again, Emma.'
Tildy Crawford was standing at her door in company with Emma Duggins watching the two small
boys playing in the yard.

The other woman smiled thankfully, 'Yes, they am.
Thanks to you, my duck.'

'Thanks to Doctor Taylor's medicines more like,' Tildy
replied, and then lifted the bottom edge of her long white
apron and used it as a fan. 'Pheww! I could wish for a cool
breeze. Do you know I've never known the weather to
stay as hot as this for so long.'

'That's what Doctor Taylor reckoned was wrong wi' my
bairns,' Emma Duggins stated. 'He said it's this heat that
causes the bad airs to rise up from the ground to give us all
these ailments. He says it's a mi . . . mi . . . mi, summat or
other.'

'A miasma.' It was Charles Brown who supplied the
word, as he came to join them from the workroom. 'Personally I'd be more inclined to blame the bad airs rising from
that Big Pool. I'd wager that the gases it gives off into the
atmosphere cause a good many of the fevers and bowel
ailments that the people who live around it keep suffering
from, including your little ones, Mrs Duggins.'

A horse and cart came breaking past Salters Yard from the
direction of the Big Pool, and Tildy saw that their neighbour, Pat O'Leary was its driver. He halted his vehicle at the
gateway and dismounting came into the yard.

'By Jase, 'tis hot enough to melt a man away!' he grinned

cheerily. 'I'll have to take a sup of ale before I travel one yard further. Me troat is parched, so it is.'

'Have you a long journey ahead of you, Master O'Leary?' Tildy enquired.

He wiped his broad florid sweating face with a colourful bandanna. 'No, Missus Tildy, I'm only travelling as far as the Chapel Yard.' He indicated a long narrow box on the back of the cart which was covered with a tarpaulin sheet. 'I'm taking that fella there to his final resting place, God ha' mercy on his soul.' He crossed himself. 'It's the poor devil that drowned hisself in the Pool. Parson Clayton is going to bury him,' he grimaced, 'and not before time either. His feet were starting to stink, if you get my meaning. In this heat mate goes rotten very quick, don't it?'

'That's true, Master O'Leary, but nevertheless I'm surprised that he is being buried so quickly. He was only taken from the Pool yesterday morning, after all. I would have thought that there would have been a little more time allowed in case someone could be found who could have identified the poor fellow.'

The bulky-bodied Irishman shrugged. 'Well, from the look of him, he could ha' bin a sailor, Master Brown. And that being the case, then God only knows how far he could be from his home, wherever that is.'

'Then he has no one to follow him?' Tildy observed, and a fleeting sadness crossed her features. 'What a shame, to be buried among strangers without a single person to shed a tear.'

On impulse she told the Irishman. 'Go and have your sup of ale, Master O'Leary, and I'll fetch my shawl. I'll follow the poor soul.'

Charles Brown smiled warmly at her, 'And I'll accompany you, Tildy.'

Tildy went back into her house to re-appear in moments with a dark shawl draped over her glossy head, and a bunch of wild flowers that she had gathered early that morning to sweeten the rooms.

She laid these on top of the tarpaulin covering of the

long narrow box, and when the cart lurched onwards she and Charles Brown followed respectfully behind.

John Clayton showed surprise when he saw the two followers, and as soon as the coffin had been lowered into the grave in the paupers' corner of the Chapel Burial Yard, and the first clods of earth were rattling down to cover it, he came to Tildy. 'Did you know this man, Mistress Crawford?' he asked with a curious eagerness.

She shook her head, 'No, Parson Clayton. My neighbour, Master O'Leary, said that the poor fellow had no one to follow him. So myself and Master Brown did so.' She sighed gently, 'At least his loved ones may perhaps one day discover that he did not go completely unmourned into his grave.'

Clayton smiled at her. 'Your charity does you both much credit, Mistress Crawford.' He stared keenly at Charles Brown, who as he normally did, was standing a little apart, as if unwilling to socialise. 'Is Master Brown new-come to this Parish?' he asked.

Tildy nodded. 'Yes. He works with me at the needle filing.'

A faint frown of puzzlement showed momentarily on Clayton's ugly face as he heard this information, and for a moment or two he studied Charles Brown curiously. There was something in the man's bearing and appearance that made him appear different from the usual run of soft workers. Then Clayton mentally shrugged and gave his attention back to Tildy.

'And so, Mistress Crawford, I shall soon be performing your wedding ceremony.'

He smiled warmly. Although he had had clashes with this pretty woman in the past, and had always considered that she was far too proud for her lowly station in life, nevertheless he had always had a great deal of respect for her. Despite all her troubles and hardships, she had always conducted herself with a degree of propriety that John Clayton considered could have been advantageously copied by many of her female social superiors in the Parish.

Now she smiled happily back at him, and said mischievously, 'Indeed you will shortly be making an honest woman of me, sir, and my present scandalous mode of life will be at an end.'

For a moment he stared in shock, then laughed heartily, and not for the first time found himself envying Daniel Lambert.

'I, for one, have never considered you to be a scandalous woman, Tildy Crawford,' he said softly. 'But I do confess, that I could wish to see you and your family come more often to church, when your present situation is regularised.'

Tildy regarded him with steady eyes. She had a great deal of admiration and respect for this man. Sentiments which she found it very hard to feel for the vast majority of his fellow clergy. She was well aware of the opinions that the godly and respectable elements of the Parish entertained for Daniel Lambert and for herself, and did not give a hang for those opinions.

'Ah, Parson Clayton, you are like your heavenly Master. You love the sinner. Unfortunately the majority of your flock do not share that sentiment.'

'What they think is of no importance in God's house, Tildy Crawford,' he told her very seriously. 'You must not let their prejudice keep you from partaking of God's mercy.'

She gave a brief shake of her head. 'I'm sorry, Parson. But I can never play the hypocrite. I do not wish to cause you any offence, please believe that. But I have never considered that to find God it is necessary to join all those canting, sanctimonious hypocrites who go to church thrice on Sundays.'

He smiled wryly. 'I see that your tongue is as sharp as ever, Tildy Crawford. But there is some truth in what you say, that I will admit. However, the doors will always be open to you.'

'Thank you, Parson. If there were more like you filling the pews, then I would be more likely to enter those doors.'

They parted with mutual good wishes.

Charles Brown seemed preoccupied as he and Tildy walked back down Alcester Street. And finally she felt constrained to ask, 'What is it, Charles? Is something troubling you?'

'No, it's only my usual morbidity.' He tried to avoid the question by joking, but Tildy suddenly felt that she must know.

'Tell me, what is it?' she persisted.

He looked gravely at her, and said hesitantly, 'It all seemed so hasty done, Tildy. The poor fellow was pulled from the Pool yesterday morning, and now, the very next day at half past one in the afternoon, he's already laid in the grave.'

'But the heat? Surely that's the reason for this haste?' Tildy ventured.

Brown shook his head frowningly. 'No, Tildy. I cannot help but feel there may have been another reason. It's almost as if Parson Clayton was trying to hide the man away so that he could be forgotten quickly.'

'But surely not,' Tildy protested. 'After all, the body was being viewed by anyone who cared to pay a penny all through yesterday.'

'That's true,' Brown accepted. 'But you know, Tildy, I really wish now, that I had gone myself to view it.'

'But why?' Tildy questioned curiously. 'Why should you now wish that?'

Brown merely shook his head and would make no further answer.

When they arrived back at Salters Yard, Tildy and Brown joined Old Esther in the workroom, and again set to filing their needles. They had only worked for an hour when Emma Duggins came into the room. 'Tildy, can you do a favour for me?' Her haggard face was troubled. 'Can you have my little 'uns in here wi' you for a whiles?'

'Of course I can,' Tildy told her. 'But what's the matter, Emma?'

'It's our kid, our Sally. Her's bin took real badly, and me mam's sent word for me to goo up home.'

Tildy nodded, and urged, 'You fetch the kids in here, Emma, and get off right away, and don't worry about them. They can sleep with us if necessary. So if your mam needs you to stay with her overnight, then you stay. I'll look after the kids.'

'Thanks, Tildy.' The woman was truly grateful, and within seconds the two tiny children were in the work-room, and she was gone hurrying away.

'I wonder what's the matter with Sally?' Tildy pondered aloud, and at her side Old Esther sniffed loudly.

'Iffen you arsks me, 'tis likely that her's bin trying to get rid of an unwelcome stranger. It warn't be the first time her's done it, neither. Silly little cow! You'd think she'd ha' learned her lesson by now, 'udden't you?'

'They never seem to, do they,' Tildy observed with a touch of sadness.

Emma Duggins' younger sister, Sally, was one of the town's Gay Girls, who frequented the pubs and inns, drinking and enjoying themselves with a variety of men. Their promiscuity led to unwanted pregnancies, and as Old Esther had said, young Sally had had a previous abortion which had nearly led to her death.

'What a shame it is for her mother.' Tildy shook her head regretfully. 'And for Sally as well. She's a likeable girl for all her wild ways.'

'She's a bloody fool!' Old Esther snapped.

'Yes, she's that as well, God help her,' Tildy murmured. 'But then, we all can be that at times, can't we?'

The two small children came tugging at her skirts, and Tildy smiled down at them.

'Now you play nicely together for a while. And then I'll give you some sweet-suck,' she promised.

Emma Duggins came back to Salters Yard early that evening just as Tildy and her companions were finishing their work for that day. Tildy took one look at the woman's haggard face, and tear-reddened eyes and feared that the worst had happened.

'Oh Emma,' she said softly, 'come in and set yourself down for a while. I'll make you a dish of tea.'

The children ran to greet their mother, who cradled them in her arms.

'What about Sally,' Tildy asked gently, 'is she dead?'

Emma Duggins nodded, and her lank hair dangled in greasy locks down her worn cheeks, and tears spilled from her eyes. 'A few hours since, Tildy. Not long arter I got theer. Her was laying real quiet then, but me mam said that she'd bin throwing herself about and screaming out earlier on. We'se had to strip the bedding, and chuck the mattress out in the yard to dry. Everything was soaking, Tildy. And the poor little cratur looked ever so strange. Her was all dark and shrivelled looking, Tildy. I could hardly recognise her. I'se never seen one who looked like her afore.'

Tildy nodded sympathetically. Untimely deaths among both young and old were a common enough occurrence in her world, and the survivors learned to bear the loss of loved ones with a high degree of stoicism. Most parents expected to have to bury at least half of their children before they themselves died.

'Well Emma, you must try and draw comfort from the fact that the poor soul did not have to suffer for very long.'

Emma Duggins nodded sadly, 'Yes, that's a comfort, at least.'

Charles Brown had been listening intently to Emma Duggins' words, and now he asked, 'Forgive me, Mrs. Duggins, but I must ask you if it would be possible for me to go and see your poor sister's body.'

The woman looked at him with mingled surprise and doubt, and he added quickly. 'Please, I have very good reason for so asking.'

'Well, I dunno what me mam 'ud say,' Emma Duggins was still very doubtful. 'Arter all, you'm a stranger to her, Master Brown.' She shook her head abruptly, 'No, me mam 'udden't want to let a stranger in to see our Sally. 'Specially not the way the poor little cratur looks now.'

'Yes, I sympathise with that fact, Mrs Duggins,' he answered, and then turned urgently to Tildy. 'Please Tildy, could not you come with me to the house, and persuade Mrs Duggins' mother to let me examine Sally's body. I have the best of reasons for wishing to do so, that I promise you.'

Tildy was equally surprised by his request, and by the urgency in his tone. Remembering his preoccupied air after the brief burial service of the stranger earlier that day, she asked, 'Does this have something to do with the drowned man, Charles?'

He nodded and said gravely, 'Indeed it does, Tildy. Please, I beg of you to come with me and persuade the lady. It really is imperative that I see that poor creature.'

Tildy hesitated, then said to Emma Duggins, 'What think you, Emma? Would it upset your mam too much?'

The other woman shrugged her thin shoulders, 'I dunno, Tildy. I dunno what to tell you.'

'It is a matter of life and death for many people in this town, Tildy.' Charles Brown appeared to be growing increasingly impatient. 'To speak frankly, if Emma's mother will not give me her permission, then I am prepared to go to the Constable, and ask him to use his authority to enable me to see this dead girl.'

Tildy's eyes widened in astonishment. She had never seen this normally equable and quiet-mannered man behave in this manner before.

'Please, Tildy, for all our sakes, come with me and inter-cede for me with the woman.' He was almost pleading with her now.

'Very well, I'll come,' Tildy agreed reluctantly. 'But hear me well, Charles. If Emma's mother is adamant, then I'll not let you badger her. Do you understand that?'

'I pray God that badgering may not be necessary, Tildy,' he replied quietly.

Emma Duggins wiped the back of her hand across her

eyes, and said dully, 'I'll needs goo and get Charlie summat to ate. He'll goo bloody mad iffen he comes home and theer's no grub laid out for him.'

Tildy patted her shoulder, 'Alright, Emma, you do that. I'll come and see you presently.' Then she nodded to Charles Brown, and they left.

Widow Beck, Emma Duggins' mother, lived in Izods Yard, an alley of mean cottages leading off Front Hill, almost at its junction with Back Hill at the Duke of York Inn. The Beck's cottage was in a terrace row sunk some four feet below the level of the roadway.

When Tildy and Charles Brown entered Izods Yard they saw a cluster of women and children at the door of the cottage they sought. To Tildy's relief she recognised the familiar face of a young woman she had once worked with.

'Hello Molly.'

'Hello Tildy, what brings you here?' Molly Green had been a friend of the dead girl, and like her was one of the so-called 'Gay Girls' of the town. She stared curiously at Charles Brown, and whispered to Tildy. 'Who's this then? He arn't your "Fancy Man" is he?'

Tildy shook her head, but took no offence. She knew this young woman of old, and the way her mind worked.

'No Molly, he's not. But he's a good friend of mine and Daniel's. We wanted to have a look at poor Sally. Do you think her mam would mind too much?'

'No.' Molly's shaggy mass of frizzed hair tumbled about as she shook her head. 'The poor old bleeder is well out of her yed, Tildy. We all clubbed together and bought her a couple o' flasks o' gin, to help her get through this. Her was powerful fond o' Sally, and her was keenin' summat terrible, so we reckoned it was best to give her a drink to ease her sorrowing.'

Molly quickly cleared the way for Tildy and Charles Brown to enter the low-ceilinged, cramped interior of the cottage.

Old Widow Beck was crouched on a backless chair, surrounded by her neighbours, her face and eyes vacuous with the effects of the raw gin. When Tildy went to offer her condolences, the old woman could only stare blankly at her and made no reply.

The young woman's body was laid out on the bare boards of the double bed which filled one half of the room. Sally Beck had been dressed in a clean white shift, with a mob cap on her head, and her jaws tied shut with a long bandage wrapped around scalp and chin. Her features were darkly suffused and pinched looking; Charles Brown quickly bent forward and pulled back the long sleeves of the white shift so that he could see the skin of her arms.

A murmuring of resentful protest greeted his action, but he ignored it, and jerking his head at Tildy and Molly to follow him, pushed his way through the crowded room and back into the sunken passageway.

'When was Sally taken ill?' he asked her friend.

'Yesterday arternoon.' The young woman screwed up her features in the effort of remembrance, 'I'd come round to see if she was gooing out, but her said that her'd got the runs real bad. So I went and bought some drink, and we stayed in. But her got worse as the night went on. I thought it might be summat that her'd ate on the Saturday night. We was up the White Hart having a spree, and we'd bin ateing and drinking all sorts.' She sighed heavily. 'We had a real good night, so we did. Sally tried to get off wi' a sailor, but he was so bloody drunk that he shit hisself, and Nail Styler threw him out. So poor Sally had to make do wi' one o' the bloody Pointer Lads instead.'

'A sailor, you say,' Charles Brown asked with an assumed casualness, but Tildy could see that the information had disturbed him.

'Yes, he was a real Jack Flash as well, a real pretty man. I could ha' fancied him meself.'

'It wasn't the same man who drowned in the Big Pool, was it?' Brown questioned.

The young woman appeared puzzled, 'I doon't know who it was who drowned, Mister. I bin here wi' Sally since she was took badly.'

'It doesn't matter.' Brown looked about the alley, and pointed to a couple of blankets and an old flock mattress which had been tumbled over a clothesline stretched across the end of the sunken passageway. 'Is that the bedding the young woman was laying on?'

'Yes,' Molly nodded. 'It's bin put out for drying. But I reckon Widow Beck 'ull have to strip the flock out o' the mattress to do any good wi' it. It's soaked right through.'

'Thank you for your help, ma'am.' Brown bowed courteously, and walked away to examine the discarded bedding.

Molly winked saucily at Tildy. 'He's a real gentleman, arn't he. Does he need some company in his bed?'

Tildy could not help but smile, 'I'll ask him, Molly. Goodbye now.'

'Tarraa Tildy. Tell him where he can find me if he does.' Molly Green winked again, then turned back into the cottage.

As soon as they were out of the alley and on the Front Hill, Charles Brown held out his hand to bring Tildy to a halt, and then told her without any preamble. 'Tildy, that girl, Sally Beck, is dead of the cholera!'

Chapter Fifteen

'SALLY BECK, DEAD o' the cholera?' Joseph Cashmore lifted his heavy hand and rubbed his chin thoughtfully. 'That 'ull be Sally Beck from Izods Yard, 'ull it?'

Tildy nodded. 'We came from there an hour since, Master Cashmore.'

She and Charles Brown were sitting in the front room of the Constable's cottage. After they had seen Sally Beck's corpse, and Charles Brown had stated his opinion that the girl had died from the cholera, they had walked the streets of the town discussing what they should do, and had finally decided to come and talk to Cashmore.

The Constable stared keenly at Brown. 'Now then, master, how come you'm so powerful sure that the wench had the cholera?'

'Because I have had previous experience of the disease,' Brown answered quietly.

'Where?' Cashmore wanted to know.

'In India.' Brown seemed apologetic as he spoke to Tildy. 'There's much about my past life that I have not spoken of, Tildy.'

'Then perhaps it might be a good time to tell us a bit more about it.' Joseph Cashmore's expression was ambiguous as he regarded the other man. He appeared reluctant to accept what he had just been told.

'Very well,' Charles Brown nodded slightly. Then began to speak. Hesitatingly at first, but then with a noticeably increasing confidence. 'I was not always a pedlar. In my younger days I held a more elevated position in society than at present.'

Cashmore nodded, as if this statement only served to confirm a previously held opinion, and Tildy herself uttered, 'I thought as much.'

Brown smiled at her, 'Oh, I do assure you that I was never anything very grand, Tildy, but I am a Licentiate of the Royal College of Surgeons, and have served in the Royal Navy as a surgeon for many years.'

'That being the case, master, then why am you earning your living at the needles these days?' Cashmore questioned suspiciously. 'Surely you'd have a better life following your old trade.'

'What is a better life, Master Cashmore?' Brown smiled with a wry sadness. 'At least as a pedlar, or a filer or needles, I do not have to hear people screaming beneath the knife. Or to see patients die because I do not have sufficient knowledge to save them.'

'Can you prove your words?' Cashmore demanded. 'Can you prove that you'm a proper medical man?'

'At this exact moment, no,' Charles Brown admitted. 'But given a little time I can undoubtedly obtain such proof. I shall need to communicate with the Admiralty to obtain copies of my documents, and with the Royal College of Surgeons to obtain copies of my diplomas.'

'Am you certain sure that young Sally Beck died o' the cholera?' Cashmore asked at a tangent.

'As certain as I can be,' Brown said confidently. 'But naturally in an imperfect science such as medical diagnosis, errors can always be made.'

'But you'm as sure as you can be, that you arn't made any error regarding Sally Beck?' Cashmore persisted doggedly.

'I am as certain as I can be, that I have made no error,' Brown repeated.

'Right then, I wants you to come along o' me, and tell to Parson Clayton the very same as you'se told me. You as well, Tildy Crawford.'

Up until this point Tildy had successfully kept her own

fear in check, but suddenly it swept over her. 'Shouldn't we be doing something to guard ourselves, Charles? Before we leave it any longer?' she asked nervously. 'If young Sally did die of the cholera, might not we be in danger ourselves?'

The man could only shrug helplessly. 'In all truth, Tildy, I don't know what preventatives I could recommend. In my experience this disease strikes seemingly at random. I have known men to share a bed with a cholera victim, and take no harm from it, and others who have done all that they could to avoid its victims, fall victim themselves.'

'What we could do, if Master Cashmore will oblige us, is to wash ourselves thoroughly and take a dram of brandy.' He grinned and for a moment resembled a mischievous urchin. 'It's only the water I would request of you, Master Cashmore. I shall purchase the brandy myself on our way to see the Parson.'

Cashmore nodded agreement, 'You can douse yourselves out the back in the wash'us theer. You'll see the hand-pump.' Then his own dour features momentarily lightened with a brief grin, 'And it just so happens that I'se got a flask o' French brandy in the house, and I'll be happy to invite you both to take a dram wi' me.'

Whether it was the quick but thorough scrubbing she gave to her skin, or the large tot of strong-tasting brandy she drank, Tildy could not say, but when the three of them set out to go to Parson Clayton's house, she found that her fears had all but disappeared.

John Clayton listened without interruption to all that the three of his visitors had to tell him. As he listened his ugly face grew ever more serious. When they had finished he asked Charles Brown several questions to clarify certain points, and then for a while sat with his hands locked together in front of his chest, his fingers steepled, and a thoughtful frown on his face. At length, he gave a troubled sigh and looked up at his visitors.

'I must ask each of you to keep silent about this for a while longer, until I have seen my Lord Aston and received his instructions in this matter. You will, I'm sure, appreciate the reason and the absolute necessity for this request I make of you.'

Although they looked doubtful, both of the other men in the room acquiesced. But Tildy questioned in protest. 'But how can we keep silent, Parson Clayton? Surely the people must be warned what's happening in the town? If the cholera's come, then we should be spreading the news of it far and wide, so that people can be prepared against it.'

A fleeting expression of aggravation crossed Clayton's features, and again he sighed, but this time in burgeoning exasperation. 'I might have known that it would be you who would make dispute, Tildy Crawford.'

Her own exasperation burgeoned, 'I'm not making dispute for its own sake, Parson Clayton. But when such a terrible danger threatens our loved ones, then you've no right to ask us to keep silent about it. If the cholera is here, then the people have a right to know of it.'

'If it is here, Crawford?' The cleric snapped angrily. 'If?' He came out of his chair, and placing both hands flat on the top of his desk leaned over, thrusting his head towards her, 'It is still a question of "if", Tildy Crawford. We do not yet know for certain whether this unfortunate girl did indeed die of the cholera, do we?'

He inclined his head towards Charles Brown in acknowledgement. 'I will speak frankly. Master Brown's account of himself bears the ring of truth, and I am prepared to give full credence to what he has told us of his medical qualifications. But in this Parish I am answerable to the Lord Aston, and through him to the Earl himself, and to speak plain, knowing both of those gentlemen as I do, I can tell you without fear of contradiction, that they will not accept Master Brown's story concerning his antecedents without fully authenticated documentation to verify it.'

'But what does that matter?' Tildy demanded to know. 'Surely the only thing that does matter is that Sally Beck has died of the cholera?'

'But the Earl, and my Lord Aston will need that fact confirming by an accredited medical man before they will take any action concerning the possible advent of an epidemic in this Parish.'

'But that is only wasting more time!' Tildy protested angrily. 'If, as you say, you believe Master Brown's account of himself, then surely you could even now be taking steps to protect the Parish?'

'Damn it all, will you be silent, woman?' Clayton's strained nerves caused his temper to snap and he bellowed at Tildy. 'Do you not think that I too might be afraid of what threatens here? But I am only my master's servant. I can do nothing until they permit me. If I allow you now to go through the town spreading this story, then all that will be achieved is fear and panic. All trade and normal intercourse will come to a standstill, and we could well be faced with a breakdown of law and order. It has already taken place in some parts of this kingdom. I will do nothing to provoke the risk of it happening here.'

Before Tildy could make any reply, Charles Brown gripped her upper arm and hissed warningly to her, 'Hold your peace now, Tildy, I beg of you. You will do more harm than good if you continue to argue this matter.'

'Indeed she will, Master Brown,' Clayton confirmed grimly. 'And if she continues thus, then I will state frankly, Tildy Crawford, that I will have the Constable here commit you to the Lock-up, and so ensure your silence. Have I made myself plain?'

Tildy recognised that she could do nothing against his obduracy, and with ill grace, nodded, but could not resist adding, 'I have a child, Parson Clayton, and sooner than place him into a danger that can be recognised, then I will gladly go into any prison.'

The cleric's broad shoulders sagged slightly, and he shook his head wearily from side to side. 'Do not treat me as an enemy, Tildy Crawford. I swear by all that I hold sacred, that I shall do my utmost in this matter.'

He nodded in dismissal. 'My thanks to you, Master Brown, for bringing this to my attention. Remain silent until you receive further communication from me. You also,

Tildy Crawford.' He paused for a moment and studied her sullen face doubtfully, then warned, 'Remember what I have said to you. And now I'll bid you both a good day. Please to remain, Master Cashmore.'

When he was alone with the Constable, Clayton told him, 'Go and find Lucas Royston and bring him here to me as soon as you can do so. I'll have him examine Sally Beck before I involve my Lord Aston.'

As the Constable was leaving, the cleric halted him briefly to instruct, 'And afterwards I want you to go to Tildy Crawford's home, and impress upon her that she must keep that tongue of her's still.' He smiled mirthlessly, 'John Knox was quite right you know, Master Cashmore, when he wrote of "The Monstrous Regiment of Women". Tildy Crawford has always shown a deal too much pride and independence for her station in life.'

Tildy's mind was full of many wildly differing thoughts and concerns as she walked up Fish Hill. Fear again began to dominate. Fear for her son, fear for Daniel Lambert, fear for Old Esther, and fear for all those others in the town who had ever been her friends. Paradoxically she had little fear for her own well being, and now it puzzled her that she could be so fatalistic about her own possible danger.

Tildy had been a sick nurse at various times in her life, and had seen much illness and death. But this new disease, this cholera, seemed somehow more frightful, if that was possible, than anything else she had experienced.

'I suppose that's because it is so new,' she thought to herself. 'It's so mysterious, and it appears to strike with such speed and deadliness, and everybody seems so helpless before it.'

She began to question Charles Brown about his previous experiences of the cholera, hoping that he would be able to give her some comfort. But he could only confess his own ignorance and puzzlement concerning its modes of transmission, and its causes, and to admit that, as far as he knew, there was no cure. It was only God's will that decided whether those it struck down were to live or to die.

A sense of sickening despair enveloped Tildy. 'What shall I do if it strikes down my loved ones?' she asked herself, and for a while could only endure her terrible sensation of utter helplessness. But then, from deep within her, her combative and courageous spirit began to muster its resources of dogged courage and determination. 'I don't know what I can do yet,' she told herself, 'but I'll try to do something, that I'll swear. I'll not surrender to it like a coward. I'll do something to fight back against it.'

Chapter Sixteen

LUCAS ROYSTON WAS a happy man on this sunny Wednesday afternoon as he strode briskly up Mount Pleasant and past the Round House. Since the previous Sunday his fortunes had improved with an amazing rapidity. From being a man of doubtful reputation among the town's elite, he was now almost miraculously transformed into a rising star in its social firmament.

As he neared the house of Arnold Pitts, Attorney at Law, and father of the delectable Maria, Lucas Royston's lips curved in a smile of satisfaction as he mentally replayed the series of events which had wrought such a transformation in his affairs.

Late on Monday night last, he had been summoned by the Parish Constable to a small and select gathering in the house of Reverend the Lord Aston at Tardebigge hamlet. The Right Honourable Other Archer Windsor, Earl of Plymouth had presided over the meeting at which William Hemming, Henry Milward, Polydwarf Allcock and several other of the parish's richest and most influential citizens had been present, including Arnold Pitts, the Reverend John Clayton, and Doctor Hugh Taylor.

The subject under heated discussion was the death of a young woman named Sally Beck. The Reverend John Clayton claimed that he had had expert opinion that the woman's death was due to cholera, and he wanted to declare an immediate state of emergency throughout the needle district, and impose a quarantine and other restrictive measures. In this he was bitterly opposed by the Needle

Masters, and Reverend the Lord Aston, who had challenged him to identify his expert opinion giver. When the young clergyman had named Charles Brown and explained the man's claims to be an ex-naval surgeon, he had been jeeringly derided for being too credulous, and scoffed at for accepting the word of a travelling pedlar.

Lucas Royston himself had then been instructed to go to the Izods Yard in Redditch, and make his own examination of the corpse. Royston was a very shrewd man, and he had realised that he must now choose his side and in his own interest that side had got to be that ranged against John Clayton. He had ridden to Redditch in William Hemming's carriage, driven by that august personage himself, and had listened with due deference to the Needle Master's views on why it was quite unthinkable that the dread scourge should be present in this Parish.

Now Royston's smile became cynical. Those views could be translated into two words, Trade and Profit.

At the mean little cottage he had briefly glanced at the darkened, shrivelled corpse, and recognised cholera. Outside once more and mounted in the carriage, he had smiled at William Hemming, 'I'm happy to say that Parson Clayton's fears are unfounded, sir. The girl undoubtedly died from a fever brought on by the summer diarrhoea. In fairness to the Parson, ignorant and inexperienced medical quacks have at times mistaken the symptoms of the various summer fluxes for those of cholera.'

Back at the Lord Aston's Vicarage, his report was greeted with relief and applause, and although John Clayton angrily challenged his findings, Lucas Royston's bland and confident assurances were accepted with an avid gratefulness by the vast majority of those present. The Scotsman's reward was immediate. Needle Masters and Parish worthies had shaken his hand and congratulated him upon his medical skills. His advice was sought on a variety of ailments, and appointments made for him to call and examine several sick members of the families of some of those present at the meeting.

On this Wednesday afternoon it was to one of those appointments he was going. He chuckled at the delicious piquancy of it. He was en route to examine Mistress Letitia Pitts, wife of the Attorney and mother of Maria.

The maidservant ushered him into a stuffy overheated parlour where the mistress of the house was waiting to receive him. The woman was reclining on an ornate chaise-longue, swathed in voluminous lace peignoirs, a feathered turban upon her frizzed and hennaed curls.

Maria Pitts was sitting demurely on a low stool by her mother's side, her grey eyes coquettishly peeping from beneath their thick dark lashes, her soft black hair dressed in long ringlets falling about the shoulders of her virginal white gown.

Lucas Royston's susceptible heart pounded and his throat thickened as he bowed to the two women. 'Dear Christ!' he thought with a sense of shock. 'I do believe I've fallen in love with this one!'

With a gravity that belied his inner feelings he began to talk to the elder woman concerning her symptoms. He regarded the fat sweaty grey features, and the thin lips pouting with petulant self-pity, and marvelled that such an ugly and unappealing creature had carried a ravishing vision like Maria within her pendulous belly. But he smiled with an understanding sympathy that charmed Mrs Pitts to her very soul, and told her in his melodic-toned voice, 'Ma'm, you are labouring beneath the affliction that ladies of your exceptional sensitivity and high breeding are all too often so unjustifiably seized by. You have a disturbance of the equilibrium of your temporal arteries. Your concern and care for others have taxed your own vital spirits beyond their endurance. To put it simply, ma'am, your own good heart has been your undoing. You have laboured on behalf of others quite beyond the capacity of your own delicate constitution to endure.'

He paused, and gazed into her bleared, and brandy-reddened eyes, successfully managing to radiate his compassion and concern. Then his even white teeth gleamed as he smiled tenderly at her, and Letitia Pitts' heart fluttered tremulously, and she thought what wonderfully fine eyes this man possessed. 'Why, they seem to probe into my very innermost thoughts and feelings,' she told herself, and a faint blush coloured her pock-marked greasy skin as she realised the shameful carnality of some of those thoughts and feelings.

'However, ma'am, fortunately I have been consulted in good time.' Now Lucas Royston's manner became brisk and confident. 'If you will only consent to trust in me, and to give me your full confidence and co-operation, then I do assure you, ma'am, that I will in the due course of time restore you to that abundance of good health and spirits that is your just and rightful portion.'

From his small leather reticule he produced a glass phial, and carefully measured some of its liquid contents into a small silver cup. 'I want you to drink this down immediately, ma'am. It is an elixir of my own diffusing.'

Mistress Pitts frowned doubtfully at the dark green liquid. 'What is it? What does it contain?' she questioned.

Royston smiled regretfully, 'I must crave your indulgence in this matter, ma'am, but sadly professional etiquette absolutely forbids my divulging the composition of this elixir. However, since you are who you are, ma'am, I can take you into my strictest confidence, and tell you that this is the personal and private treatment of our own Royal Family.'

He became secretive in his manner, and his voice dropped to almost a whisper, 'I must confess in all honesty, ma'am, that this remedy came into my possession quite recently without the consent of His Majesty's personal physician. Therefore I must ask you to exercise the utmost discretion concerning it. It might well cause considerable resentment to be directed against me from those medical men who attend on the Blood Royal, if they were to come to know that I had been treating my own patient with it. Even though that patient is a lady of quality and great repute.'

Mistress Pitts' eyes widened and she stared with

something approaching awe at the liquid. But Maria Pitts' grey eyes danced, and she put one dainty hand to her mouth and coughed very loudly. Causing her mother to glare suspiciously at her.

The elder woman swallowed the dose in one gulp, then smacked her lips reflectively, 'I do declare that this has a tang of something familiar in it, Doctor Royston.'

He smiled reassuringly at her. 'I'll not try to deceive you, ma'am. I have added just the tiniest suggestion of the finest French brandy during the diffusion process. One of the ingredients, a most rare and costly extract from the East Indies, has a slightly bitter taste. I add the brandy to disguise that.'

Mistress Pitts nodded, then after a moment or two, declared, 'Do you know, I really begin to feel somewhat restored already.'

Royston nodded gravely. 'It is a most potent remedy, ma'am, but I fear it will take many more draughts of it before your constitution is fully restored.'

Again Maria was taken by a sudden fit of coughing, but before her mother could voice any remonstrance, there came a sudden commotion from the rear of the house, and moments later a dishevelled maidservant burst into the room wailing loudly, 'Oh Missus, come quick, the cook's bin at the gin agen!'

With an agility astounding in such a large, fat and ailing woman, Mistress Pitts vented an angry imprecation, came off the chaise-longue, grabbed a long brass poker from the fireplace, and went through the door shouting at the top of her voice, 'I'll learn you your lesson, you drunken besom-bitch! I'll bloody learn you!'

Maria threw back her head and laughed until tears started from her eyes, and Lucas Royston joined in that laughter.

When Maria's laughter calmed, she told Royston, 'And you sir, are a shameless rogue. Filling my poor gullible mother's head with all that nonsense about secret remedies and costly ingredients, and Royal Families.'

The man looked at her keenly, and noted the devils of

mischief in her lucent grey eyes, then smiled, and shrugged. 'You're right, my sweet girl. I am indeed a rogue, and have filled your mother's head full of arrant nonsense. But would she have preferred me to tell her the truth? To tell her that all she was suffering from was too much self-indulgence and insufficient bodily exercise?' He chuckled easily, 'Don't worry. The elixir contains naught to harm her, and indeed does truly contain some beneficial ingredients.'

She mock-scowled, 'I've a mind to tell her the truth of the matter.'

He sensed that boldness would pay him, and went to the girl and bending down suddenly kissed her mouth. She tried to push him away, but he held her firm, and lifted her up from the stool so that her body was pressed close against his own. The feel of her firm breasts and rounded thighs through the thin fabric of her dress sent shivers of desire coursing through him, and his mouth became more urgent and demanding. The rigid resistance of her body only lasted for seconds, and then she abruptly softened against him and returned his kisses with a fervent hunger that both amazed and delighted him.

Afraid that her mother would return quickly, it was Lucas Royston who finally broke off their embrace, to tell her urgently, 'I'm in love with you, Maria, and I want to marry you some day.' He had not intended to voice that second statement, but now that he had done so, he suddenly realised that that was exactly what he did want above all else. To marry this beautiful young woman, and spend the rest of his days loving her.

'Will you, Maria? Will you marry me?' he pressed, and after only a momentary hesitation, she nodded and told him firmly, 'Of course I will.' Inwardly she was experiencing the most thrilling moments of her life. This was the very essence of romance, but none of the novels she had secretly read had prepared her for the sheer lusty excitement of all her senses and emotions.

'When? When shall we marry?' she asked eagerly, and Lucas Royston hesitated only a second before telling her.

'Just as soon as we can, honey. I'll ask your father for your hand, and if he refuses me, then we'll run away and get wed.'

Maria almost swooned with the romantic ecstasy of it all, and again she sought her lover's mouth with eager fervour.

It was the older and immeasurably more experienced Lucas Royston whose mind began to work more sensibly first. Very gently he put her from him, and pushed her down once more onto the stool. Lifting his hand in a pleading gesture for her silence, he told her softly, 'Now let us both present a calm front to your mother, so that she'll suspect nothing. I shall make an appointment to see your father as soon as possible, and then I shall ask him for your hand. If he agrees, then we shall have the banns called directly. If he refuses,' he paused and lightly kissed her reddened lips, 'then we'll elope.'

'Oh yes. Oh yes, my love,' Maria sighed in blissful happiness.

Chapter Seventeen

JOSEPH CASHMORE WAS not a happy man that Wednesday afternoon. He sat in his wooden-armed chair in the front room of his cottage in Evesham Street, frowning thoughtfully as he watched his wife doing her ironing on the table.

Uncomfortably aware of her husband's glowerings, the small timid woman eventually was constrained to enquire nervously, 'What is it that ails you, Mister Cashmore? Is is aught I'm adoing?'

With an unaccustomed gentleness he told her, 'No, wife, 'tis naught that you'se done.' He sighed and rose ponderously to his feet. 'I'm going out.'

'I'll get your things straight away, Mister Cashmore,' she flustered, but he waved his hand to stop her.

'No, wife, I can get 'um meself. You goo on wi' your work.'

When he had put on his blue frock coat, and the ornately brocaded tricorn hat, he took up his long crowned staff of office and went to the door. Then he stopped and stared long and hard at his diminutive wife, until she twitched nervously beneath his gaze. He came back and bent to kiss her cheek, then told her huskily, 'I know I'm a grim bugger to live wi' wife. But I thinks the world on you really.'

He went through the door leaving her gaping after him with astonishment at this totally uncharacteristic display of tenderness.

Cashmore was a deeply worried man. He shared John Clayton's conviction that Sally Beck's death had been caused by the cholera. And like John Clayton, was extremely concerned at the seemingly deliberate refusal to accept that fact by the rulers of the Parish. He knew Lucas Royston from the Scotsman's previous sojourn in Redditch, and although he had no personal animosity towards him, considered that the Scotsman was not a man to be trusted when his own interests were involved.

The Constable directed his footsteps towards Salters Yard and as he came to that ancient huddle of buildings nerved himself for what could prove to be an uncomfortable meeting with Tildy Crawford.

A small group of slatterny women stood together in the cobbled front yard, and their gossiping ceased as he came through the yard gate, and they stared with guarded hostility as he used the steel tip of his staff to rap on Tildy Crawford's door.

There was no answer to his knocking, and Cashmore swung round and called to the women, 'Do you know if Mistress Crawford's gone out somewhere?'

'They'm all down at Duggins',' one woman told him, and jerked her chin towards the far end of the yard, 'down theer.'

As Cashmore walked past them, the woman who had previously spoken asked him, 'What's you want wi' Tildy Crawford then?'

He shook his head, 'That's no concern of yourn, my wench. It's Parish business.'

Inside the foetid room of the Duggins' home, Cashmore found a close press of bodies. Emma Duggins and her two smallest children were laying on the bed. Charles Brown was bending over the woman, watched by Tildy Crawford, Old Esther Smith and Charlie Duggins.

'By God, but bad news travels fast in this town!' It was Tildy who spoke, and she evinced her surprise at Cashmore's arrival, 'Who told you of this, Master Cashmore?'

'Nobody told me of anything,' he informed her. 'But what's the matter wi' this lot?'

Tildy read the unspoken question in his eyes and shook

her head. 'No, it's not the cholera.' Her velvet brown eyes hardened as they swung to Charlie Duggins. 'It's him. It's this bullying bastard. He's near killed poor Emma this time.' Tildy's voice was shaking with anger. 'If I were a man, Charlie Duggins, I'd break your head for you, for serving this poor creature so.'

Charlie Duggins' gaunt unshaven face was sullen and hangdog, and he suddenly swore vilely and pushed past Cashmore and out into the yard.

Cashmore could not help but gust a sigh of relief, and as Tildy's eyes came on him, he gestured apologetically with his hand, and offered, 'I can deal wi' this, Tildy Crawford. I canna deal wi' the cholera.'

Understanding she smiled bleakly, 'Will you commit Charlie Duggins to the Lock-up for doing this?'

She pointed to the badly cut and swollen face of Emma Duggins, and to the snivelling frightened children.

'If she'll swear complaint against him, then I will,' Cashmore answered.

'You know she'll not do that,' Tildy said angrily. 'She's too feared of him to do such.'

Cashmore shrugged, with relative unconcern, 'Then there's naught I can do about it.'

There was ample reason for his unconcern. Many men beat their wives almost as a matter of course, particularly in the poorer quarters of the town and, as the Parish Constable, Cashmore had locked up men time after time for beating their wives unmercifully, only to have the wife later withdraw her complaint, and in some cases abuse the Constable himself for intervening in her domestic affairs.

Made uneasy by Tildy's angry stare, the Constable enlarged, 'Look, Tildy Crawford. There's a deal o' this sort of thing happens every day, and unless the woman 'ull stand by her guns and press it through, then I must let the bloke goo free. And that's exactly what I has to do in nearly every case.' He paused, and then went on in a more confidential tone, 'Anyway, I wants to have a word wi' you in private.'

Charles Brown was now dressing the injured woman's

wounds and Old Esther was assisting him. So Tildy nodded acquiescence and followed the Constable out into the yard.

'Listen very carefully, Tildy Crawford,' he spoke in low-pitched rapid tones, as he went on to tell her what had occurred during the meeting at Lord Aston's house on the Monday night. Tildy's face was a changing pattern of disbelief, dismay, indignation and anger as she listened.

When his narrative halted, she burst out, 'And still John Clayton dares to order me to keep silent? To threaten me with the Bridewell if I speak out about what I fear is happening here?'

Cashmore shook his head unhappily, then urged, 'Please, Tildy, be quiet a minute, and hear me out. I went to talk wi' Parson Clayton this very morn about all on it. And he's as worried as any on us, I can tell you. Now, he can't spake out hisself, because it 'ud mean the end of his living if he goes agen Lord Aston's wishes, and I'm in the same position in a manner o' spaking, arn't I. Iffen I loses this position then I'd be scrattin' to earn a crust. I'se had to upset too many people hereabouts in the course o' me duties, for any on 'um to give me aid in finding other work.'

As she listened a dawning understanding of other concealed motives behind his words came to Tildy, and her lips curled scornfully, 'Hold hard, Joseph Cashmore!' she interrupted forcefully. 'Let me tell you what I'm thinking, shall I? You and John Clayton are too feared of Lord Aston and the Needle Masters to tell the town what is happening, aren't you. But if I'm understanding correctly what you haven't yet told me, then you and the Parson wouldn't take it amiss if I spoke out about Sally Beck, and maybe the sailor, having died from the cholera? Is that it, Master Cashmore? Tell me true now, is that it?'

Shamefaced, he nodded slowly, but then went on, 'The Parson and me both agree, that it's too late to do anything about Sally Beck, the chance has gone. But what we thinks, is that if anybody else dies sudden in the town, then perhaps you and Master Brown 'ud goo and view the body, and if it looks to be the cholera, then you could come to me, or Parson Clayton, and tell us so. We'll then approach Lord Aston, and if he still refuses to take any action, why then, me and the Parson 'udden't do anything to prevent you and Master Brown spreading the news far and wide.'

Tildy stared at the uneasy man before her with a mounting contempt, 'So what you're saying is that it would be alright for me and Master Brown to risk the anger of Lord Aston and his cronies, but you and the Parson still wouldn't dare it?'

Cashmore could only drop his gaze, and nod unhappily.

Tildy thought for only a moment, then in her turn she nodded decisively, 'I'll do it, Master Cashmore. But not for the sake of saving you and the Parson from any upset with your masters. I'll do it for the sakes of the poor women and kids in this Parish. God knows they've little enough to be happy about in their lives, but they've the right to have a chance of surviving to live them out.'

The man seemed to cheer up a little. 'Good, Tildy, that's very good. Now, what we'se got to plan is how we can get word straight away that anybody's is took badly. So that you and Master Brown can get to 'um quick.'

Tildy smiled bleakly. 'You and the Parson can make your own arrangements about that, Master Cashmore, and I'll make mine.'

He nodded quick agreement, 'Alright, Tildy, it shall be as you say. But remember now, it's most important that you comes direct to me or the Parson next time you suspects the cholera, so that we can report it to Lord Aston afore anything else is done.'

'Alright,' Tildy murmured, but inwardly had already made the decision, that the next time she saw a cholera victim, then she would immediately spread the warning around the Parish, and only then inform the lawful authorities.

As soon as the Constable had left her, Tildy went to tell Old Esther, 'I've got an errand to see to, Esther. I'll not be long.' Then she hurried down Alcester Street and swung around the Big Pool past Paoli's Row to enter Red Lion Street. At the Red Lion Inn she turned under the archway and went into the narrow winding Silver Street, debouching from its noisome confines into the equally noisome and unsavoury Silver Square.

The tall ramshackle building that was Mother Readman's lodging house was her destination, and Tildy went straight through its doors and along the dirty passageway to the big gloomy kitchen at the rear of the building. As she had expected, Mother Readman was sitting before the great inglenook in her huge thronelike chair, swathed in multi-layered black garments despite the heat of the day, with a huddle of her ragged courtiers ranged around her.

Tildy smiled and bent to kiss the tallowy raddled cheek of the massively fat old woman. Mother Readman was the uncrowned, yet absolute monarch of Silver Square and its satellite Silver Street, and for many years had given Tildy shelter here in her lodging house, whenever the young woman had been in dire straits. Tildy loved Mother Readman, and the old woman fully returned that emotion, and even though Tildy no longer lived here, they met often and knew that they could always rely on each other's friendship.

'How's the rheumatics today, Mother?' Tildy wanted to know, and the old woman's hanging jowls rippled, and her piled mass of frizzy grey hair beneath the great floppy mobcap trembled as she shook her head mournfully.

'It's bleedin' awful, my duck. Me bleedin' hips am aching wuss now, than when Readman used to bleedin' well be riding me every night.'

'Did you not rub the salve I brought you into them?' Tildy scolded. 'That's a sovereign cure for the rheumatics, Mother. Old Esther made it up herself.'

The old woman wheezed with laughter, 'It arn't bleedin' salves I needs, my duck, it's new bones.'

'Listen, I can't stay long, but I need a favour from you.' Tildy placed her mouth next to Mother Readman's ear and whispered for some minutes. Then she drew her head back and waited expectantly. Mother Readman's brown stubs of teeth showed in a grin, and she nodded slowly.

Tildy smiled as she retraced her steps down Silver Street. Despite being now virtually confined to her chair Mother Readman still commanded the most thorough and widespread network of gossip and information in the entire needle district. If anyone was to be taken suddenly ill, or to die, then Tildy knew that through Mother Readman's sources, she herself would come to know of it very quickly.

'All I need to do now, is to wait,' she told herself, and her satisfied smile widened as she thought of how Lord Aston and his cronies would react when she shattered their wall of secrecy to smithereens. The risk of their anger, and the steps they might take to punish her for speaking out was no deterrent.

'After all,' Tildy told herself, 'if it's to be a choice between the cholera or the Bridewell, then I'd much prefer the Bridewell. Better to be in a cell, than in a coffin.'

Chapter Eighteen

WEDNESDAY WAS ALWAYS slow business at the White Hart. Nail Styler's regular customers were normally all but penniless until the Saturday payday, and although he allowed the trusted ones to put their drink on the 'tick slate', still there were limits to the amount of that credit that he himself could afford to trust them with. So, apart from the scant passing trade of carriers and trampers, Nail Styler had ample leisure to sit and think.

His thoughts now in the late hours of the afternoon were troubled. He had heard of the finding of the drowned man in the Big Pool down in Redditch, and was certain in his mind that it was the sailor he had entrusted to the care of John Lea. The problem was, that he had not seen John Lea since the night of Saturday.

Styler was annoyed at the failure of the man to report back to him, but more annoyed to have heard that the drowned man had been all but naked when found. Rumour had it that the dead man might have been murdered for his possessions, and there had been a lot of wild talk concerning the lack of any pressing official investigation into the matter.

The innkeeper considered that he knew John Lea well enough to know that for all his taciturnity and lack of any sociability, he would not have robbed the sailor, and most certainly would not have thrown the man into the pool. But that being the case, the worrying question of John Lea's whereabouts still remained to be answered.

Styler decided to go in search of John Lea himself, and demand an explanation from the man of what had occurred with the sailor.

'Eppie, I needs to goo out for a bit,' he shouted up the stairs, and before the formidable harridan he was married to had any chance of intercepting him, he had pulled on his coat and broad-brimmed hat and was gone from the inn.

From the upstairs window she bawled after him, 'Doon't you goo wasting my money on boozing or betting, Styler, you barstard! You be back afore nightfall, or I wun't be answerable for what I does.'

Eppie Styler was perhaps the only person in the hamlet of Headless Cross who had no fear at all of her ex-prize fighter husband. Like many another tough brawling man, he lived in mortal fear of his wife's sharp nagging tongue and fearsome temper.

When Nail Styler reached the tollhouse at the top of Mount Pleasant he stopped for a brief word with the elderly tollman. 'Has John Lea brought his cart through here lately, gaffer?'

The old man shook his head, 'No, I'se not lifted the bar for him this day, Nail. Nor for a few days neither. To tell truth, I bin wondering wheer he's got to. He was supposed to bring me a sack o' rock-salt from Redditch. Let's see now?' The old man scratched his stubbled throat. 'It mun ha' bin Sat'day last that I seen him. Ahrr, that's it. Sat'day arternoon I seen him. He told me then that he'd bring the salt fust thing on Monday morn. But I anna seen hide nor hair o' the bugger. Mind you, that warn't much of a loss, miserable silent bastard that he is.'

'Alright, gaffer, if I see him, I'll remind him about it.' Nail Styler hid the dread that this news had caused him with a bluff grin, and went on his way down Mount Pleasant.

Lea lived alone in a small isolated cottage at the bottom of a steep eastern slope from Mount Pleasant, which could be reached by means of a sharp-falling field path. At another time Nail Styler would have enjoyed the surrounding meadow and woodland, heady-scented with grasses and wild flowers, and a myriad of birds and insects creating a pleasing music of nature. But now, as he reached the bottom of the steep path and walked along the narrow valley towards the cottage half hidden by trees and bushes, he felt tense and nervous.

The cottage appeared still and deserted, and as Nail Styler came up to its mud-walls he could hear a sustained buzzing noise. The low door stood ajar, and from within the buzzing noise sounded abnormally loud to his nerve-strained hearing. He pushed the door fully open, wrinkling his nose at the stench the low-ceilinged room emitted, and saw clouds of flies swarming around a huddled shape on the earthern floor.

Realisation and nausea hit Nail Styler almost simultaneously, and he turned and retched violently and stumbled away for a few paces. When his heaving stomach subsided and his initial shock lessened, he wiped his mouth and went determinedly back into the cottage. The flies swarmed upwards from the body in dense clouds, buzzing shrilly as if angered at this new assailant who came to drive them from their feast, and Nail Styler cursed and coughed and choked as he inadvertently took some of their clustering bodies into his mouth, and he spat and swatted furiously to clear them from his head and face, and cursed again as he looked at the features of John Lea, made almost unrecognisable by the discolouration and swelling, and the ravaging teeth of rats.

Again Styler went from the cottage, his mind in a turmoil. He seated himself on a soft mossy bank and buried his face in his hands as he tried desperately to think coherently.

Nearly an hour passed before he came to a decision.

'Theer's naught to be done for John Lea now, is there. And I mun think o' my missus and kids.'

He stood up and looked carefully at the hillsides around him. Only cows and sheep were to be seen in the hazy meadows, and no sounds of foresters' axes or smoke from charcoal burners' fires came from the stretches of woodland.

'God ha' mercy on your soul, John Lea,' Styler muttered, and walked quickly away.

Chapter Nineteen

'HOW LONG HAS you had that shirt then, Anthony?' Old Ben Wardle peered blearily at the fine cambric garment his boon drinking companion was wearing. 'That's a gentleman's shirt, that is.'

'And it's a gennulman who's awearing it, my bucko.' Anthony Spragge belched resoundingly, then hammered his empty pewter pot on the table and bellowed, 'Can I get some bloody service 'ere, or should I take me custom elsewheres?'

The landlady of the King's Head inn came bustling through into the small tap room. ''Ull you give over bawling, Anthony Spragge, you'm like to wake the dead, ne'er mind all o' Bredon.'

'Bollocks!' the old reprobate rejoined, and shook his friend's shoulder. 'Cummon now, Benjy, bottoms up.'

The other man drained his own mug, and the plump landlady bustled away to refill both.

When she had returned, and gone again, Ben Wardle eyed his friend curiously, 'Wheer's all this money acoming from?'

'What money?' Spragge demanded.

'Why this money! This money that you'm spending so free?'

'Ahhrrr, now then, that's the question, arn't it?' Spragge laid one black-nailed finger to the side of his nose and winked owlishly, 'Iffen I was to tell you wheer it come from, then you'd be as wise as me, 'udden't you, my bucko.'

The street door opened and a peculiar looking figure appeared in the room.

'Well now, look who it arn't,' Anthony Spragge declared, and waved his arm in welcome. 'Come in and set yourselves down wi' us, Your Majesty. I sees that you'se got your crown wi' you today. Wheer's you bin then? Down to London for the Court?'

The man he questioned was tall and rawboned. His clothing consisted of layer upon layer of rags, and over his shoulders he wore a filthy torn blanket in the manner of a cloak. His long hair hung down in greasy tendrils to his shoulders, and on his head there was a mock-crown fashioned from odds and ends of rusty scrap metal. His face was almost black with sun and dirt, and one of his eyes was badly cataracted and watered continuously, while the other was a bright glaring blue.

He was a harmless and homeless lunatic, who believed himself to be King William the Fourth, and was either treated as a pet, or abused by the townsfolk, according to their current moods. He spent his days wandering the environs of the town, and most of his nights sleeping among the gravestones in the Chapel Burial Yard.

'Here, missus, be so good as to bring His Majesty a drink, 'ull you?' Spragge bellowed, and within moments the plump landlady bustled in.

She smiled good-naturedly at the newcomer as she set the foaming pewter pot before him on the table. 'Here you be, King William. I anna seen you for a bit, has I. Wheer's you bin akeeping yourself?'

He grinned vacuously at her, displaying long gnarled yellow teeth. 'I'se bin walking my kingdom, missus.'

He took long gulping swallows from his pot, then set it down again, and the froth glistened on his stubbled jaws and mouth.

Anthony Spragge winked at Ben Wardle, 'And what's you seen in your kingdom this day then, Your Majesty?

Looking for a tasty young wench to share your royal bed, was you?'

The madman laughed slobberingly and shook his head so hard that it seemed his crown must fall off. Then he told them with an air of delight. 'I see'd a dead 'un, I did.'

At first his listeners treated this statement as a joke. 'What's that you say, dead 'un? Was it a wench, Your Majesty? Did you give her summat to warm her up?'

Again King William roared with laughter, delighted at being the centre of attention, and again the rusty crown threatened to topple.

'No, it warn't a wench. It was a bloke, and the rats was ateing his yed. He didn't half look a mess.'

It was the landlady who was first to realise that the lunatic might be speaking the truth. 'You tell me that again, King William. What was it you saw?'

'I see'd a dead 'un, missus, and the rats was ateing his yed. He didn't half look a mess.' The madman lifted his pot to his mouth and drained it with grunts of pleasure.

The three with him exchanged questioning looks. 'Does you reckon he might be spaking the truth, Anthony?' The landlady's plump good-natured face wore a doubtful frown.

'Tell you what, missus, you fetch him another pot, I'll pay,' Old Ben Wardle requested.

When she had done so, Wardle invited the madman, 'Now you take a swig o' this fust, King William.'

The man dutifully obeyed, and beamed with pleasure as Ben Wardle asked him carefully. 'Now this dead 'un you see'd. He warn't in the Chapel Yard, was he, being buried like?'

'Oh no,' King William shook his head, 'No, he was alaying in his house, and the rats was ateing his yed. He didn't half look a mess.'

He went to raise his pot to his mouth again, but Ben Wardle's hand shot out to grasp his wrist and prevent him. 'No, you canna drink any more until you'se told us wheer this bloke was alaying. Can you remember wheer you see'd him?'

The madman nodded positively. 'Oh yes. I remembers. He was alaying in John Lea's cottage. On the floor he was. And the rats was ateing his yed. He didn't half look a mess.'

Again his three listeners exchanged doubtful frowns. Then Wardle asked, 'What does you think? Does you reckon he really saw summat?'

Anthony Spragge shrugged, 'That's hard to say, arn't it, wi' this silly bugger.'

King William was again noisily sucking at his drink.

'Wheer is this John Lea's cottage?' the landlady wanted to know.

'It's down in that valley that lays behind the Round House, near enough,' Spragge informed her. 'I knows John Lea. Miserable bugger he is, as well. He 'udden't gi' you the time o' day.'

'What does you reckon we ought to do then?' Ben Wardle asked again. 'Does you reckon he really did see summat theer?'

Anthony Spragge suddenly grinned with malicious delight, 'Well, whether he did, or he didn't, I'm agoing to goo and tell that soddin' son-in-law o' mine about it. It'll serve the fat arsed bugger right to have to shift his lazy hide and goo and find out warn't it. This is just the right sort o' thing to spoil his supper for him, and serve the bugger right. Come on, Ben. Let's goo and fetch him out from his chair.'

Chapter Twenty

B Y THE LIGHT of a solitary lantern and three stubs of candles Charles Brown, aided by Joseph Cashmore, stripped and carefully examined the body of John Lea.

Outside the night was warm and still, and only the rustling and muted squeaking of rats in the thatched roof, the hissing of moths' wings being singed in the candle flames, and the harsh breathing of the two men broke the silence within the cottage.

'Well?' Cashmore's heavy features were sombre and fear lurked in his eyes.

'I really can't say for certain.' Charles Brown pursed his lips thoughtfully, 'With the heat of the last days causing premature corruption of the tissues and expansion of the internal gases, and the damage done by the rats, it's very hard to judge.'

A disquieting thought struck the Constable, 'You doon't think that he might ha' bin killed by somebody, does you? I mean, it's a bit strange, arn't it. That bloke being found in the Pool half stripped, and now John Lea here like this. I'm beginning to wonder if we got a bloody lunatic running round the Parish killing people.'

'No, I don't think that this man was killed by human agency,' Brown smiled mirthlessly. 'Though to be brutally frank, I could in one way only wish he had been. But there's no indications of physical violence.

'The lacerations are caused by the rats, and these discolourations,' he indicated the various patches on the body, 'are caused by the blood settling to the lowest levels, and these others are merely the onset of putrefaction. They've not been made by physical assault.

'Unfortunately, as I said before, the heat and the swelling of the internal gases makes it very hard for me to come to any judgement as to whether the cholera is involved here, or not.'

He pointed to the discarded clothing. 'And I can tell nothing from those. The natural exudation of body fluids and waste after death could be the reason for their condition.'

The Constable gusted a heavy sigh. 'God blast it!' He almost groaned the words, 'Does you know, Charles Brown, I'm starting to feel like the bloody cholera is hanging over this town, looking down at us and laughing. I'm starting to believe that it's playing wi' us all, like a cat plays wi' a mouse, and that when it gets tired of its play, then it'll swoop down like a demon out of hell, and wipe us all from the face o' the earth.'

He cursed aloud in frustration, 'God rot the fuckin' thing. If it was a man I could bloody well fight it. But it wun't come out into the open wheer we can see it. It lurks in hiding, and comes sneakin' on us like a thief in the night to steal our lives. Goddamn and blast the fuckin' thing!'

Charles Brown made no reply, only straightened the limbs of the dead man, and covered him decently with a blanket.

'What can we do now, Master Brown?' Cashmore asked with a note of despair in his voice.

'We can give this poor fellow a Christian burial, Master Cashmore. And then only hope and pray that when the next unfortunate is struck down we shall be able to fully identify our enemy, and act accordingly.'

'Does you reckon that others will be struck down then, Master Brown?' the Constable asked in a husky, subdued voice.

The other man nodded sadly, 'Oh yes, Master Cashmore.

That is as sure as the sunrise. This is merely the beginning. The opening shots of the war, as it were.'

Charles Brown was speaking the truth. The *Vibrio Cholerae*, the *Comma Bacilli*, the death-dealing legions of King Cholera were advancing secretly, silently and inexorably by water, by flies, on flecks of saliva, on the unwashed, contaminated flesh of human carriers throughout the Parishes of Tardebigge and Ipsley.

Chapter Twenty-One

NAIL STYLER WAS not able to sleep on Wednesday night, and rose early from bed on the Thursday morning, his head aching, his mood restless and nervous. Leaving his wife still snoring he went downstairs and unlocked his spirit-locker. Lifting out a bottle of brandy he pulled its cork and took a long swallow. The raw spirit burned its way down his throat and chest and spread its warmth through his belly. But although it stilled the queasiness of his stomach, it brought no ease to his mind.

Suddenly he found the surrounding walls intolerably confining, and he pulled his boots on and snatching up his coat and his bottle of brandy went hatless into the cool morning air.

The mental vision of John Lea's dead face constantly recurred and he was unable to thrust it from him.

'I shouldn't ha' left you laying theer, John,' he muttered remorsefully. 'The least I could ha' done was to see to it that you was buried like a Christian.'

He wandered almost aimlessly along the road in the direction of the Mount Pleasant tollhouse, taking frequent swigs from the brandy bottle and muttering explanations and excuses for his behaviour to the dead John Lea.

'I never thought any harm 'ud come to you, John, that I swear. I mean, I thought the sailor was took badly, but I didn't know for certain it was the cholera he'd got, did I? It anna my fault that you took it yourself, John. You can't blame me for it, in all fairness, now can you?'

The houses he passed along the way were already waking

to the business of the day, and frowsty-faced, sleep-numbed men, women and children were beginning to come out of their doors to trudge reluctantly to their work in the mills and factories and workshops of the town. The clanging of those establishments' warning bells could be heard both near and from far away, and their varied tones sounded gay and festive, in ironic contrast to the grim drudgery awaiting within their walls for those who obeyed their summons.

As Nail Styler came alongside the big Round House he was hailed by a man leaving the peculiar structure.

'How bist, Nail? What brings you down here at this hour?'

Nail recognised Davy Hughes, a young Needle Pointer who was one of his regular customers.

'How bist, Davy? I anna bin able to sleep, that's all? I thought a walk might settle me down.'

'Snap to that, Nail. I arn't had a wink o' sleep neither. Our kid's bin took bad, and I'se bin kept awake all bleedin' night by him.'

The young man's brother, Jamie Hughes, was another Needle Pointer, and a regular at the White Hart.

All Nail Styler's earlier nervous anxiety returned in full measure, and he asked quickly, 'What's the matter wi' Jamie, then?'

'I reckon he's got the summer flux.' The young man did not seem unduly concerned. 'He keeps on being sick, and shittin' hisself, and moaning that his yed pains him.' He hawked and spat onto the ground, then grumbled, 'I mean to say, he's me kin, and I doon't like to see him took badly, but he's kept me awake nigh on all bleedin' night. I'se just told him, that if he anna any better when I comes home this night, then I'm agoing to dose him up wi' laudanum. That'll keep the bugger quiet, I'll warrant it 'ull.'

Nail Styler tried to hide the fear that assailed him now, and asked as casually as he was able, 'Is he by hisself then?'

The young man nodded. 'Me and him as lived by oursen ever since the old 'ooman died. Nigh on eight months now, since her popped it.'

'Maybe I'll call in on him while I'm down here, and see if he needs aught?' Nail Styler suggested.

'Ahr, if you wants to, my old cock.' The Needle Pointer's tough features creased in a lewd grin. 'If you can stand the stink, then I reckon our Jamie can stand the pain.'

By now they had reached the fork of the Front and Back Hills where the Duke of York inn stood, and a small beerhouse named the Black Horse slightly up from it.

'I'm going in here to get a livener afore I goes to me work.' Davy Hughes nodded towards the Black Horse, 'Be you coming in?'

Styler agreed, and followed the other man through the low doorway into the black-beamed tap room.

Despite the early hour the room was filled with workmen who had also called in to take their liveners, and a hubbub of conversation filled the tobacco-fugged air.

The beerhouse keeper, John Whateley, a short, thickset, heavily paunched man recognised a fellow tradesman, and came immediately to greet Nail Styler, 'Now then, Nail, what brings you down these parts?'

'I needed a bit of a walk, John.'

Whateley handed the newcomers a glass of rum each, and waved away their offered payment. Then leaned over the tall counter to have a chat. 'Did you hear about John Lea, then?' he began.

Nail Styler's breath caught in his throat, and it was Davy Hughes who asked, 'What about the miserable bleeder?' and joked, 'has he finally spoke to somebody?'

'He'd have a fuckin' job to do that now, Davy.' Whateley's swarthy face grinned, 'They found the bugger dead in his cottage last night. Bin nigh on ate up by the bloody rats, from what I'se heard tell.'

'Gerrout?' Hughes exclaimed. 'You doon't say?'

'I does say though, Davy,' Whateley rejoined. 'I had old Anthony Spragge in here fust thing this morning, and he told me all about it.' He went on to relate the full account of what had happened, and Nail Styler heard him with an ever increasing dismay.

'And they canna tell what he died from, you say? He sought repeated confirmation as Whateley's tale came to its ending.

'No, not from what old Anthony told me. Funny thing though arn't it, that a bloke who's bin a surgeon should be working at the needle filing now?'

'Well, at least the needles doon't scream when you'm working on 'um, does they?' Davy Hughes quipped.

'Wheer did you say this bloke Brown lives now, this surgeon?' Nail Styler tried to appear casual yet again.

'Down Salters Yard, I believe,' Whateley informed him. Then asked slyly, 'Why does you arsk me that, Nail? Has you copped for summat you doon't want your missus to know on?'

Styler forced a laugh, 'That's about the strength on it, John. So doon't you goo atelling her that I'se bin asking you, 'ull you?'

The other winked salaciously, 'No, I'll not do that, Nail. Iffen I gets lucky wi' me new serving maid, perhaps I'll be needing to spake wi' the bugger mesen on the quiet, some fine day.'

When Nail Styler and Davy Hughes left the Black Horse and parted, Styler stood for some moments, uncertain of where he wanted to go or what he wanted to do. His remorse for what had happened to John Lea returned to torment him again, and finally he muttered beneath his breath, 'I'll be damned if I'm agoing to have you on me conscience as well, Jamie Hughes,' and he made his way towards the Round House.

There he went into the room where the sick man lay, and in only a few seconds came out again and started to hurry down into Redditch.

Tildy, Old Esther and Charles Brown were in the workshop at the rear of the house, and as they tongued and filed the needles they discussed at length what had occurred the previous night.

'Well, I think it wrong of the Parson to still do nothing,'

Tildy concluded. 'I think that you should have told him that the man had definitely died from cholera.'

Charles Brown shook his head, 'No, Tildy, that wouldn't have done at all. It would not be ethical.'

'Ethical, be damned!' Tildy retorted spiritedly. 'I feel as if we're all sitting on a great barrel of gunpowder that has a lighted fuse stuck in it, and nobody is even trying to put out the flame.'

Old Esther nodded agreement, and said in her cracked wavering voice, 'You'm right theer, my duck. I'se scryed all this acoming. Remember what I told you afore, Tildy, I seed death and destruction acoming. I seed Death walking towards this town wi' his great scythe over his shoulder, and his book o' names under his arm.' She appeared to relish this grim symbolism, for she kept on repeating, 'His scythe over his shoulder, and his book o' names under his arm. Yes, that's what I seed, his scythe over his shoulder and his book o' names under his arm . . .'

Listening to the old crone, Tildy was tempted to ask her to try and describe something other than this grim picture. Her own forebodings were depressing enough, without this contribution from Old Esther.

'Hello, anybody in theer?' the voice called from the front door, and Tildy shouted in reply, 'Come on through, we're out in the back here.'

Footsteps sounded on the stone-flags of the passageway, and then the workshop door opened and Nail Styler's shaven, broken-nosed head peeped into the room.

'Good morning to you, I'm seeking the man named Charles Brown.'

'I'm here.' Charles Brown laid down his tongs and file.

'Me name's Nail Styler, I'm wondering if you could come and have a look at a mate o' mine, Jamie Hughes. I reckon he might have bin struck down wi' the cholera.'

Chapter Twenty-Two

THE MATTRESS AND bedding were saturated, and Jamie Hughes' skin was already assuming a dark blue-grey hue, and was cold and clammy to the touch. His face and limbs looked shrivelled and shrunken, and his eyes mirrored his abject terror. He cried out and his body spasmed into a foetus-like position, and from his mouth and rectum he discharged a grey-white fluid resembling water that rice had been boiled in, which was almost odourless.

Tildy distinctively shrank back in horror and fear, but then, when she saw Charles Brown and John Clayton trying to aid the sick man, she felt a flush of shame for her own weakness, and went forward to the bedside herself.

'Can anything be done to help him, Master Brown?' the clergyman's ugly face was pale, and his strained tone betrayed the fear he was fighting to master.

Brown shrugged helplessly. 'I've no instruments or leeches to bleed him with. He needs to be placed in warm dry blankets, and a steady dry heat applied to the course of his spine. I want warm water, and salt, and I need hot bags to place against his limbs.'

He stared around the meanly furnished room, and sighed to see how bare it was of anything that he could use. Then he lifted the sick man's flaccid arm and felt for the wrist pulse with his fingers. His expression was very grave when he gently laid the arm down and he jerked his head at Clayton and Tildy to signal them to follow him out of the room.

Outside, in the warm sunlight Nail Styler was waiting for

them. 'Well, is it the cholera?' he demanded immediately.

Charles Brown nodded silently, and Styler cursed and in his agitation slammed one fist into the palm of his other hand.

'Can the man be saved?' John Clayton asked.

'I fear not,' Brown said regretfully. 'His vital fluid is sadly depleted, and the organs whose nerves are connected or chiefly derived from the spinal marrow are extensively deranged. Mayhap we are come too late to aid him. I need cordials and opiates and sinapisms. Also I need a full medical box so that I can administer to his body.'

'You are sure that it is the cholera?' Clayton pressed.

'I am positive of it,' Charles Brown answered emphatically. 'And now, sir, I would most strongly urge upon you the necessity to prepare for the very worst. I fear that the epidemic will shortly be upon us with its full fury.'

'I will communicate to Lord Aston what has happened here,' Clayton said. 'And await his instructions in the matter. In the meantime, to avoid spreading unnecessary panic, I would enjoin upon the three of you the necessity of remaining silent, for the time being, at least.'

At first Tildy could only stare at him in shocked amazement. She could hardly believe what she had heard him say.

'You still want us to remain silent about this, Parson Clayton?' She sought confirmation.

'Yes, Tildy Crawford. There is nothing to be gained by spreading this news through the town. You will only create disturbance and needless unrest among the people.'

Now she faced the man, and felt her cheeks begin to burn as her anger rose. 'Parson Clayton, when Master Styler here came for Master Brown and myself, it was me who insisted that we find you and ask you to come up here with us. I did this, because I thought that you would be the very man who would take whatever action is needed. But now, all you can do is to bleat to us, that we remain silent.'

He frowned at her, 'Have a care you do not try my patience too far, Tildy Crawford. I know what I am about in this matter.'

Tildy was too irate by this time to pay any regard to his threatening manner. 'Well I'll be damned if I know what you're about, Parson. You can't really believe that we are prepared to stay silent about this, while that old fool, Aston, dithers about and wastes time that should be better spent.'

'I will not be wasting time, Crawford.' Clayton's own hot temper had risen by now and his voice rose so that it brought curious faces to the windows of the Round House. 'I shall have Lucas Royston brought here, to confirm Master Brown's findings. And then I shall go post-haste to my Lord Aston, and consult with him on the best course of action.'

'And how long will this all take?' Tildy shouted back.

'How long, woman?' Clayton's features were suffused to a dull red. 'Why just so long as it does take. Will that be answer enough for you?'

'No, it won't.' Tildy's frustration with this man's obduracy caused her to clench her fists so tightly that her fingernails dug deep into the palms of her hands. 'People are at least here, and they know naught about that threat. They could at least be taking steps to try and protect themselves from this vile disease. But because of you and your masters, it could already be attacking others all through this Parish.

'Master Brown told you before that Sally Beck had died from the cholera, and you bade us keep silent, because you would have your masters decide what action should be taken. Well we did stay silent, Parson, and now a fine young man lies on his deathbed, and mayhap he lies there because we obeyed you, and kept silent. Have you not thought of that?'

'You will do as I bid, Crawford. Or I swear by my God, that I will this very day have you committed to the Bridewell,' Clayton hissed the threat, and his great muscular body trembled with the force of his affronted pride, that this woman of an inferior social class should so defy and upbraid him.

'Oh, you'll have me committed to the Bridewell, will

you, Parson Clayton.' Tildy's own voice and body trembled with her anger. 'Well then, you'd best send for the Constable right now. Because I'll tell you true, Parson, I am not going to keep silent about what has happened here, and what has gone before. I'm not keeping silent for one moment longer. The people in this Parish have a right to know what danger threatens them and their loved ones. So you may do as you wish with me, but I'm going to start warning them this very instant.'

Suiting action to words, she beckoned to the curious faces staring out of the windows of the Round House tower, and when heads poked forth and hands cupped ears, she shouted, 'Jamie Hughes has been struck down with the cholera. Can you hear what I say? Jamie Hughes has been struck down by the cholera. The cholera is come to this Parish. Spread the word so that everybody may have fair warning of it. The cholera has come to this Parish.'

Shock and alarm greeted her news, and questions were shouted back at her, but she ignored them and swung to face the glowering clergyman. Quietly she told him, 'Now you may commit me to the Bridewell, Parson Clayton.'

Before he could reply, Nail Styler intervened, 'If you'm agoing to commit Tildy Crawford, Parson, then you'd best send the Constable arter me next. Because I'm agoing to do the very same that this wench has just done. I'm agoing to spread the warning about the cholera. She's right in what she says, and you must know that in your own heart.

'Jamie Hughes lies on his deathbed because I was too fritted to spread the news o' what I feared was happening here. I reckon that bloke who drowned in the Big Pool had the cholera.'

As they all stared at him in astonishment, he went on to relate the full account of what had happened on the Saturday night at his public house, leaving nothing out.

' . . . and so that's the truth on it. And I wishes now wi' all me heart that I'd have made sure that that poor bugger was properly looked arter, instead o' trying to shift the trouble of him onto others. And then, when I saw poor

John Lea laying dead in his cottage, I was sore troubled by what had happened. I just couldn't rest until I'd done summat to make amends. Tildy Crawford is right in what she's asaying, Parson, and no matter what punishment might come on me yed, I'm agoing to follow her lead in this.'

'And I also,' Charles Brown stated calmly.

For a few moments the clergyman glowered at each of them in turn, but they met his eyes without flinching.

'You are each of you determined to be committed to the Bridewell?' he asked, and each of them nodded.

He himself nodded slowly. 'So be it.' His glower metamorphosed into a dour frown. 'I will not act like Canute, in this matter. It seems the tide is fully turned against me. Very well then, let us agree to act in some concert. I will go direct to my Lord Aston and report that the cholera is definitely arrived here.

'You, Master Styler, will go to Joseph Cashmore, and instruct him from me that he is to summon all the Church and Chapel Wardens, the Vestrymen and Overseers and the medical practitioners to attend a meeting at two o'clock this afternoon at the Chapel.

'Master Brown, could I ask you to do whatever you can to ease the plight of Jamie Hughes?'

Both men readily agreed to his requests, and he turned to Tildy, with a hint of grudging admiration lurking in his eyes.

'And you, Tildy Crawford, may continue alerting the people that the cholera is in this parish.'

She inclined her glossy head. 'I'll try not to alarm them unduly, Parson Clayton. But for the present I'll remain here and aid Master Brown with Jamie Hughes.'

'Good!' he grunted, and raised his tall black hat. 'My thanks to you all.' Then acknowledged, 'I will fully admit that I think you have prevented me from erring once again in this matter.'

With that admission he restored all of Tildy Crawford's previously held respect for him, and she smiled and told him, 'We'll do all that we can to aid you, Parson Clayton. You only need to ask of us whatever you would wish us to do.'

He nodded curtly. 'Many thanks, Tildy Crawford. I shall do so if needs be.'

With that the four of them parted.

Tildy and Charles Brown went back into Jamie Hughes, and found him once again being attacked by cramps, and discharging the white-grey fluid from mouth and rectum.

Sudden dread shivered through Tildy, as she visualised herself or her loved ones being so afflicted, and for a while she could only stand mute, and battle inwardly to stay herself from fleeing from this room.

As if understanding the inner conflict raging within her, Charles Brown patted her shoulder, and when Jamie Hughes' spasming body stilled, again sought for the pulse in the flaccid arm. The young man's sunken eyes rolled upwards in his head and he appeared to sink into unconsciousness.

Tildy by now had brought her rampaging emotions under some degree of control. 'What can we do to aid him, Charles?'

Her companion sighed, and shook his head. 'Little enough, I fear, Tildy. What you could do is to ask the neighbours if they have any dry blankets, and ordinary kitchen salt and warm water. And I need to apply dry heat to this poor fellow's spine, so ask if anyone has a warming pan, or even heated platters would do at a pinch.'

Tildy hurried to obey his instructions. She hammered on the nearest neighbour's door, and a middle-aged, motherly looking woman opened it, and stared out at her caller with troubled eyes.

'You'm the young wench that's next door wi' Jamie Hughes, arn't you?' the woman sought to know.

'I am,' Tildy confirmed. 'Please, can you help me. I need dry blankets, salt and warm water, and a warming pan if you have one. Or even some heated platters will do?'

'Is is right what you shouted out down in the yard?' the woman asked, 'about Jamie Hughes having took the cholera?'

Tildy nodded, 'Yes, it's true, I'm sorry to say.'

'Oh my God!' The woman moaned softly, her pink complexion blanched, and abruptly she stepped back into her house and slammed the door in Tildy's face.

Tildy stood for a moment, too surprised to react. Then hammered the door and called, 'Are you all right? Why have you done this?'

'You get from here!' Even though muffled by the thick wooden panels of the door, the throbbing terror in the woman's voice could be clearly heard. 'You get away. I'se got me own kin to think on. You'm bringing the cholera here, so get away.'

'Please, there's no call to be alarmed. I haven't got the cholera. And the poor man is suffering dreadfully. He needs help.'

'Get away from here!' The woman shrieked, and now Tildy could hear her sobbing. 'Get away! Get away!'

Other heads had been poking out of windows and doorways watching Tildy hammering the door, and hearing all that passed. Now, when Tildy stepped back and looked about her those heads disappeared and windows and doors slammed shut, and with a sickening dismay Tildy realised that she would get no help at all from the people living here in the Round House. Their terror of the cholera overlaid all sentiments of compassion and charity.

Still she continued to try and find someone, but no door opened to her knocking, and she hurried back to tell Charles Brown what had happened.

He evinced no surprise upon hearing her account. 'Cholera terrifies everyone, Tildy. You can't really blame these poor benighted souls.'

'I'll go and fetch blankets from my home,' Tildy told him. 'And I've a warming pan there we can use as well.'

'I'll come down with you. I'll go to the apothecary and see what he has in the way of medical instruments and necessaries. I can do nothing to combat the cholera without the proper means to hand.'

Tildy smiled briefly, 'You are becoming a surgeon once more then, Charles?'

He shrugged, 'What else can I do, Tildy. God only knows it will be little enough that I will be able to achieve against this foul distemper, but someone must try.'

As it always did in Redditch Town, news spread with an amazing rapidity, and even as Tildy entered her house in Salters Yard one of Mother Readman's ragged lodgers came panting to tell her that the old woman had heard rumours concerning a case of the cholera at the Round House.

Tildy could not help but smile wryly. 'Give Mother Readman many thanks from me,' she told the man. 'And tell her that I've just come from there myself. And tell her that it's true. There is cholera there. It's Jamie Hughes that has taken it.'

As she gathered together blankets and the warming pan, and salt and clean rags, Old Esther remonstrated strongly with her, 'You'm bloody mad, you am, Tildy, going back up theer. You'm putting yourself at risk.'

Tildy shook her head. 'You don't know that, Esther. Charles has told me a good deal about the cholera. He had much experience of it when he was in India. He says that no one knows how it spreads, or why it should attack some and not others. He says that in his opinion those who fear it, are more likely to catch it than those who defy it. He knows of cases where men have shared the beds of cholera victims, and have taken no harm. And other cases where people have fled from it, but have died nevertheless.'

She paused for a moment, and curiously examined her own emotions, and found, much to her amazement, that all fear of the disease seemed to have left her. It was not really fatalism on her part, but rather an inner conviction that she was not destined to be stricken with this disease. She shook her head in wonderment, not understanding why she should have suddenly acquired this supreme confidence in her own invulnerability.

'I'm in no danger,' she stated positively.

The old woman was unimpressed. 'Ahrr, that's what the bloody cockerel says afore it goes into the pot. It crows on its bloody dunghill, and rogers its hens, and thinks that nothing 'ull ever harm it.'

'Well thank you very much, for comparing me with a dunghill cock, Esther,' Tildy said tartly.

'How's about Davy and me and Daniel?' the old woman questioned. 'Has you not stopped to think that you might be bringing the cholera back here to us from bloody Jamie Hughes?'

Her words jolted Tildy's new-found certainty, and seeing by the younger woman's expression that this was so, Old Esther pressed on, 'You'se just said yourself that nobody can tell how the cholera gets from one to another. How can you know that you anna bringing it here into this house when you comes back from Jamie Hughes' bedside? Has you got the right to put your own child in peril, Tildy?'

'I knows that you thinks you'm acting for the best, and I admires your good heart, Tildy. But what's Jamie Hughes to you? You never even knew the bloke, did you? How can you risk your own bairn, for the sake of a stranger?'

'How can I risk Davy and Daniel, and Esther, for the sake of a stranger?' The question reverberated inside Tildy's head, and confused, she muttered aloud, 'But someone must help those in such sore need?'

'Oh yes, I'll not deny you that,' Old Esther stated emphatically. 'But let it be them who's got naught but their own wellbeings to consider. Let the old widow-women who allus acts as sick-nusses do it now. They'se already had their lives, my wench, and they'll get paid for looking arter the sick 'uns. Same as the doctors 'ull get paid. But you'm agoing out now to do it for nothing.

'You'se got a child to think on, and has you stopped to think what might happen to him iffen you was to take sick and die yoursen?

'Ne'er mind about that breaking me and our Daniel's hearts, you mun think on what it 'ud do to Davy. A poor fatherless boy, only twelve years old, to have his mam took from him as well? It 'ud nigh on kill the poor little soul, and you knows well it 'ud, Tildy. That sweet bairn worships you. It 'ud be the death on him iffen he was to lose you.'

These were overwhelmingly powerful arguments to use against Tildy Crawford, whose adored son was the centre of her world, and who had struggled to bring him up, and made any sacrifices, and made those sacrifices gladly, to ensure her child's wellbeing.

Now she sank down on a stool by the side of the table, and shuddered visibly as terrible scenes came before her mind's eye. Davy, lying like Jamie Hughes on a filthy wet bed, writhing in terrible agonies, his face a livid blue-grey, his young strong body shrivelled and shrunken until he resembled more a monkey than a human being. She drew breath sharply, and lifted her hands as if to drive the dreadful images from her. But they relentlessly persisted and strengthened their hold, and at last she buried her face in her hands, and burst into tears.

'Theer now, doon't take on so, my duck.' The old crone came to her and cradled her head in her withered arms, pressing Tildy's head close to her frail body. 'Theer now, doon't take on so,' she crooned the words and stroked Tildy's glossy hair. 'You shall stay here wi' me, and then we'll all be safe, wun't us. You'll stay here, and we'll all be safe. Davy, Daniel, me and you. We'll all stay close in this house, and keep far away from the cholera, wun't we. Then we'll all be safe.'

By the time Charles Brown came from the Apothecary's, carrying his bag of medical instruments and necessaries, Tildy had come reluctantly to the decision that she could not risk the wellbeing of her own loved ones by accompanying him back to the Round House.

Brown's eyes were kindly as he stared at her tear-stained face, and saw the shame and distress she felt for what she considered to be her failure of him.

He smiled and patted her shoulder, 'Don't distress yourself, my dear. You are doing what I would most probably do if I were in your place. You are quite right to put the welfare of your own loved ones first.'

'And you? Will you return to the Round House?' she asked quietly.

He nodded, 'I am driven to do so, my dear. I abandoned the practice of medicine once, and I thought that I had abandoned it for ever. But now it seems to have me gripped in its talons again, with all the strength that it once exerted upon me,' he chuckled grimly. 'I can only hope that I'll not to do as much harm to the helpless this time, as I managed to do before.'

Chapter Twenty-Three

'ORDER, GENTLEMEN! ORDER!'

The Vestry Room of Saint Stephen's Chapel was a seething mass of sweating, voluble dispute, and Lord Aston was forced to bellow at the top of his voice in order to be heard above the noise and hubbub. 'Order Gentlemen! I pray you let us have order here!'

A degree of quietness fell over the room, and all eyes stared expectantly at Lord Aston, who was flanked by his curates, the Reverends John Clayton and Julius Fessey.

Aston's gaze moved across the faces before him. The surgeons, Taylor, Pratt and Royston, the Church and Chapel Wardens of the Parish, William Hemming, Henry Milward, Joseph Cresswell, Charles and Thomas Bartleet, Edward Perks, Thomas Fowkes and Edward Browning, the young newly arrived Attorney. The Dissenting ministers were present as well, the Reverend Ezekial Humphreys the Congregationalist, and Mister Thomas Slack the Wesleyan Methodist, plus an assortment of other town notables. 'Thank you, gentlemen. Mayhap we can now act as gentlemen should. With due decorum and good manners,' Aston rebuked sourly, and William Hemming was quick to resent that remark.

'Damn and blast it, Aston, can you come to the matter in hand, and spare us a lecture on behaviour. Some of us are busy men and have important business to attend. We cannot do with wasting time here.'

The dyspeptic clergyman glared at his old antagonist, but realised that at this meeting the party of the Needle Masters held the numerical ascendancy, and so forebore to pick up the proffered gauntlet.

'Gentlemen, the cholera is in this Parish.' Aston hid a secret smile of satisfaction at the visible consternation his announcement brought to the face of his old enemy, William Hemming. Then went on, 'Doctor Royston has examined the patient, a man by name of Hughes, and has confirmed that the unfortunate fellow is afflicted with the disease.'

Lucas Royston was uncomfortably aware of William Hemming's accusing scowl being directed at him.

'Knowing the proclivities of this dread affliction, we can surmise with some considerable degree of certainty that other cases will quickly become manifest in this Parish. Therefore, gentlemen, it behoves us to make due and proper preparations to withstand its onslaught.' Aston paused, and immediately half a dozen voices shouted questions, but he waved them all to silence.

'If you please, gentlemen.' When they had subsided, he continued, 'the Earl is at present in London. I intend to journey to see him there this very night, and inform him of what has come to pass in this Parish.'

There were a few knowing glances and whispered gibes exchanged about this abrupt departure from the vicinity of the cholera, but to do him justice, the Lord Aston was not attempting to escape from danger, but only to act in the manner that he thought would best expedite matters.

'I shall request the Earl to immediately convey to His Majesty's Privy Council these sad tidings, and use his best influence to have an official Board of Health embodied here as soon as possible. In the meantime, and during my absence, the Reverend John Clayton will appoint and preside over a temporary Board, which will be empowered to act on my behalf, and to carry out any measures deemed necessary to combat this epidemic.

'Reverend Clayton is also empowered to swear in any Special Constables which may be required to enforce those measures. I would request of you all, gentlemen, that you will give your fullest co-operation to Reverend Clayton during my absence.'

Now it was Aston's turn to stare challengingly at William Hemming and his fellow Needle Masters. 'If those measures should include the imposition and enforcement of a quarantine in any part of the Parish, the confiscation or destruction of articles of private property, or the prohibition of traffic or exchange in goods, then so be it.'

There was a rumbling of dissent and protest, but Aston disregarded this, and told them, 'Because of the deadly nature of this disease, His Majesty's Privy Council has fully authorised the shire Justices of the Peace to carry out even the most punitive measures to combat its ravages. This I fully intend to do, gentlemen. I have the law behind me, and so do those I deputise have it behind them.'

This time a faint smile of satisfaction did touch his lips as he saw that William Hemming, although glaring at him with hating eyes, declined to accept this challenge and remained silent.

'Very well, gentlemen, thank you all for attending on me here. I shall now depart for London, and will on your behalf convey to the Earl your assurances that you will give your fullest co-operation to those appointed to direct these endeavours against the cholera.'

When Lord Aston had left the meeting, John Clayton assumed the position of chairman. 'Gentlemen, I would greatly appreciate any advice you may have to offer, on what immediate steps we should take to deal with this situation. Mr Hemming, sir, perhaps you would be so kind as to give us your views on this?'

The young clergyman's appeal and invitation served to mollify the resentment that Lord Aston's high-handed manner always seemed to invoke in his hearers and William Hemming bowed graciously, his plump florid features displaying some gratification that his position as the foremost Needle Master in the Parish should thus be seen to be acknowledged by the Lord Aston's deputy.

'Parson Clayton, gentlemen,' Hemming's cheeks

momentarily puffed out. 'We've all read or heard about the unrest among the poor that the cholera creates wheresoever it appears, so I would venture the opinion that it would be wise to swear in sufficient Special Constables at the outset to deal with any such unrest in this district.'

There was a rumble of agreement to this suggestion, and John Clayton bowed his head in acceptance.

'Secondly we must enforce a quarantine of any known cases of the cholera.' Again there was universal agreement.

'And thirdly, and to my mind, most importantly, we must endeavour to carry on with our business and trade in as normal a manner as possible. We must not hide in our cellars quaking in our boots, but must show the courage of true-born Englishmen. Goddamn it all, gentlemen, we fought and beat Napoleon Bonaparte's French Empire, did we not, and our flag flies in glory all over the world. Shall it be said that a foul foreign disease had the beating of us?'

'Indeed it shall not, sir!' a man shouted, and the whole assembly applauded rousingly.

Hemming's face glowed with satisfaction, and he bowed to John Clayton. 'I am prepared, sir, to assist you with all means in my power to put these proposals into force just as soon as you are able to do so.'

'My thanks, sir. Be assured that I shall do so,' Clayton bowed in return, but inwardly thought to himself how ironic it was that this man should gain such enthusiastic applause for voicing only the most obvious of suggestions, and without offering any ideas on the practicalities involved. 'Very well,' he told himself, 'I shall act on my own initiative entirely from this moment on.'

Aloud he said, 'Gentlemen, I think it the wisest course for me to begin to put Mr. Hemming's valuable suggestions into effect immediately. Therefore I will now declare this meeting to be adjourned. Could the Select Vestrymen, the medical gentlemen, and Master Cashmore please remain so that I may have words with them. My thanks to you all, gentlemen.'

The meeting dispersed in a babble of excited voices.

As he faced the smaller group remaining, John Clayton's mind worked with speed and clarity, and he formulated his plan of campaign like the soldier that he had once wished to become.

Firstly he addressed the Select Vestrymen, the ruling council of the Parish, Henry Milward, William Hemming, Thomas Bartleet and William Balden.

'Gentlemen, let us act boldly in this matter. I propose that we levy a Rate immediately to defray the expenses the Parish will incur in fighting the cholera?'

After some hesitation, the Vestrymen agreed to this proposal.

'The question of imposing a quarantine must be considered next,' Clayton went on. 'There are some empty decayed cottages in the Old Hop Gardens in Badger Lane belonging to Mr Thomas Vincent, if my memory serves me correctly. I think we should rent those cottages from Mr Vincent for use as a temporary Quarantine Hospital. They are most convenient to the town, but for all that are still suitably isolated from the main routes into the centre.'

This suggestion was also agreed to.

'To obtain the necessary bedding and utensils, we can employ the Town Crier to make an appeal for charitable donations of such articles. At the same time he can cry our offer of employment for sick nurses to care for the victims.'

'How many nurses do you think will be needed, Parson Clayton?' Henry Milward wanted to know. 'There's no sense in the Parish going to unnecessary expense in this matter. God knows it will cost enough to rent the cottages from Tom Vincent, grasper that he is.'

'Oh I'm sure he can be persuaded to take a nominal rent for them, Henry,' William Hemming put in with a macabre touch of unintentional humour. 'After all, if this epidemic is a bad one, he stands to make a fortune from the hiring of his hearse alone.'

Thomas Vincent, amongst his varied business interests, also acted as the town undertaker.

'I'm sure I don't know how many nurses we may be

needing at this point in time, Mister Milward,' John Clayton frowned slightly with impatience. 'We can only wait and see.'

He turned to the three doctors. 'Gentlemen, could I request you to volunteer to serve the Parish at this time?' To their credit all three of them signified their willingness without any hesitation.

'We shall need to know the locations and the numbers of the afflicted,' Clayton told them. 'And to have certain diagnosis that it is indeed the cholera. Could I ask you then to be ready to examine each case as it occurs, and to give me your diagnosis?'

Lucas Royston saw his opportunity to cement his re-establishment back in this town, and instantly seized upon it.

'Parson Clayton, my uncle, Doctor Pratt, and Doctor Taylor here, both have very large practices to consider, and already face overwhelming demands on their professional services. Would it not be best for both them, and the unfortunates who may be stricken with the cholera, if, initially, at least, I myself solely undertook to carry out this obligation?'

He smiled with a charming modesty. 'I do have considerable experience of this disease, and should I have the misfortune to become infected myself by it, then surely the town can better afford to lose my services, rather than the services of either of my esteemed colleagues. Naturally, the afflicted cases I refer to would be only those who are not already present patients of my fellow practitioners.'

He sensed the relief in the other doctors, that they now need not be obligated to go into the mean hovels of the poor for scant remuneration, and told himself ruefully, not for the first time, 'Ah well, Lucas, beggars can't be choosers.'

Clayton considered for a moment. Remembering the previous time when Lucas Royston had been the official surgeon to the poor in Tardebigge Parish, and like the Scotsman he inwardly shrugged and thought, 'Well, beggars can't be choosers, and I am in desperate need of the full time service of a medical man.'

He glanced in silent question at the Select Vestrymen, and read acceptance in their eyes, then turned to Lucas Royston, and smiled. 'Doctor Royston, you are now appointed the official Surgeon to the Poor of the Tardebigge Parish. Terms to be agreed upon at the earliest possible date.' His smile became ironic, 'Shall I say welcome back, Lucas?'

Now it was the turn of Joseph Cashmore, and this was quickly dealt with. 'Master Cashmore, will you bring those whom you select for Special Constables to me at the earliest opportunity, and I will administer their oaths. I myself will now go in search of Richard Hill the Crier and engage his services.'

'Do you need us any longer to remain here, Parson?' William Hemming was becoming impatient to be gone. 'I've many pressing matters to attend to.'

'No, Mister Hemming, sir, I think that we have done all that we can do, at this present time. My thanks to you all, gentlemen, and I'll bid you a good day.'

Outside the Chapel in the warm sunlight he asked Lucas Royston, 'Where can you be found, Lucas? At your uncle's house?'

The Scotsman shook his head. 'No. I've taken rooms at the house of Augustus Bartleet near the bottom of Fish Hill. I'm practically your next-door neighbour, John.'

'Well, that is convenient for us both, Lucas. I shall have it cried that your services will be available to all in the event of a cholera attack.'

'In that case, I'd best have fumigatory devices set up in Mister Bartleet's hallway. Because no doubt many of my callers will bring a myriad of vile stinks and other unwelcome little visitors with them.'

'Remember Lucas, Our Saviour did not shrink from the poor and unclean,' Clayton gently rebuked.

'And neither shall I.' The Scotsman's fine eyes gleamed amusedly and he chuckled, 'But I cannot help but doubt that the dainty Master Augustus will care to emulate Our Saviour and myself?'

Chapter Twenty-Four

JAMES BRAY CAME to a halt outside the castellated Lock-up, and rang his handbell until he had attracted the attention of a sizeable crowd, which gathered around him expectantly. In sharp contrast to the general seedy shabbiness of his listeners, the Town Crier was a resplendent figure in his gold-laced tricorn hat, full-skirted canary yellow coat, plum breeches and white stockings ending in silver buckled shoes.

'Oyezzz, Oyezzz, Oyezzz, let it be known by order of the Select Vestry that should anyone be thought to have taken the cholera, then a report must be made to Doctor Lucas Royston, who is to be found at the house of Mister Augustus Bartleet on Fish Hill.

'Oyezzz, Oyezzz, Oyezzz, let it be known by order of the Select Vestry, that any respectable woman who seeks employment as a sick nurse can make application to any of the Parish Officers, or to Parson Clayton for the same.'

James Bray finished his message and walked on down towards the Big Pool, where he would halt and deliver it once more. A small group of ragged urchins followed at his heels, badgering him with their appeals to let them ring his bell. The Crier ignored them, knowing from previous experience that to attempt to drive them away would only serve to make them intensify their torment.

Tildy was in Mother Readman's kitchen when one of the lodgers came in to tell them about the Crier's message.

The old woman's pendulous jowls quivered as she cackled with cynical laughter, 'Marvellous aren't it! Poor folks die o' fever year in and year out in this bloody town, and nobody takes a blind bit o' notice on it. But now they'm agoing to be dying o' the cholera instead, then the Vestry mun be told on it straight away.'

'But surely it's a good thing that the Vestry have done, to have a doctor appointed for all to be helped by?' Tildy gently challenged.

'Yes, I'll give you that,' the old woman conceded. 'But they only does so, when they'm in danger themselves, my duck. If it was only the summer flux that's took Jamie Hughes, then the bloody Vestry 'udden't be bothering to appoint no doctor, you can be sure o' that.'

Tildy sighed, and nodded, 'I'll not argue that point with you, mother.'

They were interrupted by the entrance of another man into the kitchen. He was dressed in funereal black, with a tall hat swathed with a crepe mourning band on his head, but his smiling face belied the sombre garb.

'Now then, Tommy Vincent, what does you want here? I anna got anybody waiting for your carriage,' Mother Readman greeted the newcomer bluffly.

Thomas Vincent, undertaker, pawnbroker and money-lender, grinned cheerily. 'I arn't come seeking a customer, mother. I'm looking for a few blokes who want's to earn themselves a shilling.'

Tildy stared at the stocky, broad-shouldered man, whose ruddy features glowed with good health and ample living, and who looked far younger than his fifty years. She could not help but marvel how incongruous his general air of joviality was when she considered his main profession.

He seated himself on one of the benches around the ingle-nook, facing the two women and, rubbing his hands briskly together, told them, 'Jamie Hughes popped it a couple of hours since, and his brother wants me to give him a good send off, wi' all the trimmings. They allus was powerful fond of each other, them two was, and Davy earns good money at the pointing, so he can well afford to make a brave showing. He wants four horses pulling me hearse, and mutes and plume and banner men, and me finest coffin, wi' real brass furniture. None o' your Brummagem tin rubbish. He's told me to get two score pair o' real kid gloves, and silk scarves to hand out as mourning tokens as well.'

He blew out a loud gust of breath, 'Jesus Christ! You'd think that the Hugheses was bloody gentry, and we was aburying a young Lord, 'udden't you, instead of a bloody Needle Pointer. Still, if he wants to gi' me his money like that, whom am I to try and stop him from doing so.' Again he rubbed his hands briskly, and grinned as he winked broadly at Tildy, with such an air of irrepressible, bubbling good humour, that she could not help but smile back at him.

'So, Mother,' he spoke directly to the old woman, 'how's about letting me have two or three o' your lodgers then? I needs some who'll stay sober enough, until they'se done the business. The sort o' money young Davy Hughes is willing to pay deserves steady men to carry his brother.'

'What's the matter wi' your usual blokes then?' Mother Readman frowned. 'Why anna they willing to carry Jamie Hughes?'

Thomas Vincent roared with happy laughter, and slapped his knees with his black-gloved hands in appreciation. 'By the Christ, Mother, but theer's no pulling the wool over your eyes, is there?' he exclaimed.

'The only cloth you'll ever pull over my eyes, Tommy Vincent, 'ull be me bleedin' shroud. And that 'ull be best linen, not wool,' the old woman told him with sardonic humour. 'Now you gi' me the truth on it. Why wun't your usual blokes carry Jamie Hughes?'

Momentarily he sobered, and told her simply, 'Because they'm too bloody feared to. They'll carry the banners and plumes, and they'll follow the hearse, but there arn't a one on 'um who'll put the bloody coffin on his shoulder.' He spat into the heaped ashes of the hearth in disgust. 'Bloody cowards!'

'You canna blame 'um for that,' Mother Readman remonstrated. 'The cholera is a terrible thing.'

'No more terrible than many another disease that I buries week arter week, Mother,' the man rejoined. 'They'm all feared on it because it's new, that's all. Because it's strange to 'um. I bin talking to that new-come bloke, Charles Brown, he calls hisself. He reckons he's bin a naval saw-bones, and he knows a deal about this cholera, because he's seen it afore out in India. He told me that he's known o' cases wheer men has shared beds wi' cholera victims, and took no harm from it. So wheer's the harm in carrying somebody who's died on it in a box on your shoulders. It arn't agooing to come through a good thick plank to catch hold on you, is it now?'

'Who's to say whether it will, or whether it wun't, Tom?' Mother Readman remarked.

'When is Jamie Hughes to be buried?' Tildy put in.

'Tomorrow arternoon,' Vincent told her. 'When I was sent for to goo to the Roundhouse an hour or so since, Parson Clayton was already theer, wi' Cashmore and that Scotchman, Royston. The Parson was very insistent that Jamie be planted just as quick as he could be. I reckon if Clayton could have had his own way in the matter, then Jamie 'ud be in his box and six foot under this very moment.' The man paused for a moment in his story, and then grinned. 'I'll tell you summat else. Him, the Parson I mean, and Davy Hughes nearly come to blows at one stage. Joe Cashmore had to get atween the pair on 'um to stop it.'

'Why so?' Tildy asked curiously.

'Because the Parson said that Jamie had got to be wrapped tight in bandaging soaked wi' tar or pitch, otherwise he 'udden't let him be buried in the Chapel Yard. Davy Hughes swore like a bloody trooper, so he did. He said it warn't Christian to treat poor Jamie so. He said that Jamie had got the rights to be wrapped up proper in decent new cloth, but the Parson 'udden't hear on it. Like I say, they was near come to blows, they got so riled up about it.'

'What was decided in the end?' Tildy was angry at herself for this morbid curiosity she was displaying, but was consumed by an overwhelming need to know.

'The Parson got his own way. And Davy Hughes was forced to agree wi' him, otherwise Jamie 'udden't be let lay wi' his own kinfolks in the Chapel Yard, 'ud he?' A sudden scowl crossed Thomas Vincent's jovial face. 'Mind you, that's presented me wi' another problem, as well. I'se got to find somebody to wrap Jamie up in the bloody bandages, arn't I. And iffen I can't, then I'll have to do it meself, and tar and pitch is a bugger to shift from your skin, arn't it? Not to mention the trouble I'll have to goo to, to boil the bloody stuff so that I can soak the bandaging in it.'

An old man came shuffling into the room, and coughing and wheezing made his painful way to the inglenook. Thomas Vincent studied him with a professional eye, then grinned happily, and enquired, 'Now then, Billy Boy, you'm not looking at all well. How are you feeling?'

The aged rheumy eyes glared back at the undertaker. 'You needn't start measuring me up, you bastard. I arn't agoing to croak it for a few years yet. I intends to kape on breathin', just to spite you. You greedy, grabbin' bleeder!'

Vincent howled with infectious laughter, and spluttered. 'I warn't hoping you 'ud be dying soon, Billy Boy. I reckon I'm agoing to have work enough for the next few months. I'd sooner keep you in reserve, for when business gets slack.'

The old man ignored him and instead, wheezing for breath, informed Mother Readman, 'The cholera's come to Paoli's Row, missus. All o' Tommy Cook's family bin struck down wi' it.'

Chapter Twenty-Five

LUCAS ROYSTON HURRIED from the room in which Jamie Hughes' corpse lay and, pulling out his fine gold hunter watch, saw that he had some minutes to spare before his appointment with Arnold Pitts at the Pitts' home a little further up Mount Pleasant.

The Scotsman felt a nervous tremor fluttering in his stomach as he walked very slowly towards the large house. He mentally rehearsed what he intended to say to the dour Arnold Pitts when he asked him for Maria's hand in marriage. Although there had been many women pass through Lucas Royston's life, he had never before been so completely infatuated as he was now, with Maria Pitts. He fully intended, should her father refuse them permission to wed, to do his utmost to persuade that young lady to elope with him.

He lifted the polished brass, lionhead door knocker and let it fall three times before the door was opened to him. It was Maria herself, and Lucas Royston's throat seemed to thicken and his breathing to falter as he reached out his hand towards her.

'Hello sweetheart,' he whispered huskily, 'I've come to speak with your father about us.'

Then he frowned slightly, as instead of greeting him with a loving gesture, she only stepped back into the hallway. He saw that her eyes were reddened and swollen as if with weeping, and he asked anxiously, 'What troubles you, sweetheart?' A sudden anger rose within him. 'Has someone been treating you cruelly?'

Again he reached out for her, and again she stepped back, raising her hands as if to ward him off.

Completely mystified by her strange behaviour, he questioned, 'But what is it, my love? Have I done anything to offend you?'

She covered her face with her hands and burst into tears, and as he stood perplexed, her mother came hurrying down the staircase into the hallway. The older woman looked worried and drawn, and when she saw the Scotsman she exclaimed with heartfelt relief.

'Thank God you've come so quick, Doctor Royston. Did you meet Lucy on her way down to your house?'

Lucas Royston could only shake his head and sigh in puzzlement. 'I'm sorry, Mistress Pitts, but I'm at a loss here. What troubles you all?'

'Have you not seen my maidservant, Lucy?' the older woman demanded.

Lucas shook his head, 'I've seen no one, ma'am. I've been in the Round House with Parson Clayton this last hour or so. What is the trouble?'

'It's my husband, Doctor Royston.' The woman suddenly wrung her hands together in front of her ample stomach, and began to weep with a real anguish. 'He's collapsed, and I don't know what it is that ails him so.'

A cold dread struck into the Scotsman, and he told the woman, 'Please allow me to see him, ma'am.'

In the comfortably furnished bedroom, Arnold Pitts, fully clothed, was laying on the satin coverlet of the great four-poster bed. He was conscious, his face deathly pale, and sheened with a clammy sweat. The fear and uncertainty in his eyes as he stared up at Lucas Royston was pitiful to see, and because this was the father of the woman he loved, Royston's concern for him was fully aroused. He smiled down at the man, 'Don't be feared, sir. I am come to help you.' He forced himself to speak with a confidence he did not feel. 'You will be fully recovered shortly. Now try and lie here quietly until I return in a little while.'

Royston beckoned Mistress Pitts to follow him from the

room, and closing the door behind them both, he asked her a series of rapid questions concerning the sick man. Then as gently as he was able, he told her, 'I'll not deceive you, ma'am. I fear Mister Pitts has been struck by the cholera.'

She emitted a faint cry, and her face turned ashy grey as the blood drained from it. She swayed as if near to fainting, and Lucas Royston was forced to take her in his arms to support her.

'Be of good heart, ma'am.' He desperately tried to strengthen her resolve. 'Fortunately this attack does not appear to be of the most virulent nature. I have much confidence that I can save your husband. Do you know how to prepare a mustard poultice?'

Her turbanned-befeathered head nodded slowly. 'Then you may be of great assistance to me in this matter, ma'am.' Royston spoke briskly, knowing that unless he roused her into some sort of positive action, she would most likely give way and collapse completely. 'I must go and fetch my medical chest, in the meantime I want you and Maria to heat plenty of water, to find out some lengths of clean flannel or other cloth, to prepare some warming pans, and fashion some small stoutly-made cloth-bags. Can you do all those things?'

Mistress Pitts nodded silently.

'Good, then let's go to it, ma'am!' He clapped his hands sharply together, and gently pushed her away from him and towards the head of the stairs. 'Let's go to it!'

When Lucas Royston reached the home of Augustus Bartleet, he found that willowy gentleman awaiting him in a state of much agitation. 'There you are, Doctor Royston, I am most anxious to have words with you.' The slender hands fluttered in the air, and the slender rouged features wore an expression of mingled resentment and trepidation.

'Can we postpone our conversation until later, Master Bartleet,' Royston spoke impatiently. 'I can spare no time at present.'

'But you must spare time, Doctor. Since these last two hours I have been repeatedly disturbed, and I may say, sadly discommoded, by a positive stream of callers to this door. Most of them, I regret to say, from the most unsavoury and disreputable classes of this town.'

'Will you please come to the point, and tell me what it was they wanted of me?' Royston queried sharply, irritated by being so hindered.

'They want you to attend on them. I have made note of their addresses.' The tinted lips puffed petulantly. 'If I had known of the nature of your medical practice, Doctor Royston, then I declare that I would not have acceded to your request to lodge in my house with such an amiable ease and readiness.

'God only knows what such people may carry with them here. Most of them positively stank to high heaven. I do assure you it has caused me considerable distress, I am not accustomed to being in the close proximity of such persons.'

'Will you please give me the list,' Royston held out his hand, and Augustus Bartleet thrust a sheet of notepaper into it.

Royston briefly scanned the short list, his lips moving soundlessly as he read the names and places, 'Thomas, Paoli's Row; Millington, Paoli's Row; Merry, next to Round House; Avery, the New End.' He folded the paper and put it into his waistcoat pocket, a worried frown on his face.

'What does this mean, Doctor Royston?' the other man asked.

Royston drew a long breath to calm his strained temper, and told Bartleet quietly. 'It means, Mister Bartleet, that an epidemic of the cholera is already raging throughout this town. It means that I and my fellow practitioners will from this moment on be fighting to control and defeat that epidemic. It means that death can strike without warning at any man, woman or child in this town. It means that there will be grief abounding. And lastly, it means that I do not wish to be bothered with your whinings about your discommoding and disturbance. I shall have neither time to listen to them, nor inclination. Now, sir, I beg of you to excuse me. I must be about my business.'

He went to push past the other man, but with a strength of grip that was at odds with his willowy frame, Augustus Bartleet stopped him. 'I pray you, hear me out, Doctor Royston, it will take but a moment.'

Scowling, the Scotsman demanded, 'Well?'

'Forgive my previous words, Doctor,' Bartleet apologised. 'I did not understand the gravity of this present situation. Now I do so, and I beg of you, to command me in any way that I can aid you in your fight against this foul disease.'

For a moment or two, Royston could only stare bemusedly at the other man, so unexpected was this volte-face. Then he gave a slight shake of his head, and grinned, 'Many thanks, Mister Bartleet. At present your best aid to me, would be to continue taking the names and addresses of my callers, and getting from them such details of the attacks as they may be able to impart.'

Bartleet bowed gallantly, 'It shall be done, Doctor. You may rest assured, it shall be done.'

Chapter Twenty-Six

SATURDAY, THE 25th of August was again hot and sunny, and normally, that day being payday, there would have been something of a festive atmosphere in the streets of Redditch. But the news of the rapidly spreading cholera, which was rumoured almost hourly to have claimed fresh victims, had brought fear to the streets. The wild rumours brought many people to the verge of panic, and for the more imaginative and timid among the population, every slight twinge of stomach ache or head pain was immediately feared to presage the worst.

Thomas Vincent was a disgruntled man as he marshalled his helpers for the funeral of Jamie Hughes. Instead of an imposing array of mutes, plume and banner men there were only five drunken sots, whom he had been forced to bribe heavily with free drink, tobacco, snuff and money in order to get them to agree to act as bearers. What was worse, was the fact that he himself had been finally forced to wrap Jamie Hughes in pitch-soaked bandages. He had been unable to find anyone to do that task even though he had offered a gold guinea as payment for doing it.

When the coffin was placed in the glass-sided black hearse with its four black-plumed horses, only a handful of mourners assembled to follow Jamie Hughes to the Chapel Yard. The dead man had been a popular figure, but the fear of the cholera kept many away who, if he had died of any other disease, would have come to his burial.

As the small procession traversed down Mount Pleasant and Front Hill and along Evesham Street, men doffed their hats and stood still to show respect, and women hushed their children and momentarily bowed their heads. But Thomas Vincent could sense that this normality was only a façade and that their faces showed relief when the hearse had passed them by, as if they feared that the mere proximity of the dead man could infect them with the deadly disease.

John Clayton was busy preparing the old cottages in the Hop Gardens for their role as a Quarantine Hospital; his fellow curate, Julius Fessey, was to conduct the burial service. If Clayton epitomised 'Muscular Christianity', then Julius Fessey was the epitome of its opposite. A soft-bodied, fat and effete young man, he had refused to hold the burial service in the enclosed space of the Chapel, and insisted on standing a considerable distance from the graveside, so that he would not be near to the coffin.

Because Jamie Hughes was the first officially declared cholera victim to be buried, a sizeable crowd had gathered to watch the hearse draw up at the gate of the burial yard. Thomas Vincent dismounted from his driving seat and directed his bearers to remove the coffin from the hearse. While they prepared to do so, Vincent went to have a brief word with Davy Hughes. 'I'm sorry that I arn't bin able to give Jamie a better showing, Davy.' The undertaker was genuinely regretful. If all had gone as he planned, this would have been a very profitable funeral for him. 'None o' me regulars 'ud agree to come. Some on 'um was too feared to, and the rest reckoned it 'ud bring 'um bad luck to bury a cholera case. That's why I'se had to take on these bloody hounds.'

'That's alright, Tommy. I arn't blaming you for it.' Davy Hughes was pale-faced with grief, because he had truly loved his brother, but was calm and composed. ''Tis not your fault that people am too feared to come nigh our kid.'

'Bloody cowards!' Vincent cursed with feeling, then glanced back at the hearse and suddenly ejaculated in shock, 'What the bleedin' hell?'

His bearers, ragged and unshaven, and reeking of

unwashed flesh and the drink he had been forced to ply them with, had placed the coffin on the ground, and tied short lengths of rope to the brass handles, by means of which they were now lifting the coffin to carry it to the open grave.

As Vincent hurried to them, the Chapel bell began its mournful tolling, sounding preternaturally loud in the still air.

'What does you think you'm doing?' he demanded angrily.

Charlie Duggins, drunk and quarrelsome, acted as the bearers' spokesman. 'We'em gooing to carry the bugger underhand. I anna putting my yed next to him.'

Davy Hughes and the other mourners crowded around the coffin. 'You arn't going to carry my brother to his grave, as if he was a dog,' the Needle Pointer shouted angrily. 'It's a bloody insult to him.'

The bearers lowered the coffin back to the ground and reacted with sullen scowls and shakes of their heads in refusal.

'I arn't getting me yed next to him.'

'I'se naught agen you, Davy Hughes, but I anna risking catching the cholera.'

'Nor me.'

'Nor me neither.'

'Look, I'll pay each one o' you an extra shilling,' Vincent offered but still the men sullenly refused.

'He get's carried underhand or not at all,' Charlie Duggins stated flatly.

'He wun't bloody well be carried underhand!' Davy Hughes asserted angrily, and a chorus of growled agreement came from his fellow mourners.

Vincent looked into the Burial Yard, where two grave-diggers and the Sexton were standing by the heap of clay dug out of the open grave, with the Reverend Julius Fessey some distance from them. 'Parson Fessey, could you come here a minute, please?' he called in appeal.

The fat clergyman came hesitantly towards the gate,

coming to a standstill some fifteen yards distant from the group around the coffin.

'What is it? What's causing this unseemly delay?' he fluted nervously, and when Thomas Vincent explained, Fessey only fluttered his plump hands nervously and bleated, 'But the man must be buried as quickly as possible.'

The Sexton and the gravediggers came forwards, and Vincent asked them. ''Ull you help me carry the coffin?'

All three initially refused, but then the Sexton offered, 'I'll carry it underhand, if you like.'

Among the curious onlookers were several who now began to voice their opinions that the dead man should not be buried in the Chapel Yard at all. But taken to some isolated place where the danger of infection from his grave would be less.

'That's right,' others began to agree with them. 'Nobody ought to be buried in this yard who's bin took by the cholera. It's too near the houses. He ought to be buried elsewheres.'

There were a group of youths in the crowd, and hearing these protests they scented a possibility of excitement, and more from mischievousness than from malice, they began to chant, 'Take him away! Take him away! Take him away! No cholera here! No cholera here! No cholera here!'

Others took up the cry, and fuelled by fear the mood of the crowd suddenly altered perceptibly, and the earlier curiosity and sympathy metamorphosed into an aggressive hostility towards the dead man.

'Take him away, no cholera here! Take him away, no cholera here! Take him away, no cholera here!'

The chant became a bawling chorus and fists were shaken, and a couple of missiles thrown at the group around the coffin.

Faced with this sudden threat to his safety, the Reverend Julius Fessey's scant store of courage abruptly ran out, and gathering the skirts of his long billowing cassock in both hands, he scurried from the Burial Yard and disappeared into the Chapel.

Thomas Vincent kept his head. He realised that this situation could at any moment get completely out of control, and ordered the bearers, 'Put him back in the hearse.'

Charlie Duggins spat onto the ground, 'Put him back yourself, I'm off.'

Suiting action to words, he walked away, and was quickly followed by the other bearers.

Helped by the mourners, Thomas Vincent re-loaded the coffin into the hearse.

'We'll have to get out o' this quick,' he told Davy Hughes, whose earlier anger was now overlaid by his bewilderment at the turn events had taken.

'What can we do?' Hughes asked anxiously. The undertaker thought for a moment, then told him, 'I'll take him down to the old Hop Gardens. Parson Clayton's theer now. He'll know what best to be done. You lot follow me down theer.'

He whipped up the four horses, and the hearse went swaying and clattering through the jeering hostile crowd and disappeared down the steep slope of Fish Hill. Once it had gone from view, a curious hush fell over the crowd, and men who only moments before had been shaking their fists and bawling threats, now seemed shamefaced, and reluctant to meet each other's eyes.

As the small party of mourners made their way towards Fish Hill, a man wearing the Needle Pointers rig stepped up to Davy Hughes. 'I'm real sorry, Davy,' he shook his head as if bewildered. 'I'm real sorry for this. I 'udden't have insulted your Jamie for the world. I dunno what come over me.'

Davy Hughes stared for a long long moment, then shrugged, 'That's alright, Joe. Jamie couldn't hear or see you insulting him, could he?' His glance flickered over the silent crowd. 'I reckon there 'ull be more nor a few o' this lot, who'll be remembering this day to their shame, when they comes to bury their own kinfolk who'll be dying o' the cholera.'

Chapter Twenty-Seven

YOUNG DAVY CRAWFORD had been a witness of the events at the Burial Yard, and now he excitedly related to his mother and Old Esther all that he had seen.

They listened without interruption, and when he had come to the end of his story, Tildy sighed sadly, and shook her head. 'Fear drives folk mad, doesn't it. I feel really sorry for Davy Hughes. They say that he thought the world of his brother, and it's terrible enough to lose him like that, without all this happening as well.'

The door to the front yard was open because of the heat, and Tildy saw her neighbour, Pat O'Leary, halt his horse and cart in the roadway and come through the gate into the yard. He looked into the room and hailed her, his broad red face smiling genially, 'How bist, missus? Is it hot enough for ye?'

'It's too hot, Master O'Leary. It makes me feel like doing nothing in the way of work,' she answered.

He stood at the open door, and asked them, 'Did you hear about the trouble at the Burial Yard?'

'Yes, Davy's just been telling us of it. Were you there yourself?' Tildy questioned.

'No, I was not. But iffen I had a bin, then I reckon that I might well have acted like the others.'

'Then you should be shamed o' yourself,' Old Esther told him sharply. 'It's wicked to refuse a poor soul a Christian burial.'

'Well, that's as maybe, missus,' the Irishman retorted.

'But from what I bin hearing this day, I reckon we'll all be having enough troubles while we'em still living, so I can't really find it in me heart to concern meself too much about them that's dead. They'm well out of it.'

'Oh you'm a wicked bugger, Pat O'Leary!' the old crone snapped. 'I'll wager there'll come a day when you'll be wishing that you'd bin a better-living man.'

'That's right, me old duck. I surely am so,' his genial grin shone once more, and he winked broadly at the old woman. 'And if wishes were horses, then beggars would ride.'

'What is it you've been hearing then, Master O'Leary?' Tildy wanted to know.

'That the cholera is spreading through the Parish like wildfire, missus. It's at Headless Cross, and down in Ipsley at Sweet Turf, and all about the Round House and down Mount Pleasant right to the bottom 'o Front Hill, and all along Paoli's Row.'

'God save us!' Tildy ejaculated softly.

'It's only him that'll be able to, missus. Because it doon't look like the doctors are capable o' doing so,' the Irishman said soberly, then suddenly grinned once more. 'Mind you, I've bin told of a sovereign prevention for it.'

'What's that?' Tildy asked eagerly, and he chuckled richly.

'Why, it's brandy, missus. Good honest brandy,' he winked at Old Esther. 'That's the drink for wicked buggers like me, me old duck. And by the Christ, I intends to take plenty of it, as well.'

'I'm going down to see to my pony,' young Davy announced. His beloved pony was kept stabled down in Bredon at the small factory that Daniel Lambert and Brandon Whittle were partners in.

For a moment Tildy was tempted to stop him from doing so and make him stay here in the house with her. The news about the rapid spread of the cholera worried her greatly, and she was afraid that her son might well become infected if he went in the vicinity where the disease had taken hold.

Then she realised that she could not keep him a virtual prisoner, and nodded, 'Very well then. But don't you go near anywhere where the cholera is. Do you hear me?'

'I won't, mam. I'll not be long. Bye Nanny Esther, bye Mister O'Leary.' With that the boy went running off.

Old Esther smiled lovingly after him and seeing Tildy's worried face, scolded gently, 'Now stop werritin' do, my wench. You canna keep the bairn locked up here day in and day out.'

'I know,' Tildy nodded. 'But I get frightened when I think that he might wander among people who are infected, and catch it himself.'

'That's only natural, missus,' Pat O'Leary looked very serious. 'But it's in my mind that it don't seem to be any use trying to hide from the cholera. If it wants ye, then it comes and searches ye out, no matter where you might be hiding.'

From outside a raucous voice shouted, 'Wheer's you hiding yourself, O'Leary? Be you trying to sneak off wi'out giving me me housekeeping? Wheer are you, you drunken barstard?'

The Irishman rolled his eyes upwards in comic appeal, 'Swate Jasus, would ye hark at my missus. Hasn't she got the voice of a nightingale? That's one the cholera 'ull never take, you may be sure. The bloody thing 'ud be too fritted to tackle the cow.'

Tildy and Esther laughter together as he went out to meet his formidable spouse, then a cold shiver suddenly ran through Tildy, and she was assailed by a terrible premonitory sense of looming disaster.

'Tildy? What ails you, my duck?' Old Esther asked with concern.

Tildy stared at her companion, her velvet dark eyes wide and frightened. 'I don't rightly know, Esther. I've just had the most terrible sense of doom. It was as if something was telling me that I'd had too much happiness these last couple of years, and now it was going to be taken from me again.'

Chapter Twenty-Eight

ALONG PAOLI'S ROW the night was made lurid by the flaming tar-barrels which had been fired to fumigate the air, and thick clouds of acrid black smoke hung low, causing the group of half a dozen men to cough and choke as they made their way along the sunken front pathway of the Row.

Leading the small group was Lucas Royston and Joseph Cashmore, and bringing up the rear was Thomas Vincent, dressed in his undertaker's clothing, with his tall crepe-swathed hat on his head. On the roadway above the sunken path Pat O'Leary sat on his cart-seat, swaying drunkenly and hiccuping loudly at frequent intervals.

Cashmore coughed raspingly as a particularly thick swirl of smoke entered his lungs, and he cursed savagely. 'Fuck this bloody smoke! Arn't theer any other way to keep the air purified?'

Lucas Royston could not help but smile at the unconscious humour of this paradox, and smothering his own cough, he said, 'You must just keep on telling yourself, that it's better to choke on tar fumes, than to die of the cholera, Master Cashmore.'

The Constable glared sourly and retorted, 'I'm beginning to wonder about the truth o' that, Doctor Royston.'

Outside the door of Thomas Cooks' cottage a knot of neighbours were gathered. Slatterny women, rough-looking men and dirty, scald-headed children.

Joseph Cashmore wielded his long crowned staff of office

to clear them from the doorway, 'Come on, gerron out o' the way. Let the doctor through, will you.'

Lucas Royston held his lighted bulls-eye lantern high as he entered the foul-smelling room, and directed its beam around the mean interior. All four of the Cooks family were lying on the ragged filthy coverlet of the bed. The doctor frowned and his features, drawn and pale with fatigue, were momentarily tinged with despair. A glance was enough to tell him that the small girl and her brother were both dead, and that Thomas Cooks and his wife were far gone in the coma stage of cholera.

He emerged into the smoke-laden air and shook his head at Cashmore, 'The two children are dead. We'll needs to move the parents to the Quarantine Hospital immediately.'

Peering through the iron railings that separated the sunken path from the roadway, Royston shouted, 'Master O'Leary, bring the cart along here.' He turned back to the men with him, and for a moment his lips curled in distaste as he saw their drunken state. They were the very dregs of the town. Shiftless, thieving, drunken ruffians, but they were all he could find to help him in this dread task, and for money and drink they were prepared to dare the cholera. Then the Scotsman's distaste became overlaid with something nearer to respect. At least they were ready to risk their own lives, which was more than could be said for many of the respectable townsfolk, who would only stand well back out of any danger to themselves, and proffer unasked for and unwanted advice on how best to deal with this awful situation.

'Right lads, bring the man and the woman out and lay them in the cart, and be gentle with them,' Royston instructed, and the men tied pieces of vinegar-soaked rags around their mouths and nostrils and went stumbling into the cottage.

'Where do the Millingtons live?' Royston asked Cashmore. The Constable led him two doors further on. Here the room was full of people all gathered around a man lying on a bed.

'Make way for the doctor,' Joseph Cashmore ordered, and tough, unshaven faces made wolfish by the light of the guttering tallow dips, glared with hostile resentment.

'Wheer's you bin, 'til now?' one man, big and rawboned, challenged aggressively. 'You was sent for hours since.'

Lucas Royston stared wearily at the man, but it was Joseph Cashmore who answered the question. 'Does you reckon that you'm the only family that's got cholera in the town, Sam Millington? Me and the doctor arn't stopped for a single minute this night. Theer's people being struck down all over the bloody Parish, so you'se had to wait your turn, like everybody else.'

'I'll bet the fuckin' gentry didn't have to wait their turn, did they?' the big man growled with resentment, and others mouthed agreement with this statement.

'That's enough from you, Sam,' Cashmore told him firmly, but not unkindly. 'Are you forgetting that I bin a mate o' your dad since we was kids together? We come as soon as we could.'

Steven Millington, the sick man, had been one of the foremost prizefighters in the needle district in his youth and even now, ill as he was, and wasted by the terrible ravages of the cholera, he was still a big and powerful looking man. He was moaning with pain, and periodically he threw himself from side to side, as his body cramped in agonies.

'We'll needs move him to the hospital,' Lucas Royston instructed.

'Why?' Sam Millington, the eldest son demanded aggressively. 'Why canna you look arter him here in his own home?'

'Because it's not convenient,' the doctor replied impatiently.

'What d'you mean by that?' The other man seemed ready to physically attack the doctor, and Joseph Cashmore interposed his sturdy bulk between the two men, and warned Millington.

'Just let things be, 'ull you, Sam. The doctor knows

what's best to be done.' He paused, and for a few moments the two men were eyeball to eyeball, then Cashmore asked levelly, 'Can we take your dad wi' us then?'

With an ill grace the other gave way, but muttered, 'He'd better be well took care of, because if he arn't, then I'll be seeking somebody's blood.'

Lucas Royston went outside and called to his helpers to come and fetch the sick man, and when Cashmore joined him there, he grinned sarcastically at the Constable. 'Do you know, Master Cashmore, I'd forgotten just how charming these locals can be.'

The Constable regarded him dourly, and then grunted, 'Wheer does you want to goo next?'

Royston considered for a moment, then suggested, 'Perhaps we should go down to Sweet Turf and see what's to be done there?'

Cashmore looked doubtfuly, 'But that's Ipsley Parish, Doctor. I dunno what the Select Vestry 'ull have to say about us taking Ipsley Parish cases into our quarantine. They wun't be pleased about having to pay for their treatment.'

Lucas Royston swore softly, 'Bugger what the Select Vestry will have to say about it, Master Cashmore. We shall go to Sweet Turf.'

Now the Constable grinned with a grudging respect at the other man, and grunted, 'You'll do for me, Doctor Royston. You'll do very well. Sweet Turf it is.'

Inside the Cooks' cottage, Thomas Vincent finished measuring the small corpses of the children and coming out of the room, he closed the door and using a lump of chalk marked a huge letter 'C' on its rough panels. Then told the watching neighbours. 'If you'll take my advice, you wun't risk gooing in theer and seeing what you can lift, my friends. Because if you should do, then it's a fair bet that I'll be coming back to measure you up next.'

Whistling happily he went after the departing cart and the rest of the doctor's party as they skirted round the Big Pool and headed down the long gentle slope of Ipsley Street.

Chapter Twenty-Nine

AT THE BOTTOM of the steep Fish Hill, almost opposite to the main gates of Samuel Thomas's mighty British Needle Mills, was the entrance to the long narrow straight lane known as Badger Lane. Towards the western end of the lane was a stretch of land surrounded by high hedgerows which had once been used for the cultivation of hops. A row of three badly decayed cottages stood in the old Hop Gardens, and John Clayton had been working for many hours to fit these cottages for use as the Quarantine Hospital.

To his dismay he had found that only one of the cottages could be made at all habitable in the time at his disposal, and so he had directed the hired workmen to concentrate all their efforts on that one.

Now, as Lucas Royston and his helpers brought in the first cartload of cholera cases, John Clayton stood waiting to receive them in company with the two old women who had offered themselves as sick nurses. By lantern light the groaning patients were carried into the cramped, low-ceilinged rooms where makeshift beds had been prepared for them. The walls were still wet from a freshly applied coating of limewash.

The clergyman showed Lucas Royston around the rest of the site. 'There is the water supply.' He pointed to a small pool which was fed by a streamlet running along the ditch at the base of the hedgerow. 'The privy is just over there behind the end cottage, and the rubbish tip is next to it. I suggest that if need arises the shed can be utilised for a temporary dead house.'

Lucas Royston strained to peer through the darkness and could just make out in the faint starlight the darker shadowed hulk of a tumbledown shed.

John Clayton sighed unhappily, 'I've got Jamie Hughes lying in there at present. You know of course about what occurred at the Burial Yard this morning?' The question was only a formality. By now the entire district knew what had happened.

'We must resolve the question of burial without delay,' Lucas Royston pointed out forcefully. 'If the bodies remain unburied, then I consider them to be a very dangerous source of infection.'

Clayton nodded, 'I've already taken steps to rectify this unfortunate situation, Lucas. I've had the Old Burial Yard next to the Abbey ruins re-opened. And I've got two grave-diggers there even at this moment preparing a grave for poor Jamie Hughes. I shall inter him with all due reverence tomorrow morning before I take the service.'

'How about the other dead? I've left two children in Paoli's Row, and a woman at Sweet Turf.' He paused for a moment. 'And to speak frankly, John, these poor souls that I've had carried here this night are most of them near to death. Obviously I shall commence their treatments imme-diately, but I'm not very confident as to the amount of success I may enjoy in saving their lives.'

The clergyman frowned with worry, 'I fear the difficulty may arise that once we have begun interring the cholera dead in the Old Abbey Yard, then we shall have problems with keeping the gravediggers to their task there. They will become afraid of the infection travelling through the very ground. Also there is the time factor involved in actually digging the graves. If it goes badly here, and we lose many people, then we may find that there will be a virtual pile-up of corpses awaiting interment.'

'Then put every man that you can find to digging a couple of mass graves there now,' the doctor suggested.

Clayton looked doubtful. 'But surely that will only increase the terror that is already running rampant through the Parish? People will think that they are all doomed if we are seen to be making such a vast preparation for burials?'

Lucas Royston made no answer for some moments, then when he did speak, his voice was filled with a genuine remorse. 'I hold myself much to blame for our present lack of preparedness to deal with this situation, John. To ingratiate myself with the Needle Masters and others of their ilk, I deliberately lied about young Sally Beck's death, when I denied that she had had the cholera.'

John Clayton interrupted him, 'Do not judge yourself over-harshly for that, Lucas. I also allowed what I considered to be my own best interest to let this situation develop as it has. All we can both do now is to ask Our Lord for His forgiveness, and do all that lies in our power to help the afflicted.'

Up in the town in Salters Yard, Tildy Crawford was also tussling inwardly with a sense of guilt, as she carried a bowl of mutton broth into Charles Brown's room in the Widow Sprake's house. The man was laying fully clothed on his narrow trestle bed, his normally florid face grey with exhaustion.

Tildy stood for a moment in the dim light of the tallow-dip spluttering smokily in its wall-holder, and stared down at the man. Judging him to be asleep she quietly laid the bowl of broth and a hunk of bread on the box which served as his table, and turned to creep quietly from the room. His eyes fluttered open and he blinked dazedly at her retreating back, then called softly, 'Tildy, I'm awake. Don't go.'

She turned in hasty apology, 'I'm sorry if I disturbed you.'

He smiled and shook his head. 'You didn't. I was only resting my eyes for a few moments.' He looked at the bowl of steaming broth, and sniffed its savoury aroma. 'By God, but that smells good. Did you prepare it?'

'No,' she admitted wryly. 'That's Old Esther's work. I

fear I shall never be able to match her skills as a cook. I swear she can conjure up a feast fit for a king from next to nothing.'

'Don't go,' the man entreated. 'I'll enjoy some company while I eat this. I've only seen and heard an abundance of grief and pain these last many hours.'

Tildy smiled at him with a mingled sympathy and admiration. Knowing how hard he had fought to save Jamie Hughes' life, and how he had worked ceaselessly all through the previous night and this day to aid those who had come seeking for him.

Many of the poorest people in the town had never known a doctor's services. Unable to afford any fees, they had always relied on cunning men and wise women to treat their illnesses. The word that Charles Brown was a new-come cunning man, who was greatly skilled in the treatment of the cholera had brought a swarm of people into Salters Yard to beseech his help; he had given that help freely and unstintingly.

Although the Town Crier had spread the news that the Parish had appointed a surgeon to aid them, a large proportion of the town's poor were too suspicious of any official offer of aid, to take advantage of it. They preferred to continue in their normal practices. And so, when they feared cholera had stricken one of their kin, they had come to Charles Brown, instead of to Lucas Royston, or Alexander Pratt, or Hugh Taylor.

Tildy's present sense of guilt was engendered by the fact that she had done nothing in her turn to aid Charles Brown, even though some of those who had sought him out were old acquaintances and a few even friends of hers. When she saw him now, utterly exhausted as he was, that sense of guilt nagged unbearably at her.

When he had satisfied the first cravings of voracious hunger, she asked him, 'How has it gone with you, Charles. Are there many stricken with the cholera?'

To her surprise he smiled and shook his head. 'Not as many as you might think there to be, Tildy. A good number of those I've attended on, have merely been suffering a summer flux, or a fever brought on by too much raw gin. Mind you, this is always so. Whenever cholera is in a district every man's slightest ache or stomach pain is feared immediately by him to be the *Cholera Morbus*.'

Tildy was suddenly assailed by an intense curiosity about the disease, and now she began to ask a spate of questions concerning it. She learned from Charles Brown, that contrary to popular belief it was not always fatal. That in fact about half of those afflicted eventually recovered from it.

'The most deadly stage is within the first twenty-four to thirty hours,' the man informed her. 'If the patients can survive the initial attack and the cramps, and live for longer than thirty hours, then they have a good chance of surviving. With the proper care and nursing of course. Sometimes however, they do appear to be getting well, and then suffer a relapse which is invariably fatal.'

'Is there any treatment which stands a better chance of curing them than other treatments?' she wanted to know, and he grinned ruefully.

'My dear girl, any and every treatment that is tried has to my own knowledge given no such indication. All that the medical man can do is to try whatever he feels may be most efficacious in the individual circumstance, and after having judged the condition of the patient.'

'And still no one knows how this disease is conveyed from one to another, or why it strikes some, and leaves others free from harm?' Tildy was mystified.

'There is an abundance of theories offered by an abundance of self-styled experts,' Brown said, and his eyes suddenly clouded with sadness. 'But none of those theories have yet been proven to be true.'

'I feel so guilty about hiding away like I am doing and offering you no aid,' Tildy confessed.

'Do not do so,' he told her very firmly. 'Believe me, Tildy, when I tell you, that if I were in your position, then I would do exactly the same. I have my own reasons for fighting the cholera.' A bitterness entered his voice, and edged into his sad eyes.

'What are they?' Tildy was irresistibly impelled to probe.

At first he made no reply, only sat staring blankly. Then, abruptly, he shuddered visibly and anger displaced sadness. 'This foul evil destroyed my happiness, Tildy.' Hatred throbbed in his voice. 'It took my wife and children from me not many years since. I was serving with the East Indies Squadron and my wife and little ones were living in quarters in Calcutta. There was an outbreak of cholera, and I lost all of them within a space of two days. Despite all that I could do in the way of treatment, they died in my arms, one after another.'

His voice grew husky and tears brimmed in his eyes. 'Something within me died with them, Tildy. I had always believed in the value of my profession to mankind. I had trusted in what I had been taught as a medical student, and I truly believed that man's knowledge could conquer disease if that knowledge was applied with wisdom and understanding. But when that knowledge failed me and I lost my loved ones, I lost faith in my professional ability, and indeed, in that same profession itself.'

A bitter smile briefly played across his grey face, 'I suppose in a sense, I was like a priest who had lost all his faith in his religion. Who felt that the God he worshipped had been proven false. And, after a time I abandoned the practice of medicine, and instead became a pedlar, and now, a filer of needles.'

'Yet you have started to practise your profession again?' Tildy challenged gently.

He grinned ruefully at her, 'I suppose like any unfrocked priest, the need to don the cassock and give the communion strikes with irresistible force at intervals, and like him, I am drawn temporarily back into the fold of the faith.' He emitted a bark of angry laughter, 'And the need to cross swords once again with my old enemy is something I am powerless to struggle against. If only for the sake of my loved ones, I owe it a beating.' He sighed heavily, and murmured as if to himself, 'Yes indeed, I owe it a beating.' Then his head slowly drooped forwards, and his body slumped back onto the bed. 'Forgive me, Tildy, but I am sorely tired.'

His mumbled words were almost unintelligible, and Tildy whispered, 'Go to sleep now. I'll see you after you have rested.'

A rumbling snore answered her, and she smiled in sympathy and crept silently away.

Chapter Thirty

IT WAS LATE on the night of Saturday the eighth day of September 1832 that Daniel Lambert returned to Redditch from his sojourn in Sheffield. He rode over the Pigeon Bridge which marked the town's northern boundary and noted to his left hand side the flickering lights of moving lanterns which he judged came from the entrance to the site of the ancient Abbey of Bordesley.

'What are they doing there at this late hour?' he wondered curiously, but then put the matter from his mind and urged his tired horse to a faster gait towards the bottom of Fish Hill, eager to reach his home and his beloved Tildy. He reached the dark looming mass of the British Needle Mills and smelled the acrid smoke of burning tar and wood.

Next to the Needle Mills was an ancient half-timbered public house, the Royal Oak, standing some three feet below the level of the roadway on the corner of a lane leading to a brickyard. The smoke that Daniel Lambert had smelled was billowing from two flaming tar barrels placed in the middle of the lane, in front of the long terrace of mean cottages that lined the lane opposite the tall side walls of the mill.

Daniel reined in his horse and for a moment or two stared at the flaming barrels, wondering why they had been set alight so close to where people dwelt. From the interior of the public house, which he knew was much frequented by Needle Pointers, there struck up a rousing song, the tune of which Lambert recognised from his soldiering days as 'The Campbells are Coming'. But the bellowed words which

carried to his ears were different to the ones he knew, and he
listened curiously to their ranting choruses.

'The cholera's coming, oh dear, oh dear,
The cholera's coming, oh dear!
To prevent hunger's call
A kind pest from Bengal
Has come to feed all
With the cholera, dear . . .

The people are starving, oh dear, oh dear,
The people are starving, oh dear.
If they don't quickly hop
To the parish soup shop
They'll go off with a pop
From the cholera, dear.

The cholera's a humbug, oh dear, oh dear,
The cholera's a humbug, oh dear.
If you can but get fed,
Have a blanket and bed
You may lay down your head
Without any fear . . . '

As the last ranting shouts died down, Daniel heard a
man's voice roar out, 'Three cheers for King Cholera, my
lads.' And a howling of jeering laughter and mocking cheers
rang out from the public house.

'May God forgive them for their wickedness!'

At first, unseen by Daniel a sombrely dressed man had
come to stand nearby. Daniel recognised him to be the
Reverend Ezekial Humphreys, the minister of the Congregationalist Chapel in Evesham Street.

'Has the cholera come here?' he asked the newcomer, but
already knew the answer he would receive.

The minister's face was shadowed by his wide-brimmed,
low-crowned hat, but his eyes when he stared up at Daniel
caught reddish glints from the smoky flames of the barrels.

'Indeed it has, sir. For more than a week now it has

ravaged this Parish. As the Psalmist tells us, it is the "Pestilence that walketh in darkness, and the destruction that wasteth at noonday".'

Sudden fear for Tildy's safety clutched at Daniel's heart, and he told the other man, 'Then I must leave you, Reverend. I have loved ones to enquire after.'

'Indeed, sir, then God speed you. It is to their own everlasting shame that those wicked men inside that den of foul iniquities do not remain at the sides of their own loved ones, instead of behaving as they do, wallowing in drink and sinful debaucheries. But then, as Job tells us, "Their hearts are as firm as stone, yea, as hard as a piece of the nether millstone".'

Gusts of raucous laughter sounded from the public house, and a woman shrieked a torrent of filthy abuse.

'Hark to them!' Humphreys exclaimed in bitter disgust. 'They should be on their knees cowering before the wrath of God, and begging for His mercy.'

Daniel could not help but speak the words that suddenly came to his lips without any conscious volition, 'Perhaps they have decided that "Isiah, Twenty-Eight", suits them better, sir . . . "We have made a covenant with death, and with hell are we at agreement".'

He urged his horse onwards up the steep Fish Hill, using his riding whip unmercifully to quicken its flagging pace. Crossing the Chapel Green the animal suddenly started and shied, almost unseating Daniel, and he cursed angrily and peered down to see what had caused the horse's fright.

A man was lying huddled on one side in a foetus-like position. For a moment Daniel hesitated, torn between his pressing desire to see whether Tildy was safe and well, yet reluctant to leave someone unaided who might have been suddenly struck down by the cholera.

He soothed his nervous mount, and then slid down from the saddle and bent over the supine figure. Even as he bent the fumes of brandy filled his nostrils, and the man stirred and mumbled.

'Drunk! Blind drunk!' Daniel grinned bleakly. 'Ah well,

you'll come to no harm here. The night's warm enough, and you're well off the beaten track, so no cart will run you over, my buck.'

Daniel remounted, and pressed on the final few score yards to Salters Yard. The huddle of tenements was quiet, and no lights gleamed in any of the windows. Daniel stared anxiously at the windows of his own house, and saw to his relief that the ground floor curtains were not drawn together.

'Thank God, there's been no deaths here then,' he sighed thankfully. If there had been a death in the house, then the curtains would have been closed. Even the most unrepentant, irreligious and feckless of the townspeople always closed the curtains in time of death. It was an infallible sign of bereavement.

He decided to wake Tildy and let her know he was safely home before taking the horse back to its stable in Bredon. He knocked on the door and waited for the glow of the lit candle to appear through the windows, his throat and chest tight with the anticipation of seeing Tildy once more, and of holding her in his arms.

'Who is it?' The sound of her soft voice brought a lump to his throat, and for a moment he was hardly able to reply.

'It's me, Daniel.'

He heard her exclamation of delighted surprise, and the bolts rattled and the door was flung wide, and then she was in his arms, her body covered only by the thin white night-shift, pressed close to his, her warm moist lips crushed against his mouth.

'Are you all well?' he whispered urgently.

'Yes, we are. Esther and Davy are asleep. And you. Are you well?'

'Yes. Now that I'm back with you, I'm very well.'

Now that she was in his arms, the scent of her in his nostrils, the taste of her on his lips, all Daniel craved to do was to take her into their bedroom and fill her with his hungry, urgent love.

Tildy could sense the fierce desire burning through her

man, and her own desperate longing roused in answer. Then over his shoulder she saw the horse standing with drooping head. Exhaustion emanating from every line of its muddied flanks. Pity enabled her to thrust back her own desires.

'See to the horse first, honey,' she whispered. 'And while you're gone I'll have everything prepared for you. Are you hungry?'

He smiled tenderly at her concern. 'Only for you, sweetheart.' With an obvious reluctance he held her away from his body.

'I'll tend to the horse. The poor beast is worn out. Will you heat some water for me to bathe when I get back. I want to be fresh and clean for you.'

She chuckled throatily. 'At this moment, I wouldn't care how dirty you were, honey.' She lightly kissed him, then spun out of his encircling arms and pushed him towards the door. 'Go now, but come back as quickly as you can.'

She hummed happily to herself as she kindled the fire beneath the big copper in the wash-house, and filled it with water she drew from the well in the front yard. Then she filled the copper kettle and set it on its trivet above the hot ashes of the kitchen fire. Daniel had a passion for tea, despite it being so expensive to buy. She also took a flask of rum from the wall cupboard, smiling mischievously to herself as she set it beside the cup and saucer upon the table. Rum always kindled Daniel's amorous fires, and tonight she wanted those fires to burn fiercely. She took cold boiled beef and bread and salted butter and laid those articles on the table also, then settled herself to await his return.

After he had bathed himself, Daniel pulled on a robe and sat with Tildy, drinking tea laced with rum, eating nothing, but feasting his eyes on this woman that he loved above all else in this world.

She told him what was happening in the town. How each day brought reports of fresh cases of the cholera occurring. Of the different ways that people were facing up to the terror induced by the disease. Some drinking and carousing, others becoming promiscuous. Some helping the afflicted among their neighbours, others turning from the sick, and shunning them. How some of the wealthier townspeople were sending their families away to safer areas, and how certain assuredly sinful people were turning religious. How some acted as if the epidemic was non-existent, while others were fearful even to breath the air in case it carried the deadly infection.

In the bedroom they faced each other, and Daniel let his robe fall and stood naked before her. Tildy saw his rampant manhood, and trembled with the need to feel it filling the hungry void within her. Slowly he lifted the hem of her shift and drew it up from her body and over her head.

While she stood proudly before him, the wavering candlelight casting shifting shadows across her full firm breasts and thrusting nipples, her rounded belly and thighs, he held her close and moved his lips slowly and tenderly over her soft warm flesh. Kissing and gently sucking her nipples, her breasts, her belly, her thighs, knelt on his knees, his arms around her hips and buried his face in the dark triangle that was her womanhood, breathing deep of her scents, tasting with his probing tongue, his hands gently cupping and kneading the firm globes of her buttocks.

Tildy gloried in his silent worship, gasping softly as his eager tongue and greedy lips sent delicious tremors of pleasure through her body, pressing her fingers against his head as if to crush his searching mouth into her very being, and absorb him completely within her. She pulled him upright and they clasped each other and sank back across the bed.

Tildy moaned with her wanting, and she parted her rounded thighs and her hands sought for his manhood and guided its throbbing pulsation deep into her, and they thrust in concert, gasping with a mutual ecstasy, and fused into a seemingly indissoluble union and became one flesh.

Later, when Daniel had fallen asleep, Tildy lay studying his face in the silver moonlight. Loving each imperfection, each wrinkle, each scar, each sign of his harsh early life and of his sufferings, and silently begged God not to take him from her.

Chapter Thirty-One

LUCAS ROYSTON ROSE from his bed and stared out of the leaded casement window at the blue cloudless sky. His bedroom faced over the garden and he opened the window and leaned his head out, sniffing the warm flower-scented air with pleasure.

Dotted around the garden, half-hidden by flowering shrubs were what looked to be fragments of ancient ruins, arches and broken stretches of wall, and what appeared to be a pavement of Roman Mosaic, and a votary shrine to an unknown deity. Royston grinned to himself. These were not ancient ruins at all, but merely the fanciful follies of his landlord, Augustus Bartleet, built from stonework he had had taken from the ruins of the Bordesley Abbey.

'Maria will enjoy seeing them,' the doctor thought to himself, and his lips smiled tenderly as he thought of her.

Their marriage was now practically assured. To his own secret amazement, Lucas Royston's treatment of Arnold Pitts had been very successful, and that gentleman was now convalescing and, although still weak from the after effects of his ordeal, seemed to be getting stronger with every day that passed.

Royston was now a frequent and welcome visitor to the Pitts' household and Mistress Pitts was openly talking of his shared future with Maria, while Arnold Pitts had intimated that he would have no objection to a match being made, once these present troubles had gone from the Parish and Lucas Royston had built up a good practice.

The Scotsman moved from the window to examine his face in the mirror fitted to the wall above the wash-stand.

He frowned anxiously as he saw the patternings of faint lines freshly engraved around his eyes and mouth, and the purple shadows beneath his fine dark eyes.

'Ah well, perhaps when I can once again get an unbroken night's sleep, these will begin to disappear,' he grinned wryly, 'and if they don't, well at least they lend character to my face.'

A solitary grey hair almost hidden among his thick dark locks suddenly took his eye; automatically his fingers caught and plucked it from its follicle.

'I can well do without you, sir,' he told it, as he brushed it from his hand into the waste basket.

A knock sounded on his bedroom door, and Augustus Bartleet's sour-visaged housekeeper, Mistress O'Dell, called, 'I'se brung your shaving water, Doctor Royston. And theer's a message come for you.'

'Come in, Mistress O'Dell.' She entered the room, and Lucas regarded her squat dumpy figure with distaste, thinking, 'I hope to God my Maria never begins to look like you, woman.'

He smiled charmingly at her pimpled face, and asked, 'What is the message, Mistress O'Dell? Is it from the hospital?'

Yesterday, Saturday, had been a busy day, with four new admissions to the Quarantine Hospital.

'No, it's from Mistress Pitts, up Mount Pleasant. She asks could you goo up theer straight away. She sends word that her husband has been took real badly agen.'

The Scotsman frowned in concern.

''Ull you be wanting breakfuss afore you leaves this morn?' Mistress O'Dell asked, and he shook his head.

'No, I'll just take some coffee. You may leave it in the Music Room, I'll be down directly.'

As he lathered his jaws and throat, and shaved with his ivory-handled razor, Lucas Royston mentally reviewed the treatments he had already given Arnold Pitts.

Ammonia, and warm carminatives with alkalis to relieve his diarrhoea. Mustard plasters along the spine to restore from their derangement the nervous organs which had their bases there. Active doses of mercury to afford relief to his head pains, followed by opium and brandy when the pain and distress of the stomach became unbearable.

As he was sipping his hot coffee in the Music Room, Mistress O'Dell came again to tell him that a messenger had arrived from the hospital. It was John Clayton's man-servant, who informed him that one of the patients admitted yesterday had died during the night, and that another one seemed on the point of death.

'Very well,' Royston sighed wearily, 'I shall be along presently. I have to call on an urgent case first.'

The man scowled and muttered something beneath his breath as he turned to leave. Royston stopped him sharply, 'Hold hard, what was that you just said?'

The man glowered sullenly, but made no answer.

'You'd best tell me, my man, or I'll be having words with your master about your manners,' Royston warned.

For a moment or two the man's face worked with mingled resentment and nervousness. Then he mumbled, 'All I said, was that the cases in the hospital never seems to get treated as urgent, does they. Even though they'm dying like bloody flies in theer.'

Anger flared in Royston, and he opened his mouth to verbally blast the man. Then, next moment he closed it again without voicing anything. What the man had said was true. People were dying in the hospital, and he, Royston, was helpless to prevent them from doing so.

He jerked his head in dismissal, 'Get you gone, and in future, mind your manners.'

Taking his medical bag from the hallway, Royston left the house and headed up the hill towards the town centre. As he walked his mind dwelt on this present situation. Lord Aston was still down in London, and no official Board of Health had yet been authorised for the Tardebigge Parish by the Privy Council.

Although the Select Vestry of the Tardebigge Parish had levied a Special Rate to pay the expenses incurred in treating the cholera victims, and for renting the cottages, purchasing the necessary medicines and drugs, etc that money had proven hard to collect, and what had been collected had already been spent, and although he was urging John Clayton to force the Select Vestry to vote more money to him, the clergyman was meeting strong opposition from the Vestrymen to do so. They wanted to wait until an Official Board of Health was authorised for the Parish by the Privy Council, and then they could claim a large proportion of what would be spent back from the government fund which had been allocated for that purpose.

'In effect, at this present moment, I seem to be fighting a one man battle against this epidemic,' Lucas Royston concluded morosely.

His uncle, Doctor Alexander Pratt, and the handsome Doctor Hugh Taylor, were only treating their existing panels of patients, and the burden of treating the cholera cases among the poor was falling mainly on Lucas Royston's narrow shoulders.

Now he grimaced, as he considered that burden. The cholera appeared to be confined to certain defined areas and segments of the Parish's population. These were the slums, and the slum-people. Only a handful of the wealthier and more respectable among the population had been attacked as yet by cholera. These were not forced into the Quarantine Hospital, as were the poorer patients, but were being treated in their own homes by the established doctors.

Lucas Royston drew a certain macabre comfort from the fact that proportionally, despite having the advantages of ample fees, home comforts, and servants to call upon, the other doctors did not appear to be having a much better rate of success in treating the disease than he himself.

When he reached the Pitts' house and tugged on its bell-rope, the door was answered by Maria herself. Lucas Royston stared at her reddened eyes and wildly agitated features with shocked concern.

'What's the matter, my love? What has happened?'

She flung herself into his arms, and buried her face against his chest. Between her sobs she choked out that her mother had collapsed and her father seemed to be dead. The cook and the maidservant had run away in terror, and she had been alone in the house for more than an hour with her sick parents.

He tried to soothe her while moving into the hallway. Then seated her bodily on a chair there. 'Where is your mama?'

The girl pointed to the room that was used as a parlour.

'And your pa?' Her slender arm swung upwards.

Now don't be distressed any longer, sweetheart.' He patted her cheek, which was wet with tears. 'I'm here now, and I shall deal with everything.'

Her grey eyes were huge in her pale face, and love welled in his heart as he gazed at her pathetic defencelessness. Even in the midst of her grief, she was so beautiful that he could hardly bring himself to leave her.

He ran up the stairs and into Arnold Pitts' bedroom. One look was sufficient: the man was dead.

Royston hurried back downstairs and into the parlour. Mistress Pitts was laying on her back, vomit smeared across her mouth and face, her voluminous petticoats drawn up almost to her waist, displaying her vastly fat thighs, encased in their white cotton stockings.

The vile stench she emitted told Royston that she had voided her bowels, and for a brief instant he pitied her loss of whatever dignity she had possessed. Her eyes were closed and she was breathing in bubbling, choking snorts, her complexion darkly flushed and congested as if the blood were forcing itself into her head and creating unbearable pressures within it.

He knelt beside her and tried to raise her mountainous bulk, but was instantly forced to realise that he was not physically capable of doing so unaided.

He returned to the hallway, and told Maria Pitts, 'i'll need help straight away, sweetheart.' He stopped to consider briefly exactly what had to be done. 'Is there a bedroom we can place your mama in?'

She looked at him questioningly, and shrugging unhappily he told her gently, 'Your pa has gone, sweetheart. I cannot put your mama in their bedroom.'

Maria's features twisted, and she emitted a howl of anguish, and her head and body started to shake uncontrollably. Royston cradled her shaking body in his arms and stroked her unkempt hair, crooning softly to her, 'There, there, my sweet. There, honey, there, don't grieve so, I'm here, and I will never leave you. There, honey, there . . . '

His mind was racing as he tried to plan a course of action. He knew that he could not leave this girl alone in this house in the state she was now in. Equally Mistress Pitts was in instant need of aid and treatment, otherwise she could well die quickly. He was in desperate need of help, but as he cast about in his mind for those he might obtain that speedy help from, he experienced a growing sense of angry frustration.

Very few people were prepared to aid those whom they were not related or close friends to, and Lucas Royston was forced to accept that the Pitts lacked both relatives and friends. He whispered urgently to the crying girl, 'Is there anyone you can think of who would come here and help us now, immediately?'

She drew a shuddering breath and asked, 'Would not your uncle, or Doctor Taylor come?'

He thought for a moment, then was forced to dismiss that idea. 'They are both fully committed with their own patients, my dear. Besides, it's not another doctor I need, but a woman who is unafraid of the cholera, and a couple of men to aid me to carry your mama upstairs.'

With an immense effort of will, Maria fought back her distress, and choked out. 'There is one who might help us.'

'Tell me,' he begged.

'She is a friend of mine.'

Lucas Royston instantly visualised the vacuous pretty features of Charlotte Benton and mentally cringed, knowing that there was no possibility at all of that simpering silly creature being of aid to anyone.

'Tildy Crawford. She will help us; I'm sure of it.'

Royston heard Maria's words, and suddenly his heart lifted. 'But of course. Why did I not think of her. She is an excellent sick nurse, and years since I gave her a deal of training in that field.'

Maria Pitts was much calmer now, and appeared to have regained full control of her emotions. 'I'll go down to Salters Yard and ask her myself,' she stated.

'Yes, you do that, my love,' Lucas Royston gladly seized on this suggestion. 'In the meantime I will attend to your mama, and prepare a room upstairs for her. Go quickly now, sweetheart.'

Maria fled from the house, coatless, bonnetless, dressed only in her gown and bootees, and people stared curiously at her as she ran past them, wondering what was causing this young gentlewoman to act in this totally unladylike manner on this Sabbath morning.

Tildy and her family were all seated around the kitchen table at their breakfast of boiled eggs, bread and coffee, and Daniel Lambert was describing to a wide-eyed Davy the wonders of Sheffield. A city of forges, furnaces and flames.

'Have you completed all your business there?' Old Esther wanted to know, and her nephew shook his head.

'No, I've brought one set of dies back with me so that Brandon can begin using them straight away, but they want me to return and help them with the design of another set.' He paused, and once more gave a slight shake of his head, 'But I shan't go back yet awhiles. I can't leave you here to face this epidemic without me.'

Paradoxically, Tildy was both pleased and disturbed to hear him say this. Pleased that he should love them enough to stay and face danger with them, yet disturbed because while he was away she had only Davy and Old Esther to worry about becoming infected with the cholera.

Daniel smiled lovingly at her, 'I'm going to see John Clayton this day, and arrange our wedding. The banns are called now, and there's naught to stop us getting wed straight away.'

Normally Tildy would have been happy to hear him say this, and would have acceded to his wishes without hesitation. But now, unaccountably to herself even, she instantly rejected the suggestion. 'No, Daniel. Let's wait awhile before we get churched.'

He frowned in surprise, 'But why? The banns are called, are they not? Why should we delay any longer? God only knows we've waited long enough as it is.'

She sighed unhappily. Embarrassment made it hard for her to explain that she was filled with a superstitious dread; that if she and this man were to consecrate their happiness at this time, then something would occur to take that happiness from them.

'Sweetheart, what is it? What's the matter?' His face was filled with worry, and her heart bled to see the distress she was causing him. Knowing that he did not deserve such treatment from her.

Again she sighed heavily, and then hesitantly tried to explain. 'I know you will think me stupid to say this, Daniel. You will call it superstitious nonsense, and mayhap rightly so. But I cannot help but feel that if we flaunt our happiness and contentment in each other by getting wed while so much death and suffering surrounds us, then something will happen to destroy that happiness.

'Let's wait awhile, honey. Let's wait until the cholera is gone from this Parish. Then I'll wed you, and gladly.'

Lambert could see how agitated she was, and his love for her was such, that rather than add to that agitation, he was prepared to fall in with her wishes, even though it meant delaying once again the thing he desired and craved above all else in life: to make Tildy Crawford his wife in the eyes of both man and God.

He nodded agreement, and forced a grin, 'Alright then, sweetheart. But mind my words now, the very minute the cholera has left this parish, I'm going to carry you physically into that Chapel if I have to.'

She smiled in grateful relief, and joked, 'You'll not need to carry me, Daniel, I shall be running there in front of you.'

To dispel the slight air of tension that had been engendered in the room, she turned to young Davy. 'Come on now, son. You should be on your way to school.'

'But it's Sunday, mam!' the boy protested, and his white teeth gleamed in his sun-burned rosy face and he laughed at her momentary confusion. Then Tildy joined in his laughter, and Daniel and Old Esther smiled, and the tension went from the room.

A hammering came on the door, and a voice called anxiously, 'Tildy? Tildy Crawford, are you in there?'

Tildy opened the door and exclaimed in shock, 'Maria, what's the matter, child?'

The girl babbled out a torrent of explanation and pleas for help, and Tildy's initial reaction was the panicky wish to close the door in her face and hope that she would go away and take with her the dangerous threat she represented.

Then, as she stared at the frightened eyes so reddened and swollen with crying, and the soft cheeks stained with tears, shame flooded through Tildy, that she should even consider turning away this terrified young girl, who so desperately sought her help. She thought of how she herself would feel, if any of her loved ones fell victim to the cholera, and no one would come to help her.

'Dear God, what sort of a woman have I become?' she asked herself with a fast-mounting feeling of self-disgust. 'Trying to hide from something that there is no hiding from, if truth be told. Where would I be now, and where would my Davy be, if people had turned away from me when I most needed their help?'

Aloud she said, 'Calm yourself, my dear. Of course I'll come with you.'

She turned to meet Daniel's questioning stare, and offered, 'I have to go and try and help her, Daniel. God knows I'm feared of the cholera. But there's no hiding place from it, is there?'

Sudden certainty in the rightness of her decision flooded through her, and she felt her old fighting spirit re-asserting itself. 'We have to strike back at this vile thing, Daniel. We have to do anything we can against it.'

Loving pride overlayed the anxiety in his face. 'I'll come as well, honey.'

Old Esther scowled doubtfully, 'Be you sure you'm adoing the right thing here?' she challenged. Tildy nodded decisively.

'But supposing you was to bring the infection back wi' you, and it was to strike down young Davy? How would you be able to live wi' yourself then?' the old crone argued stubbornly.

'Suppose I turn this girl away, and stay hiding in here, and then the cholera strikes down Davy, or you, or Daniel? How would I be able to live with myself in that case?' Tildy counter-attacked. 'How could I go seeking aid then, after I'd refused to give aid myself? Tell me, Esther, how could I?'

The old woman's lipless mouth pursed in annoyance, but she was forced to acknowledge grudgingly, 'Ahhrr, you'm right theer, my wench. I mun gi' you that. You'm right theer.'

'Then there's no more to be said,' Tildy told her. Then added, 'Listen, Esther, you're a skilled wise woman, why don't you now begin to search through all your cures and charms, and see if you can find anything among them that might be of help against the cholera?'

The old woman looked doubtful. 'I anna done much in the way o' that for years now.' Suddenly she scowled angrily at Tildy and Daniel, 'And that's your fault, that is. You 'udden't let me practise me charms and spells, 'ud you, in case I was took up for witchcraft.'

'Well we're not trying to stop you from doing so now, are we?' Tildy told her, and coaxed, 'Come now, Esther, try and help.'

The old crone's toothless mouth worked as she muttered silently to herself for some seconds, then she grinned and nodded. 'Alright then, I'll see iffen I can sort summat out that might be o' use in this.'

When Tildy, Maria Pitts and Daniel reached their destination, all of Tildy's earlier trepidations about the cholera returned in full force to torment her, and her breathing became shallow and quick and her throat tightened nervously as the three of them entered the house and went into the parlour.

They found Mistress Pitts lying on her back, but now with a blanket covering her legs and hips.

Lucas Royston greeted them thankfully, 'I'm happy to see you. Now, I've arranged a bed of sorts upstairs for this lady, and I've made an attempt to cleanse her.'

Maria looked shocked that a man should have taken such intimate liberties with her mother's flesh, and Lucas Royston told her apologetically, 'Don't be concerned, my love. I am a doctor, am I not? To me a sick person is not a sexual being. Besides, I could not leave the poor lady lying in filth, could I?'

As he finished speaking the fat woman groaned and writhed and started to retch violently. Gouts of grey-white fluid issued from her mouth, and Maria Pitts uttered a piercing shriek.

Tildy took the girl's arm and led her from the room and into the rear of the house. Maria was sobbing and moaning incoherently and knowing that hysteria was threatening, Tildy shook her hard, and spoke sharply to her, 'Stop this, Maria! You must not act in this way when your mother is in need of all the help you can give her. Stop this nonsense!'

Maria hiccuped and stared at Tildy with wild eyes, and again Tildy told her harshly, 'Stop behaving like a silly child! You must help your mother now, not give way to your own weakness.'

She glanced around the kitchen, then told the younger

woman, 'See there, fill those pans with water and put them on to heat on the cooking range. Get a fire kindled beneath the copper in the wash-house and fill that with water also. Then, when you've done that, find out as much clean flannel cloth as you can, and blankets, sheets and coverlets.'

Maria Pitts stared dumbly at her, and Tildy forced herself to feign an anger that she was far from feeling.

'I'll not tell you again, you little fool!' she shouted threateningly, and once more shook the slender body as hard as she could. 'Get on and do what I have told you to do! Right now!'

After a moment, the girl began to mechanically perform the tasks Tildy had set her, and when she was satisfied that Maria Pitts would be alright, Tildy left her and returned to the parlour.

The effort of generating a false anger had enabled Tildy to force back her own trepidations, and now when she re-entered the room and saw the writhing woman, crying out as the agonising pains tore through her body, Tildy's perception of this disease suddenly altered. Death was not a mysterious stranger to Tildy and neither was illness; now the cholera became just another illness, that carried with it at times the familiar concomitant of death.

'I've met with you before,' Tildy spoke defiantly in her mind to these familiars, 'and I didn't fear you then and I do not fear you now. For all that you have come here with a fresh name and in a fresh guise. You are still the same thing that I knew before, and I can still fight you, as I did before.' She smiled inwardly with a sardonic contemptuous bravado. 'The worst that you can do to me, is to kill me. And I'm not feared to die. So how can you ever really defeat me, or gain a true victory over me?'

Lucas Royston stared at her curiously and Tildy abruptly became aware of his staring, and grew flustered. 'Yes, Doctor, what is it?' she questioned, fearing that she had been voicing her thoughts aloud.

He shrugged and told her, 'Nothing really, Mistress Crawford. It is only that your attitude seems curiously uncaring of what faces us here. Are you not afraid of the cholera?'

Tildy was able to smile, and to answer with complete honesty, 'Naturally I'm afraid of what it might do to me, Doctor Royston. But I'm not afraid to face it and to fight it.'

Admiration dawned in his fine eyes, and he smiled, then suggested, 'Come then, let we three bear this poor lady upstairs, and put her into bed.'

Chapter Thirty-Two

'**H**ER'S GONE, PARSON.' Old Mary Monk took her short blackened clay pipe from her toothless mouth, and with practised fingers closed the sightless eyes, then she placed a tiny feather upon the dark blue lips of the young woman lying on the bed.

The feather did not move, and John Clayton sighed, 'Yes, she's gone, may God have mercy upon her soul.'

Ezra Edkins, his manservant, entered the low-ceilinged room, and Clayton enquired, 'Did you see Doctor Royston? Is he coming here?'

The man shook his head. 'Not yet, he anna, Parson. He said that he'd bin called to an urgent case that he mun see to first.'

The man's eyes moved to the woman on the bed, and his lips writhed in a spasm of pain. 'Mary Andrews gone, has her?' he sought confirmation.

'Ahr, so her has. Not twenty-four years old, and leaves five little 'uns wi'out a mam.'

'You doon't need to tell me that, Mary Monk,' Ezra Edkins rejoined sourly. 'The wench is first cousin to me. Her was more like me younger sister, than me own sister was.'

'You'd best go and fetch Tom Vincent to measure her and the others,' John Clayton instructed, and thought aloud to himself, 'let us see now, that's William Freeman, Mistress Merry and now this poor soul died since yesterday morning.' His heart sank within him, and he sighed despairingly as he looked around the cramped, bad-smelling confines of the cottage. 'This place is totally unsuited for its present purpose, I fear.'

Ezra Edkins and Mary Monk exchanged a meaningful glance, and then the manservant ventured tentatively, 'If I might make so bold, Parson?'

'Yes, Edkins, what is it?' John Clayton replied absently, as if preoccupied with other matters.

'Well, sir, theer's a lot o' wild talk agoing round the Parish, about this place.'

Clayton frowned and asked sharply, 'What sort of talk?'

As Edkins hesitated, the clergyman snapped curtly, 'Come on, man, speak out.'

'Well, sir,' still the man was hesitant, 'the talk is, that theer's all too many o' the ones we brings here am dying.'

Clayton rolled his eyes heavenwards in exasperation. 'That is a piece of information of which I am already full well aware, Edkins.' A sense of his own helplessness weighed heavily on him. 'But what can we do to save them, Edkins? That is an answer I should like to have from you?'

'Oh I knows 'tis no fault o' yourn, Parson, or of the medical gentlemen, but like I said, theer's a lot o' wild talk going round the Parish, and there could well be trouble because of it.'

'For the love of heaven, will you speak plainly, man?' John Clayton's patience strained by lack of sleep and worry, finally snapped. 'Don't prevaricate any longer, Edkins, but speak out plain and clear, will you.'

'Alright, Parson. The talk is that them who're dying here, well, that their bodies is being sold to the hospitals up in Brummagem for the surgeons to practise on. Talk has it, that theer's some on 'um who died in here who could ha' bin saved, iffen they'd bin cared for proper.'

The man's words did not cause Clayton any undue surprise. He knew already that similar rumours had been circulated in the other districts of the country where the cholera had taken hold. Rumours that the doctors were conducting risky experiments in treating the cholera to the detriment of the pauper patients on whom they conducted those experiments. Rumours that the bodies of the dead were being sold to the teaching hospitals for students to practise anatomy on. Rumours that large numbers of the sick poor were being deliberately allowed to die, to ease the burden of the Poor Rate on the better-off classes. Clayton mulled over the information for some time, then asked his manservant, 'Who are the most active in spreading these rumours, Edkins?'

'Well, Sam Millington's had a lot to say for hisself just lately. He took his dad's death very hard, you know, Parson.'

Clayton nodded. Steven Millington had died shortly after being brought into the Quarantine Hospital.

'Sam Millington reckons that he should have been let give his dad a proper Christian burial, in the same grave that his grandad lays in, up in the Chapel Yard. He reckons his dad should have bin laid in earth, not in quicklime,' Edkins went on. 'He's saying that because the box was sealed, he warn't even give the chance to pay his proper last respects to his dad, and that now he arn't even sure that his dad was buried at all, but might well ha' bin sold to the Brummagem Resurrection Men, and a box filled wi' stones and suchlike laid in the Abbey Yard. He says that the reason you'm burying the stiff 'uns in the dark o' night, is to hide what's really gooing on.'

'Yes, yes, very well, Edkins,' Clayton had heard enough, and he bitterly resented the sheer injustice of these vicious rumours.

All the measures that the ignorant were suspecting and complaining against, were being taken solely for their own protection. The dead were wrapped in pitch or tar soaked bandages and placed as quickly as possible into their sealed coffins to avoid the risk of the corpse spreading infection. Each coffin was laid in the mass grave and covered with layers of earth and quicklime, again to lessen the chances of spreading infection through the soil.

The mass graves now being utilised in the old Abbey Yard, were because of the numbers now dying, and the lack of gravediggers prepared to work in the burial yard. The interments were conducted at night to avoid disturbing and frightening by their very frequency the rest of the Parish population, and Clayton himself was taking great pains to conduct each burial service with as much reverence and dignity as was possible given the extreme circumstances surrounding them.

He bowed his head and uttered a short prayer above the body of Mary Andrews, and then told Edkins, 'Go and tell Thomas Vincent he's needed here, please, Edkins.' To Mary Monk he said, 'Just cover the poor girl and leave her in peace, Mistress Monk. Mister Vincent will see to the necessary offices when he comes here.'

Clayton walked through into the adjoining room, just as evil-smelling, low-ceilinged and cramped, and spoke to the man and woman lying together on one of the three beds that filled all available floor space.

'And how are you feeling this day, Cook, and you Mistress Cook?'

Both of these first victims of the cholera had miraculously survived the agonising cramps, extreme dehydration, and collapse into coma, and were now beginning to show signs of recovery. Both of them pallid-featured, wasted and gaunt, but very much alive. They nodded at the Parson and mumbled something which he could not catch.

Clayton regarded them with something akin to wonderment. They were under-sized, drunken, weakly slum-rats, and yet they had survived an onslaught that the tough, mighty-muscled Steven Millington had succumbed to in only a matter of hours.

'Why should that be so?' Clayton asked himself silently, as he stared down at them. 'It's a mystery that has no answer, I fear.'

He turned and looked at the two other beds, both with two patients in them, women in one, men in the other. One of the men was lying comatose, his skin darkly hued. His bedmate was tossing himself from side to side, crying out in pain and muttering in delirium, while the second sick nurse, an ancient pauper named Widow Westwood, was trying ineffectually to wipe the vomit from his mouth and face, her head shaking with palsy on her withered neck, the short clay pipe in her mouth belching out fumes of rancid-smelling smoke.

Both of the sick nurses constantly smoked their strong tobacco as a prophylactic against the cholera, and John Clayton could see no harm in letting them do so, although he himself doubted the efficacy of that protection.

The two sick women were both in the coma stage of the disease, and Clayton considered secretly to himself that they would not live for very much longer. He was also beginning to think that this establishment of a makeshift Quarantine Hospital had been a grave mistake. The idea was sound, but the buildings were not suitable, and the lack of equipment and medicines, of laundry facilities, of proper cooking ranges, of nurses and other attendants combined to ensure the failure of its purpose.

Sixteen patients had been brought here during the last weeks. Ten had died, and of the six remaining, he guessed that only the Cooks might live. Lucas Royston had told him that for those cholera victims who survived, a convalescent period of up to a month might be required, before they could be safely discharged from the hospital.

This thought brought a further grimace to Clayton's face. Sheer lack of space would begin to create insurmountable difficulties should the survival rate of the patients here begin to increase. He had hoped to have the other two cottages made sufficiently habitable by now to give the extra space needed. But the workmen refused point-blank to carry on with the necessary repairs and renovations once the first cholera patients had been brought here, and so only this one building would ever be in use.

A feeling of utter weariness swept over the clergyman, and for a moment his head swam with a sickening dizziness. The overwhelming need to escape from the foul air, and the sights and sounds of suffering forced him to blunder outside.

He stood in the fresh clean air, drawing great draughts of

it into his lungs, and waited for the dizzy spell to pass. The fear that this vertigo might be the initial symptom of a cholera attack momentarily touched him, but he forced the thought away, telling himself that it was only lack of rest, and failure to eat for the last two days, that had brought on this sudden weakness.

'But I am going to need to eat and sleep very soon,' he realised. He knew that even his exceptional strength and stamina could not last out indefinitely under the immense demands he was making of his physical resources.

'I'll wait and have a word with Lucas Royston, and then I'll rest awhiles,' he decided. He thought about Lucas Royston for a moment or two, and smiled wryly. 'What an example of a black sheep becoming whiter than white.'

He found himself admiring the way that the Scotsman had thrown himself whole-heartedly into the battle against the epidemic, and frowned as he thought of those others in the Parish who could have been expected to set an example to the lower orders of selfless commitment to the struggle, but had signally failed to do so.

An old broken bench was set against the outer wall of the cottage, and John Clayton seated himself on it, enjoying the warmth of the sunlight on his face. He closed his eyes and almost instantly slipped into a fitful doze.

'Now then, Parson, shouldn't you be up at the chapel for morning service?' It was Tommy Vincent's voice that brought John Clayton back to a stupefied wakefulness. The clergyman blinked and peered blearily at the undertaker's bluffly grinning face. He pulled out his hunter watch from its waistcoat fob and exclaimed in shock as he saw the time displayed on its ornate face.

'I must go, I'm very late,' he rose, and again his head swam as vertigo assailed him.

'Be you feeling alright, Parson?' Vincent asked with concern.

John Clayton mastered his reeling senses by sheer force of will, and nodded, 'I'm perfectly well, Master Vincent. It is only lack of sleep.'

The other man regarded him shrewdly, and told him, 'Iffen I was you, Parson, I'd goo up the wooden hills to Bedfordshire arter you'se took the service. 'Tis no use you making yourself badly by overdoing things like you bin adoing. We can't have you falling ill on us, can we now. You'm the captain of our army here, and we'd be in a right mess if we hadn't got you to direct us,' he laughed heartily. 'Arter all, just look at what happened to the French when they lost Old Boney.'

'Did Edkins tell you what is required of you?' Clayton found that this man's seemingly inexhaustible fund of good spirits was beginning to irritate him. He wished just once that the man could display a more seemly gravity of demeanour in the face of so much untimely death.

'Ahr, so he did, Parson. Theer's three fresh 'uns, arn't there?'

'Yes,' Clayton answered shortly, and walked away.

Vincent watched him go, and a hardness came into his eyes as he muttered to himself, 'Starting to get you down, is it, Parson? All these buggers dying on you. Well you'll just needs to try and get used to it, my bucko, because I reckon we'll all be seeing a deal more on it afore it's all over and done with.'

He stood at the door of the cottage, calling out merrily, 'Are you theer, Mary Monk, my own sweet dumpling, and wheer's the lovely Milly Westwood? Who's you got for me today? Nobody I'm too fond of, I hope. I doon't like losing friends this time o' day. I'd sooner have that happen when I'se had a few gins in me later tonight. I can stand the grief better than. Mind you, theer's more nor a few that I 'udden't mind measuring up at any time.' He roared with laughter at his own sally, and went inside.

Chapter Thirty-Three

IT WAS SIX o'clock in the morning of Tuesday the 11th of September, and Mistress Pitts had reached the collapsed stage of her illness. In the grey dawn light Tildy, pale-faced with fatigue, looked pityingly at the woman, and marvelled at the change in her physical appearance that the last few hours had wrought. The woman's face and neck was like a grotesque bluish mask, horrible to look upon, the skin hanging from the skull in rivelled layers, and the fat body resembled some monstrous balloon that had had all the air let from it and was reduced to a flaccid, formless heap.

Standing at the woman's head, Lucas Royston lifted the limp arm and felt for the wrist pulse with his fingers. He pursed his lips and gave a slight shake of his head, then told Tildy in a whisper, 'I fear we're losing her, Mistress Crawford.' He beckoned Tildy to take the sick woman's other wrist and feel the pulse for herself.

Tildy did so, and it was some seconds before her finger-tips could detect a faint thready pulsing.

'Is there naught else to be done for her, Doctor Royston?' she whispered.

He considered for some time, then said gravely, 'I think it necessary to administer a profound shock to agitate her vital fluid, Mistress Crawford. I propose to carry out venesection, then a transfusion of saline broth directly into the same vein that I shall bleed her from.'

'Have you used that treatment before?' Tildy wanted to know.

He shook his head, 'No, but I have heard that it has been

used with considerable success in India by our army surgeons there. Come, I'll show you what you must do to aid me in this.'

Under his directions Tildy prepared a solution of five pints of warm water with common salt dissolved into it, into which Lucas Royston also dissolved some alkali powder.

His next instructions caused her to stare at him in shock.

'I'll have to go to my uncle's house, Mistress Crawford, I need to borrow his apparatus for the transfusion. While I'm gone I want you to boil some meat, beef preferably, and when the meat is cooked, then drain off the liquid into the saline solution.'

Seeing Tildy's expression, he explained, 'Mistress Pitts is greatly weakened, and the juices of the beef will give her much needed restoration of strength and energy.'

Tildy saw the logic in what he said, but still, deep in her mind doubt persisted. Alone in the kitchen she sorted out a piece of beefsteak from the cold-box and cut it into small pieces before placing it in a pan of boiling water.

Her doubts as to the wisdom of what the doctor proposed to do strengthened as time passed. Tildy had always been fascinated by the treatment of illness and injury, and over the years from a wide variety of sources she had garnered a considerable amount of knowledge concerning illness and its varied treatments. From Old Esther particularly she had learned much of plants and their healing qualities, and from medical men, including Lucas Royston himself, she had learned their different remedial methods. Some of those methods she rejected without hesitation, her own common-sense telling her that they were useless. Other methods, she was forced to accept as the doctor knowing best, but she still had her own doubts about their efficacy. She had worked as a sick-nurse before, and from her own experience had concluded that doctors invariably killed more patients than they cured. But aware of her own lack of education, and ignorance, she was loth to dispute what the medical men propounded as their established true wisdom.

It was some two hours before Lucas Royston returned,

carrying with him a large tin jug which had a small brass nozzle in its base. Over this nozzle Royston slipped a long narrow leather tube, which in its turn had a pinch-cock attacked to its end. A thin-tubed brass canula which would form the connection between the vein and the leather tube completed the apparatus.

In the bedroom Mistress Pitts appeared almost moribund. Her skin was very dark, her eyes deep-sunk and half-slitted to show a gleam of white, and her breathing could hardly be detected.

Lucas Royston frowned unhappy, 'I fear we may be too late. Still, there's naught to be lost by trying, is there?' He paused, and enquired of Tildy, 'Maria, is she asleep?'

Tildy nodded, 'I looked in on her a few minutes since.'

The man showed his relief. He had dosed the girl with laudanum the previous night, to ensure that she would obtain some degree of respite from her mental sufferings.

Tildy watched while Lucas Royston tied the arm and cut into the vein with his lancet. A turgid trickle of blood issued, oozing down the mottled skin into the bowl beneath and Tildy drew in her breath in surprise as she saw how tar-like it appeared. The bowl filled with a painful slowness, until Royston stated, 'There, that's fourteen ounces. That should do it.'

The tin jug had been set on a tall pot-stand so that it was some five feet above the sick woman's head. Lucas Royston took the thin rounded end of the brass canula and inserted it deep into the opened vein, then turned the pinch-cock and released the saline infusion.

It took almost five full minutes for the liquid to be absorbed, and then Royston tied up the open wound, and they both waited. For perhaps half an hour Tildy stood motionless, breathing shallowly, watching for she did not know what to happen. Then she nearly cried out in shock as Mistress Pitts shuddered violently, opened her eyes and looked at the man at her side.

'How do you feel, ma'am?' Royston's voice trembled, for his shock had been as great as Tildy's.

'I feel much better, Doctor, much better indeed,' the sick woman told him in a weak breathy whisper. 'I'm very thirsty, Doctor. My mouth and throat burns with thirst.'

His eyes were wide with an amazed delight as he looked at Tildy to tell her, 'Fetch some water, Mistress Crawford, quickly now.'

Tildy hurried downstairs and drew fresh cold water from the pump in the wash-house, then came running back upstairs with it. She poured a glass full and held it to Mistress Pitts' dry cracked lips, supporting the woman's head with her arm.

The woman sucked at the cold liquid, some of it dribbling from her mouth and down her chin. Then with a weak motion of her hand signified that she had drunk enough; Tildy gently laid her back upon the pillows.

'How do you feel now, ma'am?' Royston enquired urgently.

'Much better, Doctor. I feel much better.' Her eyes closed and slowly her head rolled to one side. A long gurgling breath escaped from her open mouth, and she died.

At first Tildy could not comprehend what had happened, and she felt dazed as she watched Lucas Royston desperately trying to revive the woman. Then as he shook his head in despair, and straightened his body, a sudden anger burgeoned in Tildy.

'No!' she cried out in sharp protest. 'No! It's not fair! It's not fair of death to take her in this way. Not now at the very moment she was feeling so much better. It's not fair!'

A feeling of bitter hatred rose within her directed against this disease that struck with such merciless savagery, and in such a squalid and filthy manner.

Lucas Royston gaped at her in surprise as she faced him with her fists clenched and bright spots of colour burning in her pale cheeks from the force of her anger. 'We can't let it beat us like this!' Her voice was strident. 'We can't let it win in this way.'

He could find no words to answer her, and only shook his head helplessly.

'There has to be some cure for this cholera,' Tildy declared passionately. 'There has to be some way to defeat it.'

She thought back over the long, long hours without respite that she had spent tending this woman, massaging the cold flesh with turpentine, applying mustard plasters along the spine, heating bran and filling bags with it to warm the body; cleansing the foul discharges and changing the soaked and soiled bedding seemingly constantly, dosing her with calomel, opium, brandy and quinine. While Lucas Royston had slept, while Maria Pitts had slept, Tildy had worked on alone, taking neither drink nor food, nor rest. And all for nothing.

The Scotsman reached out to pat her shoulder sympathetically. 'You are over-wearied, Mistress Crawford, and near to exhaustion. That is why you are feeling so over-wrought about this. Go you home now, and sleep. When you have rested you will feel more philosophic about Mistress Pitts' death. I will arrange matters here and see to Maria.'

When she seemed disposed to argue against him, he pointed out, 'Your loved ones will be anxious about you, Mistress Crawford. It's many hours since you have left your home.'

He smiled encouragingly at her, and urged gently, 'Please, go home now. I don't wish you to be taken ill at this point. I shall be needing you to aid me further. You are the finest sick-nurse I have ever encountered. Go now, please.'

Abruptly a wave of weariness passed over her and she felt herself sag with sheer bodily weakness engendered by too long sustained an effort. Reluctantly, she was forced to accede to his wishes.

As Tildy trudged slowly down Mount Pleasant her mind, tired though it was, would still not allow her any peace. Thoughts came and went with dizzying rapidity, and constantly the visual image of Mistress Pitts opening her eyes and telling the doctor how much better she was feeling repeated itself.

Tildy experienced an eerie sensation that at some point in the long purgatory of Mistress Pitts, the cure for the cholera had presented itself to her, Tildy, and that she had failed to recognise it. Frustration at the inability of her tired brain to marshal her thoughts and recognise that cure now plagued Tildy unbearably, and she felt like screaming aloud.

'It can be beaten. The cholera can be beaten.' This conviction now laid a firm hold on her, and although Tildy recognised that perhaps it was purely wishful thinking on her part, nevertheless she allowed the conviction to dominate her thoughts. 'The cholera can be beaten. It can be. It can be beaten . . . '

The repetition of that single thought, became a chanted refrain in her mind and her footsteps marched in tempo with its cadence, and that cadence stayed with her even after she had reached her home, and gone thankfully to her bed.

Chapter Thirty-Four

ON THE AFTERNOON of Thursday the 13th September, John Clayton called a special meeting of the Select Vestry and the medical practitioners at Saint Stephen's Chapel. Once they had assembled in the small vestry room, the clergyman asked Joseph Cashmore to report the latest cases of cholera.

'Mistress Wilkes, Mistress Wilkes' daughter. Jacob Warner's youngest child, William Bennet, Thomas James's wife, Mistress Hughes, Parson Shuley, Benjamin Pearce's wife, Charles Ludgate, Benjamin Pearce hisself, Mistress Matthews, Mistress Matthews' daughter, Tom Freeman, Mary Clarke, Mistress Hughes' child, William Louch's child. Of them Mistress Matthews and her daughter, Will Louch's child and Parson Shuley are already dead.'

Lucas Royston, his features drawn and grey-looking, spoke up, 'I regret to add that Maria Pitts has also fallen victim to the cholera.'

Knowing the Scotsman's love for the young woman, John Clayton looked at him with concern. 'Is she dead, Lucas?'

Royston shook his head, 'No, but she is gravely ill. I fear for her life.'

'When was she taken ill?' Clayton enquired.

'Yesterday forenoon. Her mother died the previous day and I think the shock of that, following so closely on the death of her father, precipitated the attack.'

'Where is she now?' The clergyman's interest was fired

because the Pitts family were the first of the upper classes of the Parish to be so cruelly savaged by the cholera.

'At her home, I have engaged Mistress Crawford as sick-nurse to her.'

'Well gentleman, there you have it,' John Clayton addressed the meeting at large. 'With these latest fatalities, there is a total of nineteen deaths that can be attributed to the cholera in this Parish. Add that number to those who are afflicted by it and we have something like forty men, women and children who have fallen victim. Plus of course those others in the Ipsley Parish, for whom at present we have assumed responsibility. The question before us is what can we further do to fight this increasingly deadly peril?'

Those present remained silent, even the normally more assertive of the Vestrymen, such as William Hemming and Henry Milward, only sat with grave faces and offered nothing.

John Clayton felt a stirring of resentment as he waited for suggestions which didn't come. He considered that those present, with the exception of Lucas Royston and Joseph Cashmore, were all shirking their responsibilities as leaders of the community. Just as he considered that Lord Aston and the Earl of Plymouth, in their capacities as the largest landowners and County Magistrates, were also shirking theirs by being in London while the cholera was raging in Redditch.

Up until now the main burden of combating the cholera had fallen on the shoulders of himself and Lucas Royston, and their handful of helpers such as Joseph Cashmore, Thomas Vincent, and the two aged crones who were acting as sick nurses down in the Hop Garden cottages. For two weeks Clayton had toiled ceaselessly in his fight against the disease existing on hurriedly snatched meals and scant hours of sleep, and he knew that his handful of helpers had been subject to the same demands on their strength. But no matter how willingly it was being given, that strength was finite, and now Clayton was ready to demand that these others around him should take their fair share in this work for the common good.

'Well, gentlemen,' he invited. 'Has anyone any suggestions to make, or aid to offer?' His hard eyes went from one face to another, and men shifted uncomfortably in their seats, some refusing to meet his accusing stare.

'Well? I am waiting, gentlemen?' He pressed relentlessly and it was inevitably William Hemming who replied.

'What would you have us do, Clayton?' His own self-guilt made him aggressive. 'I thought it was already fully agreed that we wait until an Official Board of Health has been appointed before we take any further action in this matter?'

Clayton's own aggression burst forth. 'This matter, as you so term it, Mister Hemming, has gone too far for us to wait any longer before taking further measures. We know that at least forty souls have been stricken in little more than a sennight, and of those at least nineteen are dead. If we do not exert our utmost endeavours immediately, then God only knows what terrible tragedy may follow.'

'But what more would you have us do?' William Hemming challenged angrily. 'We have already paid to have a hospital established, and we have appointed a surgeon to treat those among the poor who fall victim. We have purchased medicines and comforts, donated bedding and furnishings, and employed nurses. How many have the Parish buried at its own expense so far?'

He answered his own question, 'Nearly every one of the dead, that I'll warrant. It's not cost the paupers a single penny piece to have their dead buried in the Old Abbey Yard, has it now? So I can't think that they have anything to complain of concerning what we have already done for them. But then, it is ever so, is it not, the pauper classes always bite the hands that feed them. Personally speaking, it's in my mind that a good number of the cholera victims have brung it on themselves with their drunkeness and whoring. I think that they've only themselves to blame.'

He paused to look around the table, as if inviting

applause, his fat face rubicund with health and high living.

It was the smugness of William Hemming's expression as he did this that caused Lucas Royston's over-strained nerves to snap. The sufferings he had witnessed during the last weeks, the deaths he had been unable to prevent, the long hours without sleep, the lack of any proper nourishment, and lastly the illness of his beloved Maria, had taken an insidious toll of his mental and physical resources. He had been near to breaking point for some days, although he had refused to accept that fact himself, attributing his state of tension purely to overwork and lack of rest. Now he jumped to his feet.

'You callous bastard!' he hissed venomously. 'How dare you insult a young lady such as Miss Maria Pitts with such statements as you have now made? You smug, callous bastard!'

He hurled himself bodily across the long table at which they were seated and caught William Hemming's thick fat neck between his hands. The impact of his body sent William Hemming's chair toppling backwards and the two men sprawled onto the floor, Hemming bawling out in pain and fright, Lucas Royston hissing curses between his clenched teeth.

John Clayton was the first to react. He came in a rush to hook his arm around Royston's neck and tried to heave him away from the other man. The Scotsman's maniacal rage imparted to his slender body a fearful strength however, and Clayton could not break Royston's hold on Hemming's throat.

The instant he realised this, the clergyman acted without hesitation. He released his grip and clubbed both his fists, then brought them downwards with a terrible force against the base of Royston's skull. The Scotsman was knocked senseless and fell across the gasping, choking William Hemming.

Clayton lifted the inert body as easily as if it had been a small child's, and gently laid the unconscious Royston on his back. The two doctors present, Hugh Taylor and

Alexander Pratt came to minister to both the combatants, and Clayton stood aside to give them room.

He scowled at the rest of the men in the room, and thundered with a furious disgust. 'Before the God I worship, gentlemen, I demand of you to tell me what is happening to us all? People are suffering and dying in this Parish hour by hour and day by day, and all that we, the so-called better class can do, is to fight one with another as if we were brutish ignorant Needle Pointers. What in Heaven's name has happened to us? What have we become?'

'What have we become?' The same question was reverberating in Tildy Crawford's brain, and the same furious disgust filled her being as she stood in Salters Yard looking down at the woman and child lying on the cobbles. It was Agnes Dolton and her son, a boy aged about eight years. The woman's husband, Arthur Dolton, was a stone mason and the family had rooms in the middle tenement of the row.

A group of the neighbours were gathering around Tildy, who had only this moment entered the yard on her return from the Pitts' house, where another nurse had relieved her at the bedside of Maria.

'What's happened here? Why are Agnes and her boy laying here like this.'

Tildy could see that both of them were semi-conscious, and judging by the state of their clothing were both in the grip of the cholera.

'Fuckin' Arthur Dolton chucked 'um both out o' the house, not two minutes since.' It was Charlie Duggins, his breath reeking with raw gin, his thin unshaven face wolfish with anger, who vouchsafed this information. 'And him a fuckin' ranting Methody pisspot, as well. So much for Christian charity, aye!'

'What?' Tildy could hardly believe what she was hearing, 'Arthur Dolton has thrown his own wife and child from the house when they're ill like this?'

'Well, it's more nor likely it's the cholera they got, arn't it. And I reckon that Methody barstard is shittin' hisself in case he catched it from 'um. That's why he slung 'um out.'

Charlie Duggins seemed uncaring about the disease, but some of the other neighbours started nervously when they heard the word, and drew back from the woman and child.

Duggins knelt by Agnes Dolton and felt the skin of her face and forehead, and asked her, 'Wheer's it paining you, Aggie?'

She grunted incoherently and the man rose and stated positively. 'Yes, theer's no doubt on it. They'se both took the cholera.'

'Dear God save us all,' one of the women moaned in frightened tones, and Charlie Duggins swung on her and spat out contemptuously.

'It anna bit o' good asking that bastard to save you, missus. We has to save ourselves down here in the Salters Yard.' He pointed down at the woman and child, 'See theer, that's what one o' God's favourite children has just done. Chucked his own missus and kid out on the fuckin' cobbles, because they'se took the cholera. I says fuck him, and fuck his bleedin' God, as well.'

Again he knelt by the sick woman and told her with a rough kindliness, 'Doon't you moither yoursen, Aggie, I'll ha' you took into the hospital. They'll be able to look arter you and your babby theer. You'll be alright. Just try and hold on whiles we gets you down theer. That's all you'se got to do.'

Tildy stared at the man in wonderment, contrasting his present behaviour with the savage, wife-beater she knew him as.

He became aware of her staring, and grinned drunkenly at her, 'Ahrr, Tildy Crawford, I anna all bad you see.'

She could not help but retort waspishly, 'Then it's a pity you can't show the same sort of kindness to your own wife and kids, Charlie Duggins.'

'Horses for courses, missus. Horses for courses!' he

answered airily, and cupping his hands around his mouth bellowed up at the O'Leary's windows. 'Am you theer, Paddy? Come on, rouse your fuckin' self, 'ull you.'

The Irishman's broad red face poked out from the casement. 'Jasus, Joseph and Mary, can't a man get any bloody slape in this soddin' hole. What d'ye mean wi' waking me, Duggins, ye noisy, big-mouthed bastard ye?'

Duggins pointed at the woman and child, and Pat O'Leary's features twisted with sudden pity. 'God save the poor souls. I'll be down directly.'

Once again Tildy was forced to marvel at the strange contradictions in people's natures. Here were two wife-beating drunkards showing a willingness to aid a stricken woman and child, whose own husband and father had been considered a paragon of domestic virtues, yet had acted towards her and her child with a vile cruelty when they most needed his aid.

Within a very few minutes Pat O'Leary had fetched his horse and cart to the yard and he and Charlie Duggins gently laid the woman and child on its floorboards.

'Do you need me to come down to the hospital with you, Paddy?' Charlie Duggins offered, but the Irishman shook his head.

'No, there's no need, Charlie. There'll be people there to help me unload these poor craturs.'

Once the cart had lurched away up Alcester Street there was a sudden metamorphosis in the mood of the neighbours. Anger against Arthur Dolton began to be voiced and the mood of the group to turn ugly.

'That bastard anna fit to dwell among decent people.'

'He deserves hanging for what he done.'

'The bastard should be taught his fuckin' lessons.'

'Wheer's he at now?'

'Skulking in his fuckin' house, I reckon.'

'Let's have a look at him then.'

Charlie Duggins went to the Doltons' front door and began to hammer on it, shouting at the top of his voice, 'Come on out here, Dolton! We wants words wi' you.'

All was silent within the curtained room, and old Widow Sprake jeered contemptuously.

'The bugger's too fritted to show hisself.'

'Let's goo in theer and fetch him out then,' a man suggested, and this was greeted with a concerted howl of agreement.

'Goo and fetch your hammer here, Jakey.'

Jakey Simmons, who worked as a blacksmith's striker and wore the fringed leather apron of his trade, was quick to run to his own rooms and reappear within moments hefting the long handled sledge hammer.

'Giss it here,' Charlie Duggins snatched the tool and swung it with all the strength of his wiry body. The big iron head crashed against the flimsy wooden panelling and smashed it inwards. Several more blows in quick succession left the splintered wreckage of the door hanging from its hinges, and while the crowd cheered, Charlie Duggins and Jakey Simmons disappeared inside the room.

Tildy, although as angry and disgusted with Arthur Dolton as the rest of them, nevertheless could not help but feel a twinge of pity when Duggins and Simmons came back out into the yard dragging the screaming, struggling, terrified stone mason with them.

Duggins brutally cuffed the man across the face and Dolton cried out and cowered down low to the cobbles, trying to shield his head with his arms.

Jakey Simmons' normally pleasant expression was a ferocious mask of jeering contempt as he grabbed Dolton's hair and forced his head back so that he could spit into his face.

Dolton began to sob and beg for mercy, and Charlie Duggins bellowed, 'Mercy is it, you yellow-gutted barstard? It's mercy you wants, is it? Like what you showed your missus and kid, you Methody pisspot?'

Moaning and sobbing Dolton shook his head wildly, 'I was feared! I was feared o' the cholera! I couldn't help mesen! I couldn't help it.'

'No, and neither could they, you rotten bugger!' Widow

Sprake yelled, and with howls of fury the mob closed around the crouching cowering man and rained a hail of kicks and blows upon him, while he shrieked, and on hands and knees scrabbled frantically in a vain attempt to escape them.

Tildy stood motionless, helpless in the grip of a mental dilemma. The darker, more primitive part of her personality lusting to join in this assault, the other part, gentler and more influenced by the religious indoctrination of her childhood, regarding it with horror and repulsion.

'Come away, Tildy! Come away now!'

She felt her arms gripped on each side, she turned her head first one way then the other, and she saw that Charles Brown and Old Esther had hold of her. She allowed them to draw her away and back to her own front door without resistance; there the three of them stood and watched what was happening.

'Shouldn't we try and stop them?' Tildy asked Charles Brown, but yet deep within herself she knew that she had no real desire to try and do so, and thought with a rueful resignation, 'I might as well accept the fact that deep down I'm just as much a savage as any one of them.'

Almost defiantly, she silently challenged whatever deity might be cognisant of her thoughts, 'Why should not Arthur Dolton receive punishment for what he did to his helpless wife and child? We are taught from birth by our so-called betters that all punishment should be left to God, and to his appointed agents on earth, namely themselves. But they are only too eager to punish someone who offends against themselves and their kin, or takes their property, or challenges their right to rule. They don't care what happens to the women and children of the poor, and the proof of that can be seen in every slum court and alleyway in this Parish. So be damned to what You or anyone else might think of me, I am pleased to see Arthur Dolton get his just deserts.'

By now Arthur Dolton had collapsed, and was lying face downwards, arms widespread, blood already pooling on the cobbles as it oozed from his broken nose and lacerated mouth and a dozen other cuts and abrasions.

It was Charlie Duggins who called the others off from their assaults. 'Leave him now. The bastard's had his lumps.'

He hawked and spat onto the bloodied head, then in final token of contempt he unlaced the cod-piece of his breeches and deliberately urinated on Dolton's head and body.

Beside Tildy, Charles Brown exclaimed in disgust as he saw this. 'Goddamn it, that man Duggins is worse than an animal!'

Tildy made no reply, she was momentarily too appalled by the realisation that a small part of her being had applauded that final gesture of contempt.

Brown left her side and went to the fallen man, and untying the kerchief from around his own neck, used it to try and wipe the blood from Dolton's head wounds so that he, Brown, could assess the damage done.

'Leave the bugger lay!' Duggins growled and others agreed with him.

'Yes, leave him.'

'Let him bleed.'

'Serves the bastard right.'

Brown ignored them, and totally disregarded the darkly threatening glares and gestures that some of the group directed at him. Instead he called back over his shoulder to Tildy. 'Will you bring me a bowl of water and some clean rags please?'

Tildy's first impulse was to refuse. A deep anger still burned in her directed against Arthur Dolton. Then, quite suddenly the sharp visual memory of her first encounter with a battered and bloodied Charles Brown came into her mind, and the anger left her, and Arthur Dolton metamorphosed into just one more sorely injured human being who needed help.

She went into her own house and brought out a bowl of fresh water and a large piece of clean flannel, then helped Charles Brown to pull Arthur Dolton clear of the pool of blood and urine he lay in, and stood by while Charles Brown cleansed the sounds.

The neighbours watched in silence, and made no move to prevent Tildy from bringing Charles Brown's medical chest to him, from which he took needle and thread to stitch the deeper cuts, and salves and plasters to cover the abrasions.

Charles Brown worked in silence, only once breaking it in order to say to the now loudly groaning and complaining Dolton, 'Hold your noise, man. Try and show some courage for once in your miserable life, will you.'

When Dolton's wounds had been dressed, Tildy and Brown lifted him to his feet. He offered no word of thanks for their aid, but only cursed viciously and shook his clenched fist at the faces around him.

'I'm going to fetch the Constable to you lot. You wicked bleeders! I'm going to have all on you put in the Lock-up. You just see iffen I wun't.'

With that he went staggering out of the yard and towards the Chapel Green.

Charles Brown grinned wryly and shook his head, 'A most unpleasant fellow, that one. He really is not deserving of help, is he?'

'Then why did you help him?' Tildy challenged.

He smiled at her, and riposted, 'Why did you help me to help him, Tildy?'

And to that, she could find no easy reply.

Chapter Thirty-Five

FOR MORE THAN a week Maria Pitts had fought for her life with a tenacity that both astounded and humbled Tildy, who had not believed that a flighty young girl could display such a quiet dogged courage. She endured her sufferings without complaint, and even when writhing in the agonies of cramps did not scream and rail against her fate, as did so many others.

Every moment he could spare from his other myriad duties Lucas Royston spent at the girl's bedside, and Tildy only left her to snatch a few hours of sleep and hurried meals.

Royston stuck to the gentlest methods of treatment that he could devise, and mindful of the example of the death of Mistress Pitts, made no attempt to bleed or transfuse the girl, or carry out any other such shock remedies.

There were days when it seemed that the crisis had passed, and that Maria had weathered the storm. Then there would be a relapse, and again death would threaten to snuff out the flickering flame of life. The only thing that in her lucid hours Maria Pitts did complain of, was the burning thirst that she could never seem to assauge, no matter how much fresh cool water she drank in effort to gain relief from its torments.

Although worn and wasted by her illness, Maria Pitts still retained traces of her beauty; Tildy found the lucent grey eyes shining from the gaunt face almost unbearably poignant. She could not help but contrast the girl as she had been such a short time past with what she had now become.

There were several occasions during the long days and nights that she spent tending the sick girl that the eerie sensation she had previously experienced following the death of Mistress Pitts returned with full force into Tildy's mind. The vague feeling that the cause of, and cure for, this dread disease was presenting itself to her, and yet, try as she might to rack her brain until it wearied and dizzied within her skull, Tildy could not take a firm grasp of that feeling. Always it tormented her by its very elusiveness, seeming like some perverse entity that delighted in hovering on the fringes of her consciousness tantalisingly close, yet always able to slip away when Tildy came near to grasping and imprisoning it in her mind.

Paradoxically, although she was working for such long hours tending the sick girl, and then in her scant periods of freedom from the sickbed looking after her own loved ones, Tildy had never felt in better health or stronger in her life, and her physical appearance and appetites matched her feelings. At times she felt ashamed of her own hunger for Daniel's loving, and said as much to him one night after they had made love. He had only laughed tenderly and drawn her close. She rationalised her hungers by deciding that, surrounded as she was by sickness and death, it was only natural that her own life-force should intensify in all directions as a reaction to the situation.

It was now half-past eight o'clock in the morning of Monday the 24 September 1832, and Tildy was due to report back to the Pitts' house in Mount Pleasant to relieve the old woman who had acted as Maria Pitts' nurse during the night. She left Salters Yard with Davy, and side by side the two of them walked in warm and close companionship towards the crossroads of the Chapel Green.

Davy was on his way to Henry James school in Evesham Street and Tildy was following what had become her daily practice, which was to go and read the list of new cholera cases which were posted on the door of the Saint Stephen's Chapel every morning by John Osborne, the local printer.

As they traversed the sunlit town Tildy found herself

marvelling at its air of normality. Shopkeepers arranging their wares or bargaining with early-shopping white aproned and mobcapped housewives with their big willow baskets on their arms. Schoolboys in tasselled caps and carrying their satchels of books, skylarking and hooting their way to their lessons, artisans and tradesmen with bags of tools slung over their shoulders trudging to their various places of work, a solitary sweep, tall-hatted and liberally sooted, his tiny climbing-boy pathetic in rags and filth following at his heels like a cowed puppy, some horses and carts, and a resplendent young dandy parading like a peacock in all his garish finery.

'Do you know, Davy, you would never think that there is such trouble and grief in the town, to look at it this morning, would you?' Tildy remarked.

Her fine tall son grinned at her, and her heart melted as she saw how handsome he was becoming, with his dark eyes and fine teeth and thick black curly hair.

'Old Henry says that the cholera is the visitation of God upon this Parish as punishment for its wicked sinfulness. He says that until men turn once more to the Lord, and walk in the Paths of Righteousness, then we shall never be free of it.'

'He would say that, wouldn't he?' Tildy smiled with sardonic amusement, visualising the grim old 'Hellfire and Brimstone' schoolmaster.

'Is he right, mam? Is the cholera God's visitation on this Parish?' the boy asked her, very seriously.

Tildy sighed heavily, 'I don't know, son. To me it seems more like the work of the Devil.'

'Arn't you feared of catching it yourself, mam?'

Tildy smiled at him, and shrugged, 'At times, I am, Davy. But mostly, I just think to myself that it's all a matter of chance.'

'But what is it really, mam? What causes the "Blue Vomit"?' He used the term for the disease that had been coined by the Needle Pointers.

Tildy could see how intensely he hungered for this knowledge, and she hesitated before telling him, 'In all truth, Davy, nobody seems to really know what it is or what causes it. Some say that is is bad food or drink or poison, others that it's bad air, or a miasma that arises suddenly from water, or from the earth. Some say we infect each other, and others say that we don't. It seems to me, that you may pay your money and take your choice.' She smiled ruefully, and then asked him, 'What do you think it is, honey? What do you think causes people to catch it?'

His face was deeply thoughtful. 'Well, Old Henry says it is the visitation of God, but then the Parson tells us when he comes to the school that God is Love, so I can't really believe that God would do such a terrible thing to people as to give them the Blue Vomit, can you?'

Tildy shook her head, 'No, I can't really believe that myself.'

Davy went on, 'One of the monitors at school told me that a fly carries it. The fly enters the mouth of someone when they're asleep and lays the "Cholera Eggs" inside. And then, when the person dies, the fly crawls out of the person's eye and flies off to find another victim.'

He grinned as Tildy grimaced and shivered involuntarily, 'That's horrible, Davy.'

'I think my friend Sammy Crook has got the right explanation though, mam. Because you know how clever he is at scientific things.'

'Oh yes, and what does Sammy Crook think it is?' Tildy smiled with a grim humour, and waited for yet another shudder-invoking revelation.

'Sammy says that it's caused by the "Miasmatic Electric Effluvium".'

'The what?' Tildy exclaimed.

Davy was mischievously delighted by this reaction of his adored mother. 'The "Miasmatic Electric Effluvium",' he crowed and hooted with laughter, then went on excitedly, 'Sammy says that the electrical fluids in the air make the body fluids turn acidic and thus produce the cholera. He says that before every epidemic there are lots of flashes of lightning to be seen in the skies, and all this lightning diffuses into the air and is absorbed into the bodies of the victims. He says the proof of the matter is that the blue vomit kills very quickly, and it leaves its victims all black and shrivelled just like a lightning strike does.'

His eyes glowed with admiration as he told Tildy, 'Sammy is really brilliant, you know, mam. I'm sure he's right. What do you think?'

She chuckled fondly, and reached out to ruffle his thick black curls. 'Well, I suppose it's as good a reason as any that I've been told of, honey. Go on now, run or you'll be late, and then it won't be lightning that strikes you, but Henry James' cane.'

He submitted impatiently to her brief kiss on his cheek and then ran ahead of her with the speed and grace of a young hunting animal. Tildy watched him go and her heart welled over with the love she bore him.

At the Saint Stephen's Chapel a knot of people were gathered around the great double doors, staring at the sheets of poster paper nailed to the thick, black-painted planking.

Tildy moved through them until she was close enough to read the words printed on the posters in heavy black type. Firstly she turned her attention to the list of the latest cholera cases, and felt a chill of apprehension as she read, 'William Aston, Cornelius Styler.'

Aston, she knew, lived on the stretch of road that joined Headless Cross to Crabbs Cross, and Cornelius Styler was better known as 'Nail' Styler, the landlord of the White Hart inn at Headless Cross.

'Mistress Emms, Ebenezer Morris' son, and his daughter, and his wife.' These were the family of the Poorhouse Master at Webheath hamlet, and one of the pauper inmates.

'William Aston's daughter, Richard Mence, Mistress Prescott, Joseph Webb's daughter, Henry Aston's son and daughter, Thomas Dolphin, May Dolphin . . . '

There were a few other names on the list, mostly unknown to Tildy, but from those she did know, and the ones she remembered from the onset of the epidemic, she was able to see that the cholera was widening and strengthening its grip throughout the entire Parish.

Something else also struck her, and that was the pattern of the homes of the people named. It seemed that these outbreaks formed distinct pockets of close locality.

'If that's the case, then Charles Brown must be wrong when he says that the cholera isn't contagious. They must be infecting each other,' Tildy thought, but then was forced to consider the fact that people like herself, Lucas Royston, Charles Brown, Tommy Vincent, Pat O'Leary, and many others in constant contact with the disease had not been infected by it.

Black crosses had been marked against the names of those who were already dead, and tears stung Tildy's eyes as she saw that several of the smaller children had been taken.

'God comfort their poor parents,' she murmured, then turned her gaze to the next poster and began to read, 'At the Council Chamber Whitehall, 21 September 1832. By the Lords of His Majesty's Most Honourable Privy Council. It is this day ordered by their Lordships that a Board of Health be constituted for the Parish of Tardebigge in Worcestershire. Consisting of the following members, viz . . .

The Right Honorable, the Earl of Plymouth.

The Right Honorable, Reverend the Lord Aston.

Reverend John Clayton.

The Churchwardens, Chapelwardens and Overseers for the time being.

Surgeons. Mr. H. Taylor.

          Mr. A. Pratt.

          Mr. L. Royston.'

Tildy scanned the appended list of names of the various wardens and overseers numbering fifteen in all, and grimaced cynically as she thought of how much they would claim from the Parish in expenses, and how little they would do to actually aid the fight against the epidemic, notwithstanding the final stern admonition on the poster.

'. . . And the said Board are to proceed in the execution of the duties required of them accordingly.

signed. C.C. Greville Esq. Clerk to the Privy Council.'

'Well, at least now that we've an officially appointed Board of Health the Select Vestry will have no excuse for not voting more funds to fight the cholera with,' she thought.

Tildy turned to find Augustus Bartleet standing close behind her. In the morning sunlight he presented a bizarre spectacle, with his painted lips, rouged cheeks and enamelled hands, and his bright blue coat with its hugely padded shoulders and wasplike corseted waistline. He raised his tall white tophat and his long flowing locks waved gently in the breeze.

'Good morning to you, Mistress Crawford. Might I have a private word with you?'

She nodded and moved a little way with him until they were out of earshot of the people reading the posters. Although many townspeople mocked Augustus Bartleet for his foppish appearance and mannerisms and derided his way of life, Tildy had conceived an ever increasing liking and respect for him during the epidemic. He had given his time and aid unstintingly to help the stricken, and had shown a courage that many of his detractors sadly lacked. Now he told Tildy sombrely, 'I am the bearer of sad tidings, Mistress Crawford.'

She knew with an absolute certainty that he was going to tell her of Maria Pitts' death. 'It concerns Maria Pitts. Sadly she died early this morning.'

The news brought grief to Tildy's heart, and also that familiar hot and angry resentment that once again the cholera had gained the victory.

'I was with her when it happened,' the man went on. 'I had gone to take a message to Lucas Royston. It seemed to me that death took her with a merciful lack of suffering at the end. Her life went gently from her. God rest her soul.'

'Amen to that,' Tildy sighed sadly, then asked, 'And Doctor Royston? How is he bearing up?'

'Very hard. He is sitting with her now, and refuses to leave her side. I think it best that he be left undisturbed until he has come to terms with his grief.'

'I'll go there now and see what I can do to help him,' Tildy said.

'Little enough, I fear,' Bartleet told her. 'In fact I was on my way to your house to tell you that there was no need of your going to the Pitts' house. Lucas asked me to tell you that he would prefer to be left alone at this time. And truly I think it best that we all respect his wishes in this matter, Mistress Crawford. After all, there's nothing can be done for the poor young lady now, and nothing that can be done to bring comfort to Lucas. He must be given time to grieve.'

Tildy saw the sense in what he was saying, and accepted it. 'Very well, Master Bartleet. I'll not go there then.'

A sudden curiosity caused her to ask. 'What happened exactly, to bring on her death? Only when I left her yesterday evening she was feeling a little more comfortable and seemed to be improving.'

'She had a relapse and began to vomit again, and then slipped into coma. At least, that is what the old woman informed Lucas had happened. She said that after you had left Maria was complaining of thirst, and drank a deal of water.'

Tildy nodded. 'Yes, she was complaining of thirst all through the afternoon, and drank much water then. She wouldn't take anything else, only water, cold fresh water.'

A thought suddenly burgeoned in her brain which at first she could only marvel at as a complete nonsense. 'Water? Cold fresh water?' she murmured, and the man stared at her curiously.

'What's that you say, Mistress Crawford?'

She glanced at him, her lucent brown eyes wide and wondering. 'Water, Master Bartleet, I was thinking of water.'

Abruptly she told him, 'Good day to you, Master

Bartleet,' and hurried away across the central crossroads and up Evesham Street.

Outside Joseph Cashmore's cottage she halted, and stood for a moment or two. 'He'll think me mad,' she realised, and doubt rose in her.

While she stood a young woman came hurrying along the street and up to Cashmore's door. 'Is he home?' she asked Tildy.

'I don't know.'

The young woman knocked on the Constable's door, and Cashmore opened it. He recognised his visitor. 'It's Meg Wilkinson, arn't it?'

'Yes Master Cashmore. I'se just come to tell you that Old Mother Cater has just fell down wi' the Blue Vomit, outside the Toll House up Mount Pleasant.'

Tildy gasped with shock; Mother Cater was the old woman who had been helping her to nurse Maria Pitts.

'Alright Meg, I'll get the cart up theer and have her fetched down to the hospital.' Joseph Cashmore told the girl, then spoke to Tildy.

'Now then, my duck, what can I do for you?'

As with Augustus Bartleet, Tildy and Joseph Cashmore had conceived a deep mutual respect and liking for each other during the course of the epidemic, and the man's eyes were warm as he looked at Tildy.

'If you please, Master Cashmore, do you have the full list of cholera cases here?'

'I do,' he informed her. 'Why does you ask me that?'

'Can I see it please?'

'Surely, you come on inside, and you can look it over whiles I'm fetching Mother Cater down to the Hop Garden.' The man raised his voice and shouted back over his shoulder, 'Wife, see to Mistress Crawford, 'ull you. Bring that list o' names that's on the dresser for her to see.'

Tildy sat at the table and carefully scanned the list of names. She knew enough of them to be able to picture their homes, and a sense of excitememt began to build in her as she thought that she could discern a distinct pattern. Vague ideas swirled around in her brain, and with her eyes still fixed on the beautifully written copperplate list, she tried to steady and grasp those swirling ideas and clearly formulate them.

She could see that there were groupings of cases, and she racked her memories to try and visualise exactly what the locations looked like where the groupings occurred. Mostly those locations were slums, and Tildy could appreciate the theory of a miasma being responsible for the disease in those slum areas. But the Pitts' house was not in a slum area. It stood alone, in one of the most healthy and salubrious quarters of the Parish. There could be no miasma created as a result of filth and ignorance there.

She sat upright in the straight-backed chair and a sensation of tightness constricted her chest and caused her breathing to become fast and shallow.

'If cholera is contagious, then why have I not caught it from the Pitts family? Why has Mother Cater caught it and not me, or Lucas Royston?' Her thoughts raced in wild spirals, and among those spirals one single word reappeared again and again and again. Water. Water. Water. Water.

Memories of both Mistress Pitts and Maria Pitts begging for water came sharply into Tildy's consciousness, and more memories of how after drinking that water varying intervals had elapsed before they had suffered relapses, and had again begun to void and vomit.

She considered Paoli's Row and the number of cholera cases there. 'They all draw their water from the Big Pool, don't they, and that man was found drowned in the Big Pool. Sweet Turf down in the Ispley Parish part of Bredon had also suffered many cases, and she recollected that the people there drew their water from another surface pool, which was partially fed from the same stream that helped to fill the Big Pool.'

The certainty that she was on the verge of discovery suddenly exploded in Tildy's mind, and she felt dizzied with it. Her initial impulse was to run to Parson Clayton and the various doctors and tell them of her discovery. Then she forced herself to remain seated, and consider the matter more calmly. For long, long minutes she sat and struggled to calm her turbulent emotions and slowly she regained control of herself.

'I think that somehow or other the cholera travels through the water, and people drink it and become infected,' she now concluded, and was surprised at how calmly and rationally she could accept that conclusion, now that the first waves of dizzying excitement of discovery had exhausted themselves.

'Now, the Pitts' house draws its water from a well, and just below it the Round House is almost in a straight line, and there have been cases of cholera there. Does the same stream feed both wells, I wonder?'

She marvelled at how clearly her brain was able to evaluate what scant information she had of the water supplies, and decided in the same instant that she needed to know more about the water supply at each focal point of the separate outbreaks of cholera in the Parish.

Tildy was alone in the cottage, Mistress Cashmore having gone out on some errand. She thought briefly, and decided that she could safely borrow the list of cases for a few hours.

'I'm going to go to every household that's had cholera and find out where they take their water from. Then, when I go to tell the Parson and the doctors of what I've discovered, I'll have the full information for them to act upon.'

A sudden exultation of battle filled her being at the realisation that if she was correct in her assumptions, then she would be striking back at this terrible disease, and perhaps on the way to gaining victory over it.

'If I'm right, then we shall begin to know you.' The cholera became a single malignant entity in her imagination, and she hurled her defiance at it. 'If I'm right, then you will be beaten, just as I always said you would. You'll be beaten!'

Chapter Thirty-Six

THE APPOINTMENT OF an official Board of Health made it possible for John Clayton to enforce his wishes upon the Select Vestry in the matter of a fresh levy for funds, and for him to appoint a paid secretary to the Board in the person of John Osbourne the Printer.

John Osbourne was a man in his mid-thirties. Tall and very thin, his face badly pitted by old smallpox scars, and his teeth rotting in his head, Osbourne had not lived in Redditch for long. He was a native of Gloucestershire and his speech was a rustic drawl, which caused the locals to mock him, but he was possessed of abundant energy and drive, a shrewd and acute brain, and was an educated and multi-talented man. All these attributes aroused the antagonism of the more xenophobic of the local-born parishioners, whose loyalties were fiercely parochial, and who deeply resented the fact that a newcomer should be given powers to direct them in their conduct of affairs.

Osbourne threw himself into his new duties with tremendous zeal, working through the night in his printshop to produce the varied forms the Government in London required to be used for its official returns and archives. He attended each daily meeting of the newly appointed Board and kept detailed minutes of the proceedings. He took it upon himself to become the messenger of the Board in imparting its decisions to the public at large, and to those in particular whose services it required. He also put forward many suggestions of his own concerning the measures to be adopted to deal with the epidemic, one of which was to divide the Parish into districts and for each district appoint an Inspector who was authorised to visit the houses in that district and report back to the Board of Health on whatever he found there that could be termed a danger to the public health, such as fresh cases of illness, heaps of filth and rubbish, neglected and choked privies and sewage drains, animals such as pigs kept within the rooms, etc., etc. . . .

Although he had gained the confidence and trust of John Clayton, and through him of Lord Aston and the Earl of Plymouth, and was increasingly empowered by them to put his ideas into action, John Osbourne very quickly succeeded in arousing fierce resentment and antipathy among many of the town's leading citizens. But it was not the leading citizens of the Parish who confronted John Osbourne with the first open defiance of his new-found authority.

By the first day of October Osbourne had completed his preparations to step to the forefront in the battle against the epidemic and now, at half-past five o'clock on this drizzly grey Monday morning, he mustered his helpers in front of the doors of Saint Stephen's Chapel. There were six aged paupers borrowed from the Poorhouse at Webheath and liberally dosed with gin and brandy, every man wearing a mask of vinegar-soaked flannel over his mouth and nostrils and carrying buckets, shovels and cleansing materials. Henry Pardoe, one of the newly appointed Inspectors, stood next to them.

Pat O'Leary was there as was Thomas Vincent, each with their respective horses and vehicles, and Joseph Cashmore and three of his Deputy Constables, armed with their staffs of office. Standing apart from the rest, swaying visibly from the effects of too much brandy, was Lucas Royston who, ravaged by his grief for Maria Pitts, now spent all his waking hours drinking and working, with no social intercourse and seemingly with little or no interest in his own wellbeing.

John Osbourne looked over his small army with a satisfied

smile, and then placed himself at their head and led them down towards their objective, Paoli's Row.

The inhabitants of Paoli's Row had been giving John Osbourne much cause for concern these last few days. Since the onset of the epidemic many of them had fallen victim to the cholera, and at first they had allowed their sick to be taken to the hospital and into quarantine. But many of those so taken had died, and now the remaining inhabitants were refusing to admit the newly appointed Inspector, Henry Pardoe, into their homes.

The various bells of the needle mills and factories were ringing out to call in their workers as the small procession went down Red Lion Street. It was only these bells that were now permitted to be rung in the Parish, the Chapel bells used to toll the knells of the dead were now silenced by order of the Board of Health, it being considered that the frequency of the mourning bells were causing too much alarm and despondency among the populace.

The workers coming out of their houses in Red Lion Street and Paoli's Row, stared at the procession with open hostility, and one man ran back under the archway at the side of the Red Lion inn, and along the length of the foetid Silver Street rousing its denizens with shouts of, 'The Resurrectioners am acoming! The Resurrectioners am acoming!'

Joseph Cashmore could hear the shouts echoing down the narrow crooked alleyways and he frowned with worry. He was well aware that there had been an upsurge of malicious rumour-mongering sweeping through the parish these last days concerning the Quarantine Hospital and the treatment of the cholera dead. It was being said, and by many believed, that the doctors were deliberately allowing the patients at the hospital to die, and then selling the corpses for purposes of dissection. Some rumours even had it that the unfortunate patients were in some cases being murdered by poisoning, and yet others that there had been cases of people being buried alive in the Old Abbey Yard because of the doctors' inefficiency.

In the short time it took the procession to traverse Red Lion Street and come up to Paoli's Row, the inhabitants had boiled out from their mean hovels, and armed with pokers, clubs, and whatever else they could lay their hands on, they were now standing in a mob on the roadway above their homes.

Cashmore went to John Osbourne's side. 'I doon't like the looks o' this, Master Osbourne.'

The pock-marked face of the other was pale with apprehension. 'Neither do I, Master Cashmore. But we have our duty to perform. Mayhap when I've explained why we're here like this, then they'll allow us to proceed with what we must do.'

Cashmore looked at the mass of savage faces glaring at him, and shrugged doubtfully, but only said quietly, 'It's best you spakes soft to 'um then, Master Osbourne. They looks to be in an ugly mood.'

Osbourne stepped towards the crowd and held up his hands placatingly. 'We are only here for your own good,' he began, and was instantly interrupted by Sam Millington, who pushed through to the forefront of the crowd.

'All we wants from you, is to be let alone.' His unshaven face was implacably hostile. 'Now I'm telling you straight, Osbourne, and you Joe Cashmore, you anna coming into our houses.' He pointed at Lucas Royston, 'And that murdering bastard can fuck off from here right now. We doon't want any bloody doctors here.'

'You'd best mind your tongue, Sam Millington,' Joseph Cashmore warned. 'And you'd best not try and hinder us. We'em only doing our duty here.' A howl of execrations met this statement and makeshift weapons were waved threateningly.

'You'll only come in here over our dead bodies, Osbourne!' a man yelled, and was supported by a roar of approbation.

By now there were spectators hurrying from the adjoining streets and alleys to see this confrontation, and Cashmore recognised many notorious trouble-makers among their rapidly increasing numbers. In an undertone he told John Osbourne, 'We'll needs tread very careful here, or we'll have a bloody riot on our hands.'

The other man's face twitched nervously as he felt increasingly uncertain of how he could assert his authority in this situation.

Joseph Cashmore shared the resentment felt towards this newcomer by many of the native townspeople, and now he was torn two ways. One part of him wished to see this self-important Johnny Newcome brought low, but the other part knew that authority must be asserted if the rule of law was to prevail. 'I reckon you'd best let me handle this, Master Osbourne,' he suggested, and the other man was quick to agree.

'Yes, that might be for the best, Master Cashmore.'

The Constable walked alone up to the crowd and halted face to face with Sam Millington. 'Now then Sam, let's you and me talk this over sensible,' he said quietly. 'I was a friend o' your dad long enough for you to be able to trust me, surely?'

The young man nodded with a grudging surliness. 'I trusts you, Master Cashmore. But not that bloody doctor, or that new-come bugger. He's too bloody uppity by far. He anna bin in the town five minutes and he's atrying to tell us what to do. Well, we anna standing for it, Master Cashmore. We anna standing for anybody atelling us what's to be done. 'Specially not some fuckin' foreigner from Gloster.'

The Constable grinned bleakly, 'I appreciates how you feels, Sam. And I'm summat in agreement wi' you on that score. But the thing is, the Board of Health has ordered certain things to be done, and as the Constable, I anna got no choice but to obey them orders.'

'And we anna gooing to let any more of our people be took down to that bloody hospital, to be soddin' well murdered theer,' the young man retorted angrily, and his words brought savage growls of support from his companions.

'How many have you got here now, who're badly, Sam?' Cashmore asked.

The young man scowled and shrugged, and at first would make no answer, but Cashmore pressed him, and eventually he said, 'Theer's a couple, and me mam is feeling badly as well this morn.' He shook his head angrily, 'But I anna agooing to let no bloody murdering bastard of a doctor come nigh her. I'll care for her meself. And that goes for the other two as well. No doctor shall come nigh 'um, and none of 'um are gooing to be took down to that soddin' hospital. They all stays here and that's final, that is. You'll needs kill all on us here fust, afore you'll take anybody from here to that hospital.'

'So be it, Sam,' Cashmore nodded acceptance. 'But 'ull you let us fumigate the rooms wheer the cholera's bin, and clear away the muck? That wun't hurt any o' you, 'ull it? And it might do some on you a bit o' good.'

The other man turned to see what reaction his companions showed, and they signified their agreement to this proposal.

'And theer's one more thing, Sam, which I must insist on,' Cashmore stated very firmly. 'Iffen I stops the Inspector from bothering you all, then in return you must all gi' me your solemn oaths, that iffen anybody dies, you'll let me know straight off, and let the undertaker come and take 'um for burial as soon as he can.'

'And 'ull you gi' your word, Joe Cashmore, that they 'ull be buried clane and decent, and not took to Brummagem for the bloody doctors to cut up?' a woman questioned.

Cashmore nodded emphatically, 'I gi' you my word on that.'

'Fair enough.' Sam Millington stood aside and gestured to his friends to clear a way. 'You can send in your cleaners and muck carters then, Master Cashmore. But no doctor, and no Inspector, and not that bloody Johnny Newcome either. He'd best bugger off quick, or I might be learning him his lessons.'

The Constable went back to John Osbourne. 'Did you

hear all that passed, Master Osbourne?'

'I did, Master Cashmore.' Now that the situation appeared to have eased, Osbourne had regained something of his previous bumptious confidence. 'But I can't say as I'm entirely happy about the agreement you'se just come to wi' that lot o' ruffians, Master Cashmore.'

'Why not, Master Osbourne?' The Constable frowned dourly.

'Well, we shanna be following the regulations properly, shall we, Master Cashmore.'

'Bollocks to the regulations!' Joseph Cashmore growled, and signalled to the cleansing squad. 'Get in theer, you lot, and get to work. The rest on you can all bugger off,' he glared at John Osbourne. 'And that includes you as well, Master Osbourne. Because I reckon if you hangs about here much longer, then we 'ull have a riot on our hands. They doon't like you over well down here, Master Osbourne, so for your own sake I'd waste no time in gooing iffen I was you.'

As the unwanted ones walked away the cleansing squad went to work in those rooms where the cholera had dwelt. Firstly scrubbing with lye soap and boiling water. Then lime-washing. Then fumigating by heating sulphuric acid and common salt and black oxide of manganese, and when they had used up these substances, by heating ordinary house-bricks and throwing strong vinegar on them which bubbled and steamed and filled the tainted air of the rancid rooms with its acid vapours.

Chloride of lime was poured into the grossly offensive smelling privies and drains and its acrid fumes set men and women coughing and choking and cursing. When they complained vociferously to Joseph Cashmore, he only told them, 'It's making me cough me lungs up as well, arn't it?' And with that they had to be satisfied.

The daylight hours passed and night fell, and once again the tar-barrels were set aflame and the black clouds of acrid smoke hung over the streets of the town like a funeral pall. In Paoli's Row a child died, in Red Lion Street a man wept by the bedside of his stricken wife, and at the end of Evesham Street where the cottages of New End nestled at the bottom of Front Hill, another man and three women and a child began to vomit and void and scream in agony as the vicious cramps of the cholera tore through them.

But the taverns still rang with drunken song and laughter, and the Chapels resounded with hymns, and families ate their suppers, and lovers walked arm in arm through the warm darkness and took delight from each other's flesh in secluded shadows, and a baby was dragged bloody and whimpering from its mother's womb and its midwives crowed their delight from toothless mouths as they saw its new born perfection.

Chapter Thirty-Seven

TWO WEEKS HAD passed before Tildy managed to visit each household where cholera had attacked. Each day had brought news of fresh outbreaks, and she wanted to gain as much information as she possibly could to support her theory. In the meantime she insisted that none of her loved ones drank any water that had not been previously strained through clean rags and boiled. Although Daniel, Old Esther and Davy thought that she was being foolish in this, nevertheless they humoured her and did as she begged them.

By Friday the 5th of October Tildy considered that she had amassed enough material to support her theory, and she went first to talk with Charles Brown about her discoveries.

'Water? The cholera is carried by the water supply?' Charles Brown exclaimed doubtfully.

They were in his room at Widow Sprake's house. The man's once florid features were now grey-hued and his eyes ringed by the dark shadows of exhaustion. Although he was not one of the Board of Health's officially appointed doctors, nevertheless many people preferred to come to him when the cholera struck down their loved ones, and his success rate was slightly better than his fellow medical practitioners. He was managing to save some fifty per cent of his patients, as opposed to the forty to forty five per cent the official Board of Health doctors were achieving.

Now he asked Tildy, 'What proof do you have of this, Tildy, when you say that the cholera is in the water?'

She explained how many of the cases were occurring in

close locations where the households shared a common water supply.

'But if that is the case then why doesn't everyone in that locality fall victim to the cholera?' he challenged.

She shrugged, 'I don't know, Charles. Mayhap some people are naturally resistant to it. But I have another thought about this point. Just consider who are the majority of the victims. Women and children and the very poor. Now you know as well as I that all those who can afford it tend to drink very little plain water with their meals or for refreshment. We drink ale or cider or small beer, do we not? I doubt if the rich taste well water more than a couple of times in their lives. But in the poor families, where there is little money, then it is the men who drink whatever can be afforded, and the women and children have to make do with water.'

He pursed his lips reflectively, and nodded slowly, 'There may be something in what you say.'

Encouraged by this, Tildy went on excitedly, 'Consider the Pitts family, and old Mother Cater. Mistress Pitts and Maria seemed to be rallying at times during their illness, but then they would drink copiously of fresh water, and afterwards they would relapse. Mother Cater also used to drink water from the pump at the house there.'

'But did not you and Lucas Royston also drink water from that pump?' Brown pointed out.

Tildy shook her head. 'I only drank it once. I didn't like the taste, so after that I always took a flask of ale or cider with me. And I don't think Lucas Royston ever tastes water from one year to the next. He always drinks wine, or whatever other spirit is available.'

Charles Brown mused over this for some time, and Tildy grew impatient and pressed him, 'Well, Charles, what do you think? Could I be right?'

He sighed and shrugged, 'Well, you could be, Tildy. But then, so could all those others who say it is caused by miasmas or electric effluvium or cholera flies or bad air.'

'That's as maybe,' Tildy was slightly annoyed by his reaction. 'But there's naught that can be done about electric effluvium or miasmas or cholera flies, is there, Charles? If I am right and it is the water, then something can be done to guard against it.'

'Such as what?' he demanded, his weariness making him speak sharply.

'We can try and purify the water. We can strain it, and boil it before use. We can prevent people drawing water from the wells that we know carry the infection.' Tildy's own heightened emotions made her almost plead with him, 'At least we can do something to fight back against this foul thing, Charles. Instead of standing helpless while it takes the lives of men, women and children.' She paused for a moment, staring at him with huge eyes, and then begged, 'Come with me to the Board of Health, Charles. Support me in this, and help me to persuade them to take measures to purify the water supplies in the infected areas. Please, Charles, help me in this.'

The man thought hard for some moments, turning over in his mind all that she had said, and was forced to admit that it was an appealing idea. At length he told her, 'The Board meets at ten o'clock in the forenoon, does it not? It's too late now for us to go to them this day. But I'll go there with you tomorrow . . .'

'Water? Carried in the water? What arrant nonsense!' Henry Milward's plump pink features mirrored the scorn he felt at hearing such a statement. 'It's preposterous! Utterly preposterous!'

Judging by their expressions the majority of the men sitting ranged round the long table in the vestry room of Saint Stephen's Chapel were in agreement with him.

'How can you say that, Mister Milward?' Tildy challenged, her cheeks burning with mingled embarrassment and anger as she heard sneering gibes directed at her, and saw the contemptuous smiles the men were exchanging between themselves.

'How can I say it, Crawford?' The Needle Master puffed pompously. 'I can say it because I've been drinking the water in this parish for more than fifty years, and I don't look as if I've taken any harm from it, do I?'

Charles Brown had accompanied Tildy to this meeting of the Board of Health out of friendship. Although he did not fully believe in her theory of water-borne cholera, nevertheless he was prepared to keep an open mind about it, and as he had already told her, he considered it to be as likely as any of the other theories being bruited abroad.

Now he felt his own resentment rising at this cavalier treatment the Board was meting out to Tildy, and he spoke out, directing his words towards John Clayton. 'Gentlemen, I do not think we should so lightly dismiss what Mistress Crawford has said concerning this matter. She has presented a well-reasoned argument, based on her own very thorough investigations, and to my mind her theory is as feasible, and mayhap in some ways more feasible, than the other explanations currently being offered as to the causes of this present epidemic. I would ask Mister Milward what qualifies him to dismiss so scathingly what Mistress Crawford has put forward?'

Doctor Alexander Pratt, sallow-faced and lanky, wearing a full-bottomed tie-wig beneath his tall black hat, was quick to take up this challenge on behalf of his patient and old friend.

'Mister Milward is qualified . . . by virtue of his . . . standing in this Parish . . . sir.' He spoke in short staccato bursts. 'And I support him . . . in what he says . . . by virtue of my professional . . . qualifications, sir.'

'Do you indeed,' Charles Brown's spirit was now fully roused, and he committed himself fully in Tildy's support. 'And by virtue of my own professional qualifications, I support Mistress Crawford in what she says.'

'Your professional qualifications, sir?' Henry Milward openly jeered. 'And what are they, pray? You came into this Parish as a cheapjack, I believe, so where have you gained these qualifications that you boast of? I didn't know that there existed a Faculty of Medicine in Salters Yard.'

This last gibe brought roars of mocking laughter from the

Board members, and a dull flush of anger suffused Brown's face. While the Board members continued to laugh and poke fun at him, he walked to the head of the table where John Clayton, in stark contrast to his colleagues, was sitting in grim silence. Brown took a flat oilskin-wrapped packet from the inside pocket of his coat and handed it to the clergyman. 'Could I ask you to peruse these papers, Reverend Clayton, sir, and tell these gentlemen what information is contained within them.'

The laughter stilled and a silence fell upon the room as the clergyman unwrapped the oilskin and taking out the sheets of parchment it contained, closely scanned them. When he had done so, he frowned, and held them high. 'These documents, gentlemen, confirm that, Charles Claude Brown, Esq., is a Licentiate of the Royal College of Surgeons, and late Surgeon in His Majesty's Royal Navy.'

Audible gasps of surprise sounded around the table, and John Clayton frowned at Henry Milward, and invited tartly, 'Would you care to examine these documents yourself, Mister Milward, and perhaps after doing so, you may think it only befitting in a gentleman such as yourself, to offer an apology to Doctor Brown for having doubted his veracity?'

Milward snatched at the parchments and scowlingly examined them. Then he laid them on the table and grudgingly muttered, 'I offer my apology for having doubted your word, Brown.'

Charles Brown nodded curtly in acceptance.

It was John Clayton who now asserted his leadership. He smiled at Tildy, and invited her, 'Mistress Crawford, concerning this theory you are propounding, could you now please once again explain your reasoning to the Board?' He aimed a sarcastic barb at the men around him, 'It may well be that some of the points you have already so ably made were not fully appreciated by these gentlemen. After all new theories are sometimes difficult for untrained minds to grasp without constant repetition.'

Tildy's colour heightened and her heart thudded as she faced the silent men. She could sense the hostility and resentment that emanated from them towards her. She knew that she was arousing all their innate prejudices by asserting herself in this way, and offending against their indoctrinated belief in the superiority of man over woman, and rich over poor.

'I think that the cholera is carried by water, because . . . ' she began hesitantly, and stumbled over her words. But as she continued to speak her belief in what she was saying gave her confidence, and she spoke with an ever increasing certainty and fluency.

' . . . and so, gentlemen, I think we must immediately seal off those wells which are infected, and make the people strain and boil all the water that they use. We could also take further measures, such as purchasing for those who have no money, ale and cider for their drink.' She fell silent, and stood waiting apprehensively for a reaction.

John Clayton nodded and smiled at her, 'Many thanks, Mistress Crawford. May I congratulate you on having presented your arguments so concisely.' He looked around the table. 'Well, gentlemen?'

Henry Milward was still seething inwardly at having been forced into apologising to Charles Brown. Now he seized his opportunity to strike back. 'Purchase ale and cider for the paupers to make merry on? That's a fine thing to be told we must do, to be sure!' he exclaimed scathingly, and with a sneering smile enquired of Tildy, 'And should we also purchase tobacco for them, Mistress Crawford, and best beef and white bread, and other dainties for their stomachs so that they will have strength enough to enjoy getting drunk at our expense?'

Abruptly he slammed his plump hands down on the table top, and thundered angrily, 'I'll be damned if I've ever heard the like of it, gentlemen! It appears that it's not sufficient for the lower orders that we maintain a hospital, and doctors and nurses at our own expense, and supply them free and in abundance with all the medicines, and the other necessities. Oh no,' he shook his head until his hanging jowls quivered violently. 'Oh no! We are now told that we must buy them their pleasures as well. We must purchase the means for them to follow their usual course of getting swinish drunk at each and every opportunity that presents itself.'

Again he paused, glaring around at his colleagues, his bulbous eyes bulging in his pink sweating features. 'Well, I for one will never do such, gentlemen. And I consider it to be naught else but rank insolence that they should see fit to demand this from us, their benefactors and betters.' A storm of applause greeted his words, feet stamping on the floor, fists pounding on the table.

Tildy could only stand and stare with blank amazement, that her words should be so deliberately and grossly misconstrued, and the faces of Charles Brown and John Clayton mirrored the disgust that they were both feeling at this exhibition by men who were purportedly the social elite of the Parish.

It was Charles Brown who was first to recognise the certainty of inevitable defeat. Going to Tildy he took her arm and jerked his head towards the door. 'Come, my dear. We serve no useful purpose by remaining here a moment longer.'

She began to protest, wanting to stay and continue to press for acceptance of her theory. But he overrode her and drew her with him from the room, and out of the Chapel.

Outside, on the short flight of stone steps he smiled bitterly at her, 'It's no use, Tildy. You will never persuade them. They do not wish to hear you, or to believe you.'

Tildy was now feeling angry. 'But why should they behave like that? All I was trying to do was to fight against the cholera, and perhaps save some of their lives. Why should they so deliberately misunderstand what I was saying?'

Before the man could reply, Tildy's name was shouted, and both turned to see where the voice had come from. It was Charles Duggins who came hurrying towards them. 'I was told I'd find you here, Tildy Crawford. You'd best get home straight off. They'se just brought your man back from his work. The Blue Vomit's took hold on him . . . !'

Chapter Thirty-Eight

AS I WAS awalking one morning by chance
I heard a maid making her moan;
I asked what was the matter,
She said in a flutter,
I'm obliged to lie tumbling alone, alone,
I'm obliged to lie tumbling alooonnne . . . '

Thomas Vincent sang merrily as he hammered the final
nails into the lid of the coffin which was lying on trestles in
the shed behind the Quarantine Hospital.

The old crone who was standing in the open doorway
chuckled wheezily, 'You'm in fine fettle this mornin',
Master Vincent.'

He grinned at her, 'Indeed I am, Widow Smout.' He
stepped back to admire his handiwork. 'There now, that's a
real tidy job, arn't it? It fits as snug as you'd wish. There'll
be no worms getting free passage into this box.'

The crone's blackened stubs of teeth showed in her lipless
mouth, and she cackled with laughter. 'Oh yes, and I'm
sure Ellie Dickens is grateful for it fitting so snug as well.
Her couldn't abide a draught, could Ellie. Her allus
reckoned her could feel a draught through four thicknesses
o' blanket.'

Again her laughter cackled out as she came to the coffin
and rapped smartly on its lid. 'How bist in theer, Ellie?
Can you feel any draught?'

Thomas Vincent joined in her laughter. 'Her's hardly
likely to, Widow Smout.' He held up his pitch-blackened

hands. 'Her's got a double wrapping o' pitch-sheet around her. That 'ud keep out a bloody gale, ne'er mind a poxy little draught.'

'She'll be put down tonight I take it?' the old woman sought to know.

'She 'ull, Widow Smout. Burial within twenty-four hours o' dying. That's the order give out by the Government in London. And we obeys it. Let's see now, her's the fourth nurse to die here arn't her.'

'Ahr,' the old woman confirmed, 'and theer's bin more nor twenty others die in this place as well.'

The undertaker nodded reflectively, 'There don't seem to be much good being done here, does there. Near upon every poor cratur who comes in here, leaves in a box.' He tapped the coffin lid. 'Even them whom come here to look arter the sick 'uns.' He glanced at his companion with a speculative gleam in his eyes. 'Arn't you afeared that you might be leaving in the same way as your old mate here?'

'Not I, Master Vincent,' the old crone scoffed. 'I takes these twice a day.' She rummaged in the pocket of her shabby black gown and produced a small tin box, which she opened to disclose some large pills coloured a bright blue. 'These be Morrison's Anti-Cholera Lozenges. Two o' these a day 'ull keep the Blue Vomit away, and I'm the living proof o' that, Master Vincent.'

'That bloke Morrison must be making his fortune,' Thomas Vincent observed enviously. 'Them pills on his be selling like hot cakes all over the Parish.'

'He anna the only one amaking his fortune out o' this bloody cholera, is he Master Vincent?' The old crone peered slyly at the undertaker.

He grinned and replied, 'Well, I must admit that I'm adoing a fair bit o' business meself these days. But it's the bloody doctors who am making the fortunes, Widow Smout. Not me. Does you know that they'm getting five guineas a week each for calling on the new cases?'

'Oh ahr, I'se heard that, Master Vincent. But they anna deserving on it, am they. Because there anna one on 'um who knows how to cure the cholera, is there, and that Doctor Royston is walking around like a bloody turnip-yedded mawkin these last days. I doon't reckon he's drawn a sober breath since that young wench he was keen on went and died. What was her name now?'

'Young Maria Pitts,' the undertaker told her, and sighed regretfully. ''Tis a terrible shame to see a pretty young wench like her was be took by the Blue Vomit, arn't it?'

'Ahr, so it is, Master Vincent. So it is. But I reckon we'll be seeing a sight more pretty young wenches took by it, afore it's all over and done wi'.'

'I reckon so, my old duck,' Vincent agreed, then said, 'Well now, I must be off, I'se got business in the town.'

'Another 'un to box up, is it?'

'Yes, in Salters Yard, Daniel Lambert. By Christ, he went quick didn't he. Got struck ill yesterday morning and afore midnight he'd gone. I feels sorry for his woman, Tildy Crawford. She's a real good wench, and she's already had more than her share o' troubles in life.'

'That's a woman's lot in this life, Master Vincent,' the old crone stated. 'Every woman I'se ever knowed, including meself, has had more nor her share o' troubles. I wish I'd bin born a man, I'll tell you. You has it easy compared to us.'

'I'll not dispute that wi' you, Widow Smout.' Vincent smiled wryly, and bade her goodbye.

'Tildy?' Old Esther gently touched the younger woman's shoulder, 'Tildy, Tommy Vincent's come.'

Tildy was sitting by the side of the bed she had shared with Daniel Lambert, and on which his sheet-covered body now lay. She looked up at the old woman, and Esther Smith's heart felt ready to break as she saw the utter desolation in Tildy's dark eyes.

'Come on now, sweetheart,' she urged gently. 'You come on wi' me out into the kitchen, and leave Tommy Vincent to do what's necessary.'

'No,' Tildy shook her head. 'I'll stay here and help him.

278

'It'll be the last thing that I'll ever be able to do for Daniel.'

Old Esther studied her with concern. Tildy had not wept, or voiced her grief at losing this man she so loved. She seemed dazed and lost, and her face had become a thin-drawn, pale mask of silent anguish.

'Oh Tildy, doon't stay in here,' the old woman begged. 'It arn't a sight you should be seeing. Daniel 'ull have to be wrapped in pitch-sheets. 'Tis not good having that as a memory of him.'

Tildy rose to her feet, her hand absently caressing the sheet covering the dead face. 'Daniel gave me a happiness that I'd never believed I could ever have, Esther. That's the memory I'll always have of him. What's left here,' she touched the sheeted face, 'isn't Daniel any more. It's only the body that he used here on this earth. Daniel's just the same as he ever was, but he's somewhere else now, that's all, Esther. He's gone somewhere else, and please God he's waiting for me to join him there when my own time comes.'

The old woman shook her head worriedly, and muttered, 'You'm so calm, my duck, it anna natural to be so calm.'

Tildy's dark eyes held a strange light as she stared at her companion, but she only told her quietly, 'Tell Tommy Vincent to come through to here, will you, Esther. But don't let Davy come through. Keep him with you in the kitchen.'

The old woman nodded, and went back into the kitchen where Davy was seated at the table, pale-faced and woebegone. Old Esther was not unduly concerned about the boy. He had wept bitterly when Daniel died, because he had loved the man like a father. But youth is very resilient, and Old Esther knew that he would quickly heal, and his grief would soon become muted and easy to bear. It was Tildy that worried her. The younger woman was too calm. Something would break unless she vented her grief.

Thomas Vincent was standing by the door with his helper, holding a coffin upright on its end between them.

'Goo on through, Master Vincent,' Old Esther told him, and silently the two men carried the coffin into the further passage and along to the bedroom.

Davy stared at the long box with fearful eyes, and Old Esther stroked his thick black curls and told him, 'Doon't let that old box distress you, my lamb. 'Tis only a box when all's said and done. There arn't naught to be fritted on about it. It's just used to make everything look decent and tidy, that's all.'

Tildy could smell the gin on the breaths of Thomas Vincent and his helper, a runty-bodied, simple-minded youth known in the town as Sarft Ned.

Vincent stared at the beautiful woman with genuine sympathy. He knew how well she had nursed Maria Pitts, and how unstintingly she helped others in need. It seemed a harsh blow of fate that she should now lose the man she loved, while others who refused to lift a finger to help the stricken apparently bore charmed lives and suffered no loss.

'Look, Missus Crawford, 'udden't it be best if me and Ned here does the business by ourselves. It arn't a pretty sight to see somebody you cares for being wrapped in pitch-sheets.'

Tildy shook her head, 'I want to do this for Daniel, Mister Vincent.'

He had sense enough not to argue the point.

The coffin was laid down by the side of the bed and the lid unscrewed to disclose the pitch-soaked sheets. Vincent opened the sheets out so that they became a black oily receptacle within the coffin.

'It's best that we does this quick, Missus Crawford, and I wants you to wear one o' these around your mouth, if you 'ull.'

From the leather satchel he carried slung around his neck he produced lengths of vinegar-soaked flannel, which he and Sarft Ned tied around their faces to cover mouth and nostrils.

After a moment of hesitation Tildy did the same, but the acrid sour taste of the soaked flannel caused her to momentarily gag and she tore it off and handed it back to Vincent. 'No, I can't wear this.'

He shrugged, 'So be it. Now listen very careful to what I'm agoing to tell you, my wench.' Vincent's voice was somewhat muffled by the flannel. 'And doon't doubt me words, because I knows what I'm atalking about.'

His shrewd eyes studied her briefly, and he waited until she nodded acceptance, before continuing, 'Sometimes when we'em moving the dead 'uns about, then their arms and legs suddenly moves as well, and their bodies twitches and jerks as if they'm still living. I doon't know what causes 'um to do this, Missus Crawford, but it's happened more nor a few times wi' the cholera cases. It's something peculiar to this bloody evil thing that causes it, I reckon, because I've not sin it afore. But be sure on one thing, my wench. Be sure that they'm dead, and not still living. No matter that they moves like that, they really am dead.'

He frowned behind his face-cloth as he saw that she displayed no apparent reaction to his words, but only nodded listlessly, and he experienced a sense of disquiet at the strange gleam in her lucent dark eyes.

'Right then, you take his yed, Missus, and you take the feet, Ned. I'll lift the middle part.'

He pushed the coffin right against the side of the bed and instructed. 'I'm agoing to pull his covering off, then as I gives the word, we all mun take hold and lift together and put him straight into the coffin. Right then . . . ' He jerked the covering sheet free and tossed it aside. 'Now lift!'

Daniel Lambert's body was shrunken and darkened into a hideous caricature of the fine man he had been, and his weight seemed negligible to their combined strengths. In a split second he was enveloped in the black oily pitch-sheet, and with deft rapidity Thomas Vincent wrapped around the overhanging cloth around the blue-black face and mercifully hid it from view. As he did this the body seemed to jerk upwards, and Tildy cried out, 'Noooo! Noooo! He's moving! He's still alive! Get him out from there! Get him out!'

Before Thomas Vincent could stop her she had thrown herself down on the open coffin and ripped aside the black cloth from the dead face, and was kissing the soiled cheeks and forehead and lips and sobbing and screaming out, 'I'm sorry, Daniel. I'm sorry! Forgive me, my love! I'll take you out of this! I'll take you out! I'm sorry. I'm sorry. I'm sorry!'

'Oh fuck it! I was afraid this 'ud happen!' the undertaker cursed. 'Get ahold on her, Ned.'

The youth was very strong for all his runtishness, and now he grabbed Tildy's arms from behind and dragged her away from the dead man. Thomas Vincent went to the door and shouted.

'Missus Smith, come on in here right away, 'ull you.'

Almost immediately the frightened faces of Old Esther and Davy appeared at the door, and Vincent helped Sarft Ned to pull the struggling, sobbing, screaming Tildy out of the bedroom and into the passageway.

Old Esther told Davy, 'Run and fetch Charles Brown.' Frightened though the boy was, he retained enough control to obey her instantly, and by the time the three of them had wrestled the hysterically shrieking and fighting Tildy into the kitchen, Charles Brown was coming through the outer door.

His experience caused him to act instantaneously and his hands whipped backwards and forwards across Tildy's face, hurting and shocking her from the fit of hysteria. For a moment she stared at him with wide, tear-streaming eyes, then she suddenly slumped downwards and sank to her knees, her hands covering her face, her shoulders heaving as she vented heart-rending cries of grief and pain.

Old Esther nodded in satisfaction, and drew Davy close to her to tell him, 'Now doon't worry, my lamb. This is the best thing that could have happened. Your mam 'ull be alright now. She'll be alright. Her's letting all her grieving come out now, and it's for the best. It's what her should ha' done hours since.'

Pale-faced and shaken though he was, Davy was able to

understand and accept what the old woman told him. He went to Tildy and knelt by her, and put his arms around her in comfort, and she choked out, 'Oh Davy. I'm sorry I behaved so badly. I'm sorry, honey.'

They stayed clasped in each other's arms and slowly Tildy's sobs quietened and her heaving shoulders stilled.

Thomas Vincent went back into the bedroom with Charles Brown and Sarft Ned, quickly re-wrapped the body and screwed down the coffin lid.

'This bedding 'ull all have to be burned, wun't it?' he asked Charles Brown, who nodded.

'I'll see to having that done, Master Vincent. Do you want a hand to take Daniel out to your hearse?'

The undertaker smiled mirthlessly. 'No, theer's no need, Master Brown. When somebody dies o' this bloody cholera, then they doon't weigh a good pennyworth. But I wun't be coming to fetch him until arter dark. So he'll needs rest here 'til then.'

He frowned with worry, 'I hope that there'll be somebody here to keep an eye on Missus Crawford. Only sometimes in these cases when we'se had a bit o' jerking about like wi' Daniel Lambert here, then the family tries to unscrew the lid and see if the dead 'un is really dead, and arn't bin screwed down alive.'

'That won't happen here, Master Vincent. I'll stay with them myself until it's time for the burial,' Charles Brown assured him, and then began to roll up the bedding and straw mattress preparatory to removing them to be burnt.

By the time he had finished his task and returned to the kitchen, Tildy had recovered some degree of composure.

'I'm sorry for the way I behaved,' she started to apologise to him, but he held up his hands to stop her.

'No, Tildy. Say naught about it. It was only natural.'

She busied herself in brewing a pot of tea, and the four of them seated themselves around the table and sipped the steaming liquid from the small deep-sided bowls.

Tildy's face was very pale, and deep shadows under-marked her eyes, but when she spoke her voice, though tremulous, held no trace of hysteria or imbalance.

'I can't understand why he should have fallen victim,' she mused aloud. 'I strained and boiled every drop of water that we used. I just can't understand it.'

Charles Brown was feeling very unhappy about Daniel Lambert's death himself. It was he who had treated the sick man, utilising the whole battery of various treatments, all to no avail. Now he sat pondering over this failure. Repeatedly going over in his mind the treatments and the chronological order of their application. Wondering if he himself had inadvertently worsened Lambert's condition with the doses of drugs and liquors, the application of sinapisms, and use of harsh purgatives and enemas.

Unable to restrain himself, he voiced his own sense of guilt that Daniel should have died, but Tildy smiled wanly, and would not accept this.

'You did all that could be done in the light of our present knowledge, Charles. You have nothing to reproach yourself about.' She sighed tremulously, 'We just have to accept that we don't know enough yet, to defeat the cholera.'

A spark of her normal fiery spirit suddenly flared, 'But one day we will. Of that I'm certain. And until that day I intend to go on fighting against it in every way I can think of. I owe that to my Daniel. I owe it to him to go on fighting. Tomorrow I shall go and see John Clayton and offer myself to work as a nurse in the hospital.'

This outburst of defiance gave Tildy renewed strength of purpose and comforted her with the knowledge that at least she would still be defying the foul evil thing that had taken her loved man from her, and carrying on the battle against it.

As the hours passed, many people came individually to the house to offer their condolences, and to see if Tildy needed help of any kind. When she expressed her surprise at the kindness being shown towards her by so many diverse personalities, Old Esther smiled and told her, ''Tis only the bread you'se cast on the waters coming back to you, my duck.'

An old friend of Esther, Tildy and Davy came unexpectedly, late in the afternoon, Zeke Pickering, the poacher, looking hale and hearty. He and his Romany woman were camping in the woodlands out by the Beoley village, and as he told Davy of the small herd of fine ponies and horses he had now amassed, the boy's eyes sparkled and it seemed that his grief for Daniel Lambert's death visibly eased.

When Zeke Pickering tentatively suggested that Davy should stay with him at his camp for a few days and help him to break some of the young horses the boy's eyes shone, and Tildy gratefully accepted the man's offer, knowing that this would help her son to recover more quickly from losing Daniel, because in many ways Zeke Pickering himself had been a surrogate father to the boy until she had come to live with Daniel Lambert.

Another reason, which influenced Tildy in favour of Davy leaving now with Zeke Pickering, was that there had been no cases of the cholera where Zeke Pickering lived, and the isolation of his camp's area was such that she considered there to be little likelihood of any such cases occurring.

When the man and boy had left, Old Esther told Tildy, 'I reckon you did the right thing theer, my duck. 'Tis best for the boy that he should leave this house o' mourning for a little whiles. But I canna help but think that you should ha' kept him back to goo to the funeral fust?'

Tildy looked at the old woman with steady eyes. 'I think not, Esther. What could Davy gain by seeing a long wooden box put down into a big hole in the ground?' She shook her head, 'No, let him see young ponies and fine horses galloping through the woodland, full of their joy of life. That will do him a sight more good than watching a dead man be buried. I want Davy to remember Daniel as he was, full of strength and joy, not as a wooden box being lowered into a clay hole.'

The old woman thought on this for a time, then nodded, 'Ahr, I can see the sense in what you says my duck.'

Charles Brown smiled warmly, 'Of course you're right, my dear. Going off with Zeke Pickering is by far the finest medicine I could ever prescribe for Davy's happiness at this time.'

Tildy's own heart was filled with a fresh sense of loss, and she could have wept as she watched the boy walking away. But she knew that when he came back, he would still be hers, and that she had done the right thing in letting him go.

A wave of utter weariness swept over her, and she could not repress a yawn. Charles Brown took her hand and insisted. 'You will go to my room, and you will sleep for a short while, Tildy.'

She shook her head and protested, 'No, I must stay close to Daniel. I can't think of sleeping now. Not until I've laid my man in his final resting place.'

He saw her determination, and let the matter lie.

Chapter Thirty-Nine

B Y THE SILVER light of the moon and the golden gleam of a lantern, the coffin of Daniel Lambert was lowered on ropes held by drunken, pipe-smoking men into the mass grave in the Old Abbey Burial Yard, while the Reverend Julius Fessey stood twenty yards distant from the graveside, his fear causing him to gabble and stutter and make a mockery of the majestic sonority of the burial service, and behind him in the lane another two groups of mourners waited to commit their own loved ones to that same mass grave.

For Tildy, numbed by grief and exhaustion, it seemed that she was enmeshed in a nightmarish dream, and when it was over she walked in silence back to Salters Yard, and laid herself down on the bare boards of the bed she had shared so joyously with Daniel Lambert. For seemingly endless hours she lay sleepless, her mind filled with memories of the man she had loved so dearly, and lost so cruelly. At intervals she wept, but in contrast to the wrenching bitterness of her earlier torments, these were gentle tears that soothed and eased her agonies.

At last sleep came, and in that sleep came dreams. Daniel was at her side once more. Daniel as she had always known him, strong and vibrant and intensely alive. Once more she felt his arms enfolding her and his mouth on hers, and the clean scent and the warm fresh taste of him filled her senses.

'Did you really think that I would leave you, honey?' she heard him asking. 'Did you really think that I could ever do that?'

'No. No. No,' she told him over and over again. 'No, Daniel, no my love. I know that you will never leave me.'

'I've only gone a little way ahead of you, sweetheart,' he whispered tenderly. 'And I shall be waiting when you come.'

'When will that be?' she questioned urgently. 'When, my love, when?'

'When it is the time to do so, honey,' he told her softly and gently kissed her. 'There is much you have to do before then. Davy must be raised to manhood, and there will be others come into your life who will love and need you. Much will happen and many years will pass, before you and I are reunited.'

'But we will be reunited, won't we, honey?' she eagerly sought assurance. 'Tell me that one day we shall be together again, Daniel. Promise me.'

She heard his fond chuckle that she knew and loved so well, and felt the firm loving caress of his strong arms.

'Yes, sweetheart, we will be.' His voice seemed to be growing fainter as if he were moving further and further away. 'Never doubt it, my only love. We shall one day be together once more and then we shall never be parted again. I know this now and that is why I feel happy. I know this now.'

Tildy came awake, and lay staring into the darkness, her heart filled with yearning love and her mind with wonderment at what had happened to her.

Doubt filled her mind, 'He couldn't have been here. He couldn't have. It must only have been a dream.'

Her hands reached out and her fingers felt the bare wooden boards beside her. There was warmth there. Warmth as if someone had been lying beside her. She held her breath, concentrating all her senses, trying to discover some trace of Daniel's presence. And then, in her mind, she heard him speak as if from a far distance.

'We'll meet again, sweetheart. Of that be sure. We'll meet again.'

Tildy's eyes brimmed and tears fell, but through those tears she smiled, as certainty filled her heart . . .